ME, AN OLD PILOT, AND A THREE-LEGGED DOG

ME, AN OLD PILOT, AND A THREE-LEGGED DOG

A Novel by

ROCKY MORRISETTE

Illustrated by

SCOTT LOETHEN

iUniverse, Inc.
Bloomington

ME, AN OLD PILOT, AND A THREE-LEGGED DOG

iUniverse books may be ordered through booksellers or by contacting:

iUniverse
1663 Liberty Drive
Bloomington, IN 47403
www.iuniverse.com
1-800-Authors (1-800-288-4677)

ISBN: 978-1-4759-7958-9 (sc)
ISBN: 978-1-4759-7960-2 (hc)
ISBN: 978-1-4759-7959-6 (ebk)

Library of Congress Control Number: 2013904062

Printed in the United States of America

iUniverse rev. date: 04/04/2013

Luckily for me, I married an English major.
To my best friend, Sheila Grace.

To the Literary Community

This is *my* book; it does not belong to the literary community. I wrote this book and I know what I meant by every word of it. In the military we would call it clear, ungarbled text. You do not have my permission to interpret it; no interpretation is necessary. You do not have my permission to try to convince your students that there are secret messages in it. There is nothing in this work of fiction that covertly symbolizes anything else. An erupting volcano is just an erupting volcano; a plane flying into a deep, V-shaped valley is just a plane flying into a deep, V-shaped valley. You'll find no rusty bicycle pumps or ladders behind the garage. That is all.

Rocky Morrisette

My sincere appreciation to
Susan L. Jenner, DVM;
Elizabeth "Buff" Peters, RN;
J. Patrick Carroll, professional pilot;
Ken Kellogg, CFI.
Olivia Kelly, aspiring writer.

Contents

Prologue

"*Mayday, mayday, mayday*! This is Cessna three-three-one X-ray Papa. I'm declaring an emergency. *Mayday, mayday, mayday!*" There was panic in my voice.

"Cessna three-three-one X-ray Papa, this is Salt Lake Approach; state the nature of your emergency."

The plane was shaking so hard I could barely hold the yoke steady. "I think my engine exploded. I am shutting it down now."

"One X-ray Papa, say your type and location."

"Salt Lake, I'm a Cessna 152. My flight plan is on file. I'm twenty minutes out of Wendover."

"X-ray Papa, are you on fire?"

"No, umm . . . negative, Salt Lake, but my engine nearly shook itself off before I could shut it down."

"One X-ray Papa and Salt Lake approach, this is Dennis Air."

Denny! I was so happy to hear his voice.

"I am this student pilot's flight instructor. Salt Lake, will you stand by?"

"Salt Lake standing by, Dennis Air."

"Summer Rose, can you talk?"

"Yes, but I have almost full left rudder in, and the aircraft isn't responding well."

"Okay, Summer Rose, talk directly to me, and only when you have time."

"Denny, I'm bleeding." My voice was shaking.

"How bad are you hurt?"

"I don't know; there's blood everywhere."

"Try to stay calm, Summer. You've got to keep flying the plane no matter what else. You know what to do; we've done lots of emergency drills."

"I know, Denny, but we never practiced what to do if the airplane won't fly right! I don't know what to do."

"You're already doing it. You haven't lost control. You've communicated and confessed, and now you have to comply. You remember what the most important thing is now, right?"

"Yeah, maintain positive control of the aircraft until the last piece stops moving."

"That's right. Summer, I know this looks bad, but remember your training. You're an excellent pilot; you can do this. Just try to land like you do back here. When you soloed last month, we gave you a full bag of luck and an empty bag of experience. What do you say we use some of that luck now and put something in the experience bag?"

"Okay."

"What's your airspeed?"

"I can't read it. The windshield is gone and my eyes are all blurry."

"No problem. Just pretend I've covered up your airspeed indicator. You're going to have to slow down in order to land. Trim the plane so that it starts slowing down. Just feel it, just like slow flight practice. Keep your head up and looking outside. Don't worry about your instruments."

Slowing down made a big difference in the way the plane flew. "That's better, Denny. That took a lot of pressure off the rudder, but now I'm having trouble keeping the wings level."

"Summer Rose, let's keep this simple. Let's make this a no-flaps landing."

"Okay . . . okay, that's a good idea."

"If the airplane starts to become uncontrollable, just lower your nose a little. We already know your airplane will fly at your current airspeed. Have you followed your flight plan?"

"Yeah. I'm over the salt flats between Desert Peak and Crater Island."

"Salt Lake, this is Dennis Air, did you copy?"

"Salt Lake copies all. We're updating Life Flight and the sheriff's department."

"Thank you, Salt Lake. You're looking for a red-over-white Cessna, and Salt Lake, this may have been a midair."

"Roger, Dennis Air, we are already checking all flight plans now."

"Okay, Summer Rose, help's on the way. We've done everything we can down here. It's all up to you now. You are the pilot-in-command. How much altitude do you have?"

"Less than a thousand feet. Denny . . . I can't keep the wings level!"

"Your right wing is about to stall! Lower your nose a little. Summer Rose, move your fuel selector to off and call us when you get down."

Funny, I thought, *how we never say the word "crash."*

"Summer Rose, kill your master switch now. Don't worry about the avionics."

I reached down and flipped the switch off. That cut all electrical power so there'd be less chance of a postcrash fire. Now the radios went silent. I felt very, very alone. I continued to fly until my right wing hit the ground and the aircraft cartwheeled.

When everything finally stopped moving, I still had my hands on the yoke and my feet on the pedals. A thick cloud of dust swirled everywhere. I couldn't see a thing. I was absolutely covered in dirt and blood and . . . feathers? It was totally quiet now except for my gyroscopic instruments, which were still winding down. Only seconds ago there had been so much noise.

I unbuckled and tried to open my door, but it just jammed into the hardpan. The passenger door was blocked by something. I started to panic but then realized I could just crawl out through the broken windscreen.

I climbed over the control yokes, shimmied the rest of the way out, and just dropped to the ground where the engine was supposed to be. On the way down, my left side hit a broken piece of the engine mount. I smelled fuel, so I moved away from the airplane and sat down on salt flats. I sat there with my head in my hands and tried to think.

I checked myself out. I was covered in blood, but the only place *I* was bleeding from was a nasty gouge on my left rib cage, where I had hit the engine mount. I also had some nasty scrapes on both shins, and it felt like my left wrist was sprained. When I started trembling, I realized I was about to go into shock. I laid out flat and tried to calm down. All I could think of was how much trouble I was going to be in. I had completely destroyed the airplane!

Mom is going to freak! She'll never let me fly again. I've got to radio in that I'm okay.

I limped back to the airplane and discovered there was just a tiny puddle of fuel that had dripped out of the fuel line. I figured it would be safe to turn the power back on. I looked inside, and the first thing I noticed was a dead white pelican in the luggage compartment. *This had all been caused by a bird strike!?*

The entire back of the plane had torn free and was twisted around. It was now smashed up against the passenger's side of the airplane. My com antennas were on that part of the plane, which meant my radios wouldn't work, so there was no need to risk turning the power on.

I walked around the plane, or what was left of it. The left landing gear was folded back and smashed flat. The left wing was bent and the tip was dug into the caliche. The right wing had been ripped off and was lying about fifty feet away. I made my way over to it and discovered parts of two more pelicans.

I found the engine about two hundred feet behind the aircraft. *Odd, it should have been in front of the plane.* I limped back to it and found parts of another pelican. That is when I got my bearings and and realized I was in front of the wreck only the fuselage had spun around so I was looking at it from the rear. The main fuselage was pointed back toward Wendover.

I went back to the fuselage and reached in through the luggage compartment to gather up my flight kit and backpack. Then I crawled back out and sat under the shade of the left wing. As I waited, I started to get hyper again, and my ribs were starting to kill me.

I had to calm down. I took some deep breaths, drank some water, and remembered help was on the way. I was not *seriously* injured—I mean, I still had all my arms and legs. Then I thought about the wrecked airplane and realized I was totally screwed. That didn't help my emotions any.

It seemed like my life had been going downhill ever since my brother, Stephen Nephi, left for his mission last September. He was my best friend, and I missed him a lot. Then Dad got his deployment orders around Halloween. Dad is a helicopter pilot, and the army needed him again. As an army brat, I was used to Dad being absent. Well, you don't really get used to it. You just come to accept it. I hated it when Dad had to leave home.

Most civilian kids really have no idea what it's like to live in a home where something called the army takes your daddy away. It seemed the army always wanted him to go away around Christmas or my birthday.

Short little TDYs for training or advancement were bad enough, but overseas deployments were the worst. He may have to be gone for a full year or more. I was angry at the army for taking him away from me again.

You have to find ways to cope. Some kids rebel and get into trouble with the law. Other kids run away or get sent to live with relatives. Some kids turn inward and suffer depression. Many children of deployed soldiers are terrible students.

But up until this deployment I had handled this stress in an entirely different way. I demanded more of myself. I wanted to have something good to put into my letters to him. I wanted Dad to be proud of me when he came home. This was especially true about my schoolwork. The only time I wasn't studying or reading something was when I went to church.

At church, I became president of my various classes. I volunteered for every service project. I sat on or chaired every youth committee. I never missed a meeting. I begged the bishop to let me give youth talks during our worship service.

That was how I coped in the past. But this deployment was different—so much worse than all the others rolled together. For the first time I realized Dad was not only going away, I now had a grasp on how long a year was. Even worse, I now realized there were people over there trying to shoot him down. They wanted to *kill* my father!

Around Thanksgiving I began falling into a deep funk. I was getting physically ill, even losing weight. I started using that as an excuse for staying away from school and church. I prayed as hard as I knew how, begging God to end the war or take Dad's unit out of it. I even began begging Dad not to go.

One morning, just before Christmas, I got up early and stood behind Dad's car so he couldn't back out of the drive. He got out of the car and just held me. There was nothing he could say. There was no other way I could communicate any stronger that I didn't want him to leave in January.

Or was there?

Mom finally came out in her robe and separated us and took me back into the house.

My depression started turning to anger. I got mad at Mom for not making him stay home. I got mad at Dad. I even got mad at God for not answering my prayers.

Christmas morning I just sat on the couch with my arms folded. I frowned the whole time. I wasn't putting on a childish show; that frown had become permanent. After that morning I basically locked myself in my room and stayed there. I only came out to eat very late at night when everyone was in bed.

One night Dad was waiting for me in the kitchen. He lit some of Mom's favorite decorative holiday candles that were still on the table. He made us ham sandwiches, and we ate in the near darkness. We talked and talked. We talked about everything but . . . his deployment. We both knew there was nothing left to be said on that topic.

That is the night that he told me that if I wanted, Grandpa Gus had offered to pay for my flight training for a private pilot's license. He was already paying for Stephen Nephi's flight training. The deal was he had to promise to go to college in exchange for the flight training. But all of that would have to wait until he got back from his mission. He got one semester in before he got his mission call.

This offer cheered me up quite a bit. Then Dad said, "You'll have to make him that same promise. This means you're going to have to straighten up your act at school. You can't afford any more grades like you got on this nine-week progress report."

I gave him my most sincere, "I will."

Grabbing the almost-empty bowl of Christmas candy, he said, "Let's go sit on the couch."

We moved to the living room and talked for another hour. Finally he said, "We've been missing you at family prayer; would you like to kneel down with me now and pray?"

That's when reality hit me again. Dad was leaving in just a couple of days. I suddenly started crying and said, "No! No more praying." I got up and without another word left him alone on the sofa.

On the day Dad was to leave, there was the usual big ceremony in one of the hangars on base. Dad's unit was lined up in parade formation in front of a parked CH-47 Chinook. A military band was playing some patriotic songs. A speaker's podium had been set up facing all the families, who were seated in chairs behind a yellow rope.

We all knew that yellow rope meant we were no longer allowed to hug or kiss or talk to our soldiers. It was as if they were already deployed, only we could still see them. The band stopped playing, and the group was called to attention.

Then the general stepped up to the podium. The soldiers were given the command that put them at "parade rest." Their feet moved apart, and they crossed their hands behind their backs. They all did it in unison and as smartly as they would give a salute. Their faces were all forward and expressionless. No one moved. No one scratched an itch. No one shrugged a shoulder to loosen a muscle. No one shifted their weight from one foot to the other to restore blood flow to their feet. No one whispered a word. This is when it really sank in that Chief Warrant Officer (CWO-3) Russell James Watson was *first* a soldier and then a husband and father.

There was always a hip-hip-hoorah speech given at these things. The general told us about God and country and patriotism and the storied history of his unit. He told us how proud we should be of our soldiers, how proud our nation was of them.

When I couldn't take anymore, I shouted, "Don't make them go, General!"

I had become a spectacle. Everyone craned their necks to see who had dared express her feelings. You could feel the tension in the hangar rise. Mom put her hand in mine. I looked over and saw her crying.

The general paused in his speech for just a moment. Then he smiled and continued on. I realized I had heard this speech before—the last time Dad deployed, and the time before that.

The general didn't know who had dared breach military etiquette but I wanted him to know. I stood up, and at first Mom tried to get me to sit down. Then she put her hand on the small of my back in a supportive way.

I stepped out of our aisle and moved right up to the edge of the yellow rope. I said again, "No, General, don't make them go!"

Everyone except some photographers stood still and speechless. I was so full of adrenalin, I was pretty much out of control. I looked over at Dad—I mean Chief Warrant Officer Watson. He didn't move a muscle, and his face remained expressionless. At that moment, I almost hated him.

I knocked over the orange cone in front of me. Half a dozen photographers were taking my picture as I stepped across the yellow rope that was now on the floor and I walked halfway to the podium. "General, do you see my dad over there? He won't even look at me because he's such a good soldier." Then I lost control and started crying.

"General, please don't make them go," I begged, and then I sank to my knees and started sobbing.

When I saw a soldier moving toward me, I figured they were going to throw me in the brig or something. But he was just the chaplain. Mother had now crossed the rope, and the two of them helped me to my feet and led me toward a row of chairs by the back wall of the hangar. He remained behind me and ever so gently put his hands on my shoulders. I wasn't sure if he was trying to comfort me or restrain me. I heard other children crying now, asking their parent why their father or mother had to leave. Several mothers and one father got up, with their upset kids, and walked back to where we were seated.

But the general finished his speech and the hangar doors opened. We could now see the C-17 cargo plane that was parked on the ramp. This was the plane that would take our soldiers away.

The band started again. There was some fancy drumming while the soldiers were called to attention. Then, on command, the band started playing an upbeat march, and the soldiers started filing out through the hangar doors. The families all got up out of their seats and moved up to the rope. They cheered and waved and held up signs and threw confetti as their good soldier marched past them and out to the ramp of the C-17.

It was like I was standing on the event horizon of a black hole. Once they marched up the ramp into that plane, we could no longer see them. I had the most sickening feeling that, like a real black hole, my father would never escape it. I would never see CWO-3 Watson again.

I was brought back to the present by the sound of a real helicopter. I got out from under the wing and slowly stood up in the heat. Now my neck, as well as my ribs, was hurting.

I could see a Chinook helicopter coming up from the south. At first I started jumping up and down and waving, but that hurt. Besides, I realized it was headed straight for me anyway. It must have homed in on my ELT. I had never been so happy to see a Chinook in my life. I suddenly gained a small appreciation for what my dad does for a living.

I sat back down next to the broken fuselage and watched as the helicopter circled me. Two soldiers were leaning out of an open door, looking down at me.

The chopper started to settle some distance away from my wreck. Before it was fully on the ground, four soldiers jumped out and came running toward me.

It looked like an army recruiting commercial on TV.

They asked me where I was injured.

"I've got a cut on my left side and my neck hurts. The rest of this blood belongs to the pelicans I hit."

One said, "Well, that would explain all the feathers." There were now half a dozen soldiers around me.

I told them I could walk and tried to get up, but they gently pushed me back against the broken fuselage. The lieutenant said, "No way. You'll be traveling first class."

While the lieutenant asked my name and some other questions, two of the soldiers started washing the blood off my face and gave me Gatorade. Then they put one of those collars around my neck, lifted me onto a stretcher, and buckled me in. Even my arms were strapped down.

Four of them lifted me up and carried me into the Chinook. The flight crew had stayed with the helicopter. The engines and blades were still turning, so the heat from the engines' exhaust was deflected down as we went up the ramp. It was extremely noisy.

They secured my stretcher into some hooks on the wall. It was a lot darker inside the helicopter, and it took a minute for my eyes to adjust. An enlisted flight crewmember put a headset on me and pulled the mic boom down in front of my lips. He tapped it with his fingers, pointed to the flight deck, and made the "talk" sign with his other hand. He put the mic switch in my hand.

I pushed the button, "Pilot, this is your passenger."

The pilot said, "I have your flight instructor on the horn."

"Summer, this is Denny. Are you okay?"

"I'm all right, Denny, but I think I have whiplash."

"You said you were bleeding?"

"It's mostly pelican blood. I hit like a half dozen pelicans. Denny, I'm sorry. The plane is a total wreck. Would you call my mom?"

"She's on the phone with me now."

"Can I talk to her?"

The pilot interrupted, "Sorry, guys, we need to cut this off. We are bingo on fuel and need to get going."

That was our cue to stop talking.

Once we were airborne I heard the pilot tell Denny that they were taking me to the unit hangar on base and an ambulance would take me from there to the emergency room. "Our ETA is twenty minutes. Muskrat Three-Three, over and out."

I heard the engines come up to speed, and the whining noises increased in volume. The vibrations in the airframe let me know the blades were also turning faster. Then I felt the helicopter lift off. The engine fumes were still being blown into the helicopter.

They closed the ramp. It really didn't get any quieter, but now I could hear new and different sounds the helicopter made. It got even darker until my eyes once again adjusted.

Then the pilot asked me, "Are you *the* Summer Rose Watson?"

"Uh, I guess."

"You're Chief Watson's daughter?"

"Yes, I am."

"Well, it's a privilege to have you onboard. You're kind of famous around the unit."

"Me?"

"Yes. The general has two photos on his credenza, in one of those bifold frames. One picture is of you with your words, 'No, General, don't make them go!' It was taken when you crossed the yellow rope. You know, he has a tremendous amount of respect for you."

"He does? Who's in the other picture?"

"General Douglas MacArthur. Under him is his famous quote, 'No one hates war more than a soldier.'"

Wow—he does know who I am!

CHAPTER 1

ABANDON ALL HOPE

I was traveling alone—*and* since I was only fifteen, I was considered an unaccompanied minor and had to be escorted. I'd been handed off from gate agent to flight attendant and back to gate agent again. It was really quite embarrassing. I was put in a "secure" waiting room at the Seattle–Tacoma airport. I would rather have been in the USO lounge. The room was filled with games and activities for little kids. About the time I found an old teen magazine, I was led to the underground tram that would take me the south terminal, where there was no possibility of escape.

Like a lot of other incorrigible military brats, I was being sent to live with an older relative. Unfortunately, my grandfather lives in Alaska. I really didn't want to go to Alaska. I felt like I was going to prison.

As we waited for the next tram, I thought above the gates of hell: *"All hope abandon, ye who enter here."* An automated voice announced the next tram was about to arrive. When the doors opened, we stepped on like shackled prisoners boarding the boat to Alcatraz. I was doomed to spend the rest of my summer in Alaska. As the automatic doors closed, I had the most awful feeling of a prison door closing.

Two minutes later the tram doors opened again, and we were below the remote terminal. We stepped onto the escalator and I thought about condemned prisoners climbing the stairs to the gallows. *Dead man walking.*

I was preboarded almost immediately and shown to my preassigned seat—21F. About halfway through the boarding process, another girl showed up; she was assigned to 21D. She was beautiful and wearing a very . . . let's say *summery* top. When she reached up to put her carry-on in the overhead compartment, several men seated near us really enjoyed the view. She settled in, looked over at me, and smiled. I smiled back.

I guess it's a primal thing that makes women size each other up. She had an athletic body but I was better built, if you know what I mean. She looked about five feet, two inches. That meant I was six inches taller than her. On the other hand, I have the dental braces thing working against me.

Our preflight safety briefing started, but it was unlike any I had ever seen. The cabin attendant announced we had two very special passengers with us. "They are the two oldest residents of the Alaska Pioneer's Home and are returning from a wild week in Seattle." Everyone laughed and applauded.

Then the two old ladies stood up and faced us. One was up front and the other one was about halfway back, nearer to us. They were so short I could barely see the one up front. They did all of the arm waving and pointing that would normally be done by the flight attendants. Actually, the taller flight attendants were standing behind the older ladies, doing what they would normally do. The passengers roared with laughter.

Then they showed us how to fasten and unfasten our seat belts and demonstrated how to put on our masks *in the unlikely event of cabin pressure loss.*

When it came time to demonstrate how to use our life preservers (*because we would be flying over water*), the old lady nearest us got all tangled up. Throwing hers down, she turned toward the steward behind her and wrapped her arms around him in a comic, romantic hug. Pursing her lips, she started smooching the air, begging for a kiss. She even reached up and tried loosening his tie. The steward could barely finish the briefing because he was laughing so hard. The lady would not let go of him until he bent down and gave her a proper kiss right on the lips. Everyone cheered. Finally letting go and fanning herself, she was brought back to her seat. Then the steward properly demonstrated the life vest thing, and we were off.

I enjoyed sitting behind the wing because I could see the control surfaces at work. As we took the runway, I watched the flaps being lowered and could associate some of those pump sounds with what was going on. It was fascinating to watch the flaps retract and the landing gear come up.

As land disappeared from view, I watched the ailerons and spoilers work as the pilot made several turns before climbing up out of the Seattle area.

About a half hour into the flight, I spotted a ship traveling between some islands off the coast of Canada and said, "Oh, look, a cruise ship!"

The girl in the aisle seat asked if she could look out my window and I invited her over. I have always been considered pretty, but I felt as plain as a mud fence next to her. She looked Latina and reminded me of a young version of a movie star whose name I couldn't remember. Her face was close to mine as she peered out the window. Looking at her mouth, I realized boys would do just about anything to kiss those lips, and I wished I had lips like hers. And that hair! It was just like a movie star's—long and full-bodied. It was a two-tone copper and caramel color.

Jessica Alba! That's it. She looks like a younger version of Jessica Alba.

A man in the row behind us said, "That's not a cruise ship, that's the M/V *Columbia*."

The girl sort of stood up and turned around to speak to the man. "I have ridden on the *Columbia*."

I looked up at her and could see her rock-hard abs—her abs . . . and a lot more—under her short top. I was definitely better endowed.

I asked, "So what's the *Columbia*?"

Turning to me, she said, "The M/V *Columbia* is one of the larger ferries on the Alaska Marine Highway. It is a super deluxe ferry with staterooms sort of like a cruise ship, just not as fancy."

"You mean like a car ferry?"

Sitting down in the center seat, she said, "Yes. There are only a couple of ways to get cars up to Alaska. You can drive them up the Alcan Highway or have them shipped up on a barge or put them on the ferry. The time I rode on the *Columbia*, Dad had just bought his Jaguar from a dealer in Seattle. We flew down to get it and came back up on the ferry.

"By the way, I'm Esperanza."

"Hey, my name is Summer Rose."

She smiled. "That's pretty. Is Rose your last name?"

"No, my last name is Watson. Rose is my middle name, but everybody always calls me Summer Rose—like a double first name. I really like your name too. Doesn't *esperanza* mean butterfly?"

"No, I think butterfly is *mariposa*. I don't speak Spanish, but I do know esperanza means hope."

"I've had a couple of semesters of Spanish classes, but I don't really speak Spanish either," I said with a shrug.

"Where do you go to school?" she asked.

"Salt Lake City, Central. I'm going to be a senior this year."

"Oh, I thought you lived in Alaska. You visiting somebody?"

"Yeah, sort of. I'm being forced to spend the rest of the summer at my grandpa's cabin in a town called Palmer. It has a lake, and there's a giant mountain behind it. But there's no cable TV, and Stephen Nephi says my cell phone won't work there. I don't even know if he has a computer or anything. I've been to it a couple of times for short visits, but I was younger then."

"Man, that sort of sounds like a prison."

Yeah! That's what I've been saying.

"Who's Stephen Nephi?"

I reached down, got my wallet out of my purse, and unfolded my pictures. "He's my brother," I said, pointing to a photo. "He left for his church mission in South America last fall. I really miss him a lot."

"He's cute. Is Nephi an Hispanic name?"

I kind of laughed. "No, it's actually an ancient Israelite name. So you live in Alaska?"

"Yeah, I live in Peter's Creek. That's, like, only twenty miles from Palmer. I've been outside for two weeks."

"Outside?"

"Outside is how Alaskans describe everyplace *but* Alaska," she replied. "I've been in Denver—one of my cousins got married. That's kind of a problem Alaskans have. Hardly anyone has extended family up here. We always have to fly out for things like weddings and funerals and graduations and stuff. I flew down with my parents, but I stayed for an extra week, so I'm traveling back alone."

She raised her arms like a cheerleader and said, "This is the first time I've traveled as an *adult*," using her fingers to put quotation marks around "adult."

She showed me a picture of her parents. "They adopted me when I was a baby, and they're a lot older than most of my friends' parents, but they're pretty cool. Our last name is Harris."

Her mother looked black and her father white, but I tried not to looked shocked or anything. *Back in Utah we don't see many interracial couples.*

I looked at the house in the background. It was huge and made of logs and had a big stone wall that I guessed was the backside of a fireplace. It also had huge picture windows. "Is that your house?"

"Yeah, it's pretty cool, huh? We're kinda rich."

She was very casual about the "rich" thing and didn't appear to be bragging.

"We can see Mount Susitna from the living room windows, and on a clear day we can even see Mount Spurr from the deck. It's really cool when there's steam coming out of it."

"You mean like volcanoes?"

"Yeah."

She said it so matter-of-factly, like everybody can see volcanoes from their front porch.

"There's also a really awesome canyon just behind our house, with a really sick waterfall called Thunderbird Falls. I think it's in a state park or something."

Flipping through her pictures, I saw one of Esperanza standing next to a hunk. "Wow! Who is that?"

Looking over, she said, "Oh, he's so 'last semester.' His name is Bruce. He's cute, but a real jerk. He's a running back for our high school football team and really thinks a lot of himself. He has rushin' hands and roamin' fingers." She pulled the picture out of its sleeve and tore it up.

The flight attendant and little old lady got to our row with the beverage cart. We each took a diet drink from the little old lady. She was such a crackup.

Esperanza got quiet as she looked through more of my pictures. "What's your dog's name?"

I looked over and said, "Oh, that's Ammo. He's Grandpa Gus's dog. His full name is Ammo Mark Two Mod One."

"Ammo what?" Esperanza asked, with a puzzled half-smile.

"He's named Ammo after his sire, Ammo Mark One Mod Zero. Grandpa got the first Ammo from the bomb dump at Galena Air Force Base."

She said, "I know Galena; it's on the Iditarod Trail."

"Cool. Anyway, Mark Two Mod One is the military way of saying version two point one."

"Okay, I understand why he's Mark Two, but why is he Mod One?" Then she shrieked, "He only has three legs; how freaky!"

I guess she's never seen a three-legged dog before.

I started explaining. "When Ammo Mark Two Mod Zero was a puppy, he got kicked by a moose. His right front leg was torn up so badly the vet had to take it off. He also took out Ammo's shoulder. When Ammo healed, it looked like he'd never had a right front leg. There was no stump or lump or anything—just the smooth curve of his ribs. His hair eventually covered up the scars, and now it looks like he was born with three legs, and that's why he's a Mod One."

Esperanza had repositioned herself to get a better look at me, and I felt a little self-conscious looking into her eyes. She showed me pictures of her dogs. They were gorgeous. I'd never seen such expressive faces and beautiful markings. One of the dogs had bright blue eyes, and the other had one blue eye and one brown eye. "Are they malamutes?"

"No, they're Siberian huskies. They're really good dogs. We've had them since I was about twelve. The one with one brown eye is Denali, and the other one is Kenai." I asked about their blue eyes. She said, "Most Huskies have two blue eyes, but some are mixed, like Denali's."

Esperanza was flipping through more of my photos when she saw a picture of me standing next to a Cessna 152. "What's this picture all about?"

"That's the airplane I got my flight training in. It was taken on the day of my first solo flight."

She looked at me oddly, like she was waiting for me to tell her I was joking.

I finally said, "Really, that picture was taken on the day I became a pilot."

"No way."

"Really, I *am* a pilot."

"Do you have a pilot's license?"

"No, I had a mishap in May, and my doctor grounded me so I haven't finished all my requirements. Besides, I have to wait until I turn sixteen to get my license."

"Sixteen? I thought you're going to be a senior next year."

"Yeah, I know. I skipped second grade when we lived in Illinois. During my fifth-grade year we moved to Ft. Rucker, Alabama. The state of Alabama rates, like, second to last in U.S. educational standards, and I tested so high they just put me in sixth grade. Because of that, I've always had a hard time fitting in with my peer group. Or maybe it's that I couldn't figure out which peer group I belonged to. In school I hang out with my classmates, but at church I'm forced to be in classes with kids my own age."

Then there is the problem of how tall and developed I am. Most people think I am much older than I am.

"Wow, even though I'm homeschooled, I've always gotten to spend time with kids my own age. I turned eighteen in March."

Esperanza looked at the picture again, and I could tell she wanted to know more about my being a pilot.

"My father has a pilot's license, and I learned to fly before I learned to drive. I can totally fly the airplane alone, but I have to be supervised by an instructor pilot on the ground, so I can get solo time. I can't take passengers up yet, but once I turn sixteen and finish up a few last requirements I'll have my license. But get this! Back home, we have a stepped system for getting a driver's license. That means I have to have an adult with me when I drive to the airport, where I can get in an airplane *alone* and fly anywhere in the United States! I can fly anytime, night or day, and I can even have passengers. I don't think that's made me mad yet, but I'll bet it will once I get my license."

Esperanza gave me a big grin and said, "No, duh. So what did you mean when you said you had a mishap—you mean, like a crash?"

"Yeah, but we never say 'crash.'"

"Did you get, like, hurt and stuff?"

I told her the whole story and realized several people around us were listening too.

"You broke your ribs! Really?"

I discretely lifted my shirt and showed her my scar.

"Word! Is that the reason you're coming to Alaska?"

"No, that's a different story."

Sensing something juicy, she leaned a little closer and almost whispered, "What could be worse than a plane crash?"

I told her about my little rebellion after Dad deployed. Then I lowered my voice and said, "I just stopped going to church and had missed so much school I had to take a makeup chemistry lab. I met this Goth kid in summer school and started hanging out with him. My mom had no idea about him.

"One night I snuck out and met him. He drove us up into the canyon to a place where you can see all of Salt Lake City. It was kind of cool at first. We sat on the hood of his car, but then he tried to get me into the backseat.

"I refused and got into the front seat and told him I wanted to go home. He got behind the wheel and lit up a joint and tried to get me to chill out with him. He kept pushing it toward my face, so I got back out of the car. He totally freaked out and left me standing there alone.

"I started walking back down the canyon road without even a flashlight. I kept hoping he would come back and get me. About fifteen minutes later I saw headlights coming up the road. I thought it was him but it ended up being a police car.

"I didn't get arrested even though I'm sure they smelled the pot on my hair and clothes. When they found out how old I was, they took me to the police station. When we got there, Mom was waiting for me—I'd never seen her so upset. I tried to explain nothing happened but I guess she'd had enough of my rebellion."

Esperanza said, "That blows, but you make Alaska sound like a prison. Is your grandfather mean or something?"

"No, he's really cool; he's the one who's paying for my flight training. I don't know, I guess just the idea of having to live out in the woods. You know? No malls or theaters, and I won't be able to go to the Lagoon."

"What's the Lagoon?"

"It's a water theme park near Salt Lake City."

"Girl, we've got malls and theaters and really anything you want. You know what? We should get together this summer! I have my own car, and we don't live that far apart. We don't have a Lagoon, but I live a couple of miles from Mirror Lake. My friends and I hang out there a lot—there's a bike path all of the way out there, and we've got extra bikes.

"I'll bet you've read the book called *Williwaw*, right?"

"Yeah," I said. "By Tom Bodett."

"And I'll bet you think all of Alaska is like the part of Alaska that Ivan and September lived in, don't you?"

"Well, I've never really studied it, but I guess in general I do."

She held out her wallet and said, "Here are some pictures from a party we had at Mirror Lake last summer."

"Wow! This isn't like Grandpa's lake. I don't think his lake even has a name or anything. It's just a neighborhood lake with a couple of houses around it. Does the water get warm enough to swim in?"

"Yeah, as long as you don't swim out to the middle or dive too deep."

We swapped addresses and phone numbers and promised to stay in touch.

"I'll be around all summer," Esperanza said, "except for one week when I'm at cheerleading camp."

"Wait, I thought you said you were homeschooled?"

"I am. Homeschooling is very popular in Alaska. We form co-ops—like, my mom is a retired doctor, so she's really strong in the life sciences. Someone else's mom or dad may be strong in math or a foreign language. In fact, one of the boys in our co-op is from Russia, so his parents are teaching us Russian for our foreign language requirement. The state also allows us to attend regular school part time, so we can use the science labs or participate in extracurricular activities. So even though I'm homeschooled, I'm considered a rising senior at Chugiak High School, and I'm on the varsity cheerleading squad." She raised her arms and shouted, "Wooo, go Mustangs!"

Someone in the back of the plane shouted back, "Chu-Chu-Chuuuugiak." Esperanza sported a big grin and then jumped up into the aisle and shouted back, "Muuuustangs" and did that bouncy thing cheerleaders do.

Somebody else started chanting, "UAA, UAA, we are the Seawolves, and we've come here to play!" Then someone else called out, "UAF—Nanoooooooks!" It seemed as if everybody on the plane was cheering. Someone would holler out the name of a school, and a small crowd would cheer for that school, and then the next and the next. Then all kinds of songs and chants started being thrown back and forth. It was like we were at a pep rally. Different groups were trying to out-sing the others.

This went on for about five minutes. It wasn't like a riot or anything, but it had to be the noisiest airplane in the world. And then there were more than a couple of people getting up and moving around in the plane, acting like wannabe cheerleaders.

It was like these people were happy to be going back to Alaska.

The seat belt sign came on, and one of the stewardesses got on the intercom and asked us all to take our seats and buckle up. Then I noticed a very handsome man in a pilot's uniform walking down the aisle from the front of the airplane. He was tall and wearing his hat, so he was quite a sight. He came about halfway back and just stood in the isle, very near our row. I figured we were in trouble, but then I saw him smiling. People slowly started quieting down and mostly just looked at him.

Over the intercom, a man identified himself as the captain and announced, "Ladies and gentlemen, we've just crossed latitude fifty four-forty. Welcome to Alaska." There was a muffled cheer and a smattering of applause. I guess the response was subdued because the other crewman—the copilot I now guessed—was still standing in the aisle.

Then he took off his hat and started singing in a beautiful tenor voice! It was shocking because of its clarity and because it was so unexpected. "Eight stars of gold on a field of blue—Alaska's flag. May it mean to you . . ."

It was chilling. I got goose bumps, and the effect on the other passengers was immediate. He paused for just a second, as if asking for everyone's attention. His voice was as clear as a trumpet. "The blue of the sea, the evening sky, the mountain lakes and the flow'rs nearby; the gold of the early sourdough's dreams . . ."

Then, as if on cue, it seemed like most of the passengers joined in. "The precious gold of the hills and streams. The brilliant stars in the northern sky."

Even Esperanza was singing. "The bear, the dipper, and shining high . . ."

The man in the aisle—with his powerful voice still loud and clear—now had an entire chorus accompanying him. "The great North Star, with its steady light, over land and sea, a beacon bright. Alaska's flag—to Alaskans dear, the simple flag of the last frontier."

When the song ended, there was a respectful applause—no whistles or "woooos." The copilot, still smiling, turned and walked back into the cockpit. The passengers all returned to their quiet conversations and remained in their seats.

I asked, "What was *thaaat*?"

Esperanza said, "That's Alaska's state song."

I looked at her in disbelief and said, "Nobody sings their state song. I don't even know what Utah's state song is."

"Well, we sing ours," she said. "The words are about our state flag. It was designed by a young native Alaskan orphan by the name of Benny Benson. In Alaska, he's as famous as Betsy Ross."

Who knew?

The beverage cart came by a second time—the little old lady was taking her job so seriously.

Esperanza said, "I haven't heard you say anything about your grandmother."

"Grandpa lives alone except for Ammo, but he does have a girlfriend. Her name is Sister Baker. She lives on the next road, in another cabin sitting at the other end of the lake."

Esperanza asked, "Why is she called Sister; is she like a minister or something?"

"No, in our church we call each other brother and sister."

Esperanza picked up my wallet again and looked at the last few pictures. "This must be your mom. She looks nice. And this has to be your dad."

"Yeah, and that's his helicopter. He's halfway through his third tour in the sandbox."

"The sandbox?"

"Sorry, that's army talk. The sandbox is the Middle East—you know, Iraq, Pakistan, Afghanistan, and probably some other 'stans.'"

"That must really be a bummer. I'm sorry."

She really means that.

"This your grandfather?"

"Yes, everybody calls him Grandpa Gus."

Looking closely at another picture, she said, "That's weird. This guy kinda looks familiar, but I don't know why."

I shrugged. "That's my Uncle Chris; he's the only one of my aunts and uncles who still lives in Alaska. He lives in Trapper Creek and has his veterinary clinic in Willow. He's also a professional dog musher. He has this huge pickup truck with dog kennels built onto the bed. He's also got a big flatbed trailer with a winch and a hoist that he can tow behind his truck."

As I went on, I noticed Esperanza was staring at me, her mouth sort of hanging open.

"Uncle Chris races in all the long-distance sled races in Alaska—the Tustumena 200 and the Kuskokwim 300 every year and the Yukon Quest every other year. He even finished the Iditarod once, but now, instead of racing, he volunteers his vet services every March. He uses his Cessna 185 Skywagon to haul injured or sick dogs from some of the remote checkpoints along the trail."

Esperanza got this look on her face. You know, that "lightbulb just came on" look.

"Are you talking about Doc Rock? Oh, sick! He's, like, so totally famous around here! You're related to Doc Rock?! The flying vet, right? Shut up! Did you say his name is Chris?"

Now I didn't know if she was joking with *me*. "Yes, his full name is Christian August Rockwell."

"Shut up." Then she went off again. "Doc Rock is so cool! He goes around with his sleds and dogs and does presentations at schools and stuff. And during Fur Rondy, he gives rides on real dogsleds. I got to ride in his sled one winter. Oh! Oh! And during state fair, he hooks up his dogs to, like, a go-cart thing with big tires. He's so totally cool. I totally had a crush on him when I was younger. I can't believe he's your uncle! My friends will just freak out!"

She finally started slowing down, just a little. "Do you know about the Iditarod? I mean, how it got started?"

"I guess. Uh no, I guess I don't really."

"We start learning about the Iditarod race and the serum run to Nome when we're in the first grade," she started. "Back in 1925, a diphtheria epidemic broke out up in Nome. There was just one doctor in town, and he had only enough serum to treat one patient—even though there were hundreds more who would probably need it—so he telegraphed for help. There was lots of serum in Anchorage—but it was January. There are no roads to Nome, and the ocean was frozen. It was way too cold to fly any of the few open-cockpit planes up there. The only way to get the serum to Nome was by dogsled, on the mail trail. Part of the trail is down frozen rivers and part of it even crosses a bay on the Bering Sea. Twenty mushers raced in relays for six hundred seventy-five miles. It took five and a half days, but they saved the town."

"Wow, I had no idea," I said. "So that's how the Iditarod started?"

Esperanza nodded. "The Iditarod is to Alaska what the Kentucky Derby is to Kentucky. They have everything from serious stuff like the economic impact of tourism to silly things like car dealers and furniture stores having Iditarod Race Days sales events.

"When I was in grade school, we had a contest called the I-Dit-A-Read. There was a big map of the race trail posted on the wall. Whenever you finished reading a book, you could move your little paper sled along the trail to the next checkpoint. Whoever read the required number of books the fastest won the I-Dit-A-Read race.

"Actually, just like in the real race, there are no losers—every musher who finishes the race is considered a winner. In the real race, the last musher is given a special award at the awards banquet—a red lantern—'cause they're like the caboose. We had our own little awards party at the end of our reading race, but we had to wait until the last student finished reading. We all colored red lanterns and gave that person a great big cheer."

She finally stopped talking. I just looked at her and said, "Okaaaayyy." Then we both cracked up.

Just then the pilot came on the intercom and told us that passengers on the right side of the airplane could see College Fjord. He told us there are thirteen glaciers in the fjord, all named after east coast colleges like Harvard and Yale. There was quite a bit of excitement and picture-taking going on. It was pretty easy to tell who the tourists were. Esperanza explained that Alaskan residents all know to get seats on the right-hand side of the plane when flying to Alaska.

So I guess it wasn't chance that I'm sitting where I am. I saw the remarkable glaciers, and the deep fjords they had carved into the mountains. They were steep-sided canyons that descended right into the ocean.

Esperanza and I kinda got talked-out after a while, so I pulled out my journal and she turned on her iPod. A little while later, I heard the engines throttle back a little and felt the pilot push the nose over. The steward then started his announcements about preparations for landing. The little old lady and her stewardess companion came by and collected our trash.

We dropped down into the Anchorage Bowl—it was so beautiful. It sort of reminded me of Salt Lake City. After landing, Esperanza and I said our good-byes and promised to call each other. She grabbed her carry-on and moved down the aisle with the rest of the "adults." When the other passengers had cleared out, I was finally escorted off the plane.

The three flight attendants, the two old ladies, and the copilot said good-bye and wished us a happy stay in Alaska. I was *once again* escorted to a private secure area. The plane ride had almost made me forget I didn't want to be in Alaska.

When Grandpa showed up, I played it cool and just shook his hand.

He didn't react but just smiled his "grandpa smile." He told me how happy he was to see me and how good I look with my new braces.

Gah! I hate my braces!

When we walked out of the secure room, guess who was standing right outside—Esperanza!

She said, "The last time I landed at this airport I was just seventeen, so they stuck me in the same area. That's how I knew where to find you."

I introduced her to Grandpa and started telling him all about her as we headed to the luggage carousel where we met her parents. Esperanza made all the introductions and told them how we'd met and stuff. Then Grandpa suggested we all go out to dinner.

This is not exactly what I expected on my arrival. I still felt like I had just gotten off the boat at Alcatraz Island.

Esperanza asked, "Dad, Summer Rose and Mr. Rockwell live out in Palmer. Can we go out there and eat at Turkey Red's?"

Grandpa said, "That is the restaurant that serves local organic produce, right? I've heard it is a great place to eat. I am always up for a new restaurant."

So it was agreed, and after getting our luggage, we headed out in our separate cars. It was so good to see Grandpa again, but I didn't want him to know that. He'd been such an important father figure to me, especially when Dad was overseas. Mom and Stephen Nephi and I have visited Grandpa several times during school breaks, but since I'd been a kid, this time was like I was seeing Alaska for the first time. Grandpa tried to get me into conversations, but mostly I remained quiet and looked at the mountains. After all, I didn't want to get to chatty with my prison warden.

We met the Harrises at the restaurant. Esperanza told us she eats there every time the Mustangs have a game out in the valley. The restaurant has a real brick oven for things like pizza and bread. We all had some awesome Italian dishes. Then came the desserts—unbelievable! They had the most wonderful "healthy" desserts. Grandpa had a hard time sorting through all the yogurts and vegan dishes but finally found a carrot cake he thought he might like.

Esperanza told her parents Grandpa Gus was Doc Rock's father. *Funny—she called him Grandpa Gus.* As we talked, we found out Mrs. Harris was retired from the public health service. She had traveled all over the state providing health care in remote villages. Grandpa talked a little about his military career and his flying experiences.

When Grandpa slowed down, Mr. Harris said, "I'm a retired airline pilot. I flew for the old Reeves Aleutian Airline."

"What did you fly while you were in the air force?"

"I started out flying in MATS in the Douglas C-124 Cargomaster, and then I later flew the Douglas C-133 Cargomaster IIs. I finished up flying some old Lockheed C-130As along the DEW line."

Grandpa said, "All targets, eh?"

"Yes, and proud of it; you know what they say, 'You call, we haul.' How about you?"

"I flew bug smashers—the O-2 Skymaster."

"Ahh, those little targets."

Trying to keep up with them, I asked, "Why do you call them targets?"

Mr. Harris said, "Because some pilots think there are only two kinds of airplanes—fighters and targets. Your grandfather and I were not fighter pilots, so we flew targets. Gus, I could tell you some stories."

Mrs. Harris said, "Maybe another time, Robert." She then turned to me and said, "Please tell us about yourself, Summer Rose."

I wasn't expecting that and didn't know what to say.

Grandpa turned to me and said, "Bob, she is one of our sisters, and a future astronaut."

"An aerospace pilot, Grandpa. Astronauts are just SPAM in a can."

Mr. Harris clapped and said, "I haven't heard that expression since the Mercury Program ended in 1963."

Mrs. Harris turned to me and said, "So you're a pilot too." It was cool because she didn't say it with surprise or disbelief.

When I glanced over at Esperanza, I saw her silently mouth the words, "An astronaut!"

CHAPTER 2

THE BUTT SISTERS AND A GOOSE CHASE

My first couple of days in Alaska were kind of awkward. I was still not happy about being here. There sure weren't any malls in this neighborhood, and I discovered Stephen Nephi had been right—my cell phone didn't work at the cabin. There was only one phone in the house, an old-fashioned desk phone with the curly cord. It sat on a table right next to grandpa's recliner.

There was a computer in the study, but it was only connected to a DSL line. *Like totally useless.* There was a TV, but it was just a small one and worked off rabbit ears. It only picked up four channels, and MTV wasn't one of them.

The best thing about my prison was Ammo. Ammo is, like, the coolest dog I've ever known. He's a black Labrador retriever. I have always enjoyed playing with him when I came to visit. He is pretty old now and has lots of gray hairs on his face and the tip of his tail. He's the smartest dog in the world—at least that's what Grandpa says, and I think he's right. He even looks smart.

Some dogs just mope around—you know, sleep a lot and don't want to be bothered—but Ammo's different. When he sits, he sits up very straight, and his chin sticks out, not down. He's always looking around like he wants to learn something or do something. Even when he's asleep, his ears move around in the direction of the least little sound. I call it his radar. He loves swimming in the lake and going for boat rides.

So far we started each day the same way. Ammo would come in and wake me up by sticking his head under the covers and putting his wet nose on my tummy. So I would roll over and he would start licking my ears until I got out of bed.

Grandpa cooked eggs and bacon and real biscuits every morning. He didn't even ask what I wanted for breakfast.

After we ate, I cleaned up the kitchen, and then we went out to the front porch. We would each have a cup of hot chocolate and some leftovers biscuits. This morning, Grandpa was wearing a beautiful pair of moccasins that his girlfriend, Sister Baker, had given him, and one of his anoraks. I had on a sweater and a pair of fat fuzzy moose slippers with soft little moose antlers and big roly-poly eyes. A summer morning in the Mat-Su Valley—a sweltering fifty degrees!

In the Anchorage area this time of year, the sun comes up at four thirty and doesn't go down until eleven thirty. The sun had actually been up for four hours, but because Grandpa's cabin sits in the valley, the sun was just now peeking over the Talkeetna Mountains. It felt good on my face. Ammo was sprawled out in a pool of sunlight in front of the swing.

Ammo and Grandpa started their regular morning ritual. Ammo had slowly worked his way toward Grandpa's feet. Lying there with his chin on his paw, he looked up at Grandpa without moving his head—just looking up with his eyes. Then his tail started thumping on the floor.

Grandpa had casually placed his hand behind Ammo's bacon grease-soaked biscuit, which was sitting on the front edge of the porch swing. Grandpa pretended not to see him—the tension slowly increased until Grandpa finally flicked the biscuit with his finger. It flew straight for Ammo's face. He snapped it up like the fox that ate the gingerbread man, licked his jowls, burped, and then got up and went on his morning walk along the lake.

Grandpa was reading *Mother Earth News* and had several other gardening magazines on the swing beside him. I'd brought out a book from Grandpa's library—an atlas kind of thing about the different regions of Alaska. As I flipped through it, I came to the section on the Aleutian Islands.

Since I was in "general population" of the prison this morning, I decided to talk to Grandpa a little bit. "Grandpa, have you ever been to the Aleutian Islands?"

He thought for a minute and said, "Let's see . . . I guess I have spent close to a year out there, if you add up all my trips."

"Wow. What did you do?"

"Well, I could tell you, but then I would have to shoot you," he said with a grin. "Much of that year I was on the Island of Shemya because of military duties."

"You mean because of the Cold War, don't you?"

"Yes, but I never liked that term. The Cold War was a lot hotter than you might think. Anyway, besides my time on Shemya, I took a fishing trip out to Attu and . . . let's see, I was hunting for World War II plane wrecks on Buldir and back again on Attu. I spent almost three weeks on several islands when I did some volunteer work for the US Fish and Wildlife Service."

"About the only thing I know about the islands is what I had learned back in sixth grade," I said with some confidence. "They're the Bering Land Bridge."

Putting down his magazine, he said, "You're a little confused, Granddaughter. "They have nothing to do with the Bering Land Bridge. Let's straighten you out on that point, and then we can talk about the islands.

"First of all," he continued, "I'm surprised they still call it a land bridge. Its proper name is Beringia, and it's a vast region of continental crust that is currently submerged under the Bering Sea. Several times in Earth's history, it was exposed by low sea levels, and during those periods we know that it was forested and at least parts of it were glaciated. The last time sea levels were low enough to expose it, was about seventeen thousand years ago, but we're currently in an interglacial period, and sea levels have been rising ever since then. Geologists have brought up core samples that yielded sandy beaches, rock-strewn river beds, and even freshwater frozen lakes. They've also brought up a bunch of organic material that has been carbon-dated at fifteen thousand BP."

I was having a hard time believing I was wrong about what I had learned in sixth-grade geography class. "Grandpa, are you sure?"

Grandpa chuckled and said, "Yes, I am sure. It is all in that book you're holding. I know it is hard to unlearn something, but I promise you, your teacher was wrong."

I sat there for a moment with my mouth open. "Wow, I never thought about a teacher being wrong before."

"Don't get me started on that," he said, shaking his head. "Anyway, even today most of Beringia is only one hundred to one hundred fifty feet under water."

"Don't you mean *thirty to fifty meters*?" I teased, smiling. Grandpa thinks the United States should have converted to the metric system back in Benjamin Franklin's day.

"As a matter of fact, yes I *do*," he said, smiling back. "By the way, part of the Bering Sea covers oceanic crust too. The Bowers Basin is twelve thousand feet—I mean *four thousand meters* deep.

"But we started this conversation with the Aleutian Islands," he said, leaning back again in the swing. "They're different from the rest of Alaska, in a lot of ways. The temperature is very mild—it stays chilly in the summer but doesn't get very cold in the winter. It rains almost all the time, except sometimes when it snows, and it's almost always foggy and windy. Weathermen call it 'the birthplace of storms.' Another name could be 'home of the forty-knot fog.'

"Let's see, what else? All the islands are covered with tall grasses and sedges, and there aren't any trees on the western islands, the ones closest to Russia. Oh, and there aren't any indigenous land mammals, but the islands are a natural breeding ground for all kinds of migrating birds—snowy owls and bald eagles and all sorts of ducks and eiders and petrels and coots. Also, gulls and puffins and too many other kinds of birds to remember. Geese, too—but I'll tell you about the geese in a little while."

"Wow, Grandpa," I said. "So you said you worked for the US Fish and Wildlife Service?"

"No, I said I *volunteered*." He held his mug toward me. "If you get me another cup of hot chocolate, I'll tell you the whole story."

"Okay!" It only took a minute, and then I brought out Grandpa's fresh mug and sat again on my end of the swing.

He took a big slurp and settled back. "I guess this story actually starts back in the early 1900s, when wearing fur was considered fashionable. Women wore fur coats, stoles, muffs, and hats. Even men sported fur trim on their leather coats. Fox fur was especially popular.

"American fur farmers got rich—and looking for a way to get even richer, they saw the Aleutian Islands as perfect low-overhead fox farms. They got permits to plant breeding pairs on their own private islands. The fox couldn't run away and had all the free food they could eat. A few summers later, the farmers came back to harvest the animals. At the same time, they also captured several vixens and traded them with other farmers, to keep the gene pool healthy. The most common breed was the Arctic blue fox."

"*Blue* fox? Really, Grandpa?"

"Actually, Arctic fox come in two varieties. The mainland or northerns are brown in the summer and pure white in the winter. The Aleutian or blue fox are brown in the summer and gray to blue-black in the wintertime. They were harvested in the summer because of the color of their pelts.

"Anyway, you might think this was a smart way to farm fox, but there was a problem no one thought about back then. The birds that migrate there all nest in the tall grass or in burrows, where the fox could easily predate eggs and chicks. Aleutian Canada geese nearly went extinct and had to be placed on the endangered species list."

"What about the other birds, Grandpa. Weren't they being killed too?"

"Yes, they were—but I call this story 'The Great *Goose* Chase.'" He chuckled and then went on. "Only one thing kept *all* the birds from going extinct—some of the islands had no beaches, just cliffs rising straight up out of the sea. There was no way farmers could plant fox on those islands, which meant the birds were safe there.

"So," Grandpa said, shifting in his seat, "during the Great Depression, people stopped buying fur. The fox farmers just abandoned their islands and let the animals go feral. Without natural predators, the fox population exploded. Since they had already driven the birds away, they survived by scavenging fish and breaking open clams and sea urchins.

"The Alaska Fish and Wildlife Service saw the problem as early as the 1940s. If they were going to save any of the endangered species of birds, the first thing they had to do was get rid of the fox. At first the eradication was only done on some of the islands, and it took many years."

"*Eradication!* That's sad, Grandpa. The fox weren't to blame—they didn't ask to be put on the islands! It's not fair." I was sorry for those fox—first the farmers "harvested" them and then the wildlife service eradicated them.

Grandpa looked at me for a moment. "I know, Granddaughter, but not much *is* fair in nature."

"I'm sorry, Grandpa. I know you're right."

"Okay," he said with a smile and patted me on the knee. "By 1962 all the fox on Amchitka had been eradicated, but the geese still hadn't come back. So during the 1970s, the US Fish and Wildlife Service released breeding pairs that had been raised in captivity, and in the 1980s they translocated wild geese to the island. They then left the island completely alone for ten years. No one was allowed on the island without a special permit, so the geese wouldn't be disturbed. They hoped the translocated geese would return to the island for the next mating season—then perhaps the second generation of geese would come the following year—and so on."

"So what happened, Grandpa?"

"Well, in 1994, the wildlife refuge manager was ready to see if the geese had reestablished themselves on Amchitka. They hired seasonal workers with a background in wildlife management to do the count—but they also advertised for volunteers in the Anchorage newspaper. I saw the ad and volunteered.

"I hopped on a military supply flight to the Island of Kodiak and then caught another flight that shuttled supplies and personnel out into the Aleutians." He paused. "You know I can hop planes like that, right—as a military retiree—if there's room?"

I nodded, and he continued. "The next day I continued on to the Island of Adak. There were about a dozen of us. I was the only volunteer to make it out there. We met the director of the wildlife refuge on Adak. We spent the night waiting for the R/V *Tiĝlax*, the research vessel that

would take us to Amchitka. *Tiglax* is a native word for 'eagle'. The *Tiĝlax*
is very modern, *but* it doesn't have a gangway. To get onboard you have
to use a Billy Pugh basket."

"A what?" I asked. "A *billipew* basket?"

Grandpa chuckled, "Billy Pugh—that's the inventor's name. It's kind
of like a big string bag with a rigid bottom and an outside rim to stand
on. Anyway, you just throw your gear inside the basket and then stand
on that outside rim and hold on. A crane picks the basket up and swings
it off the dock and onto the main deck of the ship.

"Pretty soon the ship was headed out to sea. We went up to the
highest deck above the bridge and watched Adak disappear behind
us—and almost as soon as we left the harbor, we saw pods of porpoise
escorting us."

"That's so cool! I'd love to see something like that!"

Grandpa got quiet for a minute and then started smiling and rocking
the swing sideways. With each sideways swing, my slippers rubbed
across Ammo's back.

"Grandpa, what're you doing that for?"

"Oh, just a pleasant memory from that trip. Unlike cruise ships, the
Tiĝlax doesn't have roll stabilizers. I really enjoyed sitting in a hammock
chair that hung on the fantail. The chair was suspended by just one rope
and would swing back and forth as the ship rolled in the sea. After just
a few minutes, it felt like the *chair* was stationary and the *horizon* was
rocking back and forth. That kind of sensory confusion can kill a pilot."

"I don't understand. How?"

"Well, my *mind* knew the chair was swinging back and forth, but
the fluid in my ears was convinced it was the horizon that was moving,"
Grandpa explained. "Hasn't your flight instructor demonstrated that for
you?"

"No, sir."

He let out a little harrumph and pulled at his anorak. "Are you
getting as warm as I am?"

"Yes, sir, I am."

"Well, I'm going to change and then go out to the garden. Would
you like to join me?"

"Sure, Grandpa."

"Okay. Then I'll meet you out in the shed?"

A few minutes later I walked out back and in the open door of the shed. I'd never been in the shed before. It served as a gardening center, wood shop, mechanic shop, and recycling center. It was neat and tidy and well-lit. Some interesting things hung on the wall. He had an X-Files poster. You know, the one with a UFO and the words I Want to Believe. There was old metal road sign that said SLOW CHILREN, PLAYING and my favorite was a real Klingon bat'leth!

Grandpa was putting on work gloves and knee pads and offered me the same. I guessed we were going to do some weeding. We headed out to the garden and I couldn't believe my eyes. It was the fanciest garden I had ever seen. It was just like the ones in the gardening magazines.

"Grandpa, it's beautiful. I've never seen a garden that wasn't just all straight rows." Things were growing in clusters and raised boxes and even in some barrels. Everything could be tended from little gravel paths that wound through the garden. You never had to step in the dirt.

He walked me over to one of the clusters. "I am trying companion planting for the first time. You see here—this raised area is where I have several dozen tomato plants, but all around them I have planted carrots. Carrots and tomatoes actually fight off each other's pests.

"Over here I have several clusters of beans and potatoes—they also help each other. And do you see all the herbs and flowers planted everywhere? They are planted throughout the garden to act as insect repellants and as pollinator attractors."

We walked over to another raised bed, and he showed me his cabbages. "They are protected by rings of onion plants—rabbits hate onions. I have also learned that I can sprinkle just plain old cayenne pepper on the ground to keep the rabbits out."

"Wow, Grandpa, these cabbages are huge!"

"Yes! I am preparing them for show at the state fair. Let me introduce you to these three. Girls, may I introduce you to my granddaughter, Summer Rose Watson? Summer, these are the Butt Sisters—Bertha, Beulah, and Bathsheba."

I fake curtsied and said, "It's nice to meet you, ladies. Grandpa, sometimes you're just a big kid."

"Thank you, I'll take that as a compliment." He then slapped his right fist and made it spin around and bonk me on the head. I broke into my Curly imitation and gave him my best "nyuk-nyuk-nyuk-woob-woob-woob-woob."

After we got the Three Stooges out of our systems, Grandpa started talking to me about Alaskan farming. "Most of us gardeners here in the valley put our plants in the ground over Memorial Day weekend, but lots of us actually start growing them in early April. I had plants all over the house, in near almost every window, and even the airplane hangar was full of flowers.

"What do you say we get to work? If you can't tell the difference between a weed and an herb, just let me know."

We started pulling little weeds.

"Do you use any pesticides or fertilizers?" I asked.

"Fertilizers, no. This soil is unbelievably rich. Pesticides—we will have to see. If everything I read is true, I should not need any. That is, except for the worst garden pest of all." He looked at me with glaring eyes and said, "Moose."

We worked on, and after a while we had moved down separate paths and were in different parts of the garden. "Grandpa, are these weeds?"

He looked up and said, "No, those are an herb called borage. Have you already pulled some of those?"

"Yeah, I think I did, sorry."

"That's okay. Just stick them back in the ground. Throw me one, would you?"

I saw him tear off a leaf and pop it into his mouth. He looked at me and said, "Try one."

I hesitantly put one in my mouth. "It tastes like cucumber!"

He said, "Yep," and went back to work.

We worked on a little longer, and then he said, "How about some lunch?"

He offered to fix it and suggested I sit out here in the garden and just enjoy life. He got up and headed into the cabin.

There was some fresh straw lying in a small pile near the middle of the garden, and I went over and laid down on it. I was surrounded by all kinds of flowers and vegetables. I felt a little like Alice in Wonderland.

As I lay there, I became aware of some honey bees buzzing around the flowers, and then a hummingbird flew up right in front of my face and buzzed around my head before it flew off to another part of the garden. I watched it as it flitted from flower to flower. The garden smelled so wonderful. As the wind gently shifted, I smelled flowers and then some aromatic herbs.

Grandpa soon came back with our lunch and a couple of lawn chairs. We set them up in the garden and ate.

Another hummingbird flew back around my head.

Grandpa said, "It must be that red headband of yours."

"Grandpa, I didn't know Alaska had bees and hummingbirds."

He put his finger to his lips and said, "Shhhh. We do not want the word getting out."

"Oh, I get it; you're trying to keep the riffraff out."

"No. Heavens no. We *are* the riffraff; we are trying to keep the morons out. The more people who think Alaska is a frozen wasteland, the fewer will move up here.

"The hummingbirds are regular summer visitors, but the bees are imported. Sister Baker and another neighbor keep small apiaries. Some people try to winter them over in heated sheds, but around here they just let the hives die off every fall.

"Would you like to hear more about the 'Goose Chase'?"

I nodded with a mouthful of peanut butter and jelly sandwich.

"Okay, let's see, where was I? Oh, yes. The *Tiĝlax̂* finally made it to Amchitka and dropped us on the island with more than enough supplies. Then it left to do other research farther west in the chain, so we were all alone out there, hundreds of miles from any civilization and more than a thousand miles from Anchorage. We were closer to *Moscow* than *New York*—even closer to *Tokyo* than *Seattle*. The only thing we had to connect us to the rest of the world was a battery powered two-way radio, which was only turned on for a short time around three o'clock each day.

"Believe me, Granddaughter; searching for those geese was hard work! Thousands of years of dead grass and sedges makes for a very thick mat called muskeg, and because of the unique climate in the Aleutians, the muskeg is always wet, so there are never any wildfires. It was like walking on a thick pile of wet mattresses—with each new step you had to climb out of the depression your last footstep made. I was a lot younger then, but I was still the oldest person on the island. I had a hard time keeping up.

"Here's how it worked," Grandpa said as he stood up to demonstrate. "We would form up in line standing a few feet apart, shoulder to shoulder, and march from our starting point to a flag some distance away. Those areas are called transects, and they were carefully mapped out. We had to stay close to each other because it was easy to miss a nest in the tall growth."

He slapped his hands on his knees. "But something was wrong—we weren't finding *any* geese! We conducted transects on many different parts of the island, but no geese. Finally, we found *one* goose! She was sitting on a clutch of eggs and had an orange band on her leg. The biologist physically examined the bird and made a note of the number on the band, so she could find out where the goose had come from and how old it was.

"The director was disappointed about how the project was turning out and made a decision to stop the goose transects. He figured their attempt to reintroduce the Aleutian Canada Goose had been a failure."

"So what did you all do?"

"Well, since the population study took a lot less time than planned, we had several days to just enjoy the nature and history of the island before the *Tiĝlax̂* came back. We also did some other things that were on the scientists' B-list."

Grandpa gave me a funny look and said, "Did I mention that back in the late 1960s and early '70s we detonated three atomic bombs under Amchitka? The joke was the island should be renamed Amka because we blew the 'chit' out of it." He chuckled.

I couldn't believe what I was hearing! "*Grandpa!* Isn't the island radioactive or something?"

"Not so far. We visited all three ground zeros. Anyway, back to my story—one day, several of us volunteers went along with a scientist to see a new part of the island. We stopped to eat lunch on a cliff overlooking a small rocky bight, and when we looked down, we could see several sea lions sunning themselves on a haul-out. Then the biologist who was with us pointed out several large black fins in the water. We—"

"*Orcas!*" I interrupted. "You saw real orcas?"

"Yes, three cows in the bight and one bull swimming back and forth across the mouth of the little inlet. After a while, one of the big sea lions rolled over, stretched, gave a great big yawn, and then crawled over to the edge and slid into the water—and one of the Orcas got *her* lunch."

Grandpa suddenly stopped and asked, "Did you feel that?"

"Feel what?"

"Oh, nothing. I thought I just felt a little microquake."

"Really? I didn't feel anything."

"Okay. Well, finish your lunch. We still have several sections to weed. Oh, and please remind me to take down those four flower baskets—they are for Sister Baker's porch.

"Remember me telling you about the B-list earlier? One of the things on that list was surveying some bald eagle and peregrine falcon nests, which were built on top of columns of rock called sea stacks. Lisa, the biologist in charge of the study had to climb up the stacks, surveying one nest at a time. After a while we lost sight of her, but then I spotted her across the cove. It looked like she was waving at us, but another scientist with us explained that she was trying to protect herself from an attacking eagle. When eagles defend their nests, they usually attack the trespasser's head, so Lisa had put her hat on her walking stick and was waving it around to confuse the eagle. We watched for a minute, and sure enough, the eagle knocked her hat off the stick."

"Grandpa, I remember seeing bald eagles on a school field trip once. They are seriously big birds! I'd be *terrified* if one was trying to attack me!"

"Well, now you know what to do if one ever does," Grandpa said. "You know, surveying the raptors' nests actually gave us a big clue about what happened to the geese—the nests and the rocks below were littered with orange bands and remains of many prey birds to include geese! It seems the geese *had* returned to the island after all, but the eagles and falcons had been eating them.

"The biologists decided to let the island lie fallow for another five years, hoping a natural balance might still be restored. They did another survey in 1999, and they were right—the program was proving to be a success after all."

"Does that mean the Aleutian Canada goose isn't on the endangered species list anymore?"

"Yes—and they were reclassified. They are now called the Aleutian *cackling* goose. Not many species that have made it back off that list."

"Yeah, like the bald eagle, huh?"

"That is correct. There are now only three islands left in the entire chain that have fox on them. More than a million acres of breeding habitat has been restored. That is a great conservation success, and I am proud I got to play a tiny part in it."

"That's a cool story, Grandpa. I think I'd like to do something like that myself someday."

He stopped digging and looked up at me for a moment. "I have no doubt you will do many amazing things in your life."

The sky had clouded up quite a bit and it looked like rain. He finished up his section and came over and helped me with the last little bit of mine. He sat back and asked if I had my logbook with me.

"Yes, sir," I said, and my heart beat a little faster.

"Good. What do you say we go out to the airport and take a few turns around the flagpole?"

"Really, Grandpa? That would be wonderful." *Hey, what kind of prison is this, anyway?*

I hadn't been up since—well, you know when. I wasn't sure how I would feel, but I was hooked on flying and wanted to give it a try.

As we drove to the airport, Grandpa told me he had read the report on my mishap. "That was really impressive flying, young lady. I doubt many students with your experience could have landed that plane. Did you know one of the birds actually bent your propeller?"

"No, I didn't. That must be why the plane shook so violently."

"Yes, indeed. In addition to the two birds that came through the windscreen, at least two others tore up the leading edge on your right wing. At normal cruise speed, the differential drag would have caused the directional control problem you reported. Then, as you slowed down, the drag became less of a problem but asymmetric lift caused your airplane to want to roll to the right."

"But, Grandpa, I totally destroyed the airplane. Why do you call that impressive flying?"

"First of all, any landing you can walk away from is a good landing. Secondly, if you had not been as good a pilot as you are, you would have been just a smoking hole in the ground. I spoke to your flight instructor, and he has nothing but praise for your skills."

"Is he mad about the plane?"

"No, he is not. It was insured, and bird strikes are considered an act of God. He did tell me something else, though. He said you needed to get back up in the air as soon as possible."

I couldn't believe my ears. Denny thought I was a good pilot.

Grandpa asked, "Do you know who Billy Mitchell was?"

"Yes, sir—he was a great early aviator."

"That's right. He was called the father of Alaskan aviation. But did you know he had multiple plane wrecks? One time, when retractable gear was first introduced, he even landed one gear-up, at Dayton Field."

"Grandpa, does Mom know?"

"Well, we have a saying up here: 'Heaven is high and the czar is far away.' She put me in charge of you, and I really do not think she will be upset with either of us."

I wasn't sure how I felt about that, but I decided to worry about it later. I was going flying! By the time we got to the airport it had started to rain. I whimpered a little.

Grandpa asked, "Are you just going to be a fair-weather pilot? A little rain never kept me from going up. But it will keep me from doing a preflight."

He handed me the keys to the plane and found a garbage bag that he converted into a raincoat for me.

Before I pushed the aircraft out of the hangar, Grandpa loaded up a folding chaise lounge and a small duffle bag. When I finished the preflight check, Grandpa came out and unceremoniously climbed into the right seat.

He directed me out to the runway and I took off. We went around twice before I remembered I had recently crashed a plane. *I guess I'm over that.* On the third go-around, Grandpa had me do a full stop on the runway.

He got out and told me he wanted me to do five more touch and goes—making the first two, full stops. "Use the thousand-foot marker as your touchdown point. I also want you to just use the right half of the runway. If you are going to be flying my airplane, I want to make sure you can land on narrow dirt strips."

He then got out of the plane and pulled the chaise lounge and his duffle bag out. He saluted me and walked off the runway.

I took off, and when I came around the first time, I cracked up when I saw him lounging in the fold-up chair, just short of the two thousand-foot marker. He was eating Oreos and had a thermos beside him.

I discovered there were no lingering aftereffects from the crash, and it felt really good to be up in the air again. I was surprised the rain didn't really affect anything other than a little reduced visibility, and I had to keep the carburetor heat on.

On my fourth go-around I realized Grandpa had packed up his chair and had apparently headed back to the hangar. I finished my assignment and taxied back in.

On the way back to the cabin, Grandpa said, "Young lady, you have worn me out. It has been a long day—did you know it's ten o'clock?"

"Ten at night?" The sky looked like it was so much earlier.

Grandpa laughed and said, "You can always tell the new guy in the neighborhood—he's the one out mowing his yard after the late-night news."

We got back home, and Grandpa went into the living room and said, "Ah ha! I thought I felt an earthquake earlier."

I went into the dining room and saw Grandpa on his knees again. Several pieces from his tin collection had fallen off the shelf.

He looked up and said, "Poor man's earthquake detector. Help me, would you?"

First I helped him get up and then passed all the cans to him as he carefully stacked them back on the shelf.

"That's a bummer, Grandpa. My first earthquake, and I didn't even feel it."

"Don't worry; it won't be your last! We probably have two or three a month." He rubbed his leg and said, "Would you mind taking your shower first? And save me some hot water—I want to soak my bones."

The next day was Saturday, and it started just like all the rest. Once we got out to the porch, Grandpa said, "I am glad to see your mood is improving. I thought I had lost my little girl."

"I'm sorry, Grandpa. It's just that I really didn't plan on being up here, and I miss my friends at church and stuff."

"So why don't you call Esperanza?"

Hmm, why hadn't I thought of that? Duh.

Then he said, "I hope you do not mind, but I signed you up for a driver's ed class. I just figured that since you are about to turn sixteen, that would have been one of the things you would have been doing down in Utah this summer.

"Tomorrow is Sunday. Would you consider going to church with me? I would love to show you off."

I thought about it for a minute and decided I at least owed Grandpa that much. I knew kids my age would be there. "Okay. Are we going to stay for the full three-hour block of meetings?"

He asked, "Is there any other way?"

So, we went to church. He introduced me to his friends before our sacrament meeting. Later I met the kids who were my age. I remembered a couple of them from my visit last Christmas. Everyone was happy—especially the boys—to have a new person at church. I was invited to girl's camp. For a little while I forgot I was angry at God.

After church everybody usually goes home and spends the day with their family. It's kind of a church thing. We went home and had a nice "lupper" (lunch and dinner combined). After that Grandpa said he wanted to study some Scriptures and then take a nap. I asked if it would be okay if I called Esperanza.

He smiled at me and said, "Sure, and you don't have to ask permission for everything you do. It is not like you are in prison or something."

Hmm, did he know how I felt?

Grandpa got out of his easy chair, dramatically dusted it off, and motioned for me to sit in the telephone seat.

Esperanza and I talked for a while, and then she invited me over. I decided to take Grandpa's advice, and without asking for permission told her I would, and then realized I would still have to ask Grandpa for a ride.

I caught him before he started his studies and he said, "No prob."

Hah, where does he get this stuff?

We jumped into the Suburban and headed for Peter's Creek. When we got out to the Glenn Highway, I was happy to see bars on my phone. I also had about a hundred messages. I turned on my navigation app and guided Grandpa right to Esperanza's house.

He looked over at my phone and said, "I could have just used my map." Then he asked if picking me up at eight would be okay.

I kinda winced and said, "Just a sec."

Esperanza was waiting for us on the deck, and when she saw us she came down with her dogs, Kenai and Denali.

I jumped out and chatted with her. Then we both came back to Grandpa's side of the car and asked if nine would be all right as long as Esperanza drove me home.

"It's okay with me; I just didn't feel like driving any later than eight. And don't forget your first driving lesson starts at nine tomorrow morning."

I reached in and kissed him on the cheek. That's something I always did when I was a kid. Then I asked, "Will you be okay alone, Grandpa?"

He smiled and said, "I'll manage," and drove off.

What just happened? In one weekend, Grandpa had gone from someone I thought was my prison warden to someone I was deeply concerned about.

CHAPTER 3

TWO NEW FRIENDS AND
MOBY DICK

Monday morning, Ammo came into my room and approached my bed. But this morning I was ready for him. I leaped up and grabbed his face and faked a big snarl. I wrestled him to the floor and tried to pin him while he pretended to eat my arm. I finally got on top of him and said, "A real gentleman would never stick his cold wet nose on a lady's tummy. It's just plain 'wude'. Our scuffle ended when he sneezed and we both got up.

"Hey, Grandpa."

"Hey, Granddaughter."

Grandpa was already dressed. He seemed as excited about my driving lessons as I was. For the next five days I was in a driver's ed course until after lunch. This was also the week of Esperanza's cheerleading camp. Her camp started in midmorning and ran through dinnertime, so my afternoons and evenings were pretty boring. On some days, Grandpa would be gone for hours with one or more of his student pilots.

It had rained for the last three days. I'd just finished reading the last book I'd downloaded on my e-reader from the Salt Lake library and was hanging out with Ammo on the porch. I was still uncomfortable with nothing to do—I was so used to always running and going. Back in Utah, there was the constant drone of the TV and the radio and the phone and the near-constant schedule of various church activities. Not just Sunday stuff—dances and service projects and committees and a dozen other things that kept me constantly busy. School activities too, and of course there was always the mall. We had to have a wall calendar to keep track of everything going on.

But up here, things just seem to get done based on the weather and the sunshine or a flight schedule. For the most part, we didn't even make plans for the day until after breakfast and our morning ritual on the porch. Tomorrow, however, was going to be a red-letter day—Grandpa's girlfriend, Sister Baker, was flying back to Alaska; she would land just after midnight.

I hadn't figured out yet that it's totally okay to just sit out on the porch and wait for a sunny day. Or to watch and wait for someone or something to walk down the road. Grandpa was out doing stuff in the shed, and I was filling the time with journaling and writing a long letter to Stephen Nephi. I also filled out about a dozen picture postcards to my friends since it was so hard to send a text. I told them the Young Women's Group leaders from Grandpa's ward had invited me to their weeklong summer camp.

Every ward in the church has a summer camp for girls. It's really a lot of fun, and all of us plan for and look forward to it every year. But, I began to wonder, why I should be excited about going to camp up here? The camp activity manual is the same everywhere. I mean, for crying out loud—I'm in Alaska! I'm a pilot. My uncle is a dog musher—and Doc Rock to boot! Shouldn't I be doing something different from what I'd ordinarily be doing back home?

Jeez, this day is just so boring!

I thought about Esperanza and realized she was the only person I knew up here who wasn't a member of my church. *Why don't I know anyone else?* I tried to justify it by saying it's summertime and I'm not going to school. Then I realized that even back in Salt Lake City, I didn't really have any friends from Central High who weren't also members of my church.

Okay, that's it! I thought. *I'm going to get to know some new people—people who don't go to my church. So . . . how am I going to do that?*

Well, that was a lot of thinking, and I once again felt the need to do something. That's when I heard the familiar sound of a rattly bumper as the mail truck came sloshing down the road, its tires splashing water out of several potholes as it pulled up and stopped at our box.

I went inside to put on my rain poncho and then walked down the drive. There was nothing for me. Looking down the road, I saw two cyclists wearing brightly colored rain gear. I could hear them talking happily with each other as they slowly pedaled along.

Here's a chance!

As they approached, I called out, "Hi, I'm Summer Rose."

That wasn't so hard.

They stopped, and we all started chatting. The girl was very short with dark hair in braids. She said, "I'm Alexis"—and pointing to the boy—"this is Robin." He had red hair and a little strip of beard, like a goatee.

He stuck out his hand and I shook it. "We've been cycling all morning," he said. "Started out from campus housing at UAA and are headed to Bodenberg Butte." He had an intriguing Australian accent.

"You're on the wrong road," I said.

They both laughed.

Alexis said, "We know. We just decided to pull off the highway to see what this neighborhood was like, and we're looking for a dry place to stop and have lunch."

Ammo slowly came down the driveway, wagging his tail and begging for attention. "That's Ammo, my grandpa's dog."

Robin dismounted, laid his bike down, knelt, and rubbed Ammo's ears. "G'day, old chap. You're a nimble tripod, aren't you? Nothing holding *you* back, eh?"

I'd seen Grandpa meet and befriend total strangers before, so I decided to give it a try. This was so *not* the way I did things in Utah.

"Would you guys like to get out of the rain and eat lunch on our porch?"

"Fair dinkum, mate," Robin said.

When I looked questioningly at Alexis, she smiled and nodded.

"If you guys can wait a couple of minutes, I'll make a lunch and join you."

They looked at each other, and then Alexis said, "Okay."

They rolled their bikes up the drive and leaned them against the side of the cabin.

Grandpa came out of the shed, wiping his hands. I suggested Robin and Alexis unpack their lunches and get comfortable on the porch. I then ran up to Grandpa and told him what had just happened.

He smiled and asked, "Am I invited?"

"Like, totally!"

"Did you offer to let them clean up?"

Gah. That never crossed my mind.

Grandpa said, "I will go extend the invitation. Do you mind making me some lunch too?"

"Woo hoo!" I ran for the side door. I'm not sure why this excited me so much, but it did.

I put the mail on the counter and made ham and cheese sandwiches as the three of them came in the front door. While Robin and Alexis took turns in the bathroom, Grandpa got out a bag of chips and poured them into a big bowl. Five minutes later, all five of us were eating lunch on the porch.

Robin opened a small jar of some kind of spread—it looked like dark peanut butter—and spread some on his lunchmeat sandwich. Grandpa saw it and said, "Vegemite! I haven't had Vegemite in decades." Even before Grandpa asked, Robin handed him the jar. Grandpa offered some to Alexis, but she just covered her sandwich with her hand. When he offered me some, I held out my plate.

"Ever tried it before?" Robin asked. When I shook my head, all three of them chuckled. "Tell you what, mate, just put the tiniest smear on one corner of your sandwich."

Ignoring the warning, I slathered a gob of it on my sandwich. Robin's eyebrows went up, and he suggested I scrape some back off, but I ignorantly said, "That's okay."

They all watched me take a big bite. They all watched as I began to chew. And they all watched as my face grew pale and panicked.

It wasn't sickening—I didn't gag—but I had a *very* difficult time convincing myself to swallow. I finally figured the best thing to do was to swallow as quickly as I could. I politely put my sandwich down, picked up my pomegranate juice, and drank half a glass all at once. My eyes were watering as I pushed my plate away. They all had a laugh.

Robin said, "It's an acquired taste, mate."

Grandpa added, "Yeah, like limburger cheese."

"Well, I guess I'm a little wiser today," I whispered hoarsely.

Robin said, "That's right—go out there and get as many experiences as you can while you're young. How many of your mates can say they've tasted Australia's favorite relish?"

Robin and I talked a little longer about travel and new experiences while Alexis and Grandpa started jabbering about the garden.

Robin said, "It's like me visiting Alaska. I daresay none of my mates have ever seen a moose."

"Yeah, I kinda understand. I'm just visiting here too. My home's in Salt Lake City."

"That's it—think of all the things you've seen that none of your mates have seen. What a wonderful experience for you, and as you said, you're a little wiser today."

Funny, I never thought of this as a wonderful experience.

Fifteen minutes later, Alexis and Robin pedaled back down the drive and down the road, rain and all. They wanted to climb the butte and get back to town before the sun went down. (Well, you know what I mean.) Grandpa just sat in the swing and smiled. He never said a word; he just smiled.

Finally, I told him what I had been thinking about making friends before Robin and Alexis came by.

"That's some pretty heavy thinking, young lady."

"Yeah, I know." Then, I joked, "It kinda hurt." We both cracked up. Then I asked, "Grandpa, would you be upset if I didn't go to girls' camp?"

"It doesn't matter to me. Is that what you want?"

I nodded. "I think so, Grandpa."

He raised his fingers to make quotation marks and said, "What-ever."

Where does he get this stuff?

"I should tell you I have volunteered to go out to the camp one night and perform bear guard duties. So what are you going to do?"

"I'm not sure. I know I need to study for my final-stage test and FAA exam. I think I might try to make some friends who are not from church."

He just said, "Oh, I see."

I looked down the road and didn't see anybody else coming. Grandpa stretched his neck and also looked down the road. He looked back at me, shook his head, and shrugged.

Ahhh, he got me again.

"I'm bored too, Granddaughter. Do you want to learn some new stuff?"

Anticipating something fun, I said, "Sure."

We cleaned up the porch and brought everything into the kitchen. Grandpa bagged my sandwich with the Australian sauce on it and said he would eat it later.

We headed to Grandpa's study. I love his study—it's like something you might see at Hogwarts. Like everything else in the house, it was built out of beautiful wood and logs. Tons of old books filled the shelves—the place even *smelled* like old books.

Rolled-up maps and sectionals and navigation charts lay all over the place. There was almost no free wall space, but an elaborately framed and matted photo of an old aviator hung in a small spot.

In one corner of the room sat a giant world globe. It was like a piece of furniture—with its own frame and four legs, looking like something you'd see in a painting of some Renaissance explorer. A sea monster was painted on the Indian Ocean, with a scroll that read, "There Be Monsters Here." Even though it had that old-fashioned look, the maps were modern. The globe had a light inside that made the oceans glow.

Grandpa walked over to the globe, rolled it out into the middle of the room, and spun it around until Alaska was front and center. "Let me show you some things about Alaska." He started by pointing out the Aleutian Archipelago. "Look closely."

I did and just shrugged.

Then he asked, "What is the last island in the archipelago?"

I looked and read the name of the island. "Attu."

Grandpa's voice always went up in pitch when he had something important to say. "No, it's not. Look again, and this time look at the geology, not the geography."

When he said that, I realized the archipelago didn't stop until it almost reached Russia. Now that I knew what he wanted me to see, I said, "Oh, I get it." Then I read, "Ostrov Beringa."

"Yes, that's Russian for 'Bering Island.' What else do you see?"

I saw another island and tried to read it. "Ostrov Med-med?"

"Ostrov Mednyy. That means 'Copper Island.' The two islands together are called Komandorskiye Ostrova."

"Commander Islands?" I asked uncertainly.

A big smile grew on his face.

"What commander?" I asked.

Grandpa corrected me. "*Which* commander. Why, the good Captain Vitus Bering, of course. He was a Dane in the employ of the Russian emperor, Peter the Great. Captain Bering died on the island so they named it after him. Heck, he even got an ocean named after him."

Grandpa got a twinkle in his eye and said, "Here's another one for you. Which longitude line is the international date line?"

Let's see, the Prime Meridian is zero degrees so . . . "One hundred eighty degrees!" I blurted.

"That's true—about half the time. Take a look." He pointed out the international date line and traced it with his finger.

I'll be darned! The date line wiggles east and west of the 180th meridian. I looked up at Grandpa and said, "I swear, no one ever told me that."

"I believe you. I got a million of 'em. Want some more?"

I nodded.

"Okay, here we go. Which state is the farthest north?"

I said, "Alaska!" thinking, *That was way too easy.*

"Yep." Then he asked, "Which state is the farthest south?"

"Florida!" *Another no-brainer.*

But he shook his head. "Put your finger on the tip of Florida. Now, just below Florida, you'll find a latitude line that's called the Tropic of Cancer. Leave your finger on the Tropic of Cancer and spin the globe around until you see Hawaii."

Dang! I'd forgotten about Hawaii. Sure enough, the main group of the Hawaiian Islands was south of the Tropic of Cancer. Anyway, that was kind of a trick question.

Then he asked, "Which state is the farthest west?"

At first I thought it was Hawaii again, but then I thought it might be Alaska. "Alaska."

Grandpa nodded slowly, for emphasis, and then asked, "Which state is farthest east?"

Without even looking, I said, "Maine."

Grandpa shook his head and pointed at the globe.

I looked and said, "It *is* Maine, Grandpa." I showed him on the globe that Maine was the farthest east of all of the states. I was *sure* it was Maine.

But he said, "Nope. It's Alaska."

"Nuh uh, no way."

Grandpa smiled and said, "Yeah-huh." He put his finger on Maine. Then he started turning the globe to the east all the while saying, "More east, more east, more east." He continued all of the way across the Atlantic and then all of the way across Europe until he got to the island of Attu and said, "Most east."

I looked carefully. He was right! About a dozen islands in the Aleutian chain have east longitudes. Maine's longitude is about 65 degrees west. The island of Attu has a longitude of 172 degrees east. "Oh, I get it. Alaska really *is* farther east than Maine."

Just then the phone rang. I jumped up and ran for the living room. "I'll get it, Grandpa!"

"Hello, Miss Watson. This is Doc Rock."

I giggled. "Hey, Uncle Chris. What up?"

"How'd you guys like to come out for dinner this evening?"

"Hold on, I'll ask." I put the phone down and went back into the study. Grandpa was moving the globe back into its corner. I told him about Uncle Chris's invitation.

"Sure, but don't forget I have to drive in to Anchorage tonight to pick up Sister Baker."

I ran back to the phone and told Uncle Chris we were in.

"Okay, we'll start the Caribou meatloaf around six."

"Do you have any dogs at the clinic?"

"Yes, I do. Why don't you guys meet us there about four thirty?"

"We'll be there or be square."

He started to hang up, and then said, "Hey, wait—I've got an idea. Why don't you spend the night? I'm going to be one technician short;

you could help me in the clinic. I have clinic hours in the morning and three surgeries scheduled for the afternoon."

"How cool! Yes!" I said. "*Hasta pronto*."

"Aloha," he replied and hung up.

Grandpa was glad I was going to have that experience.

"So when I am going to meet your mysterious girlfriend?" I asked playfully.

"I don't know, probably when you get back from Chris's house. I suspect she's going to want to rest tomorrow, and I know she's going to be very busy the day after that."

"Okay, cool. I'm really looking forward to meeting her."

Grandpa headed for the kitchen, probably to find some snacks. I started looking on the bookshelves to see if I could find something to read. There were so many kinds of books. One section had nothing but college text books. Another section was full of atlases. There was a big section filled with reference books. Then there was a section for classic literature, with dozens and dozens of titles I'd never even heard of. Some I *did* recognize—but only because I'd heard about them, not because I'd read them. Books with titles like *Treasure Island*, *The Call of the Wild*, and *Tom Sawyer*. And look at that! He even has all the Harry Potter books. And on another shelf was a big collection of Hardy Boys and Nancy Drew mysteries. There were all the books in the Tennis Shoes *Among the Nephites* series.

Grandpa came in, crunching some carrot sticks. He pulled down a book—*Brother to the Eagle*—and handed it to me. Looking at the cover, I realized it was the same picture of the aviator that was framed on the wall. I read aloud, "Colonel Carl Benjamin Eielson."

Grandpa corrected my pronunciation—"I-ul-son"—and said, "He crashed more airplanes than anybody I know of, except maybe for Billy Mitchell. I read this book the first time when I was a teenager. He's sort of a hero of mine." I looked at the copyright while Grandpa was talking—1952.

"I really think he's the reason I became a pilot," Grandpa said, "and he was *certainly* the reason I fought to stay in Alaska when I was in the air force."

"I'll start reading it to—" Right in the middle of my sentence, I saw *Moby Dick* on the shelf right in front of me. "*Moby Dick!* I've always wanted to read this, but I just never seem to have time back home."

When I pulled it down and opened the front cover, my jaw dropped. "Grandpa, 1851!"

He smiled and said, "Well, it *is* a keeper. That's a first edition. If you'd like to read the book, I have a modern paperback. I have to warn you—it's a difficult read."

"No thanks, Grandpa. I can just download it from the Salt Lake Library or buy it as an e-book."

I carefully opened the old volume to the first page. As my eyes fell on the first words, Grandpa said, in a dramatic voice, "Call me Ishmael. Some years ago—never mind how long precisely . . ."

I looked up at him, and he said, "I've probably read that book half a dozen times. I know I read it aloud to your uncle and aunts—and maybe your mom too, I don't remember for sure. Why don't you start it, and if you'd like, I'll read it to you too."

When he put the first edition back into its place on the shelf, I realized I was looking at a section of books that were all bound in leather. I saw at least a dozen Tarzan books. I pulled down *Tarzan of the Apes.* Grandpa said, "That year was 1912." Then he asked, "Did you know it's a tragic love story between Young Lord Greystoke and Jane Porter?"

"Oh! 'Me Tarzan, you Jane.' That Jane?"

He just smiled at me.

I put it back on the shelf and let my fingers run across the volumes. I found four Sherlock Holmes books side by side.

Grandpa said, "Come, Watson, come! The game is afoot."

Next I fingered an ancient book with a rough cover that was the same color as a pair of faded jeans, with the name Tennyson embossed in gold on the spine. Grandpa smiled and nobly quoted, "Theirs not to reason why, theirs but to do and die . . . Half a league, half a league, half a league onward . . ."

I cut in, "All in the valley of death rode the six hundred."

Grandpa looked impressed. Then he said, "All the books on that top shelf are first editions."

Next, when I came across a collection of stories and poems by Edgar Allan Poe, Grandpa said, "Once upon a midnight dreary, while I pondered, weak and weary . . ." He paused as if he were recalling and then said, "Tell me what thy lordly name is on the night's plutonian shore!"

I chirped in, "Quoth the raven, 'Nevermore.'"

Grandpa said, "So they still teach the classics."

"Well, not exactly. I know those two because they were assigned as extra credit work in one of my advanced placement classes. Grandpa, have you read all these books?"

He thought for a moment and said, "Well, I'm still working on Will Shakespeare's collection, but other than that I can say yes, I've read them all—many more than once."

I was impressed, saying, "Wow."

Grandpa found the paperback edition of *Moby Dick.* I thumbed through it, finding notes in the margins.

"Those notes are from your mom and aunts and uncle," he said. "Most are vocabulary and nautical phrases. We didn't have the Internet in those days, you know. You are welcome to keep the book, if you like. By the way, you will not find any marginalia in an e-book—nor will you find the stain from the carnation your mom pressed between a couple of pages in one of these books."

"Really, Grandpa? What book?"

"*Which* book? I do know, but you will just have to find it yourself."

"Thanks, Grandpa. This'll be the first real book in my personal library."

"A great book to start your library with," he said, handing me a carrot stick.

Thanking him for the tour, I tucked *Brother to the Eagle* and *Moby Dick* under my arm.

"Grandpa, I wish I could learn everything the way you teach me stuff."

He smiled and said, "Well, it *is* a very effective way to learn things, but unfortunately, it's not a very efficient way to teach things. Think about it—we'd have to have one teacher for every student."

"Hey, that's not a bad idea. We should hire all the grandpas in the world and make them teachers." We both chuckled. "Really, Grandpa, do you know how hard it is to learn anything in school?"

He stopped, looked right at me, and said, "No, I guess not."

"It's really bad. Nobody gets to class on time. First period is the worst because of delays at the metal detectors. We're not allowed to carry backpacks to our classrooms, so we all have to get to our lockers between most classes. They only give us seven minutes—and sometimes we *do* need to go to the bathroom, you know. Then there are disruptions during the class. Most of the time it's the same kids cutting up. Sometimes students forget to turn off their phones. The PA system disrupts us, or the office calls the teacher—right in the middle of class.

"We've had some fights in class that were so bad, the teacher had to call the police. One time this guy ran into class during the middle of the period. It turned out he was trespassing, because he'd been expelled. He was hiding from the police in our classroom!" I sighed. "It can be even harder for us girls."

"What do you mean?" Grandpa asked, giving me all his attention.

"Well, like when my biology teacher does a demonstration, all of the tall boys bully themselves in up front. We girls can't see a thing. I did have one teacher, named Richard Kelly, who always made sure the girls had a good view. He also made sure we had a chance to participate. Sometimes teachers ask us to break into groups and pick a leader. Usually, there's no picking involved—the biggest boy just appoints himself. Mr. Kelly would always announce, 'I'd better see some girl leaders.' Unfortunately, none of the other teachers even seem to realize how the boys take control in these situations.

"It was because of that teacher's example that I started insisting I have a good view or just telling some big boy that I wanted to be the leader. If he wouldn't let me be the leader, I'd join some other group that was looking for a leader. I've also told some boys to shut up for a minute and let a girl answer for once, even if I wasn't that girl. Grandpa, the worst part of it is, so much of the time I have to teach myself."

While I was talking, I'd been watching Grandpa. He was *really* listening to me. He *really* wanted to know what was going on in my life.

"What do you mean?" he asked.

"Well, do you know why I take advanced placement classes?"

"I thought I knew. Please, tell me, why *are* you taking AP classes?"

"Last year, I was in a regular geometry class. The teacher was trying to teach us how to figure out the volume and surface area of spheres and cones. Grandpa, there were kids in that class who didn't even know how to multiply! The teacher had to spend so much time tutoring those kids that some of us just got bored and worked on ahead without her. A few of us grouped together and started helping each other. The teacher saw us and encouraged us to continue working that way, since she couldn't do much of anything for us.

"It's the same in most of my classes. It's hard for a civics teacher to explain about political regions if the students can't find Scandinavia on a map. Grandpa, I mean, like, some of them didn't even know which hemisphere to start looking in. One time a student tried to correct a teacher by telling her that everyone in Africa was black. When the teacher mentioned that Egypt is part of Africa, he argued with her about that too."

Grandpa's face had changed. He looked sad.

"I told Dad what was going on and asked him to please help me. The next day we went down to the school, and he asked that I be placed in all AP classes. The counselor told us that all the AP classes were full, and there was nothing she could do. Dad got up and walked out on her, going straight to the principal's office. By the following week, I was in all AP classes. Mostly they were already full, and the school just squeezed me in—but in the case of geometry, they created a whole new class. At first there were just a few of us, but after a while that class filled up too."

"Good for your dad. We had an expression in the military—'Lead, follow, or get out of the way.' Your dad is a leader." Then he reached out and grabbed my shoulder, "You're a good leader too."

"Thank you, Grandpa."

Grandpa stretched and asked me what time it was. When I told him, he said, "I really want to know more, but I need to shower before we go. How about you?"

"Yeah, but why don't you shower first? You're so much faster, and I can pack an overnight bag while you're in there."

He smiled at me and said, "Okay, get out of the way."

Men are so lucky—it only takes them a few minutes to get ready. I'd just barely gotten into my room when I heard him close the bathroom door and start running the shower. I pulled down my overnight bag and set it on the bed.

Then something *freaky* happened. It's really hard to explain if you haven't experienced it yourself. It was such a weird feeling. It's kind of like you have another sense organ that you've never used . . . but this time the house started shaking, and I heard the empty tins fall off the shelf in the dining room again. Grandpa's earthquake detector had just recorded a small earthquake! I stood there paralyzed for a second, and then everything returned to normal. Still frozen and holding my breath,

I listened—but that was it. It'd all happened in just a few seconds. Sort of like a big truck had driven by. Grandpa was still in the shower, so I guess he didn't hear the cans hit the floor.

Then it happened again—that same weird feeling and the house began to shake and rattle—much harder this time and for much longer. There was an audible rumble. I involuntarily screamed and sort of scampered this way and that. It really scared me.

I suppose it lasted for about ten seconds, but it seemed much longer. I heard things rattling in the house—dishes, I think. I also had heard a loud snap, like a piece of gravel hitting a car windshield. My heart was pounding, and I felt the adrenaline in my system. My hands and arms trembled, and I was breathing fast.

I'd just experienced two earthquakes!

Grandpa calmly asked, through the bathroom door, "You okay?"

"Uh . . . yeah, I guess."

"Go out on the side steps, take a look at the lake."

Unbelievable! There was a wave in the lake! It bounced off the far bank—just like if you'd moved a cookie sheet with water in the bottom—and then it sloshed back to this side. It was small, but big enough that I could see it from the cabin. Then I heard Grandpa's flat-bottom boat bumping up against the dock. I watched for a moment until everything went back to normal again.

I stepped back inside and shouted, "Is it over?"

Grandpa came out of the bathroom. He looked so relaxed. "I don't know. Probably." Going over to the fallen tins, he started to restack them again. I hadn't noticed before, but he stacked them in precise but precarious positions near the edge.

I said, "That was freaky!"

"Yeah, pretty sick, huh?" he said, cracking a grin.

"Does that happen a lot up here?" I asked anxiously.

Shrugging, he said, "*De temps en temps,*" with an exaggerated French accent.

When I looked at him curiously, he held out an open hand, palm down, and rocked it back and forth.

Thinking about my Spanish vocabulary, I recalled that time is *tiempo.* Spanish and French are both Latin based languages. "From time to time?" I ventured.

He reached up, touched his nose and said, "*Oui, de temps en temps.* That's two."

"What about the one yesterday?"

"Oh, yeah, I forgot. That's what we call a 'swarm,' then."

"Do we need to look for damage or anything?"

"If you want, you can go around and open and close all the doors and windows, but I don't think you'll find anything. Maybe you could do that tomorrow, since you still need to get ready, eh?"

"I can be ready in just a few minutes. I'll take my shower at Uncle Chris's tonight—is that okay?"

"I don't care."

With that, I went around and checked all the doors and windows. The front door was dragging a little, and I found a crack in the living room picture window. I showed Grandpa.

After giving everything an inspection, he said, "I can plane down the door, but I'll have to call a contractor to replace the window. Dang! That is triple-pane glass." He stood back for a second and commented dismissively, "I guess the front corner of the cabin settled a little."

It's hard to believe how casual he was about a *swarm of earthquakes!*

But he just said, "Why don't we leave now, so I can run a short errand on the way."

I went back into my room, threw a few things into my overnight bag, and grabbed a few *more* things out of the closet. Popping back out, I called, "Ready."

Grandpa looked impressed.

CHAPTER 4

WHERE THE DOGS
ARE BEAUTIFUL AND THE
WOMEN ARE FAST

The three of us (don't forget to count Ammo) jumped into the Suburban and headed out to the Parks Highway. Grandpa said he needed to buy some firecrackers, so we drove up the hill on the outskirts of Wasilla. There were several fireworks stands. He pulled up to the stand that had a big inflatable gorilla out front.

"Coming in?"

"Nah, I'll just stay here with Ammo."

Ammo jumped into the driver's seat. I rubbed his ears and hugged him, but he didn't seem to be interested in conversation. I tried again.

"There's your master, in there buying firecrackers. Boys never seem to grow up—they all like their firecrackers."

Ammo didn't seem to care one way or the other. He was staring into the trees, like he had spotted a squirrel or something. I checked my phone and had four bars, so I started listening to my messages. After seeing there was nothing really important in any of them, I looked but couldn't find whatever had Ammo's attention.

Then I just sort of gazed *through* the trees and focused on the mountains off in the distance. At first I didn't see it, but then I noticed what looked like a column of smoke coming from behind one of the more prominent peaks.

I hopped out of the car and walked over to the trees to get a better look. Ammo came along and stayed near me. "Ammo, do you think that's a volcano? No, it can't really be a volcano; volcanoes are in faraway places."

Grandpa had walked up behind us. "Yes, Summer Rose, that is a volcano and you *are* in a faraway place. That is Mount Spurr."

"Is that what an eruption looks like?" I asked.

"No, that's just steam," he said. "See how the column has white fuzzy edges? That is hot moist air cooling down in the atmosphere, just like a jet contrail."

"Esperanza told me she's seen the volcano steaming from her deck in Peter's Creek," I said, and then asked, "Where does the steam come from?"

Grandpa explained, "Well, lava must be rising inside the volcano. That is probably what is causing our little swarm of quakes. As it rises, it heats up the rocks that are under the snow and ice pack in the summit crater. Spurr does that every couple of years, but it hasn't actually erupted since 1992. We can catch the news at Chris's house to find out what is going on." Grandpa checked his watch. "It is almost four thirty now."

About twenty minutes later we pulled into the parking lot of Uncle Chris's vet clinic. The place looked like it used to be an auto repair shop, with an office on the left and six old maintenance bays on the right. It was nicely painted and was, in places, trimmed with logs and rough-cut lumber. *Very frontiersy*, I thought.

The office was the clinic's reception room, and the large roll-down bay doors were painted so you couldn't see through the windows.

Blocking the first three bay doors were parking bumpers and half-barrels overflowing with bright flowers. Those doors obviously weren't used anymore. More flowers trailed down from wooden hanging baskets, and directly in front of the big reception room window was an old dilapidated dogsled—with even *more* flowers spilling from the sled's basket.

Painted on the glass was a simple sign: Rockwell Veterinary Clinic. Above the bay doors—across almost the full length of the building—was a giant sign that read *ALASKA*, Where the Dogs Are Beautiful and the Women Are Fast! A second, smaller sign read *WILLOW, ALASKA,* Home of the Official Start of the Iditarod Dogsled Race.

When we stepped inside, Ammo trotted right up to the front counter—well, three-legged dogs don't actually trot. He hopped up onto a lowered section of counter where pet owners could set down their pet carriers. A pretty lady with short blonde hair, wearing medical scrubs, came from the back and went straight to him.

"Hello, Ammo! How're you doing, boy?" Ammo barked in reply, and she gave him a treat from her pocket.

"Hi, August," she said, and then turned toward me with her right hand out. "And you must be Summer Rose. It's great to finally meet you! I'm Lenore." We shook hands. "Chris is with our last patient—he'll be out in a few minutes."

"Really, your name is Lenore?" I realized that was kind of rude of me.

But Lenore took no offense and said, "The story goes that my great-grandfather was a fan of Poe's. The name was passed down to my grandmother and then to my mother and then to me; there is nothing more to it than that."

Still trying to recover, I awkwardly said, "I think it's a beautiful name."

She thanked me and went to the front door and turned the CLOSED sign over. Then she went back behind the counter and started counting the money in the register. Grandpa sat, closed his eyes, and started to "meditate." Ammo continued to pester Lenore for more treats, which she laughingly gave him.

The waiting room had two window walls and two regular walls. One of the regular walls was absolutely covered with pictures and letters from young students—all thank-you letters to Doc Rock. The other regular wall, behind the counter, was filled with framed photographs of mushers and race dogs. It took just a second to see that all the inscriptions were addressed to Uncle Chris and most included the words thank you.

The photos seemed to be arranged around one picture that was larger than the rest. A little brass plate identified the man in the picture as Joe Redington Sr., the father of the Iditarod Race. Standing next to him in the picture was a bearded, long-haired, and much younger Uncle Chris—who was as good-looking then as he is today.

There were pictures of dozens of other mushers. I didn't recognize most of the names, but there were a few I knew from family stories. One picture that really caught my attention was Susan Butcher, four-time winner of the Iditarod Race, standing with my very young mother and Aunt Marie, Aunt Katy, and Uncle Chris.

I laughed when I saw a framed cartoon showing a team of sled dogs. The view was from the basket. All you could see were the dogs' behinds, with their tails held high. The caption read, "The scenery always looks the same if you're not the lead dog."

The door to the back opened, and out came an older woman carrying her fluffy little lap dog. I had to hold back a snicker—I'm not sure why, but it struck me as funny. Uncle Chris was courteous as he walked the lady out and helped her into her Cadillac. As she drove away, he came back in and locked the door. He looked over his shoulder with a big grin on his face and shouted, "Gee-haw!"

I jumped up and gave him a hug. I was blown away by the fact that I was now taller than him. "Uncle Chris, do you know about the volcano?"

"What volcano?"

We both looked over at Grandpa, and he said, "*Which* volcano. It is Spurr this time; she is venting steam."

"We've felt several earthquakes, but, no, I didn't know about Spurr. Did you, sweetie?"

Lenore just shook her head as she continued counting the till.

Chris asked Grandpa, "What are the winds?"

I realized I had no idea why that was important, but Grandpa said, "Light, but right out of the south. They're supposed to shift more to the east and pick up a little."

Using Scooby Doo's voice, Uncle Chris said, "Ruh ro." Then using his real voice he asked, "Lenore, would you bag up the computers while

I give Summer the nickel tour? Dad, would you get some bags from the utility closet and help Lenore?"

Uncle Chris waved for me to join him. Then he said, "Hey, babe, would you mind riding with Dad? I'll bring Summer Rose with me when I'm done here." Lenore finished counting the last few bills, wrote down a number, and then smiled and said, "Sure, babe."

Uncle Chris and I stepped through the door, and for a second I forgot we were inside a garage. The first bay had three treatment rooms arranged down its length—totally modern and professional. I figured out Uncle Chris had built this part of the clinic like anybody else would, except he'd built it *inside* another building. I oriented myself, and pointing to my right, asked, "Is there a garage door behind that wall?"

He nodded and smiled at me. His smile looked exactly like Grandpa's.

Then we walked through another door into what had been the second maintenance bay. On one side of the central area sat a bank of kennels of various sizes. The other long wall was filled with white counters, cabinets, storage bins, and a bookcase. Two stainless-steel tables stood in the middle. At either end of the central area was a door—one leading to a small surgery, the other to an efficiency apartment. In the middle of the far wall was a double door leading into the third bay, which looked like the inside of a barn—with large kennels, a dog run, and a corral for larger animals.

We went through another set of double doors to reach the last three bays, which still looked like an auto repair shop with the big roll-up garage doors. Where we were standing—the fourth bay—looked like a storage area. Doc Rock's big kennel truck was in the fifth bay, and his flatbed trailer was in the sixth.

"Wow, Uncle Chris, this is fantastic! And you have *got* to talk to me about 'Doc Rock.' I met a girl on the airplane coming up here, and when she found out you were my uncle, she just about flipped out. It was like I was famous just because I was your niece."

He laughed and said, "All right, I'll fill you in on my celebrity lifestyle! But right now we need to get going. Let me do a quick check on a couple of my patients, and then we'd better dash into town and pick up a few things before we go out to the house."

We went back into bay two. Uncle Chris opened the doors of a couple of the small kennels, petting and talking to the dogs. Then he brought a white miniature poodle out of its kennel and set it on one of the tables. The poor thing was trembling. Uncle Chris asked me to calm the dog down while he got a thermometer from one of the white cabinets. He talked to the poodle as he took its temperature, and I continued to pet it as Uncle Chris finished his examination. Finally he said, "I think you can go home tomorrow, Biscuits." He put the dog back into its kennel. He turned on a CD player with some soft nature sounds (birds and frogs and stuff) and quiet new-age music in the background, and then flipped off the main lights and pointed to the door that led out to the garage.

We got into the "Doc Rock" truck and headed east back toward Wasilla.

"Where are we going, Uncle Chris?"

"I've let my volcano supplies run low. I need to replace a few things."

"Why?" I asked, with just a hint of panic. "Grandpa said it was just steam."

"Well, it is right now. But that could change in a heartbeat. I just need to pick up some new tarps and tape and, let's see . . . panty hose."

"*Panty hose?*" I laughed.

"If you put panty hose over the air inlet on your car, it keeps the air filter from clogging as quickly. Most people are smart enough to stay home in an ashfall, but I have my patients and my own dogs to worry about, so I have to know I can drive safely."

"Uncle Chris, are you serious? Don't joke! This is kind of scary for me."

"Yes, I'm serious. But don't be scared, kiddo. It's gonna be okay." He put his hand on my shoulder and said, "Hey, I'll even let you buy the panty hose."

"Oh, Uncle Chris!" I growled. "Besides, I don't know what kind to buy."

"Well, my favorite shade is nude," he said with a grin, "but my truck really doesn't care."

I felt a little embarrassed by what I now realized was a silly question. Uncle Chris said, "Go for the largest size you can get." When he saw the expression on my face, he added, "There's more filter material in queen size."

We pulled into a mega-store called Fred Meyer. Uncle Chris handed me a fifty-dollar bill and said, "Get as many as you can with this. I'll be in the paint department. We don't have a lot of time."

When we got inside the store, I picked up a hand basket and Uncle Chris took a cart, and we headed off in our own directions. I could just imagine my journal entry tonight: "Today I bought panty hose for Uncle Chris's truck." I cracked up as I pulled eight packages of nude, queen-sized panty hose off the rack and threw them into my basket. Two guys showed up at the rack and started scarfing up more panty hose. "Sorry, guys, I just got the last of the queen-sized nudes." They looked in my basket and smiled. Then I headed over to the paint department to meet up with Uncle Chris.

As I walked down the big center aisle, I glanced down one of the side aisles and saw someone who totally blew me away. I was so freaked I actually zipped back behind the end of the aisle and then sneaked a peak around the end cap. She looked up and smiled. I actually shrank back and then almost ran to find Uncle Chris. When I spotted him, I dashed over and threw my basket into his cart. "*Uncle Chris!*"

"What's wrong, Summer Rose? Are you okay?"

My voice quivered when I said, "You're not going to believe who I think I just saw!"

"Who was it? Where?"

"About five aisles down. Come see!"

"All right, calm down."

I grabbed the front of his cart and nearly pulled him down the center aisle. When we were almost there, I went around behind Uncle Chris, gestured toward the side aisle, and whispered, "Is that who I think it is?"

Uncle Chris boldly stepped forward as far as I would let him. He looked back at me and said, "It sure is." He started to pull me forward, but I jerked my hand out of his and withdrew even further.

I couldn't believe it! He started walking toward her. I heard him say, "Hey, Todd." A male voice replied, "Hey, Chris." Then another voice—this time it was the woman—said, "Well, if it isn't Christian August Rockwell. It's nice to see you—it's been a while, hasn't it?"

"It has. I'd like to introduce you to my niece." Then in a louder voice he said, "If I can get her to come here."

I cautiously stepped from behind the end of the aisle. All three were looking at me and smiling. I was trapped, so all I could do was swallow hard and move forward with whatever dignity I had left.

Uncle Chris reached out for my hand and politely pulled me into their circle. "Todd and Sarah, this is Summer Rose Watson."

I stood there dumbfounded.

Todd said, "Hello. Are you up here visiting?"

I started to answer but had to clear my throat first. "Yes, sir."

Then Sarah stuck out her hand and said, "It's really nice to meet you, Summer Rose."

I finally raised my eyes up off the floor and looked her in hers. With as much courage as I had in my fifteen-year-old self, I shook her hand and said, "It's nice to meet you too, Mrs. Palin."

"So, are you going to be a veterinarian like your Uncle Chris?"

I suddenly felt some confidence. She was actually asking about me! "No, ma'am. I'm going to be an aerospace pilot." I paused and said, "An astronaut. I'm almost a private pilot, now. I'm just volunteering at the clinic because one of Uncle Chris's technicians called in sick."

"That's wonderful!" she said. "You're already working toward your goal of becoming an astronaut! Most kids your age haven't got a clue what they want to be. And it's also very nice of you to volunteer at the clinic."

Uncle Chris interrupted and said we needed to get going or supper would be ruined.

But now that I was face to face with one of my heroes, I didn't want to leave! I have to admit I didn't know a thing about Sarah Palin's politics—I just knew she was a former governor and a vice presidential candidate and she had written books. She's the kind of woman I want to be—self-confident, educated, and a real leader.

Desperate to keep the conversation going, I asked, "Mrs. Palin, are you a pilot?"

"Gosh, no! Todd's the pilot in our family! But I was once the mayor of this town," she said and laughed.

"Come on, Summer Rose. Let's go," Uncle Chris called from down the aisle. I told the Palins I hoped we could meet again and hurried to catch up to him. When we got to the checkout aisle, I tugged on Uncle Chris's sleeve to get him to lean over a bit. Cupping my hand around his ear, I whispered, "Did you know she's *not* a pilot?"

Uncle Chris chuckled a little bit and said, "No, I never thought about that. Why is that so important?"

I started to tell him and then thought better of it.

He looked at me for a moment and then said, "*Ooohhhh.* You just met one of the most famous women in America and she's not a pilot, but *you* are. No modesty here, eh?"

I realized how I had just embarrassed myself.

"That's okay," he said and patted me on the back. "Sometimes you have to ring your own bell." Then he said, "By the way, do you know what you call a student pilot with fifty hours of training?"

"No, what?"

As he put our purchases on the belt, he said, "A student pilot."

With a groan I said, "I get it."

I handed him the fifty-dollar bill back. We checked out and practically trotted for the truck. "Hurry up, kiddo," he said over his shoulder. "Lenore is going to kill me."

As we drove back through Wasilla, Uncle Chris told me the Palins live about a mile off the highway. "Would you like to drive by?"

"No, not really."

"I've known Todd for about ten years. I met Sarah about five years ago, but I used to watch her do the ten o'clock sports on TV before she got into politics. She reminds me a lot of you."

That kind of surprised me. "Really! You think *I'm* like *her*?"

"No, that's not what I said. I said *she* reminds me of *you*."

This is the type of respect and emotional support I get from my family. That was really a very nice thing to say about me.

"Is Mr. Palin a musher?"

"No, Todd races iron dogs."

"What?"

"Snowmobiles. He's a four-time winner of the Tesoro Iron Dog Classic. I was on his aerial support team when he won the race in 2002," he said. "Todd and Sarah do have a couple of house dogs that I take care of in the clinic, so I see them a couple of times a year."

"Cool." We drove past the clinic and traveled farther away from civilization. We rode along quietly as I looked out at the scenery. After a while I said, "It sure does take a long time to get to your cabin."

"Yeah, it's about 45 miles from the clinic—at about 114 mile."

"I've never understood what that means, Uncle Chris."

"We don't have house numbers this far out, so we use the highway mile markers. My actual physical address is Mile 114.2 George Parks Highway, Trapper Creek, Alaska. It is a lot easier to just say 'about mile 114' on the Parks."

I laughed and said, "This place is crazy. I love it."

As we drove, I got another good look at the volcano and noticed it had changed. "Look, Uncle Chris!" He stopped at the first place with a pull off. The volcano was spitting a billowing black cloud.

"Looks like Spurr has gone and done it. That's an 'I *ain't* ly'n' eruption."

"Oh, look, is that lightning?"

"Lightning in the ash cloud is very common. Got your camera?"

I held up my phone and took, like, a dozen pictures. "Are we in any danger?"

"We could be, but probably not like you're imagining," he said. "The biggest danger to us is ashfall. The winds are still out of the south, and that ash *is* going to hit us. Don't worry; it won't bury us like Pompeii—we're too far away. We may get an inch or two, but that's enough to do all kinds of damage."

"Like what?"

"Tons of things—people have respiratory problems, power outages, computer failures, all kinds of machines breaking down, and the sewer plants plugging up. Let's get back to the cabin."

When we got to Uncle Chris's place, we were happy to see dinner was just about ready. Lenore was setting the table and Grandpa was on the phone with Ammo at his feet. The TV was tuned to a special news broadcast about the eruption.

Uncle Chris went into the kitchen and asked, "What's up with the eruption?"

She said, "August just called the flight service station, and it looks like Ted Stevens Airport will remain open for now. The ash is going to settle right on top of us out here in the valley."

"What are we going to do?" I asked.

"Well, first we're all going to sit down and eat," Lenore said. Then she added, "But you all have permission to wolf it down!"

We sat down around the table, and Uncle Chris said a blessing over the food—then we all started gobbling our dinner like we were at a pie-eating contest.

I felt a cat rubbing against my ankles. "Oh, hello. What's your name?"

Lenore said, "His name is Danger."

"Oh! Poor boy, what happened to your tail?"

Grandpa stood up as he was wiping his mouth with a napkin. "I have to get going in case Palmer gets some ashfall too."

Lenore also got up and started clearing the table. "I'll bring the dogs into the garage."

Uncle Chris said, "Well, it looks like I get to take care of the plane and the clinic. Lenore, would you call and cancel all appointments for tomorrow? And also let the owners of the dogs at the clinic know I'll be spending the night down there." Then he added, "You'd better bag up the computers here at the house too."

He turned to me and asked, "Do you want to spend the night here with Lenore or with me at the clinic?"

I have to admit I was a bit overwhelmed, but the fact they were taking all of this in stride made me feel a little better. I looked to Grandpa.

"It's up to you, Granddaughter, I don't care."

"I'll go with you, Uncle Chris."

I looked apologetically at Lenore, and she said, "That's cool. I've got Danger and the dogs for company."

Grandpa and Ammo left first.

Uncle Chris said, "Let's go, Summer Rose," and then gave Lenore a hug and a kiss. "I'll talk to you later, honey. Love you."

"I love you too. Be careful."

Uncle Chris and I headed out to the garage. He opened a cabinet and pulled out three brand-new air filters, which he threw into the backseat of the truck. Then he opened up the hood and put one of the panty hose over the air cleaner inlet. When he'd gotten everything tightened down again, we got in and he drove out behind his house, right next to the dog yard, where we had a clear view of the volcano. What an awesome change had occurred! I could no longer see it—only a giant black smudge that obscured the mountain and seemed to rise straight up.

"The ash cloud is coming right at us," Uncle Chris explained. "That's what makes it look like it's going straight up. Also, the column is starting to drop the heavier ash along its path, which is why we can't see the mountain. It ought to be directly overhead in less than two hours, and it *will* be dropping ash on us."

"Black ash?" I asked. "Why is the ash black?"

"It's gray, actually. It only *looks* black, because the sun is behind the cloud and can't penetrate it. The same illusion happens in thunderstorms."

I looked up at him.

"You've seen really superdark storm clouds, right?"

I nodded.

"Think about it. *All* clouds are white."

Ahhh . . . I'd never thought of that.

"Uncle Chris, is everything going to be okay?"

"More than likely, but that's a *real* volcano over there. Some of the volcanoes on this end of the chain have been known to spew ash for weeks. The best news is, we're far enough away that the ash will be pretty well dispersed before it gets here. All we'll see here is a fine, powdery ash."

It took another forty-five minutes to get back to the clinic. Uncle Chris used a remote door opener and backed halfway into bay five. As he slid out of the truck, he asked me to give him a hand. He went up a set of plain wooden stairs that led to a loft above bay three. There was about six feet of space between the ceiling of the clinic and the ceiling of the original car repair shop. I saw dogsleds stored up there. He motioned for me to join him.

By the time I got to the top of the stairs, he had started moving some sleds and things around until he got to four large, bright-red tote bags. He passed the first one to me and asked me to drag it over to the edge and drop it down to the garage floor. I saw an embroidered logo that read Sporty's Pilot Shop. When we got all four bags pushed off, I asked him what they were.

"They're covers for the airplane. I usually use them to protect the plane during ice storms, but I guess they'll work for ash too."

We got all the bags into the backseat of his truck. Then we got in and pulled out into his parking lot.

"So where's the airport?" I asked.

He looked at me like I was crazy. "What? The Willow Airport is right *there*—just across the highway."

Gah! There *was* an airport just through the trees. I saw a group of industrial buildings, but from this angle I couldn't see the hangar doors—they just look like warehouses or something. I looked at Uncle Chris, put the "L" sign on my forehead, and said, "Duh."

He chuckled as he drove across the highway and up a short driveway to the parking ramp. Other people were already there covering and protecting their airplanes.

We pulled up to Uncle Chris's plane and hopped out. The ash cloud was getting closer. Uncle Chris threw me a roll of blue painter's tape and told me to seal up the cargo doors. He sealed up the main doors and all around the windows. We sealed up every seam and orifice where ash could possibly get in.

He went to the truck and opened the tote bags. There were eight custom-fit covers and sleeves that we used to cover every horizontal surface on the plane. When we finished, he tossed me another roll of tape and pointed at other planes nearby. As I began taping the doors and windows on a Piper, Uncle Chris headed back to the truck and got out some of the new blue poly tarps. Hopping up on top of the kennels, he gave a shrill whistle and waved some tarps over his head. Three people came running over, and he tossed each of them a couple of tarps. Then he went to the airplane on our left and started taping.

I finished two airplanes and was working on a third when I noticed the tape wasn't sticking like it should. I also noticed a gritty feeling in my mouth. Uncle Chris had already walked back to his truck. When I joined him, he said, "It's here. Too bad about the rest of these planes."

"Who owns those planes we just sealed up?"

"I have no idea, but I'll bet they'll appreciate not having to buy new gyroscopic and vacuum instruments."

"You mean we just helped people we don't even know? Uncle Chris, that's so cool! Who were the people who came and got tarps?"

He just shrugged. "Alaskans tend to watch out for each other that way."

I felt some ash getting into my eyes and started rubbing them with the backs of my hands.

"Don't rub your eyes!" he said urgently. "Let's get back to the clinic and we'll flush them out."

It was kind of exciting to be in a real volcanic ashfall, but I was glad to get in the truck. In just a few minutes, we were safely parked back in bay five. By the time we got there, my own tears had washed away the little bit of ash in my eyes. When we got out of the truck, Uncle Chris leaned against the front fender in a "TV commercial" kind of way.

He said, "Come here and see something." He opened the hood of his truck and removed the panty hose he had placed on the air inlet. He shook the panty hose, and a lot of ash fell to the floor. Then he removed the air filter itself and tapped it on the floor a bunch of times. A whole lot of dust fell out of it too. "You see that?"

"Yeah, and I can still feel it between my teeth."

"Do you know what that is?"

"Yeah, it's volcanic ash."

"I know, I know—but what is volcanic ash?"

"You know . . ." I shrugged. "Ash."

"No, it's not ash. There were no trees or anything else that would burn up in that volcano. What we call ash is actually pulverized rock and volcanic glass. That stuff in your teeth is called tephra. It'll ruin your teeth if you keep grinding them. It'll ruin metal surfaces in your engine and will definitely destroy the bearings in your gyroscopic instruments. It can destroy the hard drives in your computers. It'll even destroy your windshield if you use the wipers. If the owners of those planes don't know how to clean their windscreens, it will look like someone took sandpaper to them. And the finest dust can get into your lungs. This is what I meant when I said we could be in danger.

"We're lucky this happened in good weather. Back in 1989 Mt. Redoubt erupted like this on a rainy day—so the ash was embedded in clouds. No one was aware of the ash, and a Boeing KLM 747 flew *right into it*. All four engines flamed out. They lost all instrumentation. Their windshield, along with every other leading edge, was sandblasted. They eventually got two of the engines restarted—barely got the plane down in one piece."

"He lost all four engines and didn't crash?" I wished I'd been that good a pilot.

"Yep, he was lucky. We've learned a lot since then. As long as the air is good at the airport, they'll just vector aircraft around the ash. Aviation is big business, you know. The FAA will allow the airport to remain open as long as there's no danger, but airlines can cancel flights on their own. Right now," he said, "I'm more worried about animals than airplanes. If people don't get their animals out of this ash, it'll probably kill them."

Looking at my face, Uncle Chris could see I was still kind of scared. "Hey, girl, it's cool. We're going to be just fine. Now listen, we've got a minor logistical problem. This is a hospital, so we can't go into the clinic with all this ash on us. I need you to go over to bay four, take off your shoes and all your outer clothes, and then shake as much ash out of your hair as you can and head straight to the shower. There are plenty of scrubs in a cabinet in the supply room. I'll stay in bay six until you give me the all clear."

In a few minutes I was in the shower. It was amazing how much ash washed out of my hair onto the shower floor. I bent over and pinched some of it between my fingers. It didn't feel like ash at all—it felt like sand. It took, like, forever to rinse the ash out of my teeth, especially with my braces. When I was dressed in clean scrubs, I hollered to Uncle Chris that I'd be out at Lenore's desk in the reception room while he cleaned up.

While I waited, I called Mom at work. She told me she'd been through three different eruptions when she was a kid in Alaska, including the 1989 eruption that almost caused the 747 crash. She remembered collecting ash off the hood of the family Suburban and suggested I fill some baggies with ash to show my friends when I got back home.

Uncle Chris eventually came in and talked to Mom for a while. When he hung up, we went back to the apartment and turned on the TV. "No one can predict how long the volcano will erupt," he said, "but we're getting pretty good at predicting the weather. Let's wait until we get a look at the weather before we get too much more concerned."

Coverage of the eruption was on all the local channels. I watched as Uncle Chris got frustrated with "man-on-the-street" interviews and all the shaky cell phone videos. "*Come on,* show us the weather!" Finally, Uncle Chris's favorite weather lady, Jackie, came on. As soon as the first state map appeared, Uncle Chris cheered, "All right!" He didn't even listen to anything she was saying.

He immediately called Lenore. "Hey, honey, you getting any ash yet? Well, it's definitely falling here. We just got some good weather news. That low-pressure system down in Dillingham is moving into the gulf, well south of us. The winds should be from out of the east by tomorrow."

I went back to the reception room while they talked and looked out the big picture windows. I'd never seen anything quite like it. It was nearly dark outside, but I knew the sun was still high in the sky. The hangars across the highway were barely visible through the falling ash.

There was almost no traffic, but when a car went by it swirled up a light-gray blizzard of ash.

I really wanted to go outside, but then I thought about all the ash I had just washed out of my hair and decided against it. I went back and found Uncle Chris in bay two tending to one of his patients.

"So what do we do now, Uncle Chris?"

"Not much. Just hunker down and watch TV or a movie, maybe? We have a Blu-Ray and a ton of DVDs and BDs. We also have plenty of frozen meals and canned food. If the power goes out, we have an emergency generator that'll kick on."

"Wow, you're really prepared. That is so cool. Oh, you were going to tell me how Danger got his name and what happened to his tail."

"Well, he hasn't always been called Danger. His name used to be Spooky." Interrupting himself, he asked, "Want a snack?"

"Sure." We walked back into the apartment. Uncle Chris got some vegetables, a spoon, a jar of peanut butter, and a couple of little cups of ranch dressing. Then we sat side by side on a couch and started snacking.

Smearing a piece of celery with peanut butter, Uncle Chris asked, "Have you ever heard of a dog musher named Libby Riddles?"

I shook my head, crunching on a carrot.

"She was the first woman to win the Iditarod."

"I thought that was Susan Butcher."

"Nope, Libby was first. Anyway, she wrote a children's book called *Danger, the Dog Yard Cat*. It was like a Dr. Seuss book—lots of rhyming words and cute illustrations. It's a story about a cat that led a team of dogs to win an Iditarod race."

I kind of snickered.

Uncle Chris grinned and shrugged. "Well, when Spooky was a kitten, he used to go out to the dog yard, just like the story cat. He'd stay just out of reach of the dogs—he knew *exactly* how long each dog's chain was. Some of the dogs wanted to play with him, but most were pretty aggressive—they didn't like him at all. A couple would have killed him if they'd ever gotten hold of him, but that didn't seem to bother Spooky. He used to just casually walk right through the dog yard, with his tail held high, two or three times a day. So we started calling him Danger, after the *other* dog yard cat."

Uncle Chris stuck a carrot stick into the dressing. "Back then I had a wheel dog out in the yard named Ernest."

I snorted and said, "Ernest?"

"Yeah, he was named after Ernest Gruening—an Alaska territorial governor." He saw the expression on my face and punched me lightly in the shoulder. "Hey, he was a great man . . . and a *fine dog*!

"Anyway, Ernest really *hated* Danger. One day, Danger was right out in the middle of the yard again, really taunting Ernest. Poor ol' Ernest finally had more than he could take. He trotted back to his box and then ran toward Danger as hard as he could. He ran so hard that when he got to the end of his chain he flipped in the air and his hind end swung around and knocked Danger within reach of One-Eyed Jack. Jack tried to get hold of Danger but only managed to chase him right back to Ernest, who got hold of Danger's tail and bit it right off!

It took two days to get that cat out from under the shed. By the time he finally came out, his tail was scabbed over and well on its way to healing. And that, my dear," he said with a flourish, "is the story of Danger, the other dog yard cat."

I applauded Uncle Chris in a little girl kind of way. "Does Danger still go out into the dog yard?"

"Oh, yeah, he does! Just like he owns the place."

After that we got talked out and played several games of dots-n-boxes and talked until the regular ten o'clock news came on. The news was mostly a rehash of earlier reports, and I lost interest as soon as the weather was over.

I returned to the office and sat in Lenore's chair to watch the ash falling. I had moved it right up against the glass and cupped my hands around my eyes to block the room lights. The ash had totally obscured any light that might have been in the sky. The outside security lighting bounced off it and back into the room. I turned off the room lights and sat at the desk again. The whole scene reminded me of videos I had seen taken from a deep-sea submarine. It was actually quite disorienting. There wasn't even any traffic anymore to break the effect.

I decided to call Esperanza. She answered her cell on the first ring.

"Hi, Summer! Is this cool or what? Are you getting any ash at the cabin?"

"I'm not at the cabin. I'm out in Willow at Uncle Chris's vet clinic. There's ash falling all around us. It's totally sick."

"*Shut up!*" She totally freaked. I heard her shouting the news to her parents.

After I described what we'd been through, she said, "There hasn't been any ash at our place. Dad grilled halibut and we've been watching the eruption from the deck. The ash cloud goes straight up for a while and then levels off and is floating out toward Wasilla. About halfway to Wasilla, the ash starts coming back down again, and it just looks like low-hanging clouds."

All of a sudden the dogs in bay two started freaking out, and then I felt another earthquake—the strongest one so far. Esperanza and I screamed at almost the same time. (It turned out we were about the same distance from the volcano, just in different directions.)

About the time the earthquake stopped, I heard Esperanza shout, "What did you say, Dad?" I heard her running through the house and then outside. "*Holy crap,* Summer Rose, Spurr just blew its top! I mean, like, really blew its top! I'm scared—I mean, I'm scared for you."

Freaked out, I ran back into the apartment to tell Uncle Chris.

"Yeah, I know," he said. "It's breaking news, but they don't really know anything yet."

"Esperanza knows, Esperanza knows! She can see it from her house!"

Uncle Chris spoke to her for a minute. She told him what she could see from Peter's Creek. He handed the phone back to me and pulled a chair up close to the TV.

"Esperanza, what do you see?" I asked. "I'm really nervous."

"It's . . . it's . . . *awesome.*"

Uncle Chris then started shouting, "Look, look, *look!* They have a live shot from a traffic helicopter."

"Esperanza, it's on the news. I'll call you back."

I pulled a second chair over next to Uncle Chris and watched his every move and facial expression. I was worried and was taking my cues from him.

We watched while, over the next half hour, this huge mushroom cloud rose from the volcano. The stem of the mushroom rose straight up to the level the ash cloud had been before the explosive eruption—a small ring spread out at that altitude—and then the stem continued straight up and finally started billowing into a classic mushroom head. The top of the cloud turned red, then yellow, and then a bright almost-white.

"The column is so high it's catching sunlight from over the horizon," Uncle Chris explained. "That must be at least fifty thousand feet." Then he slid even closer to the screen. "Look at the base! Look at the base!" I realized he wasn't talking to *me*—he was talking to the camera operator in the helicopter. Almost as if the camera guy heard him, the camera pulled out for a wide shot and then zoomed in on the base of the column.

"There! See it? The column is starting to collapse."

Ash started falling back down right around the volcano, and the entire volcano disappeared from view.

Uncle Chris said, "That cloud of ash is moving at hundreds of miles an hour down the slopes and across the flats. It's called a pyroclastic cloud. Anything or anyone within thirty miles of that volcano will be killed instantly." Then he threw himself back in his chair. "Damn! The Yuklahiltna Lodge is pretty close to that."

"What about us?" I asked.

"No, sweetie, we're a hundred miles away." He smiled and patted me on the shoulder. "We're still okay. We're just going to get a lot more ash until the wind shifts. Jackie said the ash cloud should be out of the Susitna Valley by midday tomorrow, and the winds won't shift back for at least a week."

It was getting too dark to video the volcano, so the news just kept replaying earlier videos. Uncle Chris said, "We're just going to have to wait till the sun comes up for any more news."

He called Lenore one last time to make sure she was watching the news and to say good night. Then I called Esperanza and told her Uncle Chris said we'd be all right out here. We agreed to talk again the next day.

Uncle Chris and I made our beds on the two couches in the apartment. He went out and turned on the dogs' music again and then flipped off all but a few lights in the reception area and bay two. When he turned off the lights in the apartment, he knelt down and said his prayers. I just rolled over and faced the wall. My mind was racing, trying to sort out all the amazing things that had happened—I mean, meeting Sarah Palin *and* being in a volcanic eruption! Gah!

I lay there until I realized it was just no use—there was no way I was going to fall asleep. I quietly got out of bed, went out to Lenore's desk, and wrote Dad a letter. That just added to the things running through my head. So I opened my journal and wrote until my thoughts stopped racing.

I finally went back into the apartment. The last time I looked at the clock, it was one thirty.

CHAPTER 5

TIME TO EARN MY KEEP

One by one I dismayed them, frighting them sore with my glooms;
One by one I betrayed them unto my manifold dooms.
Drowned them like rats in my rivers, starved them like curs on my plains,
Rotted the flesh that was left them, poisoned the blood in their veins;
—Robert W. Service, "Law of the Yukon"

The clinic phone rang. Uncle Chris tried to turn on the lights, but nothing happened. It was totally dark, even out in the bay. The only light was from the red digits on the clock—seven thirty.

I heard him fumble around for the phone. "Dr. Rockwell . . . hello, Larry . . . I'm real sorry to hear that . . . how many? Yeah, sure. Are you going to bring them in now? No, I'm already here in the clinic . . . yeah, us too . . . No, I have a backup generator, but I gotta find out why it didn't kick in. Just pull up in front of bay four. Okay, I'll see you in an hour."

He hung up. "Summer Rose, you awake?"

"Yes. What's wrong, Uncle Chris?"

"Larry Gallagher had three dogs get away during the night." His voice was muffled as he rubbed his face. "He finally found them, but they're in pretty bad shape. Are you dressed?"

"Yeah, I'm still wearing the scrubs you loaned me."

I heard him open a drawer and dig around. Then he turned on a flashlight. "Time to earn your keep."

"Okay. Would you hold the light over here? I can't find my shoes."

He handed me the flashlight and stumbled off into the bay. Pretty soon, he returned with several battery-powered lanterns, flooding the room with light. I looked at the digital clock again—*hmm, must be battery backup*—and asked if it was a.m. or p.m.

"It's a.m.," he said casually, and then yawned.

Out in the waiting area, we could see weak daylight outside. Everything was covered with four or five inches of ash. Some ash had even leaked in around the threshold of the door.

Uncle Chris texted Lenore. I started to call Grandpa but remembered he just had the one living room phone and decided he'd call us when he got up and around.

Uncle Chris sucked in a big breath and briskly rubbed his face again. "Let's go check out the generator."

Back in the maintenance bays, it was pitch black. I think that's when it finally clicked for me that the only windows that weren't painted over were in the reception area. I followed Uncle Chris out to bay six and held the lantern for him. It just took him a minute. "Yep, here it is; just some switchology."

He threw the switch, the generator kicked on, and everything powered up.

We started getting everything ready for the new patients. First, we parked three dog gurneys in bay four. Uncle Chris put together a tray of things he might need and set it on a chrome version of a roll-around computer table. Then he tossed a surgical mask and cap at me. I fastened the mask and let it hang down around my neck. The cap had an elastic band, so I just snapped it on like the lunch lady does. Uncle Chris explained the caps and masks were for protection from flying ash when we opened the garage door.

"We're not going to bring the dogs into the treatment rooms. They'll be covered in ash. We'll just use bay three."

The clinic phone rang—it was Jenny, Uncle Chris's other technician. She explained there was no way she could come in. Uncle Chris told her to take care of her family and not worry about the clinic.

After he hung up, he said, "It's going to be just me and you, kiddo. I'd appreciate all the help you can give me."

"Sure, Uncle Chris."

"Just be as professional as you can. I won't ask you to do anything I don't think you can't handle. Because of the ash, you're going to have to stay in the front half of the clinic. I'll stay in the back. Bay three will be neutral territory, but I want you to sweep the floor every time someone comes in from the maintenance bays."

He rubbed his face again and looked around like he was trying to figure out what to do next. "I'd also like you to do Lenore's job, like taking any calls on the clinic phone. I'll see anyone who needs help. Tell them I can't leave the clinic—have them pull up in front of bay four and honk. Keep the outside office door locked—I don't want any ash getting into the front rooms of the clinic. And go ahead and turn the OPEN sign around and put a sign up on the front door telling people to honk, in case we have any walk-in clients. Okay?"

I could tell he was making this up as he went along. He reached down to his key ring and pulled one key off and handed it to me. "This is for the drug cabinet. Don't lay it down for *any reason*. Since you're my only assistant today, I want you to go familiarize yourself with the drawers and cabinets so you can find things when I ask for them."

Man, this is, like, for real.

I did everything Uncle Chris told me to do. I was still familiarizing myself with all the supplies and equipment when I heard a truck pull up outside and honk. I put on my mask and waited at the door of bay four. Uncle Chris pulled the chain to open the big roll-up door a few feet and then let it slam down hard. After he did this twice, I figured he was trying to knock ash off the outside of the door.

He finally raised the door just high enough to walk under without having to duck. He went out and helped Mr. Gallagher bring in the dogs. They pushed each gurney up to me, and I wheeled them into bay three. They closed the garage door and started stomping and brushing the ash off themselves. Mr. Gallagher pulled down the bandana he was wearing over his face.

I couldn't believe how bad the dogs looked. None of them were moving, and they were completely covered in ash. They looked like old rugs that had been left out in an alley for a couple of years.

Uncle Chris quickly examined each dog with a stethoscope. Then he looked at me and said, "This one didn't make it. Get him out of the way."

I pushed the gurney over by the bay door. Before covering him up, I said, "Sorry, boy."

Uncle Chris concentrated on the other two dogs. He used a big syringe to wash ash out of their muzzles and eyes. It was only then that I realized the dogs were both bleeding from their noses and mouths.

Uncle Chris told me to go into the surgery and roll out the anesthetic machine. When I returned, he instructed, "Now go into supply and find a little cart with the O_2 bottle. It's green. I'm also going to need oxygen masks for both dogs."

After I found everything and brought it out, Uncle Chris put an oxygen mask on the first dog and told me to adjust the flowmeter to two liters. After I figured out what do, I heard the oxygen flowing into the mask. Pointing to the other dog, Uncle Chris said, "Hook up Alexander to the other O_2 bottle."

I went into action and then watched Uncle Chris work on the second dog—Caesar. He was lying on the table without moving a muscle. I wasn't even sure he was still breathing until he started gagging and coughing. Such pathetic little sounds—there was so little air moving in or out. He weakly pawed at his face and gave a little whine. Then he just closed his swollen eyes, and I saw him relax and slip away.

After checking with the stethoscope, Uncle Chris said, "I'm sorry, Larry—he's gone too." He took off the oxygen mask and examined the dead dog's eyes. "Larry, come over here and take a look."

Mr. Gallagher took one look and angrily said, "Damn it!," almost like he was mad at the dog. Then he walked over to the third dog, and I heard him address the dog as Alexander. He petted the dog and talked quietly to him in a very loving way.

Uncle Chris covered Caesar's head with a green surgical drape, and I quietly rolled him over next to his teammate.

Now all our attention was turned to Alexander. He was struggling hard to breathe, his chest heaving with each effort. Uncle Chris pulled the oxygen mask off and examined the dog's mouth. "Larry, you need to see this too." Uncle Chris pulled the dog's lips back—his lips and gums were bluish. Mr. Gallagher took one look and walked a few steps away. He had turned his back to us, his hands in his back pockets, palms out.

"What is it, Uncle Chris?"

"Alexander's not getting enough oxygen into his bloodstream, even with the oxygen mask. That's called anoxia."

"Can't you operate or something?"

"Sweetie, his lungs are clogged up, and even if I could do something about that, he's also blind. The ash got into their eyes and scratched their corneas beyond all hope." I realized Uncle Chris was talking to me but also seemed to be talking for the benefit of Mr. Gallagher.

Then it got quiet. The oxygen still flowed into the empty masks. I reached up and shut one off. Mr. Gallagher walked a little farther away, almost to the wall. Without turning around, he said, "Damn this country. You'll take care of everything, Doc?"

"Like they were my own, Larry."

Mr. Gallagher sighed and said, "All right then," and walked out with his hands still in his back pockets. He never even turned to look at Alexander.

Uncle Chris put the oxygen mask back on Alexander and then followed Mr. Gallagher out into bay four. Neither said a word. Uncle Chris just slapped him on the back and opened the garage door for him. A moment later, the truck drove away.

After Uncle Chris closed the garage door, he walked back into bay three. He pushed the first two gurneys to the back of bay four and unloaded the dogs into a chest freezer. Then he walked over to me and said, "Let's get this over with."

"Get wha . . . ?" Then I realized what he meant.

"Can you do this?"

I shrugged. "I dunno—I guess." I felt anxious, but I didn't want to show it. "What do I have to do?"

"Well, I'm going to need a syringe with 5 ccs of sodium pentobarbital. The syringe is just like other lab equipment you've handled in science class—there's nothing magical about it. Besides, I'm sure you've seen syringes being loaded on TV shows."

"Do I have to inject the dog?" I asked.

"No, sweetie, that's my job."

I turned and stepped into the treatment room, with Uncle Chris following me as far as the door. I unlocked the cabinet and looked for the drug.

"It's the only one with a pink tint," he said.

When I found it, he asked me to bring it to him so he could check the label. "That's the one." After talking me through the process of loading the syringe, he watched me lock the vial back in the cabinet and return the key to my pocket.

"I'm sorry to say this is probably not going to be the last euthanasia procedure we'll do today, and I may be too busy to talk you through this again. Can you do this by yourself next time?"

My hands were shaking as I handed him the loaded syringe. I looked at him and said, "Yes, Doctor."

He smiled at me, and then we walked over to Alexander. The oxygen seemed to have brought him around a little. He was a slightly more alert and reacted to our movements.

"You can talk to him if you want. Go ahead and remove the mask."

I said his name and cradled his head in my arms. I talked to him for a second, and he weakly wagged his tail twice and rested his head against my stomach. I watched Uncle Chris insert the needle into a vein on Alexander's foreleg. "Happy trails, Alexander," he said, injecting the drug.

What happened next was instantaneous. The full weight of Alexander's head just dropped into my arms, and his tail stopped moving. He didn't moan or try to run or flinch. It was just like somebody had turned off a switch. He just ceased to exist. "Snap"—just like that he was gone. He didn't even have time to close his eyes.

"Uncle Chris! What just happened?"

He looked at me kind of surprised. "What do you mean? I thought you knew . . ."

"Not that, Uncle Chris. I knew what we were doing—I just don't understand." My eyes were filling with tears.

"Well, the sodium barbital caused . . ."

"No, no, no! What just happened? Don't you get that I don't understand *what just happened*?"

"Do you mean to his soul?"

I was a total wreck. I laid Alexander's head down and sobbed. "No, I don't think that's it—I don't know."

Uncle Chris cradled my face in his hands and looked straight into my eyes. With the same love and wisdom of my father and grandfather, he asked, "Whither hath fled that bit of animation?"

I hugged him and said, "Yeah, I think that's it. Please say it again."

"Whither hath fled that bit of animation?"

I buried my face in his chest and asked, "Where *did* it go, Uncle Chris? Where did that *life* go?"

He hugged me lovingly, and we rocked back and forth. "Well, sweetie, people have tried to answer that question since the beginning of time. I don't think you and I are going to figure it out today. As doctors, we simply don't understand what that spark of life is."

"I'm sorry, Uncle Chris." I took a deep breath and let out a big sigh. "It was just so shocking to see how quickly something can die. It isn't just about death. I mean, I handled the first dead dog without any problem, and I watched the second dog die on the table. But Alexander was different. Uncle Chris, I just wanna know what happens." I pulled back from our hug and added, "And there's something else, Uncle Chris. I didn't understand Mr. Gallagher's reactions to what was going on. Sometimes I felt like he really loved the dogs, and others it seemed like he didn't even care."

"Well, I do know the answer to that one. Professional mushers have a very complicated relationship with their dogs. Like any pet owner, they love their animals. But these dogs are so much more than pets—they're working animals. I don't know any mushers who make their entire living off racing—but many, like Larry, count those race purses as a very important second income. Larry has a young family to support. Putting down a race dog has the same impact on him as a farmer losing a tractor—and Larry just lost *three* tractors."

Just then the clinic phone rang again. I quickly blew my nose and cleared my throat. I was still wiping the tears out of my eyes as I answered the call. "Rockwell Veterinary Clinic. Yes, the doctor is in, and he's taking all walk-in appointments . . . Yes, ma'am, thirty minutes . . . please pull up in front of bay four and honk . . . Yes, ma'am, we do understand. Your dogs aren't the first we've seen this morning. Oh, Mrs. Davis, how many are you bringing in? Thank you. Good-bye."

Uncle Chris took Alexander out to the freezer. When he came back, he said, "Well, that fills up the freezer."

I reported, "Bennie Davis is bringing in Nun-Chuck and Mary-Go-Round. It sounds like a repeat of what we just saw. I hope we don't need a freezer for them too."

"Okay, let's get ready."

He showed me what a "sharps" container was, where I could dispose of the used syringe. I gathered up the leftover supplies from Mr. Gallagher's dogs and replenished the triage tray and swept bay three. When that was done, I stole a minute to wash my face and brush my teeth and hair.

This would end up being the longest day of my life. We saw patients continuously until three that afternoon. When we finally had a chance to take a break, there were seven new patients in the pens and large kennels in bay three. I had no idea how many dogs were out in bay four—the ones who had died. We also still had the three small dogs in bay two.

When the calls stopped coming in, Uncle Chris guessed that probably meant all the severe cases had been treated somewhere else or their owners had just put the dogs down at home.

Then I realized something terrible. "Uncle Chris! What about all the wild animals?"

"Well," he said, "after the Mt. St. Helen's eruption in 1980, we learned that burrowing or denning animals will probably survive the initial blast and ashfall. Any animals that had no protection will more than likely end up like the dogs in bay four. Small herbivores and insectivores will survive if they can dig under the ash to get to their food. Any large carnivores that managed to survive the initial ashfall will have to leave the ashed-out areas or die. As always, scavengers will do just fine."

"What about moose?"

"Just like the dogs in bay four," he answered. "But you haven't asked about birds and fish."

"Oh, yeah."

"Birds have a remarkably delicate constitution. Most birds that didn't escape the area before the ash started are already dead. Most fish will die off for the same reason our patients did—their gills will get fouled with the ash."

"Wow, this is really tragic."

Sounding very much like Grandpa, Uncle Chris asked me, "Is it?"

"Uh, *yeah*."

"I don't think it is, Summer. It's just part of a natural cycle. Volcanoes are part of nature, and the death of all that wildlife is also part of nature. It's all part of a bigger picture that we mere humans can't see or comprehend. Eastern religions call it 'Dharma.'"

Hmm . . . I need to look up "Dharma."

I didn't say anything. I wasn't sure exactly what I felt about what he had just said.

Uncle Chris then asked, "What about floods? Do you think those are tragic? Think of all the wildlife that dies in a flood. Not even the burrowing animals survive."

Uncle Chris looked at me, but I still didn't say anything.

"What about forest fires? What about droughts?"

I looked down and said, "I get it. I just never thought about it."

"Summer, the only thing tragic about those events is when children get in the way. In my opinion, when people knowingly build on floodplains or along fault lines or on the slopes of a volcano or deep in the forest, they become part of those natural ecosystems. Usually it's only the kids I feel sorry for."

"Gee, Uncle Chris. That's pretty harsh."

"I hope you don't think I'm harsh. It's nature that's harsh. I've just accepted it for what it is."

By five that evening, the wind had shifted enough that we had blue skies and no hint of lingering ash in the air. After we scarfed down some power bars—our first meal that day—Uncle Chris said, "We need to start cleaning up the clinic, inside and out. I'll start outside by cleaning the doors and sidewalks and a couple of parking spots. Tell all new callers that owners will have to have their animals cleaned of ash before they can be brought into the clinic."

I was amazed at how much ash had made it into the front part of the clinic, despite our efforts to keep it clean. There was even ash on the bag that covered the computer. I found a small vacuum and cleaned the obvious ash inside the office while I watched him blow ash from around the outside of the doors and windows. Then he shoveled and swept. After that, he brought around a garden hose and washed down the front of the building.

He then cleared some parking spots. I kept him supplied with drinking water and more energy bars. He looked like a zombie. He was absolutely covered in ash. We watched six big snowplow trucks come by. To his dismay, there was now a big berm of ash across the entrance of the parking lot.

Finally, at seven, Uncle Chris came into bay four, took off his mask, and closed the door, breathing heavily and limping badly. I helped him pull off his low-topped shoes. He winced in pain—both of his socks were bloody.

When we got his socks off, we discovered he had bleeding raw spots on both feet. Ash had gotten into his shoes and cut into his feet, right through his socks. While he took his outer clothes off, I placed a couple of towels on the floor just inside the treatment room so he could shuffle-skate into the apartment and take a shower. He told me to tell any callers we were closed and were not taking any new patients until tomorrow morning at ten.

Sighing deeply, Uncle Chris reported that the generator had to be getting low on diesel fuel. "I sure hope the power comes back on soon. I'm not sure there's enough fuel to get us through the night." Then he belittled himself for not topping the tank off the last time he'd used the generator.

While he was showering, I called Lenore on the clinic phone and told her what had happened. She said she'd hired several neighbor boys to clean off the walks and their dog yard. "Now all the dogs are back outside, but the garage is a mess."

"How's Danger?"

"Well, he's been using the litter box again. Listen, Summer, would you tell Chris that I'll be by about nine o'clock with hot food, and then I'm going to take him to the urgent-care clinic. Oh, hey—is the power back on yet?"

"No, and we're running low on fuel for the generator."

"Yeah, same here. Tell him I'll bring all the empty diesel cans I can find."

After we said good-bye, I called Grandpa. I filled him in on Uncle Chris's feet and the generator fuel problem. He told me the highway was still closed north of Wasilla because of downed utility wires but should be opening up shortly. He said he'd bring all the diesel fuel he could carry.

Next I called Esperanza. I wanted to tell her everything that had happened, but I knew I should be working—so it was a short call.

A few minutes later, Uncle Chris came out of the apartment in fresh scrubs—barefoot and walking on the outside edges of his feet. He sat and asked me to get him a few things he needed to treat his own feet. After he had cleaned and anointed each sore with antibiotics, he covered them with gauze and medical tape. Then he asked me to go into the apartment and get him two pair of white socks.

When I came back, I saw he was trying to get ash out of his ears. Between the two of us, we got the first pair of socks on, and then he pulled the second pair over the first on his own. He stood up and gently took a few steps around the chair. "Yeah, that's good," he said and sat again.

He looked at me. "You did some remarkable work today, Miss Watson. I really thank you. When I watched you today, it was hard to think of you as just a junior in high school."

I corrected him. "I'm a rising senior now, Uncle Chris!"

"Excuse me." He grinned. "Really, you were great. How do you feel?"

"I'm okay, but that may be the adrenalin talking."

"You ever think about going into the veterinary sciences?"

"Uncle Chris, you know I'm going to be an aerospace pilot!"

"Yeah, I know. I just thought you and I could go into business together. I'm thinking about partnering up with a younger doctor someday. Well, then, how about this—how'd you like to make two hundred fifty dollars tomorrow?"

"Uh, yeah! What would I have to do?"

"Well, you see that parking lot? I'll get a contractor out here to scoop all that ash up and haul it away. But I also need to get the roof shoveled before it rains. That's a flat roof up there. The ash is heavy enough that if it *rains* on that ash, I could lose the whole building."

I looked down at his feet. He held them out, straight-legged, like a little boy. "These are my fault. I should never have gone out there with low-topped shoes on. If you wear knee-high boots and we tape your pant legs down, you shouldn't have any problems. I hate to press you, but I need an answer right away. If you don't want the job, I'm going to have to hire someone else tomorrow."

"No, I'll take the job." Then I remembered. "Oh, Uncle Chris. I talked to Lenore while you were in the shower."

He smiled and said, "That's all right—I just spoke to her."

"And I talked to Grandpa," I added. "He's coming out with diesel fuel as soon as the highway opens."

"That's great! Team Rockwell rides again. I think I'll call him and ask him to bring his snow scoop too." He saw the question mark on my face and added, "It's kind of a shovel, but it has two handles that come back . . ."

"Oh, yeah, I know what you're talking about. I think I need a couple of things too, so I'll call him back if you like."

I called, hoping Grandpa hadn't left the cabin yet. Heck, I guess I hoped he would even hear the phone ringing in the living room. He finally answered on about the tenth ring. I told him about the new job and said I'd like to stay a few more nights. He had no problem with that. Then I asked if he had any high-topped boots I could use.

"Only if you think you can fit into the mud boots that Stephen Nephi wore last summer."

"Yeah, they'll probably be okay. I need a couple more things—for Team Rockwell."

"All right then, let me get a pencil."

I asked him for the snow scoop and earplugs to keep the ash out of my ears. Then I sheepishly asked if he would mind going into my underwear drawer.

"I raised four girls—I know what bras and panties look like. Do you need any pants and shirts?"

"Thank you, yes—and some high-top socks."

"Anything else?"

"Um, yeah, but I don't know if you want to . . ."

"Say no more—I'll bring your box of tampons."

Man, how embarrassing was that?

"That it?"

"I think so, Grandpa."

"All right, I'll see you guys in a little while." Then he hung up.

When I went into the apartment, I found Uncle Chris lying on his sofa bed with his feet propped up on the arm. He told me a contractor was coming out about seven in the morning to clean the parking lot.

We turned on the TV and watched one of the local station's extended coverage of the eruption. They started each segment with a graphic that included the word AFTERMATH and that sorta dramatic nonmusical-music, like they were a cable news station. We learned the highway was now open all the way out to Talkeetna. We also watched field reporters talking to Matanuska Electric officials about the power outage, learning that it could be days before power was fully restored throughout the valley. Another reporter was with borough officials who were taking a lot of heat about the snowplows rolling berms of ash into people's driveways. And from "Eruption Central" we heard that the roof of a senior citizen's home in Houston had collapsed and that a camera crew had been dispatched.

The anchor announced that in what was left of the hour they'd have live reports from the Alaska Volcano Observatory, the sewage treatment plant in Wasilla, and Alaska Railroad Headquarters in Anchorage. At the nine o'clock hour, they'd be covering the roof collapse live as well as talking to two different companies that were inviting the cities and borough contractors to bring ash to their quarries for free disposal.

Uncle Chris got up during the commercial break to check on his seven new patients as well as the three dogs in bay two. Several needed attention, and he asked for my help.

About the time we had them all back in their kennels, we heard honking outside bay four. "That would be Dad," Uncle Chris said. I went out and raised the door. Ammo skittered in, his whole body wiggling with excitement. Then Grandpa ducked under the door and stepped in with a whole lot of fish and chips. Man, did it smell good!

The four of us sat and ate—Ammo managed to finagle nibbles from everybody! Well into our meal, we heard the electric garage door in bay five opening and Lenore hollered, "A little help here!"

Uncle Chris and I looked at each other, remembering that she was bringing hot food. This time I was the one who said, "Ruh ro." Grandpa didn't have a clue, but he and I went out and helped her bring in all kinds of things she'd brought to make our stay a little more comfortable.

Before we went out for a second load, Lenore said, "Yum, I smell fish and chips!" She sat down with us.

When Grandpa figured out what had happened, he apologized, saying he had no idea she'd cooked.

She just shrugged it off, saying, "We'll eat my roast tomorrow."

We talked as we ate. The main topic of discussion was Uncle Chris's feet. When Lenore said she was going to take him to the urgent-care clinic, he got a little testy, telling us he could treat his own feet. "There's nothing they can do for me at the urgent-care clinic that I can't do for myself."

After that was settled, we brought everything in from Grandpa and Lenore's vehicles. Then Lenore went to shut down the generator and serviced it with oil and new air filters. While it was off, Grandpa transferred the diesel fuel from all the cans he brought with him, which just about half-filled the big storage tank. They both had to tramp through unshoveled ash to get to the generator and tank.

After loading all the empty gas cans into Uncle Chris's trailer, they hooked it to the back of Lenore's SUV. They'd have to drive back to Palmer to find a filling station that had any electricity, and then they'd have to drive all the way back past the clinic and out to Trapper Creek to fill the fuel tank on the generator at the cabin. We all met for a minute at the outside door of the waiting room. Grandpa and Lenore stayed outside while Uncle Chris and I stood inside the door. Grandpa said if he got too tired, he and Ammo would spend the night in their guest room.

The three of them came up with about six plans—discussing the merits and shortfalls of each plan all at the same time. Then they started talking in pairs (never the same two people), all trying to put together a logistical plan. Lenore finally spread her arms out in front of her in a grand gesture. The Rockwell boys fell silent.

"Here is what we'll do. August, put your Suburban in bay six for tonight. Then you and I will make the fuel run and go back out to the house. You and Ammo will spend the night at our place, and tomorrow morning about ten o'clock, we'll drive back down here to the clinic. By then, the parking lot should be finished. I'll put the trailer back into bay six, and August, you and Ammo can take your Suburban and drive on home or whatever." She stood there a moment in silence. The men had nothing to say.

I piped up, "Well, there you go. Perfect!"

Both men left the meeting, marching to Lenore's orders. I was really beginning to like her. She looked at me and overdramatically said, "There they go, and I must catch them, for I am their leader." She gave me a high five and followed Grandpa Gus out to hook the trailer up to her SUV.

After things quieted down, Uncle Chris said, "It's time for rounds. This will probably take two or three hours. You up for it?"

I answered with a question, "What do you need me to do, Doctor?"

He explained that normally on rounds his assistant followed closely, writing down orders and keeping track of every procedure. She also got whatever drugs or supplies he might need. "You and I are going to have to wing it."

Then he looked at me and said, "All my technicians are paid by the hour. You've been earning twenty-two dollars and seventy-five cents an hour since seven thirty this morning."

I looked at him with surprise. "But I'm just volunteering."

"Well, that *was* the plan—until *both* my technicians failed to show. You've done the work of *both*—and for the most part as *well* as *either* of them. And I pay a hundred dollars to any technician who spends the night at the clinic. I'll give you that for last night *and* tonight."

The matter didn't appear to be up for discussion, so I did some quick mental math. I let a little "woo hoo" slip out. "Sorry, but that's more money than I've ever made."

"And I'll bet you've never worked so hard or as long either!"

Two lab coats hung on a peg at the end of one of the cabinets. I put one on, picked up a clipboard, and said, "Ready, Doctor."

Smiling, he turned to the first patient, and I started writing.

"Patient name: Halftrack. Bill for emergency exam, nasal lavage, ear flush times two, optical flush, and application of ophthalmic salve times two. Oh, and IV sedation."

He asked me to get another bag of saline solution, a syringe, and the bottle of Buprenorphine. He examined Halftrack as I found the supplies he needed. Asking me to watch, he swapped out the IV bag. Afterward, he asked, "Can you do that?"

The "Yes, Doctor" thing had gotten old, so I just nodded.

He asked for the medication and syringe and then administered the drugs. When he was finished, he checked his watch. "That took twenty minutes. Let's see if we can pick it up a little."

We stepped up to the second cage. "Start a new sheet. Patient's name: Blaze."

We were interrupted at nine thirty by Grandpa and Lenore, who brought some really soupy Dairy Queen Blizzards. They'd also brought two bags full of milk, lunch meat, and bread and stuff—*and* a box of doughnuts for tomorrow morning. They didn't stay, and we slurped the Blizzards as we worked.

When we finished treating the dogs in bay three, we moved to bay two. Really, all we had to do there was change the pads in their cages and top off their food and water. "These two guys should have gone home today," Uncle Chris said. "Patient's names: Biscuit and Tamale. Make a note—call the owners and get them out of here.

"Stay clear of *Sven, der schwarzer teufel.*" He pointed to the Doberman puppy. "That's German for 'Sven, the black devil.' He's in quarantine because he nipped a toddler. The state says either put him down and check his brain for rabies, or quarantine him for ten days. Tomorrow he will have served his full sentence and be a free man."

Just before midnight we turned on the music and turned off the lights in both bays. Uncle Chris watched the news for any updates, and I took a shower and brushed my teeth. We were exhausted. By twelve thirty we both turned in. Uncle Chris pulled a piece of electronic equipment out of the bottom drawer of his night stand and turned it on.

"What's that?"

"A baby monitor. I set the other end up in bay three." Then he turned off the light. As he settled in, he said, "Spurr has stopped erupting."

"That's cool, Uncle Chris. Good night."

Something startled me awake at two thirty. I sat up and looked around the room in the near darkness.

Uncle Chris said sleepily, "Earthquake," and fell back to sleep almost immediately.

I flopped back down and covered my head with the sheet.

At 4:00 a.m., Uncle Chris woke me up. "Summer. *Summer Rose*, wake up."

"What?"

"Sorry, I need the key to the drug cabinet."

I couldn't get into my pockets so I had to stand up. I nearly fell back down as I searched and finally found it. I could hear a dog whimpering on the baby monitor. "What's wrong?"

"I need to sedate Alice again."

"Okay, I'll help you."

"That's okay. I can handle it."

"No, you're paying me, aren't you?"

"Alright, but I need you up *now*." Then he said, "Lights," and flipped the switch.

As I put on my shoes, I watched him limp out into bay two.

I caught up with him in bay three.

"I need 5 ccs of Torbugesic." Then he added, "For Alice."

I managed a tiny smile and then went to the drug cabinet and found the sedative. I put together a tray with the syringe and other things I thought he might need, and then carried it back out to bay three.

Uncle Chris saw the tray. "Very nice."

He inspected the bottle and set it back on the tray. He handed me bag of saline and said, "Go ahead and hang that for me."

When I finished, he injected the sedative into the IV port and then placed the used syringe on the tray.

Next he moved to Lightning. After showing me how to pinch off the catheter, he removed the IV and carefully handed it to me, using alcohol wipes to disinfect where the catheter had been on Lightning's foreleg.

"Now would you please get me four Elizabethan collars?" When I gave him a funny look, he said, "You know, those lamp shade-looking things."

"Ohhhh . . . but I don't think I've seen those."

"Sorry, they come in a flat box. Check down low over by the sink."

After I found them, he put one each on Twister, Skipper, Telstar, and Illya. I made annotations on each dog's note sheet.

Before I could ask, he said, "Normally, these dogs would have been washed as part of their treatment. These four are now alert enough that they're trying to clean themselves, which means they'll ingest a lot of ash if we don't prevent it. I hadn't thought about it before, but I suppose that means we're going to start seeing another wave of dogs with digestive tract problems later this week."

Uncle Chris started hobbling toward the apartment. "Okay, Summer Rose, drop the used needles into the sharps container, put the drugs away, and lock up the drug cabinet. Police up our trash and go back to bed."

Wow, look at me.

After I finished, I turned off the lights in bays two and three. Uncle Chris was already asleep. I turned off the apartment lights and got back under my sheets.

CHAPTER 6

JUST KICK HIM IN THE ASH HOLE

I woke up again to what I thought was another earthquake. Uncle Chris raised up on one elbow and said, "Five thirty! I wasn't expecting him till seven." That's when I realized what I'd heard was a piece of heavy equipment rumbling around the clinic.

We both sat up, stretching and yawning and rubbing our faces. I had this irresistible need to scratch my scalp. I started carefully at first but then got more and more aggressive until I was scratching like a wild woman. "*Ahhhh!*"

Uncle Chris looked over and cracked up at my now totally crazy hair. He still hadn't moved past sitting up, so I went to the bathroom first. When I was finished, I opened the door and looked out, holding my comb and toothbrush with a questioning expression.

Uncle Chris waved me off and said, "My gyros are still tumbling—go ahead."

After brushing my teeth, I started trying to comb out my hair, but it was all snarled in the back and I was having a hard time. I stepped out of the bathroom to see if Uncle Chris had gotten off the couch yet. He was still sitting there and saw me fighting my hair.

"It's the lack of humidity. Want some help?"

How could Uncle Chris possibly know how to get the tangles out of a girl's hair? He doesn't have any kids.

Almost like he heard my thoughts, he said, "I used to do your mom's hair when we were little. I got pretty good at it. I think Lenore has some detangler in the bottom right drawer. And you'll need to wet your hair a little."

I gave him a "no duh" look.

After wetting my hair, I came out and handed Uncle Chris the bottle. I knelt in front of him with my back to him. He took my towel and vigorously dried my hair. I heard him yawn twice as he worked behind me.

The heavy equipment kept moving around the clinic.

He spritzed my hair with the detangler and combed it in using his fingers. He dropped his arm on my shoulder and opened his palm several times like the itsy-bitsy spider, only lying on its back. I laid my big comb in his hand, and he went to work.

As he combed out my hair I realized this whole scene was exactly the way Mom took care of my hair when I was little, right down to the itsy-bitsy spider thing. When he finished with the big comb, he held it out in front of me, and I traded it with my fine-tooth comb.

"Would you like a herringbone French braid?"

"No, thanks. Just a ponytail please." I handed him a big scrunchy.

"Man, these would have been nice when I used to do your mom's hair."

Funny, I never thought about life before scrunchies.

He finished up and tapped me twice on the shoulder, just like Mom used to.

Once I was out of his way, Uncle Chris got up and turned the fire on under the kettle. Then he took his turn in the bathroom, shaving and putting on a fresh set of scrubs. When he came out, he was still barefoot and walked gingerly on his sore feet. He set a pile of supplies for treating his feet on the dining table and flopped down into one of the chairs.

"Summer, there's no way I can put on any kind of shoes today. I'm going to have to stay inside the clinic and ask you to do the outside stuff." He pointed to his wristwatch and said, "You're back on the clock."

The heavy equipment seemed to be operating directly behind the apartment now, backing up and moving forward a whole lot of times. Each time it backed up, that annoying beeping sound pierced right through the back wall like the machine was going to crash into the room!

We each got a hot cup of Pero and headed out into the reception room, grabbing the box of doughnuts on our way. Two very large dump trucks sat in the parking lot, each with a flatbed trailer behind it. Uncle Chris nodded with approval. "They're about done out front. They just have to pick it up and put it in the trucks."

Just then a Bobcat loader came racing around the end of the building hauling a scoop of ash. The driver dumped it onto one of the large piles along the edge of the parking lot. He then backed away from the pile and jammed it into forward so hard the front wheels came off the ground.

"Why is he driving so fast, Uncle Chris?"

"Time is money. The more parking lots they can get in, the more money they'll make. There are probably contractors coming in from Anchorage right now to try to get some of his business. Yorgy does all my snow removal, and I know he always likes to see an unexpected heavy snow. I'm sure he sees this ashfall as a blessing."

About then, a third truck pulled up into the front parking lot. It looked like there was going to be a show, so I pushed Lenore's desk chair around for Uncle Chris. I flipped her wastebasket over and slid it under his feet like a footstool. Then I sat down on the low spot on the counter, and we watched the activity.

The third truck was a service truck. The guy stretched out a hose and began refueling the first dump truck. He also changed the air filter. The guy in the Bobcat roared around the corner again with another scoop of ash. The two operators waved at each other, and then the Bobcat raced around back again. The service truck operator moved to the second dump truck. Before long the Bobcat rocketed by again, this time followed by a much, much larger front-end loader. They both emptied their scoops then parked.

"Summer Rose, go ask Mr. Jorgenson to come to the office. Tell them we have doughnuts."

When I got close enough, I saw the vehicles all had signs on them that read, Jorgenson L.L.C., Houston, Alaska. The big tractor also had the name 'Yorgy' painted on it—that's how I figured out the old gnarly guy was Yorgy. He said they'd be right in, which kind of upset me because they were all totally covered in ash. Each of them was muffed and masked and wore scarves like motocross racers—they even wore goggles.

Inside again, I asked Uncle Chris, "Do they have to come in? I mean, I just cleaned the office last night."

He said, "I've got office cleanup today. We can let them into the office and the public restroom." I looked at him like an old schoolmarm over some imaginary reading glasses.

He said, "What? I'll clean it up."

I wagged my finger and said, "I'll be watching you, young man." When I turned to look out the window again, a wad of paper went sailing over my right shoulder.

The three drivers took off their protective gear and started knocking the ash off their clothes as they walked toward us. Each was carrying a large thermos. I noticed the Bobcat driver was a lot shorter than the other two.

As they walked in, Uncle Chris said, "Yumpin' Yiminy, Yorgy, you start early!"

"Early? We've been up all fuckin' night."

Whoa! His language caught me totally off guard, but Uncle Chris didn't react at all. "Yeah, us too. We've got a full house back there. Yorgy, I'd like you to meet my niece, Summer Rose Watson. She just came up 'in country' for the summer. She's been a huge help to me."

I waved and said hi to the group, but none of them made an effort to acknowledge me or introduce themselves. Scoping me out, the middle-aged man said, "Damn, Doc, she sure is hot. 'Course all your sisters were lookers too."

I felt my face flush with embarrassment.

Then the Bobcat operator spoke up and said, "You're not so fuckin' hard to look at either, Chris."

I know the surprise must have shown on my face when I realized the Bobcat driver was a woman! Her short hairstyle was somewhere between bleached blonde and yellow, and she had piercings all over her face and ears.

Trying to ease my tension, I took the box of doughnuts over to her and then sat back down on the counter. She took two doughnuts out of the box, put the box on the floor, opened her thermos, and threw her right leg up on the next chair. I'd expected her to take the box and pass it on, but she didn't.

Mr. Jorgenson said, "Don't mind her, Summer. That's my daughter's little bitch-child, Emily. She wasn't taught any better." He walked over and snagged three doughnuts out of the box, leaving it on the floor.

Wow—Grandpa would never talk about me that way!

My revulsion toward Emily quickly turned to pity. The way the whole family talked was nothing like anything I'd ever experienced—well, except in movies. I didn't realize "real" people actually behaved that way.

I tried to change the mood by saying, "Emily, you can sure drive that Bobcat."

The other Mr. Jorgenson—the middle-aged one—walked over and grabbed four doughnuts from the box. "Hell, give a monkey a typewriter and he'll eventually spell a word."

That really seemed to amuse both Jorgenson men, but it only made me angry. I swear, I was about ready to say something, but Uncle Chris just reached up and laid his hand on my shoulder, pulling back ever so slightly.

The men were still snickering at Emily. She flipped the bird at them. The younger man grabbed his crotch and said, "You'd never go back to another A-rab."

"Shut up, Uncle William."

Yorgy shouted, "Shut up, both of yuhs. William, go finish up servicin' the tractors. Make sure you grease those front trunions on the Cat this time—they're squealin' like sick monkeys every time I tilt the bucket. Then get back here with the water truck and hose this place down. I don't want to get a call from Doc sayin' you missed a spot—but see if you can do it with just one tank full this time, you idiot."

"Yeah, sure—whatever, Dad," William said, heading out the door.

"And you, you little troublemaker. Get your ass back in that loader and bring the rest of that ash out here so I can start puttin' it in the trucks. And if you ever flip me off again, I'll break off your fuckin' finger."

"Right after I take a piss." She got up and headed for the restroom, still eating a doughnut.

Mr. Jorgenson turned to Uncle Chris and said, "You want to square up now."

It wasn't really a question.

"What's the damage?"

"Well, let's see. I usually charge five hundred just for plowin' your place. I'm gonna have to charge another two fifty for the haul-away and two fifty for the wash-down."

"I'll give you eight hundred dollars," Uncle Chris said. "The gravel quarry is taking the ash for free, and you're probably still sucking water out of Beaver Creek using the borough's pump." He got out of Lenore's chair, limped around behind the desk, and unlocked a file drawer.

Mr. Jorgenson said, "Eight hundred fifty dollars—and don't tell nobody! What's wrong with your feet, Doc?"

Just then Emily came out of the bathroom and bent over to pick up her thermos. When she did, I saw she was wearing a thong and had some sort of tattoo in the middle of her back, right at the belt line. She stood up and started to walk out when Mr. Jorgenson reached out like he was going to backhand her. When she flinched, she bumped her head against the corner of the metal door jam. It bumped hard—I know it had to hurt.

She snarled. "Damn it, you crazy old man." That's when I saw she was missing probably half her teeth. I wondered if that was due to bad dental hygiene or violence.

I couldn't take anymore. I climbed off the counter and demanded, "What did she do to deserve that?"

He pointed his finger at me and said, "Nothin'. That was just for the next time."

I barked at him, "You know there are laws against that kind of behavior?"

"Now listen here, you pretty little she-bear. I never touched her, *did I?*"

Uncle Chris put his hand on my shoulder again and said, "Sit down, Summer Rose." Then he looked at Mr. Jorgenson and said, "That's enough."

William started the service truck and drove away. A few moments later, Emily fired up the Bobcat and raced around the end of the building.

Suddenly, Mr. Jorgenson's whole demeanor changed. He looked at me and said, "Summer Rose, thanks to this volcano, I've figured out a way to catch moose that nobody else has ever thought of. I just dig a big-assed hole with my backhoe. Then I throw some of this ash in the bottom and put some peas around the edge of the hole."

I can't believe he thinks this is the first time I ever heard this joke.

"Then I stand back and hide behind a tree." He backed up a little, like he was telling this story to a class of kindergartners. "When a moose comes to take a pea . . ." He jumped at me and I flinched. "I jump out and kick him in the *ash hole.*" He busted out laughing, exposing his yellowed, twisted teeth and spraying doughnut crumbs all over the floor. I smelled his foul breath.

Uncle Chris tore the check out of the pad, "Eight hundred twenty-five dollars, take it or leave it."

Mr. Jorgenson took the check, snapped it a couple of times, and asked, "This thing any good, Doc?"

Uncle Chris just smiled and said, "If it isn't, you know where to find me. So tell me, how's business?"

"Well, if we have ten more fuckin' eruptions before the snow flies, we might break even this year. You?"

"Getting by, thanks."

"You hear 'bout them idiots down at the senior citizens center?"

"We heard they had a roof collapse."

"Yeah, they did, but they shouldn't have. That cheap motherfuckun' manager down there hired a bunch of Tongans out from Anchorage for day labor. They started by clearin' the roof over the dining hall. Just kept pilin' it up all at one end of the building till purty soon the roof under that big pile of ash just caved right in."

"Anybody get hurt?"

"Nah, the lucky sons of bitches." Mr. Jorgenson saluted Uncle Chris with the check and then turned and walked out to the big tractor. Within minutes, they were loading the piled-up ash into the trucks.

It was getting close to that time of the month when my emotions were very near the surface, and I was shaking with anger.

Uncle Chris looked at me. "You want to talk about it?" he said quietly.

"Yes . . . no . . . *yes.* I can't believe you do business with that kind of people!"

"Well, he's good at what he does. He always comes when we call, and believe it or not, he's the cheapest guy around."

I angrily snapped, "That's not what I mean."

"I know it isn't. I don't usually have that much direct contact with them. Usually, Lenore calls, they come during the night, and they get a check in the mail."

"Why didn't you step in and help me, Uncle Chris? I don't understand why you didn't stand up to them!"

"It seemed like you were holding your own." As he locked the checkbook back up he said, "I know a little about the family because I used to wrestle William back in high school. I was on the Chugiak team, and he was on the Wasilla team. William pinned me, at state, and he seems to want to lord that over me to this day. I'm surprised he didn't try to put me in a half-Nelson, just to remind me. That, and sometimes they make the local news."

"The news?"

"Yeah, the whole bunch of them can't seem to stay out of trouble. If it's not stealing borough supplies, it's a drunken car wreck or a domestic violence complaint. I guess the last time they were in the news was about three years ago. Emily got pregnant when she was about your age. Yorgy got it in his head that a Sikh boy had raped her."

"A what?"

"A Sikh. Sikhism is an offshoot of Hinduism. It started in India, *not* in an Arab country. Sikh men never cut their hair and they wear turbans. Anyway, the boy was never arrested, but one night he was beaten half to death by some 'unknown assailants.' The kid never saw his attackers, but he was sexually battered during the attack. The attackers also cut off his hair. It was all in the news for weeks. Eventually, the boy's family moved out of the valley. Whether it was rape or not, Emily had to drop out of school and is now the single mother of a dark-skinned little girl."

"That's all so totally sick. I still can't believe you—"

Uncle Chris raised his hand and in a surprisingly stern tone, said, "Hush, and listen to me. Welcome to the rest of the world. You have lived your entire young life in a cocoon. And that's not necessarily a bad thing. You've been sheltered and nurtured by a loving, caring family. You've attended good schools and had good health care, including dental care."

Suddenly I realized just how good I have it. But you know what? I wasn't in the mood to be corrected. Not that day. Not this week. Not even by Uncle Chris. My emotions seemed to be all that mattered. I didn't care if he *was* right, I just didn't feel like being wrong.

"So what does anything about *me* have to do with you doing business with those jerks?" I demanded.

"There's a life lesson here, Summer Rose. You need to learn this someday, and it might as well be here and now." His tone had calmed down just a little.

I managed a not-too-sincere, "Sorry." I wasn't feeling well and it was the best I could do.

Calmer now, he said, "Thank you, and I'm sorry too. You know, between the two of us, we might've gotten five hours of sleep last night."

"Yeah, and that's not the only thing causing me stress today."

"Yeah, I figured. I was raised around four sisters, you know." He'd changed back into the man who'd offered to put my hair up in a French braid.

About then Emily and Yorgy drove the dump trucks away, the heavy equipment in tow.

"Summer Rose, if a butterfly doesn't bust out of its cocoon, it'll die. And you, poor thing, have had *two* cocoons around you. Not only your wonderful family cocoon but your church cocoon. You've been raised in that safe environment. The boys in your church classes have been taught to respect you as a woman. You in return have been taught to dress and act with modesty. You've been taught to respect your parents and other people. You've been taught that we are all God's children, and God loves us all.

"So I'll tell you what anything about *you* has to do with those 'children of God.' They exist out here in the real world—in the mission field. You can't just switch off the TV and make them go away. You can't just not see them because they're 'R' rated. Out here in the real world, there are lots of good and bad people—and some, like the Jorgensons, who're somewhere in between. Not everyone believes in being 'honest, true, chaste, benevolent' . . ."

I joined in the next part. "'Virtuous and in doing good to all men.'"

Oh man! He just worked one of our articles of faith into a conversation. Now I'm probably going to cry.

He continued. "Back when I was in Mutual, I was taught to be *in* the world but not *of* it. I guess that means doing business with people like the Jorgensons. And here's something else to think about—Emily's little girl needs to eat too."

That's it. Here it comes.

Crying, I got up and gave Uncle Chris a hug. With a cracking voice, I said, "Uncle Chris, I love you." I couldn't let go. I held on and just sobbed. Uncle Chris didn't try to fill the pause. He just hugged me and remained silent.

I cried some more—that deep, you-can't-control-it kind of crying that seems to go away but then comes back harder and from some place you don't even know about.

I bawled, "I miss my father!" I managed to whimper, "I'm so afraid his helicopter is going to get shot down and he'll get hurt or die." Then I stood back and stomped my feet, and this time I screamed at the top of my lungs, "*I hate this war!* I just want him to come home!"

Uncle Chris stepped back behind the desk and pulled a double wad of tissues out of a box. Then he kissed me on the forehead and walked me over to the door to the back of the clinic. He held out the Kleenex. I took them and stepped through the doorway, still crying.

I went and sat in the apartment. Once I got totally cried out, I just sat in the dark for a while. Looking at the clock, I was surprised to see it was just seven o'clock. I also noticed line three light up on the phone. I guessed Uncle Chris was talking to Lenore. A few minutes later, line three went dark and line one immediately lit up. Finally, line one went dark, and Uncle Chris shuffled in, looking apologetic.

"Are you still on the clock?" he asked.

"Yes, sir."

"Thank you. Usually, I haul dead animals down to a facility on Knik-Goose Bay Road. Yesterday, my plan was to put all the dead dogs on my trailer this morning and drive them down there. But now that I'm gimpy, I can't do it. Those animals have to get out of here today—they're not frozen. The company that incinerates the animals has been working around the clock. They have a pickup of three dead cows from Harrington's Dairy about ten miles from here. They told me they can pick up our dogs *if* we can have them ready in about an hour."

"What do we have to do to get them ready?"

"We didn't have time to document yesterday," he said. "We've got to scan their microchips so Lenore and I can reconstruct the documentation later. I just can't go out into bay four with these open wounds on my feet. Think you're able to scan the dogs? All you have to do is run a wand across the backs of their necks and then read the code to me."

I thought about it for a moment. "I can do that. It might even get my mind off things."

"Okay, good! If you'd said no, I was going to have to ask Dad and Lenore to load them up and take them down to Wasilla. It's going to take me a few minutes to unwrap and boot up a computer and get some things ready. How long before you're ready?"

"I'm ready now," I said, standing up, wiping my face and blowing my nose one last time.

"Then if you'd like, you can let Biscuit and Tornado out of their cages for a few minutes. And you know what? Go ahead and let Sven out too. He's served his full sentence. While they're out, change their pads and give them fresh food and water."

Then Uncle Chris went back to the reception room to get things ready.

It was nice to see the dogs playing with each other—even Sven, though it took a few minutes for him to join the others. I was beginning to think any dog that came in was destined to die.

About ten minutes later, Uncle Chris came back into bay two and told me to get the dogs back in their cages. "If they give you any trouble, use some dog snacks to get them back in."

I put on the lab coat and got Biscuit and Tornado into their cages with just a little difficulty, but Sven kept running away from me. Uncle Chris grabbed him by the back of his neck. Sven then got calm until Uncle Chris opened the kennel door. He started barking and growling, in a puppy kind of way. He even tried to bite Uncle Chris. Once he was in the kennel, he went to the very back, walked around in a circle three times, and lay down with his face away from us. He was whimpering and shaking.

Uncle Chris said, "Quarantine is really tough on the dogs."

I hung around the front of his kennel and tried to cheer him up.

"Drop a sow's ear into the cage. You can love on him later."

We went into bay three, where Uncle Chris gave me a quick lesson on the wand. He had me wand Alice, who was still pretty much strung out on the sedative, as practice. It wasn't hard at all. Next he suggested I put on a rubber apron.

"I don't think you'll have to move any of them, but put on some latex gloves and a surgical mask anyway."

Then he handed me three cardboard tags with two thin wires at one end. Written on the tag was a long alpha-numeric code, along with the dog's name and Uncle Chris's signature. He said, "Larry's three dogs—the ones in the freezer—are to be cremated. Just use these wires to tie the tag onto one of their hind legs."

I smelled the faint odor of dog poo when I went into bay four. I walked up to the dogs—there were so many! Yesterday, I saw only one or two dead dogs at a time. When I pulled off the tarps that covered them, the dog-poo stink was much stronger, along with a strong smell of urine.

I started with the dogs in the freezer. I scanned the top dog and compared the number to those on the three tags. "Uncle Chris, it says Governor Baranov."

Still standing in the doorway, he apologized and said, "His full name is Governor *Alexander* Andreyevich Baranov."

I just rolled my eyes and tied the "Alexander" tag on his right rear leg. The next dog ended up being Caesar. I couldn't scan the third dog because he was at the bottom of the freezer.

Uncle Chris said, "No problem. The last dog has to be Balthazar—I put him there myself. If you can get to one of his rear legs, go ahead and tag him."

The dogs on the floor were much easier to scan. Uncle Chris had laid them down in such a way that I only had to touch three of them. I scanned them and read the numbers to Uncle Chris.

Before I finished, I'd scanned a total of eighteen dogs. Uncle Chris and I worked well as a team. We had no do-overs, and it didn't really take us long at all. Uncle Chris then headed back to the reception area.

I was about to cover them when I heard a big truck outside. They were early. Uncle Chris must've still been in the office, so I opened the big roll-up door to bay four and went out to talk to the guys in the truck.

The guy in the passenger seat hopped out and headed over to the open bay door. When Uncle Chris stuck his head through the outside office door, I just waved at him, and he went back inside. The man in the bay started waving his arms just like a guy marshalling an airplane into a parking spot. He kept saying, "mon-back" over and over. I'm not sure who he was talking to because the driver sure couldn't hear him over the loud backup beeper. But they were also a good team, and they got the truck backed into the bay on the first try.

Both men put on disposable paper coveralls, booties, rubber gloves, and gas masks—not just paper masks. The truck had a liftgate that dropped all the way to the floor, like a little elevator. They started piling the carcasses on the liftgate, leaving just enough room for the two of them to ride up. Then the men started two-man tossing the carcasses between the three dead cows that were already in there. This was hard to witness.

Then the men rode the gate back down for the second load. Once again they tossed the dogs in like big bags of grass seed. The driver pulled up his mask and said, "We're three short."

"They're in the freezer; they're the ones to be cremated," I said.

They pulled the frozen carcasses out of the freezer, put them on the liftgate, and, with a lot more respect, laid them at the very back of the truck.

Just then William Jorgenson showed up with the water truck and started blowing the truck's big air horns. I went out to see what he wanted. He rolled down the window, but the truck was so loud I couldn't hear him. It was obvious he wasn't coming down, so I had to step up on the running board.

"I can't wash this parking lot down with that damn truck sittin' there, now can I?"

"Then go start in the back," I said. I was actually hoping he was going to give me trouble. I was ready for it—and you already know how I feel about bullies.

"You mean he wants the back washed too?"

"Yes, that's what he paid you to do." I finished with an exaggerated voice, *"Ain't it?"*

"Well, get off of my fuckin truck and tell them to hurry the fuck up!"

As he drove around back, I walked back into bay four. Uncle Chris finally showed up at the door to bay three. He handed me a computer-generated page and said, "Sorry, I had trouble getting the printer to work. I need one of them to sign this."

I reached in the door, got my clipboard with all of last night's notes, and clipped the new page right on top. I saw all the microchip numbers were listed. The three special dogs—Mr. Gallagher's dogs—were also identified by name.

I carried the clipboard over to the driver, who had just stripped off all his protective gear. After the driver signed the paper, he said, "Thank you, ma'am."

The "ma'am" part surprised me. He was probably ten years older than me. Then I thought—I was dressed in scrubs and a lab coat, I was carrying a clipboard, and I had just directed the wash-down truck around back. I guess I must have looked like I was in charge. I thought, *Hmm, I have to remember that.*

No sooner had the truck driven away than William drove around the corner. The truck had four big nozzles in front that were dripping water. He lined up to get a pass directly across the front of the building. I heard the pump kick in, and the drippy nozzles shot out a wide pattern of high-pressure water. He started coming slowly toward me. If I didn't hurry and close the bay door, he'd have sprayed the first ten feet of the bay. I got it down just as I heard jets of water strike the door.

Running frantically toward the office, I managed to lock the outside door just as the water started hitting it. Uncle Chris was on the office phone. He had a finger stuck in his ear, trying to block the noise of the truck. Once William finished that pass, it got a lot quieter. Uncle Chris covered the mouthpiece and said, "Good catch. Thanks."

I watched as William made four more passes and then drove away. When Uncle Chris finished his phone call, he thanked me again and asked me to get a mop and bucket. I saw a lot of water had been forced under the door.

Uncle Chris made another phone call while I mopped. When he hung up, he asked, "What was William's problem?"

"Nothing. I took care of it."

Uncle Chris grinned at me and said, "Oh, you did, did you?"

Before I could say anything, I turned and ran back to bay three, hurried into the apartment bathroom, and barfed up one cup of Pero and two doughnuts, sprinkles and all.

When I came out of the bathroom, Uncle Chris was waiting with a glass of dark grape juice. "You okay?"

"Actually, I feel all right now," I said, gratefully taking the glass.

"Are you sick?"

After a couple of swallows, I answered, "No, I really do feel okay. Now I'm just hungry. I think it was just my nerves."

"I'm not surprised. You've had a pretty rough morning, and it's not even ten."

He lay down on the couch, propped up his feet, and closed his eyes. "I got a call from home when you were outside 'taking care of business.' Lenore and Dad should be here in just a few minutes."

I sank back and closed my eyes too. I was doing some mental math again. "Uncle Chris, this eruption has cost you, like, fifteen hundred dollars."

"It'll be closer to five thousand before it's over—and that's *only* if the winds remain favorable. I'm going to have to shut the clinic down in the next day or two to have it professionally cleaned and sanitized—and they're not cheap on a *regular* day." He let out a long, tired sigh. "Some days you eat the bear, and some days the bear eats you. This eruption has also brought *in* a lot of business. Not the kind of business I like, but business nonetheless. Let's see, we treated and released ten dogs. We've got seven out there that were overnighters, and a couple of those will be here several more days."

Doing the accounting with him, I said, "And there were eighteen dogs out in bay four. How do you keep track of all of that?"

"I don't. Lenore takes care of all of that. She's going to be very busy for the next couple of days. She's my office manager, receptionist, payroll clerk, supply clerk, in-house accountant, and tax person."

"Wow! That's a lot. Does she get paid?" I instantly regretted asking that and wanted to take it back, but he answered matter-of-factly.

"We both get a nice salary."

"You mean you have to pay yourself?"

"Not *me—she* writes the checks. I guess it's some sort of tax thing or social security thing or some 'thing.' And by the way, I'm giving you a raise. You've been doing the work of *three* people."

Just then my phone rang. I saw it was Mom and went out into the waiting room to talk to her. "Hey, Mom, what's up? It's awfully early for you to be calling."

She said, "No, it's noon here, and I'm on my lunch break."

"Is everything all right?"

"Yes, everything's fine. I just got a call from your dad."

"Is he okay? Is everything *really* fine?" I couldn't help being scared about Dad, even when things were supposedly okay.

"He was TDY in Germany and really sounded homesick. He's pretty tired of being away from us. He gave me some pretty exciting news."

"Yeah? What?"

"He got his follow-on assignment."

My heart sank. I'd been dreading this news. We'd been stationed at Hill Air Force Base for more than five years—all my junior—and senior-high school years up to this point. We all knew when Dad got back from the Middle East this time, we'd be moving, but I just didn't want to think about it. This move meant I'd be going to a strange high school for most of my senior year.

Mom said, "Don't you want to know where we're going?"

"Mom, please just tell me we're not going back to Ft. Rucker."

She tried to cheer me up. "Honestly, sweetie, I don't think you'll mind this post."

"Only if we're staying at Hill." I tried to add enough teenage sarcastic tone that she'd know, at least one more time, how unhappy I was about this move.

"No, it's a *loooonnng* way from Alabama *or* Utah."

I just set my jaw and waited for worst.

Then Mom quietly said, "We're going to Joint Base Elmendorf-Richardson."

It took about two seconds to sink in. I repeated it slowly in the form of a question. "Fort Richardson, *Alaska*?"

"Yeah, baby! Your dad and I have been trying to get to Fort Rich ever since we got married." I could hear the emotion in her voice. "I'm finally going back home. Your dad is going to be the battalion standardization flight instructor."

We both got quiet—and then we started squealing like a couple of kids. We were both talking at the same time and at suprahuman frequencies. The dogs in the kennels two rooms away started howling! Uncle Chris rushed in thinking something was wrong.

All I could say was, "Uncle Chris! Uncle Chris!" I handed the phone to him and said, "Here, talk to Mom."

I jumped up and danced all around. I was hopping and flapping my arms like a crazy person. Uncle Chris gave me a really weird look and then turned a little bit away from me. After he and Mom talked for a while, I saw a great big smile break across his face, and he gave me a thumbs up. He talked to her a little longer and then gave the phone back to me and left the room doing a little jig.

Mom said, "Sweetie, I don't think you fully understand about this new assignment. Your dad and I talked, and we've agreed he'll retire as soon as he's eligible, right there in Alaska."

As I tried to process that, she said, "No more moves, baby. You're home too!"

"Do you know what town we're going to live in?"

"Oh, we haven't discussed any of that yet. We just now got the news of the assignment. We'll probably have to live in base housing until we get this place sold."

Mom told me she'd gotten a couple of letters from Stephen Nephi and Dad. "I'll send them to you. Listen, I have to call your aunts and uncles, and I have to get back to work, so I'm going to say good-bye now."

"Thank you, Momma. I have so much to tell you. Can we talk again later? And is it okay if I tell everyone about the assignment?"

"Yes, sweetie, sure! Tell Grandpa—that'll save me a call. And of course you can tell your friends. I love you. Bye."

I bounded into the little apartment. Uncle Chris was standing in the kitchenette, nuking something that smelled good. I ran over and hugged him, jumping up and down.

He, like, totally surprised me when he grabbed me firmly by the shoulders and held me out at arm's length. "Whoa! You need to stop doing that!" He sat me sat down at the table and said, "Summer Rose, I never felt like it was my place to speak up. But you don't have a grandma up here and your mother is in Salt Lake. I apologize, but you need to remember you're now a healthy young woman . . . a *very* healthy young woman."

I thought about how I must have looked. I was probably jiggling as bad as Esperanza. There was one of those awkward silences, and then he joked, "So, how about those St. Louis Cardinals?"

After we both laughed, he took my hands in a very loving way, and we started talking about all the exciting news. "Uncle Chris, do you know what high school the kids living in post housing go to?"

"Yeah, they go to Bartlett."

Just then we heard Lenore and Grandpa in the front office, but neither of us got up. Lenore went straight to Uncle Chris, and Grandpa turned the fire on under the kettle and then greeted me.

Lenore fussed over Uncle Chris, asking how the night went and how his feet were. He assured her all was fine.

Then she good-naturedly said, "This place is a mess!"

"Yeah, and you haven't even seen bay four yet," he said.

"How many?"

I jumped in and said, "There were eighteen out there. I have to tell you guys something."

But Lenore turned to Chris and said, "Eighteen? Our freezer can't hold eighteen dogs. Have they started stinking yet?" Before either of us could answer, she turned to me and asked, "Were?"

Uncle Chris jumped back in and said, "There was no way I could move the dogs with my feet like this, and I didn't want you to have to do it."

Grandpa said, "We were planning on it first thing."

I waved my arms over my head, "Hey, you guys! I have some important news here!"

"They've already been picked up," Uncle Chris said. "C&S was working all night. They had to pick up three cows from Harrington's dairy, and they had room in the truck for the dogs, so they came by earlier and got them. They're not going to charge for the pickup. Harrington paid for the run.

Lenore asked, kind of panicky, "Who bagged and tagged them?"

"They waived the bagging since they were being put into the truck with the cows, and my assistant here tagged the ones that needed it."

"Did they all get scanned?"

"Yep. Summer Rose took care of that for me."

I realized the "grown-ups" were talking—and every kid knows to be quiet when the "grown-ups" are talking. I still had the clipboard with me, so I just handed it to her.

"You took notes? Summer Rose, you took notes!"

I just gave her a big smile.

Grandpa said, "That parking lot sure looks nice. No one north of here has done a thing yet."

"Yeah, Summer Rose took care of that too."

Grandpa and Lenore turned and looked at me. Then Lenore asked, "You met the Jorgensons?"

Uncle Chris said, "She sure did. When I was on the phone with you this morning, I looked out just in time to see her climb up on the running board of the wash-down truck and give William what for."

Grandpa clapped his hands and laughed. "Yorgy was here?"

Uncle Chris said, "I think if I hadn't held her back, she'd have torn his right arm off."

Grandpa was still laughing and clapping and stomping his feet. He regained his composure and then looked over at me and broke into another laughing fit. He slapped his leg and finally had to get up and leave the room.

Lenore walked over to me, gave me a high-five, and said, "You go, girl."

CHAPTER 7

BUBBLE TRUCK

I t took me two days to get the roof shoveled, but it took a lot longer than that for the Susitna valley to get back to some semblance of order. But here at Grandpa's cabin, things had already returned to normal.

Today was my sixteenth birthday! When I came into the kitchen for breakfast, I saw a new framed photograph on the table, a studio shot of a lady.

"Wow, Grandpa, she's pretty. Is that Sister Baker?"

Grandpa winked at me and said, "Yeah, isn't she something?"

I winked back at him and said, "Oh, Grandpa, you're too old to have *that* kind of girlfriend."

Pretending to be insulted, he said, "I most certainly am not." He put his left hand on the kitchen counter, hopped up in the air, and clicked his heels together. When he came down, he didn't land very well. I think he might have hurt himself a little, but he didn't say anything about it.

After breakfast we moved out to the porch.

"Grandpa, you sure do like to hang out on the porch. It must be your most favorite thing to do!"

"Hmm . . . I suppose it is, especially in good weather. I don't want to waste any sunlight—which goes *double* in the winter."

"You even sit out here in the winter?" I exclaimed. "But isn't it too cold?"

"It is not bad if I have proper clothes on." He yawned and started speaking before the yawn was finished. "Besides, it is *beautiful* here in the winter! The snow and frost turn everything into a fairyland—and there is a special kind of magic, seeing starry skies and the aurora borealis even at four in the afternoon. Alaska is an amazingly beautiful place, no matter the season. And you may not realize it, but some of the most beautiful places in Alaska cannot even be reached *except* in winter, when the rivers are frozen."

"Okay, Grandpa, I get it. But I guess I'm asking, what do you do when you're *not* sitting on the porch? I mean, when you don't have grandkids visiting and that kind of thing."

"Ohhh, all kinds of stuff. Sometimes I might have as many as twenty pilots working toward one certificate or another. I have all kinds of things that keep me busy here at the house and church and the temple. I do some volunteer work, and I try to learn something new every day. It is a good day when I learn something new—and it is a *great* day when I learn something I did not know I didn't know."

"Uh . . . you didn't know that you didn't know? What does that mean?"

"Well, here is an example. A couple of months ago, I learned there are at least ten solid scientific reasons why Pluto is no longer considered a planet. I did not even know Pluto is no longer classified as a planet! That was something I didn't know I didn't know."

Grandpa flicked Ammo's greasy breakfast biscuit off the swing. Bam! Gone.

"How would you like a moose roast for dinner?"

"Sure, Grandpa," I replied. "Sounds great. Do you hunt moose?"

"No, that is a younger man's thing. But I keep my freezer stocked with roadkill."

I wrinkled my nose. "Grandpa! Sometimes you can be so gross. And besides, don't you mean a younger *person's* thing?"

He looked at me and said, "Yes, I did mean a younger *person's* thing, but I'll still bet you a box of doughnuts it is roadkill."

"Okay, Grandpa, it's a bet," I said, and then just let it go.

"So, Granddaughter, nothing special on the calendar today? What shall we do besides sit on this porch swing?"

I can't believe it . . . he's forgotten it's my birthday.

For a moment, I couldn't think of anything to say. I was pretty bummed. I mean, I knew I wasn't going to have a party with friends and stuff, but I thought I'd at least get a "happy birthday" or something.

Grandpa looked over at me, and asked, "What's the matter? Cat got your tongue?"

"Grandpa . . . it's my *birthday*. Did you forget?"

"Oh, right . . . happy birthday," he said matter-of-factly.

When I didn't say anything, he continued. "Well, if you cannot think of anything to do on your birthday, I have a few suggestions."

When I looked at him, he smiled and said, "Since you are moving up here, why don't we go get your Alaska driver's license?"

Funny, I'd never thought about that. I figured I'd just drive on my learner's permit and not get my license until we moved here.

Grandpa said, "It is a family tradition. Your mom and all your aunts and uncles got theirs on their sixteenth birthdays."

"Let's do it, Grandpa!" I said as I stood up.

"Don't you want to study the manual?"

"Grandpa, I took a practice test in driver's school, and it's really simple. It's hard to imagine *anyone* failing it."

"Okay. Don't forget your driver's safety course certificate."

We got there ten minutes before the DMV opened, and forty-five minutes later I was handed a hot new driver's license fresh out of the laminating machine.

I thanked Grandpa, and he just smiled and said, "Well, who loves you, baby?"

"You do, Grandpa! I'm sure of that."

As we walked out to the car, he handed me the keys but held on to them to get my attention. Then he added a big, "*And*, your license establishes your Alaskan residency. You will qualify for next year's permanent fund dividend check. Your parents won't be able to get theirs for two years."

"How much is that?"

"It varies, but it's been as high as two thousand dollars. It is one of the perks of living in an oil-rich state. Did you know there are people who want Alaska to secede from the Union and join OPEC?"

"That's crazy, Grandpa."

"Yes, but that is Alaska politics." He smiled and asked, "What do you want to do now, birthday girl?"

I reached into my purse and pulled out the pay check Lenore had given me. I handed it to Grandpa and said, "I need a bank account, but I'm not a full member of society yet, so I need an adult cosigner."

"I'm an adult," Grandpa said dryly.

Gah! He's turning me into a "straight-man"!

So off we went to Grandpa's credit union. By ten thirty I'd set up my checking and savings accounts, and I was the proud owner of my very own debit card. Grandpa gave me my usual ten-dollars-per-year birthday gift, which added another hundred sixty dollars to my deposit. I now had almost a thousand dollars. This was turning out to be a pretty cool birthday after all.

When we arrived back at the cabin, Grandpa said, "I've been thinking of something else special to do today. How'd you like to drive up to the Matanuska Glacier?"

"Grandpa, that would be so awesome!"

"Good. If it's all right with you, I would like to stop by Sister Baker's house and drop off her flower baskets. You can meet her and Sister Knudtson."

"Sister Knudtson?"

"Helga Knudtson is an elderly lady Sister Baker takes care of. Sister Baker is a hospice care provider." Grandpa gave me a direct look and asked, "Do you know what hospice is?"

"No."

"Hospice is a service that provides care for people who are expected to die soon. Sister Knudtson is not expected to live until Thanksgiving."

I was shocked. "But can't the doctors do something to help her?"

"They *are* helping her, sweetie. Helga is 98 years old. She's been sick for years, but no matter what her doctors did, she just kept getting sicker. So now they understand she is terminally ill and have stopped ordering anymore painful procedures or prescribing medicines that might prolong her life.

"Instead, they are giving her medication to keep her comfortable and helping her prepare for what's coming. Hospice has doctors, nurses, aides, social workers, and even chaplains—all dedicated to helping her have the best possible quality of life in the time she has left. She has even already had her own funeral."

"What?"

"Yeah, it was a great potlatch."

"A potlatch?" I asked. "What's that?"

Grandpa said, "A potlatch is a native tradition. It is sort of a party or celebration where the host gives gifts instead of getting them."

Then he added, "Sister Knudtson said it was sad how everyone got together and said nice things about people after they had died. She wanted to hear all of that while she was still around." Grandpa chuckled. "She sat in a big easy chair in the church cultural hall, and everyone came up one by one to say good-bye to her. She gave every single one of them a gift—sometimes cash and sometimes a nice object from her home. She only kept enough money for her expenses until she dies.

"You know, I had never seen her happier! We had a big potluck dinner, and everyone brought her favorite dessert—lemon bars. She had at least one bite from all the recipes.

"Helga has even written her own obituary and already paid for it to be printed in the papers. She has also left very strict instructions—no more funerals or memorial services after she dies. She said to just bury her next to her husband and twin baby girls and get on with our lives."

"Why doesn't she go live with one of her children?"

"Well, she has outlived all of her children and most of her grandchildren. Remember, she's ninety-eight years old. And she once told me, '*Meine werzeln sind hier.*'"

I gave Grandpa a puzzled look, and he said, "'My roots are here.' Brother and Sister Knudtson were some of the original pioneers in the valley. He is already buried in the Pioneer Cemetery. There is a double headstone, with Sister Knudtson's name and birth date already chiseled into place. There's also a set of headstones for their eight-year-old twin girls who died of chicken pox. The Knudtsons lived out here when the only way to get to Anchorage was by train or dogsled."

"I don't understand. Why didn't they take the highway?"

Grandpa smiled and did one of those silent chuckles—you know, where their chest sort of jerks but no sound comes out. He shook his head and said dryly, "There *was* no road back then. The bridge across the Matanuska River wasn't completed until 1935. That is the old steel bridge that sits right next to the current bridge.

"The old Glenn Highway did not go east to Glennallen until World War II, and the Parks Highway did not get finished until the early '70s. Heck, Anchorage was still a tent city when Helga was born in Switzerland."

Grandpa slapped his knees, indicating he was done with that story, and stood up. "Ready to visit the glacier, birthday girl? I have laid out a pair of wool Swiss army pants and a wool sweater in the mud room that should fit you. Those ought to keep you dry." Then he added, "You will also need your mud boots—I hope you brought them back from Chris's."

I nodded.

"Good. I will throw a few more things together that we might want. As soon as you are ready, we will get going."

I changed into the wool clothes. Both the pants and sweater were loose and really heavy. When I came out, Grandpa said, "Perfect! Now you look the part. Today I am going to take you one step closer to becoming a real Alaskan."

"What does that mean, Grandpa?"

"You will see," he said with a mischievous grin. Then he put the moose meat in the slow cooker.

While I was dressing, Grandpa had also changed into his wool clothing and was wearing an old baseball cap that had a big "21 TFW" on the front—something to do with his air force days. Before we left, he wrote a little note and tacked it on the note board on the front porch: "We have gone up to the glacier. Roast in the pot."

Grandpa always posts a trip plan—just in case, he says.

As we walked out to the driveway together, to my surprise Grandpa led me over to his beautiful truck, instead of the Suburban. I'd never ridden in it before.

"This, Granddaughter, is a 1951 Chevy. I bought this truck when your mother was a little girl, and it was an old truck even back then. In fact, this truck and I are the same age. Your mom and aunts and uncles called it 'Bubble Truck' when they were little because of these fat round fenders."

Everyone in the family knew Grandpa loved Bubble Truck. He'd restored it to look just like it did when it was new—cream-colored except for all four fenders, which were chocolate-brown.

Grandpa had already loaded Sister Baker's flower baskets into the bed of the truck. The flowers kind of made it look like a picture on a calendar. So I got out my phone and took a couple of shots from different angles.

"Why do they still call those things phones?" Grandpa asked rhetorically, and then handed me the keys.

I looked at them for a second. "*Me? Really?* It's okay for *me* to drive Bubble Truck?"

"Why not? You have got your license now."

"Yes, but . . . but—"

He interrupted. "I have already talked to your mother—she said she trusts us both. She just wishes she could be here to see you drive it." Grandpa then went around and got into the passenger seat. He looked out the window and said, "Let's go."

As I got in, he told me, "It is basically just like driving the Suburban, but a couple of things are different. It does not have power steering or power brakes. The old-fashioned steering is not too much of a bother unless you are trying to parallel park." He held up one finger and said, "One thing you have to remember—the truck will wander down the road."

"What do you mean?"

"It won't hold a straight line—it wanders. You will get used to it. Do not worry about the brakes. The first time you try to stop by just touching the brake pedal and the truck does not slow down, your brain will tell you to push harder. The clutch is just like the clutch in my Suburban. Well, it is a little stiffer. Oh yeah, one more thing—you have to cancel the turn signals yourself."

"Grandpa," I whined.

He looked straight ahead and said, "Come on. Your mother was driving this old truck as soon as she was tall enough to reach the pedals."

I didn't answer him; I just buckled my seat belt. Seat belts were the one modern feature Grandpa had added to the truck. I adjusted the rearview mirror, stuck the key in the ignition, and turned it—but nothing happened. "Grandpa, something's wrong."

"Oh! Sorry, I forgot there is *one* other thing. The key just turns on the electrical system. You have to use the foot switch to start the engine."

"Foot switch?"

He pointed to the floor and said, "There, on this side of the gas pedal. It works just like turning the key on the Suburban. Just step on it, and when the engine starts, take your foot off."

"Okay, here we go." When I stepped on the switch, the engine started and then revved up really fast. I quickly took my foot off the switch.

"Don't worry—most people do that when they first use my truck. You accidentally pushed on the gas pedal when you stepped on the switch."

I just nodded and put it in first gear and slowly let out the clutch. We started down the driveway.

"When we get to the end of the drive, turn left. Sister Baker's road is about a quarter mile down the way."

As I got near the end of Grandpa's driveway, I pushed in the clutch and stepped on the brake. *That wasn't so bad.* I flipped on my left turn signal and took my foot off the brake—and heard a very distinct *thunk.* I stepped on the pedal and let it go a couple of more times. *Thunk, thunk.* Yep, it was the brake pedal.

I slowly let out the clutch and turned onto the road, and off we went. When I shifted into second gear, there was a grinding noise. Grandpa was still looking straight ahead and said, "Don't worry about it. This old transmission is not as sophisticated as the one in the Suburban."

When I shifted into third and accelerated, Grandpa said, "Slow down—her road sort of sneaks up on you." I reached over to turn my turn signal on and realized it was still blinking from when I turned out of the driveway.

Grandpa stretched and popped his knuckles and said, "You will get use to that too." He pointed through the windshield and said, "Turn just this side of that big yellow rock."

There was a boulder the size of a Mini Cooper beside the road. Someone had painted it bright yellow. I turned onto the road and shifted into second gear. *Thunk.*

Grandpa said, "Her house is the third one down, on the left."

As I approached the driveway, I reached down to use my turn signal, but it was still blinking from the last *two* turns. Grandpa pretended he didn't see. I slowed way down, and when I tried to put the truck in first gear, it made an even louder grinding noise than before. I stepped on the brake too hard, causing the tires to skid along the gravel. Grandpa pretended not to be interested in what was going on. I finally got it into first gear and took my foot off the brake. *Thunk.* We headed down Sister Baker's short little drive. I pulled up behind her car and turned off the key. I let the clutch out before the engine completely stopped, causing the truck to lurch a little. *Thunk.*

Sister Baker came out of the house and walked up to the truck on the driver's side. Looking right past me, she said hello to Grandpa. She looked at me and said, "I've *really* looked forward to meeting you, Summer Rose." She reached in and patted my hand.

"Yes, me too. It's nice to meet you, ma'am."

She smiled and looked at me for a second. "August has told me all about you. Oh—happy birthday, by the way! Such an important one too—sixteen!"

Gah, Grandpa had not forgotten about my birthday!

I smiled, and she said, "Oh, braces I see!"

"They're coming off as soon as I get back to the Lower 48."

She smiled at Grandpa and said, "I see you've been teaching her to speak Alaskan." Then her eyes lit up when she looked in the back of the truck. "Oh, August, they're beautiful."

Grandpa opened his door and stepped out of the truck. Sister Baker stepped back as I tried to open my door, but it was stuck. When I bumped it a little harder, it finally popped open. I was hoping someone would say something about my driving Bubble Truck, but it didn't seem to be important to either of them. That's when I realized they were both treating me like an adult, not like a little kid who managed to stay up on her bike for the first time. That made me feel kind of good—but still, part of me wanted someone to say *something.*

Sister Baker was leaning over the bed rails, kind of "petting" the flowers. Grandpa came around and stood beside her. She put her arm around his waist and said, "Thank you, August. They're so wonderful." She put her arms around him and gave him a big kiss, caressing his back. When the kiss was over, she slowly withdrew, holding on to his arm and letting her hands continue down until only their fingertips were touching. Then she moved to pick up one of the baskets.

Grandpa turned toward me and stuck out his tongue like a little boy! I had to cover my mouth to keep from laughing out loud. He reached over the bed rails and started handing the baskets out. Sister Baker and I each grabbed one and headed toward the porch. Grandpa followed behind us, carrying a third basket. I hurried back to the truck for the last one.

As I was walking back, I watched Grandpa hanging the baskets on some hooks up under the porch roof and along the eve of the house. Sister Baker's house wasn't a log cabin, like Grandpa's. It was an old house but well-maintained and very tidy. I handed the last basket to Sister Baker, and Grandpa took it from her. While he was stretching to hang the last basket, Sister Baker gave him another big, romantic hug. Grandpa brought his arms down and returned her embrace, and then they kissed again. Sister Baker looked over Grandpa's shoulder and gave me a great big smile.

I loudly cleared my throat with an exaggerated "ahem." When they both turned toward me, I crossed my arms and tapped my foot. "Please, not in front of the children."

When we walked into Sister Baker's house, I noticed an old lady in the living room, sitting bent over in a glider. She had to be the oldest person I'd ever seen. In a voice that was way too loud, Sister Baker said, "Helga, this is Summer Rose, August's granddaughter." But Sister Knudtson didn't even look up.

Grandpa walked up. "Hello, Helga. I hope you are feeling well today. Snow is coming early this year, don't you think?" He too was talking in a louder-than-usual voice. She acted like she hadn't heard him. I didn't know what to say, so I stood there awkwardly for a moment.

Then Sister Baker asked us, "Won't you both stay awhile?"

Before either of us could answer, Sister Knudtson said in a trembling voice—to nobody in particular—"Summer Rose . . . that's a lovely name, isn't it?" She never looked up, and that was all she said.

I reached behind Grandpa's back and tugged on his shirt. He took the hint and told Sister Baker about our plans to go to the glacier. "I am going to introduce her to the joys of an ice worm cocktail."

"So you *are* trying to make an Alaskan out of her," Sister Baker replied with a grin. "Then you'll need to be going." She turned to Sister Knudtson and said, "They're leaving now, Helga."

"Take care of yourself, Helga," Grandpa said loudly.

I shouted, "Good-bye, Sister Knudtson," wondering if I was too loud. Then I said, "See you later, Sister Baker," as I ran off the porch.

Like a little girl again, I looked back and said, "I'll drive, Grandpa!" Not waiting for his response, I ran for the truck and was already buckled in before Grandpa got there. Sister Baker followed him over and closed the door for him. "See you soon?"

He patted her hand and said, "Yes, you will."

"Oh," Sister Baker said, "I meant to tell you—I found some fresh bear scat down by the lake this morning."

Grandpa asked, "Been eating berries?"

"Yep." She gave me a big smile and said, "Drive careful, hon," then walked back onto the porch.

I looked at Grandpa. "A bear? By our lake?"

"I do not think we need to worry about him. He is probably just crossing the valley to get to a new patch of berries. He has plenty to eat this time of year, and besides you are too skinny for a bear to even take notice."

Like so often, I wasn't sure if he was joking.

I started to turn the key, and Grandpa reached over and stopped me. He asked, "You sure you can drive this truck up that highway?"

"Sure I can," I said with a lot of confidence.

"It gets pretty narrow and curvy about twenty miles up the road."

"I can do it, Grandpa."

"All right, then, I am sure you can."

I started the truck with the foot switch—and *this* time I didn't step on the gas pedal. As I tried to turn the truck around, I discovered it was hard to turn the steering wheel when the truck wasn't moving. *Thunk, thunk, thunk.* After a couple of tries, I finally got it turned around and—*thunk*—we were off.

"When you get out to the Glenn, turn left and go out like you are driving to the airport," Grandpa said. "The road to the glacier is about thirty miles up the valley, at mile post one oh two."

I made it out to the yellow rock, looked both ways, and then we were on the highway, heading east. I managed to get the truck into third gear without any grinding noises. Grandpa was right—the truck did wander. I was constantly moving the steering wheel back and forth to keep the truck in the middle of the lane.

At fifty miles per hour, it was too noisy in the truck to talk much, but about two miles down the road, Grandpa said, "Turn signal." My left turn signal was still blinking, so I quickly turned it off.

The valley grew narrower. Sometime after Sutton, the drop off on the right side of the two-lane highway grew steeper, while the cliff on the left came right down to the edge of the highway. The highway was also becoming more winding, and I was getting more nervous.

Around one turn, I saw a big truck coming at me. I let Bubble Truck wander too close to the guardrail, which caused Grandpa to straighten up in his seat. I was beginning to think this was a bad idea, but I didn't want Grandpa to think I couldn't do it. Tears were building in my eyes. I knew Grandpa could see them, but he just smiled, scratched his beard, and looked out his side window.

I slowed down at one hairpin turn where the road got really close to the Matanuska River. Because the terrain had been rising, the river was now flowing faster than down by the bridges. It was narrower and banked with rocks and boulders, with some large boulders in the middle of the stream. It was so beautiful, but I couldn't afford to look. Once we got around the hairpin turn, we came to a really steep hill. Grandpa just said, "Second gear."

I shifted into second, and the truck powered up the hill. Grandpa patted the dashboard and said, "This old girl really does not like that hill. Do you, girl?" Then he said, "Put it back in third." I shifted and things were normal again—near-terrifying, but normal. After about fifteen more minutes, he said, "We are almost there."

We went around a curve, and I saw the glacier for the first time. "Oh, wow!"

"Just drive," Grandpa said. "I will take care of the sightseeing."

But the glacier kept stealing my attention. It was so big and so blue! Finally, I saw a small sign for the glacier turnoff. I was so happy we were almost there! I'd stopped crying, but I was still nervous. My hands were getting tired from gripping the steering wheel, and my back was sore from sitting so erect and tense. I had never been this tense in an airplane.

I turned off the highway onto a dirt road, and *this* time I remembered to cancel my turn signal. The road was more like a driveway than a road. The truck started vibrating really badly, so I slowed down.

Grandpa said. "If they have not plowed the road in a while, it gets these little ridges called 'washboards.' Slow down, or this old truck will fall apart."

The road started going downhill and was just wide enough for one car. "What happens if we meet a car coming up the hill?" I frantically asked.

"I do not know. That has never happened to me before."

That didn't make me feel any better.

We went around a curve, and the road suddenly steeply dropped off. For a second I couldn't see the road over the hood. I realized there was no guardrail to keep me from going off the edge. We started rolling down the hill, like, way too fast! I kept using the brake—*thunk, thunk, thunk*. Each time I stepped on the brake, the back end of the truck started sliding sideways. I started crying again, and the little girl in me shouted, "*Grandpa, I'm scared!*"

"It is all right, Summer," he said. "Watch where you're going and put it into second gear. Then let your foot slowly off the clutch."

"I want to stop, Grandpa!" I yelled. I was openly crying now, and I didn't care if he saw me.

It got so noisy in the truck Grandpa had to lean over so I could hear him. At least he wasn't pretending everything was normal. He shouted, "We will be okay. We cannot stop now—the road is too narrow and steep." He talked to me the rest of the way down the hill. Finally, the road started to level out and the curves were easy again. At the end of the road was a kind of dirt parking lot. I coasted in and then shut off the engine. *Thunk*.

I just sat there crying and Grandpa got out of the truck, walked over, and sat down on an old log.

I tried to get out, but the door was stuck. I bumped it so hard my arm hurt, but it finally opened. I stomped over to Grandpa and shouted, "That was *mean*, Grandpa! *Really, really mean!*"

Since he was sitting, he had to look up at me. He had such a pathetic look on his face. "Summer Rose Watson, I am so sorry. I am so very, very sorry."

I stomped my foot, and my bottom lip was probably sticking out. I wanted to be mad at him some more, but when I saw his face, it was hard to not forgive him.

He stood up and hugged me. Rather than returning his hug, I just stood there and cried a little longer.

"Sweetie, I was not doing that to scare you or make you angry. I guess I forgot what it is like to be a young driver. I guess I forgot that driving that old truck for thirty miles can be like an eight-hour shift, especially for someone with your limited experience." He stepped back and looked me in the face. "Please forgive me. Sometimes it is hard to remember you are just sixteen."

I was still too shaky to talk much, so I just nodded. Then I cried some more.

Grandpa walked over to the truck and came back with a couple of one-liter bottles of water, a candy bar, and a little pack of tissues. He sat back down on the log again and patted it. I flopped down beside him. When he handed me a water bottle, he took my hand and opened up my fingers. I had four little crescent-shaped cuts in my palm from where my fingers had wrapped around the steering wheel. My other palm looked the same. They weren't quite cuts—I mean, they weren't bleeding. While I was drinking, he unwrapped the candy bar and broke it in half.

I'd stopped shaking and leaned against Grandpa, feeling exhausted. After I got that crying taste out of my mouth, I took a bite of the candy. It was the best chocolate I'd ever tasted. It wasn't as sweet as a Hershey bar and it felt creamier in my mouth.

"What kind of candy is this?" I asked.

"It's called Belgian special dark chocolate. I cannot get it up here in Alaska, so I have a friend mail me some on a regular basis."

"Is he in Belgium?"

"No, he lives in Seattle. A store down there sells it."

We sat quietly together on the log for a while, eating our chocolate and calming down. I was starting to feel okay again when Grandpa suggested we turn around on the log and sit facing the other way. When I turned around, the glacier truly caught me by surprise. Coming down the dirt road, all I could see was how narrow the road was. I hadn't paid attention to the glacier. It was huge and so beautiful!

"Grandpa, that's the most wonderful thing I've ever seen!" I jumped up and hollered, "Woo hoo! Let's go, Grandpa! Come on, let's go!"

"No, Granddaughter, not yet. I have not quite recovered from our trip down the road yet. Just sit here with me while we look at this marvelous sight. I have noticed that you're getting better at slowing down. Now would be a good time to practice that new skill. Please, come sit a while longer."

I wasn't too happy about it, but I did as Grandpa asked. I guess I was pretty wiggly, because it wasn't long before Grandpa finally said, "All right, let's get our mud boots on."

We went over to the truck and pulled on our boots. Grandpa put on a bright-orange backpack that he had thrown into the truck. Pulling out a bright-orange, high visibility, vest like highway workers wear, he asked me to put it on over my sweater. Then we started walking down a winding path.

Before long the trail started getting really messy. In some places it was washed away or something. There were great big muddy spots and even some big puddles where the trail should have been. In other places, big piles of gravel and dirt blocked the path.

"Grandpa, why isn't the trail better kept?"

He chuckled and said, "This is the terminal moraine of a glacier, Granddaughter. This glacier is alive. If you come back next week, this part of the trail will be altogether different. Sometimes the glacier moves forward and scrapes rock and dirt in front of it, like a bulldozer. Other times it retreats, leaving a soupy, muddy mess."

"Ohh, I get it." That's when I realized I couldn't see the glacier anymore. "Grandpa," I complained, "when are we going to get to the glacier?"

"What do you mean? It's right there."

"Right where?"

Grandpa stopped for a minute to rest. He asked, "Have you ever heard the old expression, 'You can't see the forest for the trees'?"

"Yes, but I never understood what that meant."

"It is like when you see Salt Lake City from an airliner. You can see all the different buildings—the temple and the capital building and maybe even Central High. You can see parks and the freeway, the lake, and even the Wasatch Mountains—the whole valley. But when you go to the library downtown and look out the main entrance, all you can see is the City and County Building across Washington Square."

I looked at the big pile of rocks and dirt in front of us and said, "So this is like the City and County Building in front of the library?"

"Sure is." He walked over to what looked like a big hill made of rock and dirt, with small shrubs and grass and flowers growing on it. He took out his knife and start chipping away at the rock and dirt, until I could see the beautiful blue ice under it all.

"But that's not what I wanted to see," I complained.

"Patience, Granddaughter. We will see what you are looking for in a few more minutes."

We climbed over another steep hill and there it was! The whole great big glacier was right in front of us.

CHAPTER 8

ICE WORM COCKTAILS AND HUNDRED-DOLLAR HAMBURGERS

We just stood there for a while and took in the wonder. Some of it was blue and some was white. Dark streaks on its surface went all the way up to its top, farther than I could see.

Grandpa hugged me and asked, "Is this what you wanted to see?"

"Oh, yes, sir," I said, still in awe. "What are those dark streaks?"

He explained, "The ones on the edges are called lateral moraines—giant lines of broken-off rock and gravel and dirt that collects as the ice carves out the valley. Shrubs and trees can grow on the moraine as it moves down the valley. The streaks in the middle are called medial moraines. They are created when two high-valley glaciers come together somewhere down valley. That one in the middle," he said, pointing, "is wider than a freeway."

Then he said something that totally blew me away. "Boy, I am sure glad for global warming."

"*What?*" I practically choked with surprise.

"It is true—I am. If it were not for global warming, this old glacier would be sitting right on top of my cabin."

"That's not what it's all about," I protested.

"*Ohhh* . . . you mean it is all about emissions from my Suburban? Come on, Granddaughter, you are smarter than that. You have heard the brouhaha on the news about the poor visitors who can no longer see the Portage Glacier from the visitor's center. Well, five hundred years ago, the visitor's center would have been *under* that glacier. Ten thousand years ago, all of Anchorage was under a thousand feet of ice. Please do not blame my Suburban for melting those glaciers too. Earth has been in a warming trend for the last seventeen thousand years.

"Do not let other people think for you. I can only shake my head when I think of all the people driving electric cars in New York City. They do not seem to understand that ten thousand years ago, Central Park was under a glacier. Whose cars melted that glacier?

"Scientists across the globe have documented at least five major ice ages. Between each ice age was a period of global warming. Within each ice age there were periods of glaciation and interglacations, with huge sea-level changes between them. Remember our talk about Beringia? Here we are, standing on the remnants of the last 'ice age'—the Wisconsin glacial period. We are now living in the Holocene *interglacial* period.

"We use the term 'global warming' like it is a bad word, but it is not. It is just part of a cycle that has been going on for several billion—that's 'billion' with a 'b'—years. And guess what? Sea levels are rising again. So we humans are inconvenienced in places like Bangkok and New Orleans and Venice and Bangladesh and the Jersey shore and probably a thousand other coastal areas. We need a villain to blame, so we pick on the internal combustion engine. *Puh-lease!* Do you know what the most efficient and effective greenhouse gas is?"

I figured it was a hydrocarbon but decided not to venture a guess. Golly, Grandpa was sure getting worked up.

"It is water vapor."

"Water vapor?" I repeated.

"Every sixth-grade science student is taught that clouds act like a blanket that holds heat close to the planet. Then a few years later we ask these same students to forget what they learned in sixth grade and tell them we should convert to hydrogen fuel technology because those engines emit only water vapor.

"Girl, stop and think for a minute. Be thankful for the greenhouse effect. If it were not for greenhouse gasses, we might as well be living on the ice planet Hoth riding on Tauntauns and dodging Wampas. What we do not want is a *runaway* greenhouse effect."

Wow, Grandpa knows about Hoth! When did he see The Empire Strikes Back?

"And there is something else politicians do not seem to want us to think about. We just had a volcanic eruption here in Alaska. Do you know what forced that ash up to fifty thousand feet? A whole lot of greenhouse gasses. Do you have any idea how big the tailpipe is on that volcano? And that was just *one* little old three-day eruption. There are volcanoes all around the globe going off all the time. And do not get me started on giant wildfires."

I was surprised at how worked up he was, but he was right—I'd never thought about the air pollution that comes from natural sources.

Grandpa turned and started walking up the glacier, still talking to himself. I heard him say, "That is the trouble with schools today. They do not want kids to think. They just want to teach them what's politically correct or get them ready for the next test."

He stopped and looked over his shoulder at me. "Did you know Albert Einstein once said he never taught his pupils, he only provided the environment so they could learn?" Then he continued up the slope, saying, "Public schools do not have time to let you learn."

Grandpa was trying to get me to stop believing what I had been taught all my life. I'd been taught that global warming was bad, and that it was totally caused by humans—*and* he was actually dissing public schools.

He stopped and took a deep breath, and then smiled, waiting until I caught up with him. He put his arm around me, and we just stood there looking up.

I said quietly, "It's so big."

"Nah, this is just a baby," he said dismissively. "This little thing is only three miles wide at its snout, and its top is only twenty miles away." Then he made his eyes real big and said, "You should see some of the *really* big ones."

"I did, Grandpa. Thanks for getting me on the right side of the plane." Then I asked, "Can we get on it? The icy part, I mean."

"Absolutely, Granddaughter. It's your birthday, isn't it?"

As we got closer, I felt the cold air coming off the glacier. I looked down and saw a milky-colored river coming out from underneath.

Grandpa explained, "That milky color is ground-up rock in the melt water. It is called glacial flour—the grains are so fine you can drink them.

"The particles drop out of the stream as the river slows down and settles into mud banks. In the dry season, the wind picks it up and blows it into dust storms. That dust settles in the valley—in some places that deposited silt is hundreds of feet thick! When we drive back through town, I will show you. That dust is one of the reasons giant vegetables grow in the Mat-Su Valley."

We started climbing up a slope until I could finally touch the icy part of the glacier. I was a little disappointed because the surface of the glacier was crusty and white, not the beautiful blue I'd seen from the highway.

"This white crust is actually ice crystals that have weathered out of the solid ice," Grandpa said, and then he added, "That's where the ice worms live."

"Come on, Grandpa! I'm too old for goofy legends about ice worms."

"No, really! Ice worms are real."

"No way."

"Yes way! I'll bet you a bag of doughnuts that ice worms are real."

"Another bag of doughnuts? I seem to remember you betting me doughnuts just a while ago that your moose roast is roadkill."

"So?" he replied with a grin. "I'm still right!"

"You're on!"

"It's settled then. I'll even let you find them."

It was weird, because Grandpa seemed so serious. "All right then, how do I find them?" I asked, playing along with his little game.

"They live between the ice crystals. They eat plant pollen."

"Okay, what do they look like?"

"You know—wormy, but they're *very* small." He reached inside his jacket pocket and pulled out a candy wrapper. Then he pulled out a jeweler's loupe he had brought with him. "Here, scrape up some of the ice crystals and pile them on this cold candy wrapper. Then use the loupe to find one. You will have to look very carefully."

He dug through his backpack and pulled out a wool army blanket, spreading it out as if we were on a picnic. He suggested I sit on it while I searched. Then he said he was going to take a short walk and would be right back. He walked away, going up a little canyon in the face of the glacier, his mud boots crunching the ice crystals. Pretty soon I couldn't see or hear him anymore. I used his loupe, but I didn't see any silly ice worms.

He's pulling my leg, I thought. *It's just a dumb ol' snipe hunt.*

It was completely quiet. The ice seemed to soak up all the sound. Down valley, I could just barely hear little sounds, like a bird once in a while or the sound of the breeze blowing softly through leaves. I heard a tapping sound coming from the direction of the ice wall. I thought it was Grandpa, but when I looked, I didn't see anything. I sat there listening some more . . . nothing. Then I heard a sound like an old gate swinging on a rusty hinge, followed by another, different creaking sound.

Putting the jeweler's loupe in my pocket, I got up and walked over to the ice wall. Leaning really close to the ice, I cupped my hands around my ear to hear better. I heard a whistling sound that slowly faded away, and then I heard a sound like someone dropping marbles on a tile floor.

The sounds were coming from the ice! Listening as carefully I could, I thought I heard a cat purring. Then there were a couple of popping sounds, like firecrackers going off way down the street.

Those little sounds from the valley seemed so loud now I was having a hard time hearing the glacier. I got the army blanket and carried it back to the ice wall, shook off the ice crystals, and covered my head like an old-time photographer. *Wow!* This time I heard what sounded like a woman singing a long high note, and then a baritone singing a longer low note. No, it was more like whale song—first a high squeal and then a low, low, low rumble. It was incredible!

I wanted Grandpa to know what I was hearing. When I came out from under the blanket, I saw him sitting on top of an ice hill—just sitting there with his arms crossed over his knees.

He'd been watching me! He gave a little wave, cupped his hands around his mouth, and hollered, "What are you doing down there?"

I yelled back, "Grandpa! It's crazy! I've been hearing all these weird noises. They're, like, coming from the glacier."

He grinned. "Yeah, she is talking to you."

"Yes, Grandpa! Come here and listen with me."

"Okay, here I come."

The hill he was on was about as tall as a telephone pole, but it had a nice gentle slope to it. Like everything else, the hill was covered in the white ice crystals. I watched him scoot right up to the edge of the hill and then shout, "Look out beloooooooow!"

He came sliding down the slope like he was sitting on an imaginary toboggan, yelling, "Yippee!" and then yodeling like Tarzan. His rough old wool army pants were scraping off the ice crystals—leaving a blue streak all the way down the hill! It was like he was painting the side of the hill with his butt.

About three-quarters of the way down, Grandpa hit a bumpy spot and started to fall over. He braced himself with his left hand, so the orange glove was leaving a little blue streak beside the bigger one. Ice crystals were flying everywhere. Grandpa rolled over on his back and turned sideways, making the skid mark as wide as he was tall. As he slid toward me I heard him making little grunting sounds, laughing as he slid right by me. When he stopped, he started making a snow angel—a blue ice angel. We were both laughing so hard. He was like a little kid—I'd never seen him acting so silly before.

After a while, he stopped laughing and said, "I am getting too old to do that. Come help me up, would you please?"

I went over and held out my arm. Grabbing hold, he struggled to get up, really depending on my support, which kind of shocked me. When he finally got on his feet, he brushed the ice off his clothes.

I looked up at him and said, "Everything up here is so special. It's all so beautiful."

Grandpa took off his sunglasses, and I could see his eyes were moist. Maybe it was from laughing so hard or maybe it was something else.

"Yes, yes—it *is* beautiful. But I am going to tell you the truth, Granddaughter. *You* are the most beautiful thing in this whole valley. Do you know—do you know that I have brought hundreds of kids up to this very place, and only a couple of them could be quiet long enough to hear the glacier talking?"

I didn't say anything . . . I didn't know what to say.

Grandpa sniffed a few more times, wiped the tears out of his eyes, and cleared his throat. Then he asked, "Well, did you see any ice worms?"

"No, of course not! I guess that means you owe me a bag of doughnuts, huh?"

"Not true! *I'll* just have to find them." He scraped up some ice crystals where the sun was hitting the glacier and piled them up on another candy wrapper. Asking for his loupe back, he looked a lot harder than I had. At last, he exclaimed, "Ah ha! You do remember my favorite doughnuts are chocolate éclairs, right?"

"No way," I said.

"Yes way! Come here, and I will show you." He carefully scraped away most of the crystals and handed me the wrapper. "Look right around the edge there."

I put my face right up next to the candy wrapper like I'd seen him do and focused the loupe. There were two of them! Little tiny worms! I couldn't believe it. "You mean they *are* real?"

"They most certainly are." He put his sunglasses back on and dramatically pushed them in place with just one finger. "I would like my doughnuts Sunday morning, please."

I'd had enough listening and learning. I had to go slide down the ice hill. Before I was done, there were four blue streaks on the side of the hill. I also wrote SUMMER ROSE WAS HERE with my gloved hand. We found some more ice worms, and we both went over and listened to the glacier talk for a while.

"Grandpa, where do the sounds come from?"

"They are caused by ice moving along the uneven valley floor. Sometimes the ice is compressed, and sometimes it is stretched. You can make some of the same sounds by breaking ice cubes out of an ice tray in the kitchen. Not all the ice moves at the same speed, so sometimes we hear the ice tearing itself apart, and other times we hear a piece of rock being torn right out of the mountain."

After listening a while longer, we explored up the canyon a little bit. That's when he told me I was about to take one step closer to becoming a real Alaskan. He found a puddle of fresh clean water in a sunny spot, scraped up some ice crystals, and threw them into the puddle. It looked like a blue Slushy. He pulled two bendy soda straws from his jacket pocket and said, "Have a drink."

"What? Why?"

"Because you can't be a *real* Alaskan if you have never had an Ice Worm Cocktail."

I took one of the straws and sucked some water right out of the puddle. It was so cold it hurt my teeth. I don't know if I actually drank a worm or not.

Grandpa had a drink—making a big "ahhhhh" sound—and then said, "Well, young lady, there is only one more thing you have to do now to be a real Alaskan."

"And that is . . . ?"

He chuckled and whispered theatrically, "You have to pee in the Yukon River."

"Aww, Grandpa, that's gross!"

"No, it is true. It is a *rule*."

We both laughed.

We finally gathered up our stuff and headed back to Bubble Truck. As soon as I thought about the truck, I got a sick feeling, but I put it out of my mind for a while.

Grandpa made it easy for me and never mentioned me driving back. As he drove away, I watched the glacier until I couldn't see it anymore. Once again the noise in the cab made talking too hard, so I just leaned back and napped.

I woke up about a half-hour later when we were just outside town. Grandpa had pulled over at a scenic overlook on top of a dirt cliff. The parking lot was covered with small drifts of dry dirt. We must have been at least three hundred feet above the Matanuska River. We could see miles upstream.

"You cannot see it from here, but just below us, on an old river terrace, there is an abandoned rail line. It is the old Chickaloon branch of the Alaska Railroad. They tore the track up back in the sixties. Before Chris left home, he, your mother, and I hiked the length of the branch. Some old railcars are still lying over the edge of the roadbed. Your mom was a real scrapper. There wasn't anything your uncles could do without her tagging along—and she always kept up. I suspect she passed that trait on to you."

Then he gestured at the vista. "All this dirt we're standing on blew down off the glacier. The river had to cut its way back down through the dirt. Now, look directly across the valley." He pointed out a straight line that had been carved into the mountainside. It looked like an old road cut. When I asked him what it was, he said, "That's how high the ancient glacier was when it came down this far. The scar was left when the glacier scraped up against the mountain."

Oh, I get it! That's where the rock for lateral moraines comes from.

As we got back in the truck, Grandpa said, "There is one more thing I want to show you." As we headed down into the valley, he asked me to watch the road carefully. We dropped down a little hill, and then the terrain leveled out for about a block or two. Then we dropped over another little hill, and the road leveled out again—and then another and another and another.

"What are they?" I asked.

Grandpa smiled and said, "They are seven old river banks. These terraces show the progression of the river as it cut down through the glacial deposits."

Funny—until I saw the pattern, they were just hills to me.

Grandpa checked his watch and said, "I would like to buy you a hundred-dollar hamburger for your birthday."

"A *what*?"

"I'll explain later."

I had no idea what he was talking about, so I just said, "Sure, Grandpa that sounds great."

"Let's get to the cabin and change into some casual clothes and pick up your flight kit."

Now he had my attention.

The whole cabin smelled like moose roast. I didn't realize it but the roast and cooker were gone.

We left just a few minutes later and drove to the hangar. As usual he sat in the hangar while I preflighted the plane. I came back in and reported the fuel tanks had not been refilled after the last flight.

"I know," he said. "I made sure of that, and I would have had serious doubts about your readiness for a license if you had not caught that.

"I have been talking to Denny, and he tells me you have no mountain-flying experience. Before I clear you for your cross-country solo, I want you to have at least one flight in the mountains. That part of this flight will be instruction. Then I want to see how you can handle a strange airfield. That part of this flight is a test."

My cross-country solo! Maybe I will get my license while I am up here. "Okay, where are we going?"

"We're going to fly through a mountain pass to Girdwood. There is a restaurant there called the Triple Nickel Roadhouse. It is about a thirty-minute flight. We'll eat dinner there and then come on back to the home-drome."

I asked about a flight plan, and he told me he had called Sister Baker and she knew our route and itinerary. Today we would just be VFR, which meant we could fly over here or over there and didn't have to worry about being at a particular airport at a particular time. "Make sure you have the current weather. I've already checked PIREPs and NOTAMs—we're good."

I accomplished my takeoff and departure "by the book." I called traffic, and we were on the way to Anchorage. Ten minutes later my grandfather became my flight instructor. He announced I had a simulated low oil pressure and needed to divert to the nearest airport.

We had just passed Birchwood Airport, so I turned back toward it. On final, he told me he wanted me to do a short field landing on the dirt strip and to use normal radio communications.

This didn't seem to be much of a test. I nailed it! But Grandpa—I mean my flight instructor—didn't criticize or compliment but said, "Take the second taxiway and pull up short of the hangar; we are picking up a couple of passengers."

That surprised me a little but not as much as when I saw Esperanza and her father standing on the ramp.

Before we shut down, Grandpa said, "We are going to fly up Ship Creek, and then over the pass at about thirty-five hundred feet. Then we will fly down Bird Creek Canyon toward the inlet. I will try not to say anything to you, but I will give you some discrete hand signals, so watch for them; any questions?"

"No, I think I got it all. Thank you, Grandpa; you're so awesome."

"You are welcome. And I prefer 'awful.'" He looked over and said, "Look it up—you'll have to use an unabridged dictionary, about the third definition down. Now, once you pick up your passengers, taxi out to the main runway, and do a midfield takeoff to the south."

I pulled up a little farther and shut down. Trying to be the professional, I walked over and greeted them. Once we were all belted in I could look over my shoulder and see Esperanza, and Grandpa could see Mr. Harris.

I gave them a little preflight briefing and told them where we were going. After takeoff, I snugged up next to the mountains and gained altitude. I wasn't sure which valley was Ship Creek so I looked over at Grandpa. He kept his hands in his lap, pointed to the left, and then pointed up.

So I banked into the next valley and started climbing. Grandpa gave us all a running narrative of what we were seeing. There were no headsets in the backseat so Grandpa had to talk loud enough for everyone to hear. I noticed he had pulled his left earpiece up and off his ear so he could hear them too.

I reached up and pulled my right earpiece up. I could only use my peripheral vision, but that was enough to see how beautiful it all was. The lakes were all so blue and everything was covered in a carpet of green and multicolored flowers.

At one point Esperanza said, "Look, a moose!" I started to look over to the right side of the plane, but Grandpa instantly secreted me more hand signals, pointing straight ahead and then up.

Then he asked Esperanza where it was. They talked back and forth about the moose and the flowers, and Grandpa told them to keep an eye out for bear and Dahl sheep. I cut in with a call to local traffic. I announced my location and description. There was no response. I continued flying up the valley.

Grandpa said, "Summer Rose, I want you to experience something." Then he asked Esperanza how she was feeling.

"I'm okay, thanks."

"Good. I am going to teach Autumn Rose something. It will get a little bumpy, but this demonstration will only last a few seconds."

Then he said to me, "You have been flying right up the middle of this valley. What would you do if you had conflicting traffic coming down the valley?"

"I would move over to the right, and we would pass each other on the left."

"Let's see how that works for you. I want you to keep one eye on the vertical velocity indicator."

I checked it and saw we were currently climbing at about one hundred feet per minute.

My flight instructor said, "Okay, you have simulated traffic coming down-valley. Move to the right."

I did, and we were then in the shadow of the mountain to our south. I immediately felt a flutter in my stomach and saw I was now descending at almost two hundred feet per minute!

"Okay, that is enough; get back to the middle."

As soon as I got back into the sunshine, I regained my old rate of climb.

Mr. Harris said, "I've read about that but never actually experienced it, Gus."

"What was it?" I asked.

Grandpa said, "That has killed a fair number of inexperienced canyon flyers. That was microweather. The air was settling on the shady side of the valley."

I'll file that under "good things to remember."

Grandpa then said, "We are almost there."

I saw the inlet between peaks, well below us.

Mr. Harris spotted a herd of sheep on the left side of the plane.

Grandpa slipped me a hand signal that clearly said to take the next pass. Then he wrote on his knee board "500/Min ↓." They all talked about the sheep as I shot the pass. Once I cleared the pass, I brought the throttle back and lowered the nose. This was the first time I experienced a little vertigo while flying. The inlet side of the mountains was very steep. As the mountains fell away, it felt like I was rapidly climbing.

I got a little aggressive, and Esperanza said, "Whoa."

Grandpa saw my confusion and said, "Keep your eyes in the cockpit for a minute and trust your instruments." Then he said to everybody, "There was an updraft coming up the sunny side of that slope. That is all part of canyon flying."

The vertigo passed immediately now that the mountains were slipping away behind me.

I apologized and reestablished my descent rate.

When we got out over the inlet, Grandpa asked everyone to watch out for traffic. (I knew he was talking to me.) I leveled off at fifteen hundred feet over the brown water. I had my head on a swivel looking for my unfamiliar airport.

"Is that it, Grandpa?"

"That is our destination. We are almost there, Esperanza."

I got on the radio and announced my intentions. I saw no traffic. The airport was actually in a canyon, and I realized my standard distance to the runway was going to have to be a little closer than usual. The wind sock said I needed to land back out toward the inlet. I slowed the aircraft down and turned to base. I started to roll wings level, but Grandpa applied just enough pressure to his yoke that I felt he did not want me to square off my turns.

My approach was going to be one graceful, descending turn instead of two square corners. Halfway into my turn I realized I was going to be long, so I dropped in twenty degrees of flaps and then thirty degrees.

I reached for the trim wheel, and Grandpa tapped my hand and said, "No. You don't have time. Just fly it down. Watch your airspeed."

Once I had made the field I dropped in full flaps. I started to raise the nose, but I felt Grandpa applying a little nose-down pressure. Then after a moment he raised both hands to let me know I was in full control. I flared just before I touched down. I kept the weight off the nose wheel by holding the yoke back.

Grandpa and Mr. Harris applauded my performance.

Mr. Harris said, "Summer Rose, that was textbook perfect. I had forgotten how much fun this kind of flying is."

As soon as I shut down, Mr. Harris touched me on the shoulder and asked, "How old are you?"

I smiled and said, "I turned sixteen today, sir."

That is when I realized I hadn't heard a peep out of Esperanza. I turned to look at her and realized she hadn't enjoyed the ride as much as her dad had. She looked a little pale. But when we all got out, she seemed to perk back up.

We walked over to the Triple Nickel Roadhouse, which was right inside the airport. It was built in the same style as the Harris's house, only on an even grander scale. The ceiling was lofted, and the stone fireplace was so large I think I could have walked inside it. The gable ends were nothing but large pictures windows. We sat by a big picture window, cut into the wall, that gave us a perfect view of ski slopes on the mountain to the east of us.

The nicest looking thing in the place, however, was our waiter. He was yummy. I caught Esperanza checking him out, and we both giggled.

I had the most fantastic hamburger I had ever eaten.

As we sat waiting for dessert, Grandpa said, "Bob, Esperanza is homeschooled, right?"

Esperanza and Mr. Harris both nodded.

"Well, Summer Rose has told me some very interesting things about today's public education system. I was surprised to hear a lot of what she had to say." He then turned to me and asked, "Would it be okay if we finished that conversation now?"

That kind of surprised me, but I agreed and started up my story again. "Well, Grandpa, remember what you said today about how schools don't have time to teach?"

"Actually, what I said was they don't have time to let you learn, but go ahead."

"Okay you've taught me how important patterns are—like the roots of words and patterns you see in your Crypto-Quip puzzles, or when we play Wheel of Fortune, right?"

"Right."

"Well, in my AP physics class, we had to learn all these formulas. There were formulas for electricity, mechanics, gravity buoyancy, and probably a dozen others. I was going nuts with all the different formulas!"

Grandpa interrupted, "Formulae."

Esperanza snickered and smiled at me.

"Anywaaay, I'd copy them down, and then I'd rewrite my notes. But with each new topic I had to figure it out all over again. Then one day I saw a pattern—it was so obvious, I couldn't figure out why I hadn't seen it before. But even *more* importantly, why hadn't some teacher *shown* it to me? It didn't matter what symbol we used for the variables—they all had the same formula format!

"I remember, that night I was *so mad*! I huffed into the kitchen and dished out some butter pecan—but I was so mad I accidentally put the ice cream in the fridge instead of back in the freezer! I picked up my spoon and clenched it in my fist and let out one of those 'eewwwh' sounds. When I finished my ice cream, I went in and got a second bowl—*after* I found it in the fridge."

Esperanza laughed. "Physics is the worst. So what did you do?"

"The next day I started showing all my classmates. I explained that it didn't matter what the subject was, the formula format was always $X = \dfrac{Y}{Z}$. Then it followed that $Y = XZ$. If we were studying electricity, it was $I = \dfrac{E}{R}$. If we were studying speed it was $S = \dfrac{D}{T}$. If we were studying force, it was $m = \dfrac{F}{a}$.

Grandpa interjected, "More commonly expressed F = ma."

"Yeah, that's right. I guess I got so animated, the teacher asked what I was doing. I walked up to the board and demonstrated to everybody. One of the other students shouted, 'Hey! It works for density.' I wrote on the board $D = \dfrac{m}{v}$. Then someone asked, 'Will it work for Boyle's law?' Before I could figure it out, someone else shouted out, $V = \dfrac{k}{P}$. I eventually sat down, but I don't remember anything else about class that day.

"What I *do* remember is that afternoon I ditched my last class and walked over to my old junior high school. When the bell rang, I walked into Mr. Wayne's classroom and asked why he never told us that. You know what he said?

"'There are state educational standards, and that concept is just not taught in junior high.' He looked up and to the right and said, 'Your senior year, I think!'"

I took a deep breath, and said, "Grandpa, I learned way back in grade school that area equals length times width. But no one ever taught me that length equals area divided by width."

Mr. Harris asked, "Do you truly understand what happened to you the night you figured that out for yourself?"

"I guess. I dunno. I mean, no, sir."

"You had an epiphany."

I looked at him with a puzzled expression and then looked at Grandpa.

"Look it up, Granddaughter. It has a Greek root, not Latin. It's spelled with a 'ph.' Go down to about the third or fourth meaning."

About that time our smoking-hot waiter brought our desserts.

Esperanza asked, "When did you learn about exponential numbers?"

Boy she hit a sore subject with me. "No one ever taught me about exponential numbers! I had to learn that myself with the help of my father."

She said, "Yeah, I thought that might be the case. I took my chemistry labs at Chugiak and got so frustrated because my lab teacher had to stop teaching chemistry for days because he had to teach the kids about exponential numbers."

I asked her, "When did you learn about exponential numbers?"

"I don't know, but it must have been back in seventh or eighth grade. How can you learn chemistry or physics—"

Mr. Harris cut in, "Or astronomy—"

Grandpa dramatically dropped his napkin and said, "You can't, Bob!"

I then asked Esperanza, "When did you learn about the metric system?"

"Way back. One of the parents came in with all these brightly colored blocks and containers and meter sticks. I remember how fun that was."

Mr. Harris asked me, "When did you learn about metrics?"

"Well, I was expected to know about it before I started biology, but . . . I guess Dad had to teach me that too. I learned more about metrics from him and ground school than I did during all of my public education."

Grandpa said, to nobody in particular, "And America can't figure out why we lag behind the rest of the world in math and science."

Mr. Harris stretched and said, "Gus, it's past my bedtime."

I checked my phone and saw it was nine thirty at night. *Funny how everybody still says "night" when the sun is still high in the sky.*

Mr. Harris insisted on paying and wished me a happy birthday. Grandpa graciously accepted and left a fifty-dollar tip. Then he placed three nickels next to his plate. Mr. Harris and Esperanza each found three nickels and left them on the table. All I could find was one nickel and one dime. Grandpa picked up the dime and laid down two more nickels.

Grandpa and Mr. Harris flew the aircraft back, and Esperanza and I sat in back. As we took the runway, Esperanza took my hand and held it. But it was a beautiful, smooth flight. We flew up Crow Creek to the Crow Pass, skirted the Eagle Glacier and then down the Eagle River Valley. This time I was just sightseeing.

After dropping off Esperanza and her dad, we flew back home. When we got back to the cabin, Grandpa said he was going to go over to Sister Baker's.

Before he left, I asked, "Grandpa, were those really one hundred-dollar hamburgers?"

"No, they were just twenty-dollar hamburgers with an eighty dollar cab fare."

"Ohhh, I get it."

Grandpa asked, "How about a hug from the birthday girl!"

I started to give him a big, little-girl bear hug, but I changed my mind and gave him a less "huggy" hug. I guess I actually pushed away a little.

Grandpa must have sensed the change. "Is something wrong?"

"No, Grandpa. It's just been brought to my attention that I'm a 'healthy young woman' now and that I need to be a little more careful about things like hugs and dancing around."

Grandpa seemed to be a little confused, which isn't a look you see very often on his face. Then he seemed to figure it out and said, "*Ohhhh, I get it.* Well, I hope I'll still get *some* kind of hugs from you."

"Sure you will Grandpa—forever and forever. Thank you for such a wonderful birthday."

CHAPTER 9

NAUGHT'S AN OBSTACLE

The next day was a Sunday, but that didn't change our morning routine. Grandpa once again invited me to join him for church. I went but only out of respect for him.

The Suburban was in the shop, and Grandpa drove Bubble Truck to church. I knew Esperanza was at Mass, so I was once again "imprisoned." I thought about it for a while and decided I would probably go to church next week and hook up with some of the kids there.

Oh, I forgot to mention, I completed my solo cross-country flight, and my FAA exam was tomorrow—July 23. I got out my ground school materials and studied for a while. My exam would be in Grandpa's

Cessna-172, so I brushed up on my V-speeds, performance data, and weight and balance charts. Then I got out some sectionals and studied all the terrain and emergency fields and radio frequencies in the area. I really felt like I was ready—bring it on!

I flipped through some back issues of Grandpa's aviation magazines. I found an article on a vintage aircraft called a Grumman Goose. I immediately fell in love with it. Then I took a short nap on the swing until I heard Bubble Truck coming down the road.

Grandpa came up on the porch and asked if I wanted some lunch. "No thanks, Grandpa, I'm good." He went back inside and busied himself. I knew he liked to study Scripture for a while after church, so I decided to make a run at *Moby Dick*.

I'd downloaded it into my e-reader the other day when we were in town—it just seemed more natural than reading a regular paperback. Grandpa was right; it was a difficult read, but I was determined to find out why it was such a classic.

After about an hour, I heard Grandpa puttering around in the kitchen, but he seemed to be content being alone, so I tried reading the book aloud to Ammo. After a while, I became aware of Grandpa watching me through the screen door. He came out with a tray that had two glasses of milk and a mixing bowl half-full of *something*. There was also an old-fashioned kitchen timer ticking away.

"I cannot remember—do you like chocolate chip cookie dough?"

I put on a giant smile. "Grandpa, you know I do!"

He came out and sat next to me, and we both started eating away. I also noticed he was carrying my paperback copy of *Moby Dick*. He asked to see my e-reader. I could tell he had never seen one before, so I gave a short demonstration. He seemed amused by the way you turn the pages and the bookmark feature.

He handed it back and said, "Sorry, I just don't like it. I can't feel the pages."

"Grandpa, I just don't get a lot of what is being said in *Moby Dick*. The grammar is all different and the allegories are lost on me. And the vocabulary . . ."

"Let me hear you read some."

He opened the paperback and asked where I was so he could follow along.

I read, "Come, Ahab's compliments to ye; come and see if ye can swerve me. Swerve me? Ye cannot swerve me, else ye swerve yourselves!"

He stopped me there and said, "Girl, you are not reading the Scriptures. Although Ahab *did* come from Quaker stock—that's where all of the thous and *yee*s come from—I think it is safe to say he was a lapsed-Quaker *and* he was an old salt. I find it hard to read this book sitting down or using my regular voice." He squinted one eye and used a voice that might have come from a pirate. "Arrr, let me read that same passage to ye, missy."

He stood up and made a grand welcoming gesture. In his best pirate voice he read, "Come," and then he bowed. "Ahab's compliments to ye." Then he increased his volume, and in a challenging voice, he said "'Come and see if ye can swerve me.'" Then his tone changed to sarcasm, and in a voice loud enough to shiver me timbers, he said, "'Swerve me? Ye cannot swerve me, else ye swerve yourselves!'" Then Grandpa gave a maniacal laugh, and as if speaking himself, said, "'Swerve me?'"

"Wow, Grandpa that was like watching a play."

"Well, more like an old radio drama, but I think that is what was in Melville's head when he wrote that."

I was eating *way* too much cookie dough, so thank goodness the timer went off. We headed back into the kitchen. The smell of baking cookies filled the whole house.

Yummm!

I started cleaning things up a little as he took the first batch of cookies out of the oven and got a second batch ready to go.

We sat back down at the kitchen table, and Grandpa surprised me by asking about my astronaut plans. He really seemed interested, and I wasn't sure how to start. I had never talked to anyone about it. But *he* asked.

"Grandpa, you know, NASA's space shuttle program has ended. But something else has also ended—the era of space belonging solely to national governments. Space is now fair game for corporations, universities, and even private enterprise. And I'm exactly the right age to get in on the ground floor of a brand-new job market—aerospace pilot.

"Did you know the people called payload specialists aboard the space shuttle weren't NASA employees?"

"No, I didn't."

"They were employees of whichever company bought time and room onboard the shuttle for their particular experiment or deployment. That is how companies got things done *in the past.* Can you imagine what will happen during my working lifetime?

"I can work and fly in space. We *are* going back to the moon. There *will* be permanent work colonies there. Those people will be called lunanauts. They will be laying out staging areas for our first trips to Mars. People from your generation are getting things ready for my generation *right now.*"

Grandpa asked, "You sure they are not luna*tics*?"

I started to answer him until I realized he had just taught me something new—but what?

He must have seen my lightbulb flickering and said, "It used to be believed that crazy people had been affected by the moon."

"Thanks, Grandpa, I had never made that connection before. Anyway, it will be up to my generation to work on orbit, or on the moon. And we won't be employed by NASA. We'll be employed by companies like Boeing, Virgin Galactic, Space-X, the University of Wherever, or even Hilton Hotels. Heck! Our space suits may have sponsor's logos, just like NASCAR drivers. Our space planes may have fast-food billboards painted on their sides, just like metro buses or taxi cabs."

"I see. So is Mars in your future too?"

"Grandpa, I'm too old to go to Mars."

He raised his eyebrows.

"Congress keeps pushing the Manned Mission to Mars back—right now it is not planned to happen before 2030. But private companies are moving the date up—maybe as soon as 2023. But it is not like there will be cities up there in my lifetime. Oh yeah, something else: right now it looks like they will be one-way trips. The people who go there will live and die on Mars, even raise families. They'll be like the Mayflower pilgrims."

Grandpa said, "Real Martians! So how do you become an astronaut?"

"I can tell you this. You no longer have to be an old navy or marine aviator or an old air force test pilot to become an astronaut or a lunanaut. The bureaucracy is already in place. The FAA, not NASA, already has a department called the Office of Space Transportation. You must hold an FAA license to fly, maintain, or operate in space. The FAA gave the very first civilian astronaut wings to Michael Melville in 2004."

"Who is he?"

"He was the first civilian to fly a suborbital flight into space. I guess you could say he's my generation's Alan Shepard.

"Already dozens of companies are looking to exploit space—to have a fleet of space planes to haul up their own space mechanics to repair satellites instead of just watching them fall back to earth because of a simple dead battery or a broken relay. There is already a private company called Astronauts for Hire that is training future astronauts. There are even private commercial companies that will go fix satellites for hire, or even bring them back to Earth for repair or salvage. Those companies are already looking for young people like me."

Just then the timer went off on my phone. I silenced the alarm and said, "Eight minutes."

Grandpa spun around to look at his timer sitting on the counter. "Oops! I forgot to set the timer!"

"It's okay, Grandpa. I've got your back."

We "assembly lined" the operation. I took the first batch of cookies off the cooling rack while Grandpa put the hot cookies on it. Then I spooned out the remaining dough into big fat balls on the now-empty cookie sheet.

"Wow," Grandpa commented.

"I like 'em *big* and *gooey*!" I said with a grin.

Grandpa put the cookie sheet into the oven and set his little mechanical timer. I set my phone timer too, just in case.

We sat back down and I said, "Grandpa, the best way for me to get hired as an aerospace pilot is to gain as much experience as I can here on *terra firma*, stay healthy, and start talking to Human Resource people as soon as I get into college. Did you know there are even scholarships for future astronauts like me?"

"No, I did not." He then paused for a moment like he was trying to make up his mind about something. Then he said, "It is interesting how we just read that particular passage from *Moby Dick*. Turn to it again and read the next few lines."

I picked up my e-reader and started reading aloud from where we had left off. "The path to my—"

"Eh, eh, eh. Use your old salt's voice and read it like you mean it."

I started again. "The path to my fixed purpose is laid with iron rails, where on my soul is grooved to run. Over unsounded gorges, through the rifled hearts of mountains, under torrents' beds, unerringly I rush! Naught's an obstacle, naught's an angle to the iron way."

Grandpa smiled and asked, "Can you figure out what that meant?"

"I think it means nothing could stop Captain Ahab from getting Moby Dick."

"That's right." Grandpa then got up and stepped into his study. He came back with a stack of books and papers.

"What are those?"

"These are just loaners until you get your own e-versions. These are my old Sanderson manuals for commercial and instrument ratings. I will be happy to help you get both tickets."

I started to reach for them but hesitated. I think Grandpa knew why.

He looked at me and said, "Naught's an obstacle."

I looked up at him, puzzled.

He said, "If you stay on your iron rails, I will help you as far along as I can."

I got up and gave Grandpa a kiss on the cheek and a very ladylike hug. I realized I had seen Mom kiss and hug him just like that.

Just then both our timers went off. Grandpa pulled the last batch of cookies out of the oven, huge and still gooey in the center. "I've just enough time to get a short nap in before dinner. Oh, I forgot—Sister Baker has invited us both to a Sunday picnic down on the lake. She's making the meal, and you and I just made the dessert. You in?"

"Of course. What time?"

"It'll have to be after Sister Knudtson is in bed and asleep. Probably around seven. You and I could set everything up around six, and I'll read a little more *Moby Dick* to you."

He yawned and said, "*Soy cansado. Dormirè la siesta.*"

I said, "*Hasta luego, Abuelito.*"

I wasn't sure what I wanted to do, but just then the phone rang. It was Esperanza!

She was all excited. "Would you like to go to Portage Pass for a day hike on Wednesday, with me and some of the girls from my squad?"

I said, "Hmmm, let me check if there is anything on my social calendar. Well, I'll have to have my people move a few things around, but . . . *of course I'll come!* What do I need to bring?"

"You know, just the usual stuff like water and power bars. We'll be catching some rays, so wear your swimming suit and bring suntan lotion—or, in your case, sun *block*." Esperanza laughed and said, "I'll be driving. Would it be cool if you met me at one of the girls' houses in Chugiak? It's really a small town and easy to get around in." When I said sure, she said, "Oh, and don't forget your bear bells," and gave me Tamika's address on Helluva Street.

Helluva Street. Crack me up!

"Ohhh, tomorrow I take my final exams for my pilot's license . . . thank you. Yeah, I'll be there with bells on." *Ha, I've always wanted to say that.*

After hanging up, I decided I would just journal for a while but got drowsy. I was about to doze off when Grandpa came out of his bedroom.

"Ready?"

"Yes, sir." We went in, gathered up our picnic supplies—a couple of blankets, some bug spray, and the cookies, of course—and threw them into a wicker basket. Then we each grabbed a handle and headed toward the side door. I snagged my e-reader off the table as we left. On the way down, I told him what Esperanza and I planned to do on Wednesday.

"Portage Pass is a most excellent day hike. I think you'll really enjoy it."

"Grandpa, I'm supposed to meet the girls in Chugiak at a house on Helluva Street. Could you take me there in the morning? Otherwise, the Suburban'll just be parked there all day long."

"Sure I will, but . . . you mean no boys will come out here and pick you up?"

"No, it's just a girl thing. We're going to do some sunbathing."

Grandpa and I found a flat spot right near the edge of the lake and spread out the blankets. While we were waiting for Sister Baker, Grandpa told me where Portage Pass was and all about the long tunnel we'd have to take to get there. Then he described the pass and told me about a two-thousand-foot cliff on the side of Maynard Mountain we'd see once we got up there.

"Sounds like a first-class adventure!" I said.

He smiled. "Something to write home about, for sure. Speaking of writing home, look over there on the back side of the lake."

At first I didn't see anything, but then—*a bear!* I whispered, "Grandpa, that's a Brown bear." I stood up and was ready to run.

Grandpa just sat there and said, "Calm down, calm down. It is far enough away that it has not even seen us yet—*and* we are downwind. Besides, that is *not* a Brown bear, Granddaughter—that is a Black bear."

"But . . . Grandpa?"

He held up his hand and said, "I know, it is brown in *color*, but it is not a Brown bear—also known as a grizzly. Brown bears are usually brown but can range in color. And not all Black bears are *black*. What you see over there is a cinnamon-colored Black bear."

"That's dumb, Grandpa. So how do you know it's a Black bear?"

"That is actually easier than you think. Black bears have a small head compared to their bodies, and their face is almost like a dog's. Brown bears have very large heads compared to their bodies and a flatter face. They also have a distinctive hump between their shoulders. Of course"—he grinned—"there is *another* way to tell the difference."

Oh boy, here it comes.

"If a bear chases you up a tree and then follows you up and eats you—it's a Black bear. If the bear knocks the tree down and eats you—it's a Brown."

"Ha-ha, very funny. Come on, Grandpa, let's go inside."

Grandpa said, "No, wait a minute. I want to see if that is a boar or a sow. If it is a sow, she will probably have a couple of cubs with her. Momma bears are the worst. So, if it *is* a sow, I will be happy to go to the cabin with you. But if it is a boar, why ruin a perfectly good picnic?"

Ammo raised his head and started sniffing. He started woofing . . . and then barking loudly. I don't think he could even see the bear yet—but he could smell it.

The bear stood up on its hind legs and looked in our direction. When Ammo finally spotted the bear, he went berserk. After it ducked back into the trees, Grandpa had to calm Ammo down. He stopped barking, but he remained on high alert and occasionally woofed. I loved on him a little bit and thanked him for protecting us.

"It was probably a boar," Grandpa said.

I kept careful watch of the woods but couldn't see any other sign of the bear or any cubs.

Realizing how nervous I was, Grandpa made a suggestion. "Let me show you how the Tanaina Indians handle bear watch. Rather than sitting in a circle and facing each other, they sit back to back, looking outward. Not only good for bear watching—also a good way to share body heat. It also gives them some of the close physical contact that is missing in our society. We tend to move away from each other in a group setting. Something as simple as two people's knees touching when we are sitting next to each other in the theater or on a plane makes us uneasy."

We gave it a try. At first it was uncomfortable. It took us a few minutes to settle down so one of us wasn't leaning too hard and pushing the other person forward. Grandpa was right—we're not used to touching each other. As we sat there talking, I became acutely aware of things like Grandpa's breathing and his body heat and the little movements he made. It was unfamiliar to me, but I liked it. And of course we now had a 360-degree field of view to watch for the bear.

We talked about a lot of things as we waited for Sister Baker to show up. We talked about Dad being deployed again and how difficult it was for Mom. We talked about our pending move to Alaska. And then we talked about flying and boys and church. Pretty soon, I'd forgotten all about the bear.

Grandpa sighed and said, "I have always wondered what it would be like to fly in space, but I am sure I am just too old to ever find out."

"Grandpa, John Glenn went back to space when he was seventy-seven years old. *I'll* take you into space. You can ride in my jump seat anytime."

"Thank you, Summer Rose. I am going to hold you to that." After a moment of silence, he said, "I guess Sister Baker is having a little trouble getting Helga to go to sleep. I see you brought your e-reader with you. Would you set it up so I can read more *Moby* to you?"

I handed him the reader then we settled back into our bear watch position. It was fun to listen to him—he used different voices for the different characters. He also explained some of the difficult vocabulary and nautical scenes as he read.

Grandpa stopped reading and said, "Here she comes."

When I turned, I saw Sister Baker rounding the lake with a basket in her hand. She wore a brightly colored summer dress, with a light sweater covering her shoulders. The dress swayed a little, making her look younger than she was. I could see her smile, even from where we sat.

Grandpa said, "She is so beautiful."

"Yes, she is, Grandpa. The prettiest thing in this whole valley."

"August, have you been reading *Chief Stephen's Parky* to your granddaughter? That's where I learned to sit like this."

"No, but I will recommend it to her."

She asked, "How was church? Some of the brothers came over during Sunday school and brought us the sacrament. Helga really misses going to church."

She knelt and opened her basket, handing out sandwiches and small bowls of potato salad and a three-bean salad. Giving us each a fork and a can of pink lemonade, she wedged her way in so we were sitting back to back to back. It took us a minute, but we got settled into this unfamiliar arrangement.

"Has the bear been back?" Sister Baker asked.

Grandpa had a mouthful, so I answered, "We saw him at the far end of the lake, but he ducked back into the woods when Ammo started barking." I added, "A male Black bear."

I felt so weird having a conversation but not looking at the other person. It also felt strange to have such close physical contact with a near stranger. Now I felt two people breathing, and her extra body heat was welcome. I felt like I got to know Sister Baker much better than if we'd been sitting across the table from each other. There's something very personal and yet very safe about the way we sat.

As I was eating my sandwich, I asked, "What kind of meat is this? It's delicious."

"It's the moose roast your grandfather cooked yesterday."

"Cool; what does caribou taste like?"

She said, "It has a gamier taste. Moose makes great roasts and steaks. Caribou, on the other hand, has a bit of twang to it. I always use caribou in things like spaghetti sauce or spiced-up meatloaf."

Grandpa said, "Moose is a very lean meat, and since it is wild, it has none of the hormones and antibiotics beef has these days. In short, if you're a red-meat eater, moose is absolutely the best meat to be had."

Sister Baker chuckled and said, "Thank you, August."

I felt him turn toward her and say, "N'est-ce pas?"

She leaned toward him and I heard them kiss. "Mais oui, mon ami."

After we finished our meal, Sister Baker said she would read to us for a while. She picked up the e-reader, taking a minute to figure it out. She too used different voices, and she seemed to be as well-acquainted with the book as Grandpa was. We all ate cookies as she read to us.

After a while, she laid the e-reader down, commenting, "I don't think I could ever get used to those." I was struck with how compatible she and Grandpa were and how compatible I was with both of them.

The bear never did show up, but the mosquitoes finally chased us inside—in spite of the mosquito spray. Grandpa and Sister Baker went to her house, and Ammo and I went back to Grandpa's cabin. I had to work hard to get the chocolate out from under my braces. I was at it so long that Ammo came in and lay down on the bathroom rug so he wouldn't be lonely. He even stayed with me while I showered. I wondered if he was still protecting me from the bear.

When I was finally ready for bed, I shut the house down. I decided to leave a porch light on for Grandpa—even though he probably didn't need it—and I made a point of shutting all the doors—to keep the bear out! When I got to my room, Ammo was already on my bed.

After my prayers, I got under the covers, snuggled up to Ammo, and started talking to him. I asked him what he thought about Sister Baker and what he thought about the bear. He just made one of those little sighing noises. I apologized for not sharing my chocolate cookies with him, explaining that chocolate isn't good for dogs. He didn't seem concerned. I read *Moby Dick* aloud to him for a while, but it didn't take long before I was ready to fall asleep.

CHAPTER 10

PORTAGE PASS

Tuesday morning I was up early, and we followed our morning routine. Funny, I hadn't been up here that long, but it was already hard to imagine starting a day any other way.

Grandpa asked if I had heard yesterday's news.

As usual my first thoughts and fears were something about the war. "No, what's up?"

"Sally Ride died yesterday."

I sat stunned and silent. Sally Ride was another of my all-time heroes. If there was anyone in this world I would like to trade lives with, it was Sally Ride. Now I find out that on the day I finally passed the last requirement for my pilot's, she had died. I would never forget either event.

Grandpa asked if I was all right.

I told him I was, and we headed out to the car, Grandpa gave me a pocket-sized air horn and an anklet with large jingle bells attached to it—"for the bears." He also handed me the keys to Bubble Truck and said, "I think you should get back in the saddle."

I smiled and said, "There aren't any big hills, are there?"

"Flat as a pancake."

It was only a fifteen-minute drive to Tamika's house, where we met her, Becky, and Christi and Angie (who are twins). Both the truck and Ammo were a big hit, breaking the ice until Esperanza arrived.

A few minutes later, one of the girls said, "Here she comes." Esperanza pulled up in a big black Cadillac Escalade—kind of like Grandpa's Suburban, but about twenty-five years newer.

After loading our stuff and promising to behave, we all piled into the Escalade. Grandpa walked up to the driver's window and asked Esperanza, "What time should I start getting worried?"

"Would nine be too late?"

"You don't need my permission. It is just nice to know." He smiled at Esperanza and said, "Okay, then, I will start worrying about nine fifteen." He slapped the door twice, stepped back, and off we went.

I recognized part of the drive because of trips I'd made to the Dimond Center Mall and the VA hospital with Grandpa. The difference this time was the girls were pointing out high schools along the way. Then there were stories about this game or that and this running back or that. I definitely felt out of my element. It was more than just being the new kid—I couldn't really relate to a lot of stuff they talked about. But they were all very nice to me, and I remembered my goal of making new, *nonchurch* friends. After we passed the mall, I was in unfamiliar territory.

Well, I thought I was. Esperanza said, "Hey, Summer Rose, check it out." Up ahead I saw an exit sign for Girdwood and then another advertising the Triple Nickel. Now it was my turn as Esperanza and I talked about the flight and the restaurant and especially that hot waiter.

Pretty soon we were at the tunnel. I discovered the girls didn't know the history of the tunnel, like how it was built during World War II. They also didn't know people used to have to drive their cars up onto a train that then took them through the tunnel. Grandpa had told me all that neat stuff the day before, at our picnic. But the girls didn't really seem to care.

Now the tunnel had been improved—a one-way road passed through it, but the train track was still there, just part of the road like streetcar tracks in San Francisco. That meant sometimes the train used the tunnel and sometime cars used it, but always at different times and in one direction only. Traffic usually changed directions every half hour.

We had arrived just about the time the traffic switched to a Whittier-bound flow, so we didn't have to wait in line too long, but we were nearly the last car. The trip through the tunnel was really kind of fun. Past the tunnel, we drove the short distance into Whittier. While we were there, I walked over to the dock and admired the beautiful water and brightly colored boats. When I saw everyone else climbing back into the car, I jogged over and was the last one in.

It only took a couple of minutes to drive to the trailhead back near the tunnel. Before we started climbing up the pass, everyone broke out their bear bells. Some of us were wearing the anklet type, so they jangled every time we moved that foot. Tamika was wearing a leather strap that hung freely from her waist, so her bells jingled twice as often as ours. Becky was also carrying a beautiful walking stick with some bells on it.

The bells came in different sizes. Some were brass and others were silver-colored. Becky's bells were made from some kind of metal that had rusted, and they made a clattering sound. I showed the girls my air horn, and Becky said she had a can of bear spray. I think we were as well-prepared as we could be without carrying a gun. We all hydrated ourselves and started walking to the tune of our own making: *jingle, jangle, clatter, cling-clang, donkity-donk.*

The noise of those bear bells would have scared away bears two valleys over. It wasn't musical or rhythmic, just annoying. But the steep trail quickly took my attention away from the noise, so soon I was only occasionally aware of the racket.

The farther up the trail or road or whatever it used to be we went, the more rutted and washed out it became. We had to climb into and out of some of the bigger washouts. I quickly fell to the back of the line. It's not like I was out of shape, but all these girls were athletes—hard-bodied athletes. I had strength in my legs, but I seemed to be breathing harder than any of them. I am pretty much a bookworm. I'd much rather be studying for my instrument rating than working out.

We stopped at what I guessed had to be the halfway point, where the trail was completely blocked by a rock slide. I was happy to see some of the girls take off their daypacks and break out their water bottles. I sat on a rock outcrop and gulped a half-liter of flavored water.

The view was fantastic, even just halfway up the pass. Below us was the town of Whittier and the Passage Canal, which I knew led to Prince William Sound. In front of us was a range of snow-covered mountains. Behind us was that huge two-thousand-foot vertical wall of rock Grandpa had told me about. To the right and still well above us was our destination, Portage Pass. I couldn't see its saddle because of the rolling landscape and shrubby growth.

After Esperanza put her water bottle away, she climbed over the rock pile, and the rest of us followed. Then, without notice or comment, she unbuttoned her shirt. She wasn't wearing anything underneath! Next, Becky completely removed her shirt and tied it around her waist—she wasn't wearing anything underneath either. I guess you could say I was in mild shock, but no one said anything about it. They just put their daypacks back on and started walking up the pass like it was the most natural thing in the world to be half-naked in public. (Well, you know what I mean.)

The church girl in me wanted to just turn around and go back to the car, but another part of me—a new part—wanted to belong to this group of friends. *So this is peer pressure.* I stood there a moment longer and then reached down and unfastened my second and third buttons, revealing the top of my bathing suit. *There, that's as far as I'm going.* I started to put my daypack on and then decided to pull my shirttail out first.

Becky—the last girl in line ahead of me—had just disappeared from sight when I started jogging to catch up with them. *Jingle-jingle-jingle.* I felt a little dizzy when I caught up. Saying a prayer as I trudged along behind them, I refastened my buttons. I felt like I shouldn't be here, yet I couldn't figure out why—other than I *just* shouldn't be here. There were no boys with us.

Why am I comfortable with being seen in a bathing suit at the pool but not up here in the mountains?

I took a deep breath. I felt guilty, but I unbuttoned down to number four. I felt like I was naked, yet I was still fully dressed.

We hiked on for another thirty minutes. I tried to appreciate the remarkable beauty around me, but between the bear bells and my inner turmoil, I had no focus left. I was totally walking on autopilot.

We finally reached the top of the pass. It wasn't a single high point but more like a hundred-meter-wide flattish spot. Like much of the rest of the pass, it was sort of rolling terrain. Esperanza stood on a ledge a short distance above me, the wind lifting her shirttails, revealing everything underneath. Once again I flushed and even felt a tingle of fear. Esperanza was the only one of these girls I really knew. I decided to stick close to her.

If we walked to one side of the saddle, we could see Portage Glacier and the start of the Turnagain arm, and then back toward Anchorage. The water in the arm was somewhere between gray and brown. From another spot we could see the remarkably deep-blue waters of the Passage Canal. It was like standing on the roof of your house—look one way and you'd see your own backyard, look the other way and you'd see across the street into your neighbor's front yard.

There was a slight breeze blowing in over the top of the pass. It was cool, and I'd worked up a sweat. Without even thinking, without even realizing what I was doing, I unbuttoned my last two buttons and let my shirt fly open. It felt wonderful! I was wearing a modest two-piece bathing suit, but the fact that my shirt was unbuttoned made me feel a little naughty. I guess it was just an unfamiliar feeling of freedom.

Suddenly, this new feeling was interrupted by panic! I leaned over and whispered into Esperanza's ear. "There aren't any boys coming to meet us here, are there?" I felt so weird. I was actually standing next to a girl who was practically naked from the waist up.

She said, "*Eeeeyu! No way!* Can you imagine boys coming up and just lying around in the sun? If they could keep their hands off us, they'd probably spontaneously burst into flames or explode or something."

"I know what you mean," I said, sighing with relaxation. "The boys at church nearly kill each other just to sit next to one of us who might be wearing a new top that's cut just a little lower than usual."

"Yeah, the same thing happens at my church."

I blurted, "You go to church?"—and then wished I hadn't said it quite like that.

She just laughed and said, "We all do. Let's see, Christi and Angie go to a Methodist church, and I'm a practicing Catholic. Tamika goes to that big Baptist church in Eagle River, and Becky goes to the synagogue in Anchorage. We've formed a group of about twenty girls who all go to church somewhere. We've sworn a virginity covenant with each other."

"Really?"

"Summer, the people who go to your church aren't the only ones who worry about stuff like premarital sex. Our parents have taught us since we were kids about the spiritual and physical dangers of having sex before marriage. All our priests and ministers and rabbis have warned us about promiscuity. Even though all of us belong to our own church youth groups, we've created our *own* sort of interdenominational youth group."

She gestured to herself and said, "We're just up here sunbathing and nothing else. Several of our cheerleading outfits are off the shoulder, so we just want to avoid getting tan lines."

I looked down and said, "I'm sorry, I just thought . . ."

"You mean, because we're cheerleaders?"

"Yeah, and something else. No one ever *said* this, I promise, but I grew up thinking only kids from *my* church cared about abstinence. We're encouraged to only date kids from our church—I guess I assumed it was because no other kids were abstinent."

"Yeah, it took *us* a while," Esperanza said, "but everyone in our group figured out they grew up with that same thing rattling around in their head." She smiled and added, "If it makes you feel any better, all of us up here today are on the varsity cheerleading squad, but not everybody on the squad is part of this group. Some squad members are sexually active, and some aren't religious or even spiritual. We couldn't trust some of those girls to keep our sunbathing expeditions a secret."

That made me feel a lot better. A little breeze came up, and I started to grab my shirt to keep it closed—just a reflex action, I guess. Then I just let go and let the breeze float my shirt open again. Now that I had cooled down a little from the climb, the breeze felt a little chilly—I was totally covered in goose bumps!

Esperanza looked at me carefully and asked if I was all right. I looked back at her, trying to see only her face. I said, "Yeah, but I've never done anything like this before." My eyes slipped down to her breasts. I quickly looked back up into her face. I'm sure my face was flushed again.

"It's all right, Summer. You can look at whatever you want. Cheerleaders are used to people looking."

"Yeah, but when you're cheerleading, you have more clothes on," I said a little defensively.

"Barely. You haven't seen some of our outfits. Look, we're just up here enjoying nature, *naturally.*" She stepped back a couple of steps, spreading her arms wide, and encouraged me to take in *all* the beauty. I was embarrassed at first, but then I did as she asked. I don't think I ever looked at a girl that way. She was stunningly beautiful.

As I looked at her, she slowly turned around and said, "Ta-dah!"

I made up my mind, took off my shirt, and threw it into the air. I looked at Esperanza and said back to her, "Ta-dah!" Funny, it was harder to unbutton those first two buttons than it was to take off the whole shirt.

Esperanza grabbed my hand. "Summer, you've got to *promise* to keep all this *über*-super-top secret, no matter whether you join us or not."

Then from a place somewhere inside, I said, "I think I really *do* want to be part of your group. What do I have to do?"

"Well, you qualify on the churchgoing and virginity part. All of us like you—*and* you didn't run away when Becky and I took off our shirts," she said with a grin. "There's one more thing you should know before you finally decide. One of us is a lesbian. She's out of the closet at school and church, but I'll bet you can't tell which one of us she is. Are you cool with that?"

I stood there, not sure how to answer. I wasn't even sure how I felt. *Is Esperanza telling me she is gay?* This was an awful lot for a good little church girl like me to take in.

Esperanza said, "Of course she's taken the virginity covenant too."

"Really?"

"Promise." She smiled. "So . . . we're all headed down to tarn number seven to eat our lunch and do some sunbathing. There won't be any wind there, and the water is almost hot. Coming?"

I smiled and nodded and then turned to pick up my shirt. Esperanza started back down to where the other girls had gathered. Her bear bells jangled unrhythmically as she did a cheerleader kind of skip-jog thing. That's when I noticed all five of them had now removed their tops.

Esperanza gestured them into a huddle. Just before I reached them, they broke out of the huddle and all came running toward me like a bunch of . . . *cheerleaders*. Cheering for me and offering words of welcome.

Now I have a new group of friends in Alaska—and none of them go to my church! Cool.

We walked past several tarns, but all the girls were laughing and saying, "Not number seven. Got to be number seven. This ain't number seven." Then in a chorus they all started chanting, "Se-*ven*, se-*ven*, se-*ven*." They were acting just like the girls at church camp. The only difference was the girls at church camp would have had their shirts buttoned all the way up to the second button.

When we got to what must have been tarn number seven, everyone dropped their packs, spread out small blankets or big beach towels, and started peeling off their shoes and pants. Esperanza and Tamika wore a skimpy bikini bottom. Christi kept her short cargo pants on, Angie wore a thong, and Becky wasn't wearing anything but her bear bells.

One at a time they splashed into the tarn, which was about the size of a backyard, aboveground swimming pool. They were playing like any teenage girls would play. I spread out my blanket, took off my shoes and socks, and then dropped my hiking pants. My navy-blue, two-piece swimsuit was a lot different from the other girls'—for one thing, there was probably *three* times as much material to my suit.

Taking a deep, shaky breath, I stepped up to the edge of the water, and then, without really thinking about what I was doing, I reached back, unfastened my top, and let it fall to the ground. I covered myself with my arms. I felt wicked!

The girls didn't pay any attention to me until I stepped into the surprisingly warm water. When I did, they all came over and splashed water on me.

The water was never more than three feet deep and was warmest right around the edges. Tamika and I played around, dropping down belly first and sort of swimming like a couple of polliwogs. We ended up facing each other, and I asked, "Why is this water so warm?"

"Well, because the water is shallow, bare rock slabs are at the bottom and"—she pointed up—"the sun thing. It's solar heating, Alaska style."

The twins stopped their horseplay and dropped down beside us, sitting in the water Indian style, and joining in our conversation. Eventually, Esperanza and Becky stopped splashing around and floated over to us, face up, looking at the sky as they talked to us. Esperanza pointed up and said, "Hey, look at that cloud!" We all rolled on to our backs and looked.

A whole band of puffy cumulus clouds was moving over the pass—the kinds of clouds people look up at and see bunny rabbits, teddy bears, or tall sailing ships. Pilots call them "puffy Q." They cast well-defined shadows on the ground, and as one of those shadows passed over us, the temperature dropped ten degrees. The effect on my exposed skin was immediate. I was once again covered in goose bumps, and my whole body shivered.

Sinking, I sloshed water over my chest, and some of the others did the same. But Becky and Tamika started scooping up water with their cupped hands and letting it drizzle over me. I enjoyed it for a second and then stood up like a shot. I involuntarily covered myself up again with my arms, and I'm sure the look on my face said it all. *Is Becky or Tamika the lesbian?*

A big smile grew on Becky's face. She said, "It's not me!" Everybody started giggling.

I looked at Tamika, and she said, "Uh-uh, not me, girl!" Again everyone broke out in laughter.

I looked at Esperanza, and she said, "It ain't me."

That just leaves the twins.

I looked at Angie and Christi. They shrugged and pretended not to know what was going on.

I dropped my arms as the cloud passed, and we were in direct sunlight again. We all got out of the tarn and stood on a grassy spot—like six sunflowers standing out in a field, with our faces all turned toward the sun. It was delicious. I never imagined I'd be tanning in Alaska—especially *topless*!

We all dried off and lay on our blankets and towels. Everyone started putting on suntan lotion, taking turns putting lotion on each others' backs. I couldn't help myself—I looked for any inappropriate touching, but I didn't see any. And I still couldn't figure out which one of the twins was the lesbian. Since Angie and Christi were identical twins, I thought maybe *both* were gay but one of them was still in the closet.

It takes a lot of sunblock for someone like me—with so much skin that's never seen direct sunlight—and I ran out. Christi said I could use some of hers. When she came over and offered to do my back, I immediately tensed up. Squirting lotion on my back, she said, "It ain't me."

Everybody busted out laughing. I looked over at Angie—she gave me a coy little smile and a little girl wave. In a squeaky little voice, she said, "It's me." Once again they started laughing, and this time I joined them.

We ate our lunches, and then the serious sunbathing began. We were all on our stomachs, and it got really quiet for a while. Every once in a while someone would say, "Bear bells," and we would all shake our bells. Occasionally the sun hid behind a passing cloud, and then we'd keep the chill off by covering up with parts of our blankets or whatever.

About thirty minutes later, most of the girls started rolling over—sunny-side up. Once again I started feeling like I shouldn't be there. I'm not sure why our nudity bothered me. I mean, I'd seen naked girls in the gym showers—but, then again, you *had* to get naked to shower, right? This seemed totally different. But I rolled over anyway, for all of creation to see.

The girls all had beautiful tans. I, on the other hand, was as pale as a ghost—and I knew I had to be careful or I'd burn. I applied another coat of Christi's sunblock and lay back down. After a few minutes, I began to relax. I stretched and arched my back, welcoming the sun's rays to parts of my body where the sun doesn't *usually* shine.

Esperanza was lying next to me, and we started talking. Keeping my voice low, I said, "I guess I'm okay with this sunbathing thing, but at the same time I'm, like, totally paranoid. You and I are very different about some things. You still kind of scare me."

"Why? Like how?"

"Well, topless sunbathing to start with. What else do you do? And ever since we first met on the plane, I've been aware that you don't wear a bra."

"Oh, I've got bras. And I do wear them sometimes, like when I go to church or on dates. I also have to wear a sports bra sometimes. My parents used to be 'concerned,'" she said, making quotation marks with her fingers, "but one day I heard them discussing it. Dad said he'd rather I go without rather than use a bra that makes my breasts look like bumpers on a Bel Air."

"What does that mean?"

"I don't know," she said, giggling, "but I still say it, because it sounds cool."

"We should Google it," I said, laughing. "Anyway, Esperanza, I've been taught that nudity is bad, that my body is a temple, and if I dress immodestly then I'm responsible for the impure thoughts that enter a boy's mind."

"Yeah, we've all heard stuff like that, but I think that's a crock. I've never tried to seduce anyone, and I'm *sure* not responsible for what a boy thinks. Besides, there aren't any boys here."

"You may be right, but my breasts are *way* bigger than yours. No *way* I could go without a bra." I told her what my uncle had said about the jiggle-and-bounce thing.

"Did you notice my mom's breasts?" she asked. "They are gi-normous, and she never jiggles or bounces. She buys her bras at a specialty shop. I know where the shop is. I'll take you down there sometime if you want."

I thanked her, and then we both got quiet for a while. Someone shook her bear bells, so the rest of us shook ours too.

About twenty minutes later, I was awakened by the sound of an aircraft engine somewhere in the pass. Raising up on one elbow and shielding my eyes from the sun, I finally spotted the plane coming from the west, over the pass from Anchorage. It was low enough that it was actually *in* the pass, not above it. It was a De Havilland Beaver, on floats.

Then I heard a second plane coming from the other direction! I knew this pass wasn't all that wide. Two airplanes in here could get kind of crowded. I hopped up and spun around to find the second plane. I could tell by the pitch change that both airplanes were headed into the pass—*and* from different directions. I looked all over trying to find the second airplane.

The other girls were totally unaware of the potential danger, but they too had hopped up and were dancing all over the place and waving at the first airplane, even though they were all topless! The pilot obviously saw us because he wagged his wings but just continued on. It was way too narrow a pass to circle back around.

The aircraft's sound dropped in frequency as it flew past us, but the mysterious westbound plane sounded like it was still coming. I was afraid they might collide almost on top of us. The sound of the eastbound aircraft faded away as it flew on toward Whittier, but the sound of the westbound was still coming at us. Then it *just quit*, even though *it had never passed us*. The frequency of its sound never deepened like it would've if it had flown by us. It was like a Bermuda triangle thing.

Anyway, all the activity seemed to end the sunbathing, and we all got dressed, to some degree or another. I put my bathing suit top and shirt back on but left my shirt unbuttoned. After we repacked our blankets and things we headed back down the pass. *Jingle-jangle-clatter-clang-donkity-donk.*

When we got close to the rock slide, we met a group of college kids hiking up the pass—about a dozen of them. Most of the boys were already shirtless, and several of the girls were wearing bikini or halter tops. A couple of the boys started talking to me, asking if I'd like to go back up the pass with them. I could tell they'd all been drinking and realized they were scoping me out. I buttoned up my shirt. All my defenses went on full alert.

But thankfully our two groups finally went our separate ways. After climbing over the rock slide, we found a bunch of fresh litter, including nearly a dozen empty beer cans. I just bent over and started picking up the trash, and some of the others helped.

Thirty minutes later we were driving the short distance into Whittier to get in line for the next westbound flow of traffic through the tunnel. We had just missed the five-thirty trip but were the first car in the new queue. We also found out it would be an hour before Anchorage-bound traffic would be moving through the tunnel again because an unscheduled train was messing up the schedule. We got out and walked to a little park to wait, buying snow cones from a vender on the dock. Who would have thought I would be eating snow cones in Alaska? We also browsed around a number of other vendors selling touristy things, trying on hats and sunglasses. I ended up buying a sleep mask with an Alaskan flag on it.

There was also a train yard and a big sea-going container ship. One really freaky thing was a train ferry that had railroad tracks built right onto the deck so entire trains could be pulled from the ferry to the tracks on the dock.

When the train finally came through the tunnel from Anchorage, we piled back in the Escalade and waited for the light to turn green. The trip back through the tunnel was more fun than the trip out because we were the first car through. We were all in a great mood until Becky screamed, "Look! A train is coming!" For an instant we all panicked, until she started laughing.

After we were through the tunnel, Esperanza asked, "Cold Stone, anybody?"

The girls all started cheering and rocking the Escalade as it rolled down the highway.

Cutting in, I said, "I'm buying!"

After another round of cheering, the Escalade wobbled down the road once again. Forty-five minutes later we were each enjoying our own personal favorite frozen dairy sedative in Eagle River. Eventually, Esperanza drove each of the girls home, and then it was just the two of us.

"What do you want to do now?" I asked.

"I don't know. I don't have a date or anything, and I sure don't want to be alone tonight."

"Where are your parents?"

"LA—they won't be back until Friday."

"So why don't you come spend the night with me?"

"That sounds like fun, but do we need to ask your grandfather first?"

"No, I know he won't mind. He really likes you and your family." I grinned mischievously, saying, "Besides, he doesn't have a cell phone, and he'll be with his flight students for another couple of hours."

"Okay, then let's swing by my place, and I'll pick up a few things first. I probably should call my folks too."

"Don't forget there's no cell service at the cabin."

"Oh, yeah, I forgot about that." She laughed and said, "And no cable TV either, right?"

"Nope, just the local stations," I said. "Hey, let's Google 'bumpers on a Bel Air' before we leave your house."

While Esperanza packed, I started a Google search for images of Bel Airs. Esperanza spotted it first. On 1957 Chevy Bel Airs, the bumpers had these two chromed, pointy, boob-shaped, things.

Esperanza said, "OMG, they look like Elizabeth Wilhoit's boobs! She's on the girl's basketball team."

Esperanza grabbed her boobs and tried to make them look like a bumper on a Bel Air. We both cracked up.

Then she called her mother, telling her about our plans. After she hung up, she turned to me and said, "I'm starving!"

"Yeah, me too. I know we have plenty of fruit and sandwich stuff at Grandpa's. Would that be okay?"

"Sure. I've been eating too much pizza lately."

We fed Kenai and Denali and played with them for a while and then drove out to the cabin and got settled in my room. After we put together a couple of meals, I led the way to the boat dock. We decided to eat in the boat.

As we were getting in, Esperanza asked, "You do know how to row a boat, right?"

"Uh, like, totally."

She got down in the boat and sat on the middle bench.

Explaining that was the rower's seat, I directed her to the back bench and then handed down the basket. Ammo showed up right about then, so I told him to get in, and I launched the boat.

I rowed out to the middle of the lake and stowed the oars. We ate our hodgepodge supper and talked about anything and everything.

Using his best sad eyes, Ammo finagled little bites from each of us. We must have made quite a sight—two pretty girls and a dog floating on a glass-smooth lake in the shadow of Pioneer Peak. This side of the mountain was shaded, but the peak had a glow from the sun. I wished someone could have taken a picture of us, but it was an image that I could only keep in my mind.

When I told Esperanza about the bear behind the lake, she got a little freaked out, and it was my turn to act all cool and stuff. I even told her how to tell the difference between a Brown and Black bear.

Grandpa finally came home, parking Bubble Truck next to the Escalade. He walked over to the dock and waved at us. We waved back. When Ammo caught sight of Grandpa, he got up and started whining and wagging his tale and licking my face—then he turned back around and barked at Grandpa.

Grandpa whistled and Ammo jumped out of the boat and started swimming toward him. We watched until he made it safely to shore. He shook the water off, head to tail, and then he and Grandpa headed around the end of the lake.

I commented, "Looks like he's going over to Sister Baker's house."

Esperanza said, "Well, Sister Watson, I have to go pee."

"Okay, Sister Harris." We both laughed and I grabbed the oars.

After we got inside, we took turns showering then did our face and hair at the sink, standing side by side. Esperanza asked about my braces, and I let her examine them. We worked on each other's hair. After that, we moved into my room and sat cross-legged on the bed as we worked on each other's nails.

Later, we heard Grandpa and Ammo come in. He messed around in the kitchen and bathroom for a while and then came to our door. "*La noche buena, mijas.*"

Esperanza responded, "Buenos noches," and then she whispered, "That's 'good night,' right?"

I nodded and then said, "*Te quiero, Abuelito.*"

"*Te quiero también.*" Then he went into his room.

Esperanza asked, "Why was Grandpa Gus speaking Spanish?"

"He does it with me all the time—all *kinds* of languages. Don't be surprised if he greets us in the morning in Farsi or Mandarin."

"I wish I had a grandfather," she said with a little sigh.

And so it went for the rest of the night. We talked about everything. Our favorite topic was our upcoming senior year in high school and our plans for college. She told me she was staying here and going to UAA. I hadn't thought about it, but I would be going to UAA also. We talked about flying. We talked about boys and my brother. I suggested she marry my brother when he gets back so we could really be sisters. She asked to see his picture again.

We talked about religion—well, not so much religion as spirituality. Despite major differences in the way our churches worked, we discovered we were very much alike in a hundred ways and that we were on about the same level of spirituality. We also discovered that despite our age gap, we were compatible emotionally, socially, and academically.

When I told her how angry I was at God, she showed real concern and compassion. She even convinced me to pray with her about it. She prayed a lot differently than I did, but it softened my heart and I apologized to the Lord.

That night I gained something I never had before. Esperanza became my buddy—more than a classmate or study partner or an age-mate at church. I'd never felt this close to anyone outside of my family before. Maybe that was because I was a military brat. I think most military brats are afraid to develop deep friendships because they all know one of them will be moving sooner or later. Or maybe it was because I was always the wrong age, or because I was a homebody brainiac. That night I gained a sister—something else I'd never had.

The next morning, we heard Grandpa at the door. He said, "*Jambo.*" Esperanza and I looked at each other, and said, "Swahili." We laughed and responded with our best "*Jambos.*"

When he asked if we wanted breakfast, Esperanza turned to me and said, "Check this out." In a loud voice, she said "*Da, dye-doosh-ka.*"

It was quiet behind the door for a moment, and then Grandpa said, "*Daas-vee-dann-ya.*"

Esperanza got into the spirit of the thing and said, "*Nyet, nyet, nye daas-vee-dann-ya.*"

Again silence on the other side. She then slowly articulated, "*Dawb-ra-ye oo-tra.*"

Grandpa tried to mimic the word. "*Dawb-ra-ye—*"

She then finished the word: "*Oo-tra. Dawb-ra-ye-oo-tra.*"

This time he got through it. "*Dawb-ra-ye-oo-tra.*"

Esperanza said, "*Da!*" and then applauded.

Grandpa then said, "*Spaa-see-ba, ba-boosh-ka.*"

By her intonation, I figured she finished the exchange with, "*Pa-zhaal-oos-ta.*"

The next thing I heard through the door was Grandpa getting the cast iron skillet out of the oven.

Esperanza said, "Grandpa Gus is so cool."

"Yeah, I know. What were you guys talking about?"

"Just a Russian-101, hello–thank you–you're welcome thing. He did pretty well until he called me 'grandmother.'"

We both giggled and then took turns in the bathroom. We got dressed and were ready to go when Grandpa called us to breakfast.

CHAPTER 11

JUST ANOTHER DAY IN THE NEIGHBORHOOD

A few days later, Grandpa knocked at my bedroom door, waking me from a sound sleep. "Your Uncle Chris is on the phone and wants to know if we would like to fly down to Naknek with him. Want to go?"

"Sure!" I said and flipped the covers off. "What do I wear?" I was pulling off my PJs before he had a chance to answer.

"Just some warm hiking clothes—and hurry," he called from the hall. "We do not have a lot of time."

"Okay." I got ready in record time and met Grandpa in the kitchen. He wasn't fully dressed yet—he had on socks but no boots, and his suspenders were down off his shoulders. The bacon was already frying.

Asking me to take over, he headed for his bedroom. A few minutes later he was back in the kitchen, snapping his suspenders onto his shoulders.

I said, "No biscuits or potatoes this morning."

Grandpa said, "That is all right, I would rather Ammo not have one this morning anyway." Then he added, "I will make toast."

"All righty then."

Grandpa poured hot Pero from the kettle into a thermos and set it on the counter.

I said, "We get scrambled this morning."

He faked a groan and said, "Not too dry! I like mine a little moist."

Grandpa buttered the toast while I finished frying the bacon and then started scrambling some eggs. He poured two glasses of concord grape juice and set them on the table.

"Grandpa, where is Naknek, and why is Uncle Chris going there?"

"There's an outbreak of canine influenza, and the vet down there needs some vaccine. Chris volunteered to fly it down. The village is on Bristol Bay, down on the Alaskan Peninsula."

We sat down and wolfed down breakfast. My Alaska geography was still pretty weak, so I had to ask for more information.

Between bites, Grandpa said, "It's about three hundred fifty miles southwest of here. Right on the coast of the Bering Sea."

"Really! The Bering Sea?" I asked excitedly.

Grandpa held up a finger, as if asking for silence. He was listening for something. He turned his head a little and then said, "We really need to get going. Chris wants us to meet him on Kampmeyer's gravel bar about fifteen minutes from now."

"Where's that?" I asked.

"About half a mile from here, on the riverbank."

Just then an airplane flew so low over the house I thought it might have knocked the chimney pipe off. Grandpa looked at his watch and said, "Your uncle wants to take a quick look at Lake George. He'll be back in a few minutes."

He grabbed the thermos of Pero and stuffed it in a little rucksack. Then he scribbled a note and hung it on the bulletin board on the front porch—a trip plan, of course—and told me to grab a coat, just in case.

This may have been old hat for Grandpa, but I was a little bewildered. As we got in the Suburban, I saw Ammo running up from the lake. I joked that it looked like Ammo wanted to come too.

Grandpa said, "Well, let him in."

Opening my door, I slapped my lap. Ammo struggled to climb over me and settled in the backseat.

Grandpa drove down to the end of his road and crossed the highway. Then we went over some railroad tracks and onto a really rutted fishing path. It was only about a hundred yards long, and then it just opened up onto a gravel bar, right on the Matanuska River.

I was confused. "Here?"

Grandpa went out onto the bar and drove up and down the full length of it. He parked right near the little trail we had just come down.

"Where's the runway?"

A big smile crossed Grandpa's face, and with a heavy Chicano accent, he said, "Runway? We don't need no stinking runway."

I wasn't sure if he was joking or what. Then he pointed up the river and said, "Get your camera ready." I never could figure out how Grandpa could pick out the sound of a single airplane and at such a distance. Sometimes he could even tell what type of aircraft it was before we could see it.

I finally spotted an aircraft—low, way low! It was Uncle Chris's red Cessna 185 Skywagon. A 185 is similar in a lot of ways to the Cessna 152s and 172s that I'm used to flying, but one very obvious difference is the Skywagon is a tail dragger—which means instead of having a nose wheel, it has a tail wheel. In ground school, I'd learned that taking off and landing in a tail dragger is a lot different from in a tricycle-gear aircraft (with a nose wheel), but I'd never flown one.

Uncle Chris flew by us and then banked hard away, out over the river. I took a shot with my camera.

Grandpa said, "You know those short field landings you have practiced? Well, you are about to see a *real* short field landing."

Uncle Chris flew down the river and then banked hard again, coming back across the river and lining up on the gravel bar. He lowered his flaps all the way—I'd never seen an airplane fly that slow! He looked a little too high to land, but then he chopped the throttle, and the aircraft gently dropped onto the gravel bar. I took another picture as he rolled past us. He turned around and taxied back by us to the west end of the gravel bar.

I looked up at Grandpa in a questioning way. He stuck his finger in his mouth and then held it up in the air. "*Ohh, I get it.*" Aircraft should land and take off into the wind whenever possible. There was a light breeze coming down the river. That's why Uncle Chris had flown downriver and turned back upriver for his approach. We would also need to take off into the wind, which was why he was taxiing away from us, to the west end of the gravel bar.

"What're we going to do with Ammo?"

Grandpa said, "Well, he is coming too."

Man, I love the Alaska way of doing things!

Grandpa told me to give him my coat and stuff—he wanted me to hold Ammo's collar. "Ammo is a smart dog, but I am not sure he knows what a propeller is," he said. "Ammo and I will sit in the back. You can ride shotgun." I saw the landing lights blink on the plane, and Grandpa said, "Okay, we can go—stay clear of the prop."

We sort of jogged down the gravel bar, approaching the plane from under the right wing. Ammo couldn't get in by himself, so I had to pretty much lift him in. Then I stepped back a little, and Grandpa got in next. I pushed the seat back and climbed in. Uncle Chris pointed to a headset hanging on a little hook just behind my head. I looked back at Grandpa—he already had his headset on and was just buckling in. I adjusted my mic and said, "Good morning, Uncle Chris," as I buckled my seat belt.

He smiled at me and asked if we were both ready. I said yes and Grandpa gave a thumbs-up sign.

Uncle Chris keyed his mic and said, "Local traffic, November nine-nine-seven-zero Zulu taking off to the east from the Matanuska River bank just west of the bridges."

No one responded.

I watched him as he went through his own little preflight ritual. First he set the brakes and advanced the throttle, pushing the yoke forward until I felt the tail of the aircraft lift a little. Then he set the flaps to twenty degrees, advanced the throttle, and released the brakes. I couldn't see out the windshield because the nose was so high. The takeoff roll was really bumpy—the plane rattled a lot—and then I felt the tail lift off. Uncle Chris pulled back on the yoke, and the aircraft seemed to literally *jump* into the sky! He leveled off for a minute to gain some airspeed and then raised the flaps to ten degrees. I could now just barely see over the instrument panel. He scanned the sky for other aircraft and raised the flaps all the way.

Uncle Chris did a 270-degree turn to the right. I looked out my window, and all I could see was the river. Then he rolled wings level, patted the dash panel, and said, "Thank you, girl. Well done."

Why do men always refer to their machines as "girl"?

He then blew me away when he looked at me and said, "It's your airplane. Maintain present course and heading. Climb to and maintain fifteen hundred feet. Keep your eyes open; this isn't the training area."

I couldn't believe it! An hour ago I was asleep in bed, and now I was about to pilot an unfamiliar aircraft with a dog in the backseat across the wilds of Alaska. I grinned broadly, and with authority, I said, "I've got the airplane."

Uncle Chris looked at me like he was a little surprised. He turned around and said to Grandpa, "She's a Rockwell, all right. What's in the rucksack?"

Grandpa pulled out the thermos and handed it to Uncle Chris, who then asked, "Anything else?" Grandpa then passed forward a bag of Oreos. It became obvious they'd had this same conversation many times before. I felt like I was really part of the moment and relished it.

Uncle Chris poured himself some Pero and said to me, "Turn down the Knik Arm and stay to the right. Don't forget Birchwood Airport is just down the way. You never know what you're going to see around there—everything from ultralights to big old Russian AN-2s. Don't be surprised if you see a paraglider picking his nose."

Uncle Chris keyed his mic and said, "Birchwood traffic, November nine-nine-seven-zero Zulu, Cessna 185, red over white, transitioning fifteen hundred feet, southbound on the west side of the Arm." Then he searched the skies for conflicting traffic.

We quickly passed the small airport, and he announced we were clear of the area. Switching frequencies again, he identified himself to Ted Stevens approach control and stated our position and intentions. He then asked if there were any heavies in the area. The controller answered that all was quiet at Elmendorf Air Force Base and that traffic was normal in and out of the airport. He directed us to remain at or below fifteen hundred feet. Uncle Chris got my attention by pointing to the altimeter.

Uncle Chris responded, "November nine-nine-seven-zero Zulu, roger. Will maintain fifteen hundred." A minute later, the controller came back and advised we had conflicting traffic in front of us, altitude unknown. All three of us started scanning the sky in front of us.

Uncle Chris said, "Remember, this guy has the sun in his eyes and won't be able to see us."

Grandpa spotted it first. "Yellow Super Cub, well below us."

Uncle Chris then informed the controller we had traffic in sight about five hundred feet below us.

Grandpa then tapped me on the shoulder and pointed toward the international airport. A Boeing 747 was climbing out and coming straight for us. Uncle Chris said, "It's a KAL. See the light-blue tail? Don't worry—he'll cross in front of us and be at six thousand before he gets here."

"It could be a *she*," I said.

Uncle Chris asked, "She what?"

"You said before *he* gets here. Could be a female flying that jet."

Uncle Chris and Grandpa exchanged looks, and Grandpa said, "You are right—it sure could be she." He didn't say it in a condescending way. I realized I might have just taught them something about innate sexism.

A few minutes later Uncle Chris told me to contact approach control and tell them we're twenty miles south. He pointed at the little brass plate with our call sign on it.

I keyed the mic and said, "Anchorage approach, this is Cessna nine-nine-seven-zero Zulu. We are twenty miles south."

The controller came back and said, "Seven-zero Zulu frequency change approved. Maintain visual flight rules. Have a nice flight."

Without being told, I switched back to radio frequency 123.0.

Uncle Chris asked me how I liked the 185. I told him it felt a lot like a 172.

He said, "Don't let her fool you. This isn't a 172, and she will spank you if you let her. You can fly until we get to Merrill Pass, and then I'll take over."

"Merrill Pass!" I said. "You mean the Aluminum Trail?" Uncle Chris didn't respond but shoved a cookie toward my face. He lowered my mic boom and put it in my mouth.

He said, "Normally I'd just fly across this rock pile at about nine thousand feet, but I thought I'd take you through the pass. You know about the Aluminum Trail?"

"Well, a little, I guess. I've heard people talk about it."

Grandpa joined the conversation, "The guy they named the pass for was Russell Merrill. He discovered it in 1927."

"I guess Merrill Field is also named after him?" I asked.

Uncle Chris said, "Yeah, they tend to name things after dead bold pilots. Russ Merrill crashed and burned in 1929, two years after he pioneered the pass."

I remembered what Denny had once told me—there are lots of old pilots and lots of bold pilots but very few old, bold pilots—so I asked, "Do they ever name things after *old* pilots?"

They both immediately chimed in, "No!" Then Grandpa added, "Just the *bold* ones."

Uncle Chris grinned, and asked, "Dad, who'd they name Elmendorf Air Force Base after?"

"A *bold* test pilot named Hugh Elmendorf."

I asked, "Did he ever get *old*?"

"Nope, just bold."

Then I said, "Hey! What about Amelia Earhart? She was a bold pilot."

Grandpa said, "Yes, and she never became an old pilot, did she?"

"Did they name anything after her?" Uncle Chris asked.

"Actually, quite a few things," Grandpa said. "She has two airports, one in Kansas and one in Florida. Also, there is a terminal at Logan International Airport in Boston named after her. She also has schools, and even a scholarship at Perdue University named for her."

Then I thought out loud, "Man, I hope they never name anything after me."

Grandpa and Uncle Chris both cracked up, and then Grandpa added, "Well, they just might have to if you do not start keeping a better eye out for traffic."

Uncle Chris motioned for me to look at Grandpa. I turned around and saw he was scrunched down with his floppy camo hat pulled over his face.

Using two fingers, Uncle Chris pointed toward his own eyes and then out the windscreen. I understood and started scanning for traffic, and then I reached over and grabbed a couple of Oreos.

I had a lot of questions about the airplane, so I pulled my mic back down and asked Uncle Chris, "What's this?" I pointed to the third knob—the blue one, next to the throttle.

He responded, "That's the propeller control."

"Oh! You've got a constant speed prop! Then where's the . . ."

Uncle Chris was already pointing to the manifold pressure gauge.

"Man, that's a lot of knobs. Do you ever get them mixed up?"

Uncle Chris chuckled, sounding just like Grandpa. "No. First of all, they're different colors, and each knob has a different shape. Besides, this is just a single-engine aircraft. You should see what the panel looks like on a multiengine aircraft."

Grandpa, who was still scrunched down in the back seat asked, "Have you ever heard the expression 'balls to the wall'?"

"Yeah, I think it means to go fast."

From under his hat, he said, "It does. Do you know why we say it?"

"No, I just thought it was a vulgar expression made up by a bunch of drunken pilots."

"Well, almost everybody thinks that—and maybe they *were* drunk. Your uncle just told you the knobs have different shapes. Well, back in the day, a throttle knob was shaped like a ball. If you wanted to go fast, you pushed the balls toward the firewall—'balls to the wall.'"

"It's just like saying 'pedal to the metal,'" Uncle Chris said.

Grandpa asked, "Traffic?"

Uncle Chris smiled and said, "Two o'clock low and eleven o'clock high." I looked down and to the right and caught sight of a float plane about to pass under our nose, and then I looked up and to the left just in time to see a low-winged turboprop a thousand feet or so above us.

"It's just like driving," Uncle Chris said. "You need to be aware of other traffic on the road. Alaska is a great big place, but it seems like everyone is flying to the same places."

I never thought about that.

Grandpa came on and said, "I guarantee you, we will not be alone in Merrill Pass."

Uncle Chris said, "I've got the airplane."

I responded, "It's your airplane," and then let go of the controls.

Uncle Chris said, "See the tall mountain at one o'clock? That's Mt. Spurr."

The whole mountain was covered in gray ash. The forest around the mountain was totally destroyed. The streams and rivers seemed silted up, and the water was starting to carve its way back down through the ash. The water was the same color as the ash. I thought about the salmon and other wildlife.

"Before you ask—no, we're not going over to look at it. The crater is at eleven thousand feet, and it's still not dormant. It's still under an orange aviation code. There's an active vent lower on the south flank, so we don't want to even fly around it. We'll buzz Mt. St. Augustine this afternoon. It's been steaming this week. Why don't you just sit back and enjoy the scenery for a while? Once we pass Spurr, we're going to turn west and enter Merrill Pass."

It had been exciting to have some stick time, but I really did want to see everything. I obviously wasn't doing a very good job on either task, so I decided to be content with just being a passenger. I asked Grandpa if there was any Pero left. He passed the thermos forward, and I lowered my mic to drink the last of it. Then he asked if there were any Oreos left. Uncle Chris passed the cookies to the backseat.

After Spurr slipped past us, Uncle Chris turned into a range of the most beautifully rugged mountains I'd ever seen. Grandpa calls these kinds of scenes "fiercely beautiful." A blue lake sat right at the beginning of the pass. A glacier spilled into the lake and completely across the valley.

Uncle Chris said, "That's Shamrock Glacier. The lake is named Chakachamna, but we just call it Lake Chaka."

Beyond the lake was a V-shaped valley. We were headed straight into it. Uncle Chris got on the radio and called local traffic to tell whoever might be listening that he was entering the pass from the east. A minute later someone called and told us they were headed west and had just shot the gap. I assumed that was a landmark in the pass. Uncle Chris asked the pilot if was able to stay to the right. The pilot replied that he wasn't encountering any turbulence and would stay to the right. Then things got quiet on the radio.

I became captivated by what I was seeing. We were several thousand feet above the ground, yet we were totally swallowed up by the pass, with giant mountains on either side of us. Uncle Chris elbowed me and said, "Aluminum Trail."

I looked at the valley floor and picked out several aircraft wrecks—and then several more and several more after that. One wreck had a big red X painted on it. Several others had yellow barrels sitting on the wreckage.

Uncle Chris said, "They mark the wrecks that way so searchers don't waste time searching old wreck sites."

It really was like a trail of aluminum. I must have counted two dozen crash sites, and I'm sure I didn't see them all.

I was so busy looking down, I lost track of the beauty of the pass. Grandpa tapped my right shoulder. I turned to look and was amazed at what I saw—a glacier that was up a side canyon. It sat in a valley that was high above the main valley floor. It towered so high above us I couldn't see the top because of the wing.

Grandpa said, "That is called a hanging glacier."

It was so big, I felt like we were the size of a mosquito. Within a few seconds, we'd flown past the side canyon, and the glacier went out of sight. The pass got a little narrower ahead.

The radio came alive again. It was the west-bound pilot. "Red Cessna, I have you in sight. We are at the same altitude. Do you have a tally on me?"

Uncle Chris quickly spotted the aircraft and said, "Tally, roger."

A moment later we passed each other.

Uncle Chris was flying well to the right of the center of the pass. He said, "Open your window for a second and listen."

I did and heard what I thought was another airplane. I turned and looked at Uncle Chris with more than a little concern on my face.

He said, "It's all right, relax. That's the sound of our engine echoing off the canyon walls."

I blurted out, "*That's it!* That's what I heard."

I turned to Grandpa and said, "When we were up in Portage Pass, an airplane flew through the pass, and I thought I heard a second airplane coming from the other direction. But I never saw the second plane. I was hearing the echo of its engine bouncing off the big cliff behind us."

Uncle Chris said, "Yes, I've heard that before. Me and a bunch of the guys used to go skinny dipping up there."

I snapped my head to the left and looked straight at Uncle Chris. I thought I had been discovered.

He just asked, "What? I don't skinny dip anymore."

I raised my mic boom and kept looking at his face. I decided he didn't know anything about my sunbathing trip, so I kept quiet. My secret was still safe.

Just then the radio came alive again. Another pilot called in, "Local traffic, this is Air Force, Beaver seven-seven, where are you guys?"

Uncle Chris answered, "We are about halfway to the gap, westbound, and I just passed a King Air headed east. Please say your location and type."

"Local traffic, Beaver seven-seven is an UH-60. I am westbound and have been in the pass for ten minutes."

Uncle Chris straightened up a little and Grandpa sat up, took his hat off, and turned around to look out the back window. Uncle Chris keyed his mic and said, "Beaver seven-seven, say your airspeed."

This time a female voice came back and said, "Local traffic, Beaver seven-seven is at fifteen hundred feet AGL and flying at one hundred seventy knots."

Uncle Chris replied, "Beaver seven-seven, you have thirty knots on me. Do you have a tally on us?"

"Local traffic, that is a negative, but we just passed the King Air. We have all eyes looking for you."

Grandpa said, "They're not even ten minutes behind us." He kept looking backward.

Seven minutes later: "Local traffic, Beaver seven-seven, please rock your wings."

Uncle Chris rocked the aircraft twice. "Local traffic, Beaver seven-seven, we have a tally on you."

Grandpa said, "I got him."

Uncle Chris radioed, "Beaver seven-seven, please say your intentions."

It took a minute, but the female voice came back and asked, "How would you guys like an in-flight picture?"

Uncle Chris reached over and pulled my mic down to my mouth and said, "Talk to the lady."

I radioed, "Beaver seven-seven, sounds great to us. How do you want to do it?"

"Maintain your current altitude; we will come alongside on your left."

I looked at Uncle Chris and he nodded at me. "Roger that, Beaver seven-seven."

Uncle Chris said he was going to keep focused on flying and asked Grandpa and me to watch the helicopter. I radioed, "We have a tally on you, Beaver seven-seven."

"Roger that; you're lead; we will stay on your left wing."

Uncle Chris nodded and I said, "We copy."

I watched as this big helicopter slowly pulled up alongside us. I could clearly see the pilot. In a helicopter, the pilot sits on the right side. It was the lady! I waved at her, and she nodded back. I radioed, "You go girl!" She smiled at me.

Then, their cabin door slid back and I saw four airmen kneeling in the doorway. They all had cameras pointed at us. The helicopter stayed with us for a few seconds and then dropped back behind us.

"Local traffic, Beaver seven-seven, can we come up on your right?"

Uncle Chris nodded at me.

I said, "Come ahead."

This time the male voice came on and said, "Maintain your heading and altitude. I am on your right wing."

Their cabin door was already open, and this time three cameras were pointed at us. The male voice said, "Can you bank to the left and gently climb?"

Uncle Chris complied, and the helicopter stayed with us again. I managed to get off a couple of nice shots before they dropped back behind us.

The female voice came back on and said, "Thank you, guys. Please maintain your altitude and heading." The helicopter then pulled up alongside again, and everybody waved at everybody. The helicopter then dropped below us and sped on ahead of us. She told us to stay above her flight path for a couple of miles. "This thing generates a lot of wake turbulence. What's your dog's name?"

I radioed back, "Ammo."

She said, "I'll bet there's a story behind that, but I have to get back to work. Where do you want the pictures sent?

Uncle Chris radioed, "Dr. Rockwell, PO box forty-nine, Trapper Creek."

The male voice then said, "Copy all. Have a safe flight."

I watched as Beaver seven-seven sped away. It was a big helicopter, but within minutes it shrank to the size of a gnat compared to the mountains and glaciers in front of us. Before long I completely lost sight of the helicopter.

Up ahead, the pass made a rather tight S-curve and then straightened out again. Before long, it made a sweeping turn to the left, and I saw a beautiful green landscape ahead of us. We had made it through the pass. "Wow, look at that!"

Grandpa said, "Well, I will say it, even if no one else will. I need a potty break, and Ammo's eyes are turning yellow."

"That's gross, Grandpa!"

Uncle Chris said, "Yeah, I'm sure we all could use a break. No problem. There's a rest area just up ahead."

Uncle Chris asked if I'd like to feel the controls on this landing. I knew that meant I was to just lightly feel the yoke and pedals—not fly the airplane. "That would be great," I said.

He asked if I knew how to cross-control an aircraft. When I said I did, he told me to stay with him. He reduced power and then stepped hard on the right rudder pedal and turned the yoke hard to the left. This destroys the lift over the wings. Basically, the aircraft falls out of the sky—but in a controlled fashion. Ammo definitely did *not* like it!

The windscreen was filled with nothing but the river below. Silly me, I thought we were going to land at an airport. At about one hundred feet above the ground, Uncle Chris increased power and straightened out the airplane. He opened his side window and started looking out and down at a river bar.

Grandpa was also leaning over Ammo and looking down.

"What do you think, Dad?"

"Think they have clean rest rooms?"

Realizing they were joking with me, I said, "They look clean to me."

"That settles it then," Uncle Chris said. He gently touched my left hand and said, "I don't want to feel you on the controls."

He banked the aircraft hard to the right, and then banked to the left, much harder than I would have, even at a safe altitude. He also used his rudder much more aggressively than I ever had. He lined us up on the gravel bar and then dropped in full flaps, causing the aircraft to slow down. Then he chopped power, and we dropped rapidly but gently onto the bar. I felt the main wheels rolling over the gravel, but the tail was still flying. I could see over the nose until the tail touched down. That frightened me a little, and I unconsciously started to apply the brakes, an involuntary reaction.

Uncle Chris barked, "Get your feet off the brakes!" A second later, I felt him step hard on just the left pedal and the aircraft pivoted on the left wheel. We stopped, lined back up on the bar, pointed downriver again.

He ran his shutdown checklist and finally pulled the mixture lever to full lean, and the engine stopped. He laid the keys on the dash and unbuckled. Turning to me, he said, "That's how it's done. Never touch the brakes on a landing like that. You can easily tip the aircraft up on its nose."

With a sound of urgency, Grandpa said, "Boys on the left, girl and dog on the right!" Uncle Chris hopped out and held his seat forward for Grandpa. I got out and helped Ammo.

After we'd all taken care of business, we were walking around and stretching. We saw two westbound aircraft fly over. Uncle Chris opened one of the cargo pod doors, brought out a sack of fruit, and invited us to help ourselves. A few minutes later, Ammo and Grandpa got back in the plane.

Uncle Chris invited me to do a quick walk-around inspection with him. Many of the components were similar or identical to components I was familiar with. He did a thorough inspection of the chrome, three-bladed propeller and the landing gear and then said, "Okay, let's get going."

Uncle Chris invited me to follow through on the controls as he performed a short-field takeoff from the gravel bar. He reminded me that you have to be careful when selecting a landing site because aircraft can be safely landed on fields that are too short for a takeoff.

After takeoff, Uncle Chris handed the airplane over to me again and told me to maintain a heading of two hundred degrees and hold an altitude of a thousand feet. I guessed that was just about five hundred feet above the ground. The only time I'd flown this low was on final approaches to a big fat, wide runway. This was a whole different feeling.

I had to keep reminding myself this was not a movie—that I was a sixteen-year-old almost-senior. For me this was high adventure, but for an Alaskan aviator this was just another day in the neighborhood.

Uncle Chris took the aircraft back after about a half hour. He climbed up to two thousand feet. He was looking for something off in the distance. Then he switched radio frequencies and said, "Major Tom to ground control."

I looked at him like he was crazy. Over the next ten minutes he repeated the call three more times.

Finally the radio came back, "Major Tom, this is ground control. Switch to frequency B."

Uncle Chris switched to a frequency I wasn't familiar with and waited. Then came, "Eh, what's up, Doc?"

"Uhh, I've got your crutches. We'll be in your neighborhood in about an hour and a half and thought we'd drop in for lunch."

The reply was, "Don't stand on formality; how many in your party?"

Uncle Chris said, "Four of us counting Ammo. Need anything from town?"

"Yeah, as a matter of fact. I lost my last can of lard and both of my lanterns. Have them put it on my tab. Also, would you pick up my mail?"

"Copy all, Buckwheat. See you in a bit."

Then the voice said, "*Oh tay*, Panky," and went silent.

Uncle Chris switched to radio frequency 118.3 and called, "King Salmon, King Salmon. This is Cessna nine-nine-seven-zero Zulu. I'm twenty minutes northeast, requesting current conditions."

Almost immediately a voice replied, "This is King Salmon with current weather conditions. Temp is fifty-two degrees, dew point is thirty-eight degrees. Winds are seven to ten from south-southwest. Partly cloudy in all quadrants. Ceiling is ten thousand. Altimeter is two nine. Seven two and falling. Active runway is one eight. Be advised we have some caribou inside the fence . . . see and avoid."

"Thank you, King Salmon. This is Dr. Rockwell. I have a supply of canine influenza vaccine for Doc Wilson in Naknek. Could you please call him and let him know I'll be landing there in thirty minutes?"

"Sure will, Doc. Everyone's been expecting you. Thanks for your help."

"You're welcome, King Salmon. We'll pass through your airspace at two thousand feet in about fifteen minutes. Seven-zero Zulu, out."

Uncle Chris reset his altimeter to the current barometric pressure. When he did, our indicated altitude changed by more than one hundred feet. He pointed off to about eleven o'clock. "That dark line on the horizon is the Bering Sea. If you follow the river down from King Salmon, you can just make out Naknek on the coast."

The airport was tiny. I couldn't even make it out until we were already over King Salmon. I did see a small herd of caribou grazing alongside a parking ramp just below us.

I was so excited about seeing the Bering Sea. I took a picture of the beach when we passed over it, as Uncle Chris flew out over Bristol Bay.

Grandpa asked, "How many of your friends back in the valley can say they have seen the Bering Sea?"

I looked back at him and smiled.

We'd dropped down to about three hundred feet. Uncle Chris pointed out a fishing trawler and headed for it. He dropped even lower and circled to the right so I could get a picture of it, and then he headed back to the village. He announced his location and intentions. Then he told me he'd make a normal landing on the field and invited me to follow through on the controls again, reminding me to keep my feet off the brakes.

Landing in a tail dragger really was different. Uncle Chris said he didn't really need to see forward on a runway like this. "I just use the runway side markers until I get to my taxiway." Once we turned off onto the taxiway, Uncle Chris gently zigzagged the plane. When he zigged, he could see out of *his* side window—and when he zagged, he could see out of *my* side window.

As we stopped, a truck came out to meet us. "I'll be right back, okay?" Uncle Chris said, leaving the engine running. He had already taken off his headset, so I just nodded. He got out, walked around behind the airplane, and opened a little door in the fuselage. He pulled out a small blue cooler and handed it to the man from the truck. They spoke for a minute.

While they were talking, Grandpa asked me if I'd ever seen any videos of the space shuttle landing. When I said I had, he asked, "Do you think the astronauts could see the runway once the main wheels touched down and before they lowered the nose?"

Huh, I guess they couldn't.

Uncle Chris and the man shook hands and the man ran back to his truck. He was already speeding away before Uncle Chris got back in the plane, saying he was hungry. Putting on his headset, he called King Salmon and advised them he was taking off from Naknek "International Airport" (ha-ha!) and was inbound for fuel. About fifteen minutes later we were climbing out of the plane at King Salmon.

A really old fuel truck—like from the 1960s—was already rolling toward us. Uncle Chris asked me and Grandpa if we'd run into town and pick up the things for his friend Louie. He said he'd stay with the plane.

We walked in and called for a taxi. A few minutes later an old ratty, rusted-out Ford pickup pulled up outside and honked. We walked out and Grandpa banged on the bed rails, saying, "You ride in back," as he climbed into the cab.

It took about five minutes to reach the store—the Alaska Commercial Company. I could write an entire chapter on that store, but just let me say, it looked like what I imagine a general store must have looked like in a Mark Twain story or on Walton's Mountain. Grandpa picked up the supplies and mail for Louie. I picked out a couple of postcards and three bottled waters, but when I saw the waters cost four dollars each, I put them back.

When we got back to the airport, Uncle Chris was waiting on us, Ammo already inside the plane. Before we got in, Grandpa announced that his legs were cramped and suggested Uncle Chris get in the back. Uncle Chris smiled, looked at me, and said, "It's your airplane."

As I climbed into the pilot's seat, Grandpa walked around and got in the right seat. We were once again student and instructor. "Check the Hobbs meter. You can log this next leg. I do not expect you to know it all—I will manage the prop. And during the takeoff, I will be following through on the controls."

"What's my takeoff speed?"

"I don't know. Let's find out."

I knew Grandpa actually *did* know, but he was teaching me a lesson. Although a pilot has to know her V-speeds, it's probably more important to be able to *feel* them, instead of just having the book knowledge.

"We are going to do something I will bet you have never done. I want you to trim the aircraft for takeoff and do *not* pull back on the yoke when you think we have enough airspeed. In fact, I want you to just lightly feel the yoke. Let's see what this airplane will do on its own. We have a ton of runway here, so don't worry."

The zigzag taxiing was pretty awkward, but I got us out to the runway and lined up. I advanced the throttle and we started rolling. I used the runway side markers to keep us going straight down the runway. Grandpa called out our airspeed as we accelerated. At twenty knots the tail started flying, and I could see forward again. Grandpa called out thirty knots; forty knots. Right after he called fifty knots, the aircraft just started flying on its own!

I was amazed. When I first started flying, I had a death grip on the controls. I was afraid the aircraft would crash if I didn't practically wrestle the plane into the sky. "What do I do now, Grandpa?"

"Just keep an eye out for traffic. Air speed?"

I checked and was surprised to see we were between fifty and sixty knots.

"Altimeter?"

We were at a thousand feet. The VVI indicated we were climbing at about one hundred feet per minute. The airplane was truly flying itself. I hadn't touched a thing since I advanced the throttle!

Grandpa said, "You have heard the expression, 'Never let the airplane fly you.' There is wisdom in that, but now you know that it can and will, if you ask it to. Ninety percent of all general aviation accidents are caused by the pilot, not the airplane. The airplane knows how to fly. Now let's get back to work."

I took back positive control with a whole new understanding of the relationship between plane and pilot. *Hmm,* maybe that's why pilots talk to their planes. They are in a relationship with them. I reached up and patted the dash panel and said, "Thank you, *boy*; that was well done."

I think all three of three were surprised at how easily I adapted to this new type of plane. I asked for a heading, and Uncle Chris said, "That-a-way." He handed Grandpa a set of map coordinates. Grandpa asked about my navigation skills.

"I've never used GPS, but I can get us anywhere using other nav-aids."

Grandpa smiled and handed me the coordinates and the map. Uncle Chris gave me the frequencies I needed. I marked my map with the coordinates and tuned my nav radios, so I could triangulate on my destination. Within a few minutes I'd established a heading that would get me there. All I had to do was watch two needles on my instruments. When both needles were pointing straight up, I'd know I'd arrived.

But something was troubling me. Until today all of my navigation exercises took me to an airport or town. I thought about that for a minute and told Grandpa, "This terrain is so flat and featureless. The best I can do is get us close."

"Fair enough," Grandpa said. "By the way, you have to be able to fly this plane and refold that map at the same time."

So I divided my time between map folding and flying, and for good measure I threw in a conversation with Uncle Chris. "What was all of that Major Tom stuff?"

Uncle Chris said, "Louie is a bit of a conspiracy nut, so I do it just because he asked me to. He doesn't want the government knowing who or where he is. You know, off-the-grid stuff. Speaking of that, hand me the mic and switch to 123.7."

I plopped the successfully folded map against Grandpa's belly then changed frequencies for Uncle Chris.

"Major Tom to ground control, come in please."

"Major Tom, switch to frequency C." I clicked the mic switch twice, which meant I understood.

Uncle Chris said, "Frequency 122.6. I told you he was a character."

The radio crackled, "I read you, Major Tom."

"Ground control, we'll be there in about twenty minutes. Is the beach clear?"

"Yeah, the beach is about the only thing that damn wolverine didn't tear up."

"Okay—looking forward to the story." Uncle Chris was leaning forward between the two front seats, scanning for the cabin. When he spotted it, he pointed it out to me, and I told him I had a tally on . . . *something*. I lowered the nose, and Grandpa reduced the power for me.

As the cabin became clearer, I couldn't believe what I was seeing—and what I was *not* seeing. There was no *cabin*—just two old school buses! I hadn't seen even a hint of a road since we left King Salmon, but here were two short school buses, one with a tower of some kind built on top. Some kind of windowless shed sat behind them by a little stream. A wrecked airplane was partially submerged in a lake a short distance from the camp. Then I saw a likely landing strip on the beach of the lake.

"Drop down and get a good look at the beach," Grandpa told me. I dropped in ten degrees of flaps and set up a long upwind leg.

"You are a little too close to the beach—swing out over the lake a little. Think you could take off from that same beach?" he asked.

"I don't have enough experience to know."

He smiled and said, "That is the right answer—the one I hoped you would give. Yes, there is plenty of beach there. Remember—keep your feet off the brake pedals. I will be right here with you on the controls."

I swung the aircraft around in a sweeping wide left turn. It was really thrilling to be this low and to be banked so tightly. I also experimented by being a little more aggressive on the rudder pedals. There was a little spit of land with some trees between me and the beach. I really wished those trees weren't there.

When I told Grandpa about my concern, he encouraged me. He said he wouldn't cut power until we'd cleared the trees. In this situation, I could really understand why it's important to land at the very end of the runway. *Dang those trees.*

Grandpa just told me to keep flying the airplane. "Lower your flaps, all the way—now." I lowered the flaps, and we slowed down but lifted up over the trees—but *man*, we were close! Grandpa said, "Okay, I am cutting the power," and the aircraft quickly settled onto the beach. One little bounce and then we were down. Of course, I couldn't see over the nose, but Grandpa said, "The beach is still there. Look out your side window and don't run us into the water and you'll be fine."

We were barely rolling when Grandpa said, "Now step hard on the left brake pedal."

When I did, the aircraft spun around and pointed back down the beach, just the way Uncle Chris had done it on the gravel bar.

Uncle Chris said, "Just like in the movies," and patted me on the shoulder. He looked out his window and said, "Hey, we've got a spruce bow hanging onto this wheel over here."

I screamed, "*What?*"

Uncle Chris laughed at me, but it wasn't mean-spirited in any way.

Grandpa read the shutdown checklist to me, and I went through the steps. The last thing I did was lay the keys on the dash. As I did, Grandpa laid his hand on top of mine. I looked over at him and he said, "Do you realize how far up the proverbial creek we would be if we lost these keys?"

"We ain't in Kansas anymore," Uncle Chris said.

I thought about that for a second. "Okay, I get it. Where *should* we keep the keys?"

"Definitely not in your pocket. The dash is fine. Just remember, keys always need to stay with the plane. Also, everyone needs to know where they are."

"Why?"

Grandpa grinned and said, "If you get eaten by a bear, your uncle and I are still going to want to go home."

"Gee, thanks a lot, guys!"

CHAPTER 12

JAM 'N' SALMON

A fter we all climbed out of the plane, Uncle Chris headed toward the school buses. Grandpa pulled a couple of dark-chocolate candy bars out of his rucksack, and we headed down the beach to check out the wrecked airplane.

Suddenly, we were swarmed by a million mosquitoes. No, it must have been a *billion*! They were just annoying at first, but within minutes they were actually becoming scary. I'd never seen so many mosquitoes before.

Grandpa took a bottle of insect repellant from the band on his hat and shared it with me, saying, "I told you—you're too skinny for a bear, but these mosquitoes will suck you dry."

When I chuckled a little, he said, "Granddaughter, I am as serious as a northbound train on southbound tracks. Be sure to keep that stuff out of your eyes and mouth. It is not your usual backyard insect repellant."

It seemed to do a good job of keeping the mosquitoes out of my face and off my arms, but they still swarmed my scalp—and they were biting me right through my clothes. I tried to ignore them.

"Grandpa, what kind of airplane is that?"

"A Lake."

"Ha-ha," I said. "Come on, Grandpa. I know it's a 'lake' plane since it's *in* the lake. But what *kind* is it?"

Before he answered, I saw Uncle Chris walking back with his friend. He was pulling a two-wheeled garden cart on steroids. The wheels looked like they came off a motorcycle. His friend was sitting on the back of the cart.

Grandpa and I started back toward the Skywagon, and we all got there about the same time.

Uncle Chris said, "Louie, you know Gus and Ammo—and this is my niece, Summer Rose. Summer Rose, this is Louie Black."

Louie held his hand out, and I stepped forward to shake it.

"Nice to meet you, Louie," I said, shaking his hand.

"Nice landing. Better'n *m'* last one," he said, nodding to the wreck in the lake.

Suddenly I couldn't take it anymore; the mosquitoes were too much! I frantically started slapping my back and rubbing my pant legs. Uncle Chris reached into the plane and found a can of regular grocery store bug spray. He started spraying me down all over, including my clothes. I stood there like a little kid with my arms spread out, turning around so he could do my back side too. Then I sort of danced in place, saying, "Ankles! Ankles!" After he finished, I took the can and did my scalp.

Uncle Chris grabbed a pair of forearm crutches out of the belly pod and handed them to Louie. While Louie adjusted the length on the crutches, Uncle Chris pulled the cart over to the aircraft and started unloading groceries.

Louie said, "Your uncle's a damn good man. I never know when he's gonna drop in like this. H' always brings fresh stuff. I got plenty of canned and dehydrated food, but I miss stuff like eggs an' milk an' fresh veggies. I never ask for what he brings, an' he never lets me pay for it."

"Everybody I know says those kinds of things about him," I said. "How did you guys meet?"

As Louie started telling me the story, Grandpa grabbed the lamps and lard and mail out of the backseat, and then he and Uncle Chris started pulling the cart toward the cabin.

"Shit, we met *many* years ago—both of us was mushers in a Yukon Quest race. H' saved a fuckin' foot on one of my dogs. Been friends ever since—wetted a lot of hooks together over the years."

I didn't care for Louie's foul language, but I tried to apply the lessons I'd learned when I heard it from the Jorgenson family. No matter how I tried, though, I'd already formed a negative opinion of him. I could tell Louie's right foot was really bothering him.

As we walked along, I got a better view of the wreck in the lake. It was just a few feet from the shore and partially sunk. "Louie, I've never seen an aircraft like that."

"Yeah, she was a beaut—a Lake Sea Fury, LA-270."

"What do you mean 'lake'?"

"Lake's the name of th' company that built 'er—like Cessna or Boeing. Lake built amphibians."

"Ohhh, I get it. Wow. So what happened?"

Rather than answering me, he asked, "You do preflight inspections 'fore you fly?"

"Sure."

"Well, there's a damn good reason why y' should. Th' damn flap connecting rod came loose on m' right flap just 'fore I touched down. If I'd been more fuckin' dili-gent on my walk-arounds, I might have found the problem before it almost fuckin' killed me!"

His language was so offensive, but like Uncle Chris said, I couldn't just "turn him off." "So, is that what happened to your foot?"

"This? Shit no, it was that gawdamn wolverine tha' showed up three days ago. H' almost got me big time."

"A wolverine! For real?"

"Yeah, but I don't wanna have to tell the story more'n once, so I'll wait till back at camp. I had my wreck 'bout two months ago. Just got the damn insurance mess straightened out. They totaled it, so I bought it back from 'em to sell for salvage. Th' engine alone oughta help me make the down payment on a suh-weet Grumman Goose tied up at Lake Hood in Anchorage."

Remember, I had just read an article about the Goose. I asked, "So you're multiengine rated?"

He looked at me like he couldn't believe I knew what a Goose was or even knew what a multiengine rating was.

"How old're you?"

"I'm sixteen."

"Fuck."

I already suspected he was a show-off, *just another type of bully,* so I decided to show off too. "Does it still have radials or has it been converted to turboprops?"

He nervously smiled and said, "Wouldn't own a dam turboprop. Way too expensive to maintain. 'Sides, I can work on my own radials."

I think at this point he was still trying to prove to me he was a big, bad, wooly Alaskan bush pilot—but he really wasn't sure what to think of me. Flatly, he said, "So you know what a radial engine is."

There was a definite tone in his voice, so I decided to end this little game. "Well, I know the difference between a master rod and a cam ring."

He just looked at me for a moment and said, "No shit."

I could tell I had met his challenge. He started walking away.

It took us another minute or two, but we finally made it to a high point between the lake and his camp. What I was looking at reminded me of something a couple of teenage boys might have dreamed up. Two short, ancient, school buses were parked side by side. One had a four-legged tower with a little cabin on top of it. A large tarp stretched between the two buses, making a kind of covered patio.

Caribou antlers hung all over the place, and all kinds of animal pelts were stretched out on frames. Out around the edge of the property, birch poles were nailed to the trees like rails on a giant fence. In most places, the top rail was higher than eight feet above the ground.

The whole place was cluttered with junk. Two trashed-out snowmobiles and a wrecked three-wheel ATV (minus one wheel) were sitting to one side, along with a number of sleds and wagons—or at least parts of them. Barrels and boxes and all kinds of other stuff, most of it looking broken, were scattered around at random. The dog yard had ten or twelve A-frame dog houses. I didn't see any dogs, but from the stink I could tell that dogs had lived there—*this* season.

Then there was what must have been the dump. It was full of plastic garbage sacks and one area that looked like a burn pit. I couldn't believe anyone would trash out such a beautiful piece of Alaska. I tried not to look disgusted, but I definitely didn't like what he had done to the place.

Trying to be polite, I turned to Louie and asked, "What's the tower for?"

"That's m' cache."

Oh, I get it. I'd seen a lot of pictures of old-time trapper's caches—you know, where they store food and ammunition—but this was the first one I'd seen made out of metal.

"Got the thing at a surplus sale in King Salmon."

We walked into camp, and Uncle Chris invited Louie to take a seat and let him examine his foot. They made a sort of examination table with a couple of lawn chairs and some boxes. Uncle Chris took off Louie's boot. Of course, Ammo had to inspect it also. The process was obviously painful.

"Sombitch, Chris! That hurts!"

Uncle Chris finally said, "Well, I think you're right. You've got a lot of soft tissue injury, and my guess is your fifth metatarsal has a hairline fracture. Guess you won't be doing the two-step, Louie."

"Yeah, th' two-step or the gawdamn Cotton-Eye Joe." He looked at me and sort of did a jig in his seat.

"You know, Louie," Uncle Chris said, "I really think you ought to come back with us and get some X-rays."

"Can't, Chris. A team's comin' out in a day 'r two to salvage the engine off the Lake. Gotta be here for that. An' both my damn house dogs are still fuckin' missing. An' 'sides, I 'spect I'm a wanted man in Anchorage."

Uncle Chris and Grandpa chuckled. But I believed him.

"I'll just stay off it," Louie said. "What the fuck'd they do for me in Anchorage, anyway?"

"Well, not much," said Uncle Chris. "They'd probably immobilize it in a temporary cast and tell you to keep it iced and stay off it."

"Well, there you go. I'll jus' soak it in the stream a couple times a day and use m' new crutches."

When Uncle Chris asked if he had anything for the pain, Louie just looked at him and smiled smugly.

Uncle Chris said, "I'll take that as a yes. Well, I'm warning you—it's going to hurt a lot worse before it gets better. And if you don't stay off it, Louie, it won't heal." Then he asked, "Now, tell us—exactly how'd this happen?"

"Well," Louie started, stretching out in his chair, "I was out on my dam trap line most th' day. I'd left th' bus door open, which I don't never do. I came in and was gonna take a nap. I musta walked right passed th' little bastard. I heard somethin' behind me and turned 'round. There was a I-ain't-lyin' wolverine up on m' kitchen counter! M' emergency door in back is blocked by the bed, so only way out was right back passed 'im. I reached for m' featherweight, but I'd took it out on the patio.

"Dam thing growled at me, and I knew that fur was about to fly!"

Louie looked straight at me for a moment and said, "Jus' growled right back at 'im! I grabbed one of my lanterns and threw it at 'im. Then he charged me. I grabbed my other lantern and swung it like a battle axe. It stunned the shit outta the little sombitch and I managed to kick 'im once—but he come right back at me again.

"I hopped over th' top of him. I hit the door and ran 'round front of the bus and headed for the ladder on the back bumper. Almost made it, but th' sneaky fucker just shot under the bus and hit me from behind. We got tangled up, and I fell flat on my dam back. I looked down my legs—he was comin' right at my balls like a Tasmanian Devil. I kicked 'im in the face an' that's when he latched on the outside of my right foot. I got up and hobbled toward the ladder . . . tripped but gotta hold of the bumper. Stood up and actually stepped on his face. Ha!

"I got my left foot on th' ladder and hoisted m'self up on the first rung, but that dam wolverine was still latched on. I started swinging my leg to shake 'im off, but he jus' started shaking back and forth like a damn pit bull. H' almost pulled me off the gawdam ladder—I think that's when he broke my fuckin' foot. I slammed him 'gainst the bumper two times 'fore he finally let go.

"Little mothafucka looked up at me with them evil, beady eyes an' jumped up and 'most got a hold of my *left* foot. He'd a killed me if he'd got a hold of me again. My right foot was on fire, but I climbed up to the roof by hoppin' up each rung on my left foot. I got to the roof and jus' collapsed in a heap.

"That's when the little sombitch laid siege to the dam bus. He'd prowl 'round it growlin' at me. I pulled off my boot and took a gander at my foot. Didn't break the skin, but it hurt like hell! Three hours later that beast still had me trapped. I needed a plan—thought if I could lower myself down the roof hatch, maybe I could make for my featherweight lyin' in plain sight on the patio table an' shoot 'im.

"Like he knew what I was thinkin', th' bastard went back inside the bus and looked up at me through the hatch. Th' little bastard got so fuckin' mad, h' started tearing up my stuff. Ripped up my bed and some of my clothes—and my new Redwings! Then he started in on the kitchen. Ever'time he heard me moving 'round, the little shit came boltin' out the door again. He'd look up at me an' snarl an' snap his jaws together. Jus' no way I was ever gonna get my featherweight.

"Then he found my can of lard and knocked it off the dam counter—got the lid off and jus' went right into the can, head first. That's when I remembered my old .22 single shot, up in the cache. Dam hard climbin' that ladder 'cause it wasn't bolted down at top or bottom. Comin' back down was even harder'n going up. 'Most fell twicest.

"Once I got down, I went over to the roof hatch an' looked down. He was completely ignorin' me—still head first in the lard can. I drew a bead on the sombitch, an' shot 'im right through the can. Never even squealed!"

Louie pointed to a skin stretched on a birch frame. "That's him over there."

I went over and examined it. It was beautiful yet frightening at the same time. Ammo had followed me and spent a whole lot of time sniffing the as-yet-untanned pelt.

"We hate to eat and run, Louie," Uncle Chris said, "but we need to eat and run. Where're the fish?"

"Down in the creek—still on the hoof." Louie grinned and then sniffed hard, cleared his throat, and spit.

"Dad, would you help Louie fire up the grill?"

Grandpa said, "I'll get it done or bust a trace trying."

Whatever that means.

Just then I heard a pilot talking on a radio. I looked toward the back of the patio and saw several radios stacked on top of a fifty-five-gallon barrel. When I asked Louie about them, he said he'd taken all the avionics out of the Lake. He'd hooked up one of the com radios to a battery, along with a police scanner.

When Uncle Chris stood up, I asked if he needed any help. He said, "Yeah, why don't you and Ammo come along?" As we walked down to the creek, he told me I was about to get a real Alaskan treat. "We're going to grab the fish right out of the water. We'll clean them and cook them minutes later. It doesn't get any fresher than that."

When we got down to the creek, I saw an old snow fence stretched completely across the stream. It had a chute that fish were forced to swim through, with a gate at both ends. Some fish were trapped inside the chute, between the two gates. I asked what I was looking at.

"It's called a fish weir. The natives fished this way forever. Now it's illegal even for the natives."

"So how does Louie get away with it?"

"Now you know why he has a police scanner and is so paranoid about radio communications—or at least *one* reason why."

Right next to the riverbank I saw a cleaning plank with a fillet knife stuck in the wood. Uncle Chris pointed to a fish net. I grabbed it and netted the first fish. When I swung it up out of the chute, Uncle Chris reached into the net and grabbed it by sticking his thumb right in the fish's mouth.

Ammo was definitely aware of what was going on. He stood at attention with his tail wagging, and then he barked when Uncle Chris set the fish on the board and cut off its head. Uncle Chris tossed the head high into the air; Ammo leaped up and caught it. Then he started tossing the head around like it was a toy.

Uncle Chris quickly slit the fish's belly, gutted it in a couple of quick motions, cut off the tail, and then finished by butterflying it.

"What kind of fish is this?"

"Silver salmon."

It took about fifteen minutes for us to get back to camp with six fish. Uncle Chris said, "Louie, I cleaned enough fish for tomorrow's breakfast too."

He handed the cleaned fish to Grandpa, who laid them directly on the grill, skin side down. After about ten minutes, Grandpa took a spatula and separated the meat from the skin, which stayed stuck to the grill. He flipped the meat over and laid it back down on the now curled-up skin.

"Don't overcook them, Dad," Uncle Chris warned.

"I know how to cook the danged fish," Grandpa said, feigning anger.

Louie seemed to enjoy the exchange.

Ammo came up from the creek carrying a new fish head. He lay a respectable distance from us and started picking the meat off the skull. Uncle Chris started singing a little jingle, "Fish heads, fish heads, roly-poly fish heads." Louie chimed in and sang, "Fish heads, fish heads, eat 'em up, yum."

I turned to Louie and asked, "How did you get the buses out here without any roads?"

"Shit, girl, there's roads ever'where."

I just looked at him.

Smiling, he said, "In wintertime, all the creeks an' streams an' rivers an' lakes—freeze over hard as concrete. Two an' a half years ago, I leased an ol' D4 Caterpillar tractor and hooked ever'thing up into a cat-train. Chained the buses together an' hooked the wanigan to the back."

"A wanigan?"

"Sorry—a cabin on skids."

I was still confused and he said, "That shed over there—just a giant sled with a shed on top. I pulled the whole contraption out here on ice."

Just then Grandpa passed me my plate. He said, "Eat it now, while it's hot." I wasn't sure if I was supposed to ask for bread or potatoes or vegetables—no one offered anything. I looked around for some salt or lemon or butter or something—but nothing! There wasn't even any silverware around. So I waited and watched.

Uncle Chris said, "Summer Rose, if it has fins or feathers you can just use your fingers—so says Emily Post."

Within minutes, we were all eating the fish—just fish. None of them said a word—just ate fish—and so did I. The flesh was much moister than any fish I'd ever eaten from the grocery store or at school. I can honestly say it was the most delicious thing I'd ever eaten.

Louie leaned toward me and said, "D'you know that there're men who scrimp and save their whole fuckin' lives to do this just once. An' consider themselves lucky for the opportunity." He paused and then said, "This is how I *live*, how I *make* my livin'. I jus' sold th' last of my dog salmon."

"Dog salmon?" I asked.

Louie had just taken a mouthful, so Grandpa said, "They are actually called chum. There are five species of Pacific salmon, each with its own distinct flavor. Most Alaskans agree chum is the least flavorful, so it's frequently dried and used as food for sled dogs."

Uncle Chris said, "He hangs the fish to dry on those rails over there."

"So where are your dogs, Louie?"

"After I wrecked the Lake I had to sell 'em to cover my operatin' ex-penses.

"If it ain't fishin', it's caribou or sheep hunting—an' sometimes a bear," Louie said. "During the off-season, I pan for a little gold or trap furs. I live out here 'bout seven months a year. Greatest place on Earth." He looked over at the grill and said to Uncle Chris, "Thought you said there'd be some leftovers." Uncle Chris just shrugged and ate the last of his second helping.

"I sure could use a bite of raspberry jam," Grandpa said.

I didn't know why he wanted it, but I offered to get it and asked Louie where it was.

"In the kitchen somewhere, if the wolverine didn't eat it too."

I hopped up and headed for the bus on the left, the one that served as living quarters. I was shocked at what I saw *and* what I smelled. The place was a disaster. I couldn't believe anyone could live that way! It was obvious the wolverine hadn't made all the mess. The smell alone was enough to convince me of that—a mixture of a dirty locker room, wet dog, fish, and lamp fuel.

I went into the kitchen and looked around for the jam. I just wanted to find it and get out of there! I moved a few things around on the counter and in the cabinets. That's when I saw the pictures . . . pornography! Not exactly what I imagine kiddy-porn to be, but I'm fairly certain the people in the pictures weren't adults. I froze in place. Honestly, I couldn't even move. My eyes scanned the scattered stack of photos. I saw things I'd never even imagined.

Finally, my feet started to move. As I backed out of the bus, I almost knocked the jam jar off the counter. I grabbed it just before jumping down the steps to the ground. Heading straight for Grandpa, I stood as close as I could get behind him and handed him the jar. I didn't look at Louie, but Uncle Chris saw the look on my face.

He smiled and said, "Louie should've told you it's the maid's week off."

Grandpa just chuckled as he opened the jar. He stuck his knife in and pulled out a gob of jam, carefully putting the knife-full into his mouth. I watched as he swished it around in his mouth. Then he dipped his knife again and held it up for me. I cupped his hand with mine and carefully guided the knife into my mouth. "Don't swallow it," he said. "Just let it melt all over your mouth."

Grandpa handed the jar to Uncle Chris, who got a gob and then passed the jar to Louie. I didn't look, but I assumed he had some too.

It took a moment, but slowly some magic chemistry started happening in my mouth. It doesn't matter what fish you eat, there's always some sort of fishy aftertaste. Silver salmon is no different. It's not a bad taste, but it's still fishy. The raspberry jam somehow changed that aftertaste—making it neither fishy nor sickeningly sweet. It was absolutely delightful. The flavor lingered long after I finally swallowed.

The three men sank back into their seats and closed their eyes as they enjoyed the jam. I guess I didn't understand how seriously they took the "jam 'n' salmon" thing, because I made the mistake of suggesting to Grandpa that it was getting late. He just held up his hand and said, "Hush, girl. Not while we're enjoying the jam."

I'm not sure if it was because of the tension I was feeling about Louie or what, but Grandpa's dismissal made me angry. I looked down at Ammo and slapped my leg. He got up and came over to me with a new fish head in his mouth. I reached down, got hold of his collar, and walked him away from the camp. I ran for a little way, with Ammo following along.

Making it up the rise between the camp and the lake, I sat down to wait and watched the men below. They all still seemed to be drugged by the jam. I realized I could still taste that wonderful slightly sweet flavor in my mouth, and I kept finding those little raspberry seeds.

I took a pee break behind some trees, and when I came out, the men had begun to stir. Grandpa looked around and saw me. I motioned for him to come join me, but he didn't respond. About five minutes later, he and Uncle Chris headed toward me. To my relief, Louie remained in camp. As I watched them get closer, I suddenly realized I'd left my sunglasses there.

I started walking toward Grandpa and Uncle Chris, and when I got to them, I asked if they would please go back with me for my glasses. After all, they weren't just drugstore sunglasses, they were expensive aviator glasses Stephen Nephi had bought for me! To my great disappointment, they refused. Grandpa told me to hurry, and they continued on toward the plane, leaving me standing there by myself.

I just gritted my teeth and marched back to camp. When I got to the patio, I found Louie still sitting in his chair. I didn't say anything, just looked around for my glasses. Then I saw Louie spinning them around in one of his hands. When I said thanks and asked for them, he just smiled and laid them on the table on his far side, away from me. I asked him for the glasses again, but he just kept smiling at me.

He was really making me mad. I had no desire to play his stupid game. I walked toward him, but he blocked my way by stretching out his legs. I was forced to lean over him to reach the glasses. As I did, he grabbed my arm, pulled me toward him, and started tickling me. I'm not a little kid anymore—what he was doing was wrong! I stood up immediately. I glared at him, but he just kept smiling. I was furious.

I decided to get my sunglasses, no matter what this bully tried. When I reached over him again, he reached under my shirt and pulled me into his lap. He had one hand still under my shirt when he spanked me—hard!—with his other hand! I jerked away and stood back up. I don't think I had ever been that angry before. He seemed happy to see me so upset. He pushed my glasses even farther away.

I remembered a video I'd watched at school during a PE class. I knew what I had to do. I walked back toward him like I was going to lean over again, but then I stomped hard on his injured foot.

He screamed and fell out of his chair, writhing in pain. I stepped completely over him and grabbed my glasses. When I stepped back over him, I said, "Thanks," put my sunglasses on, and then slowly and deliberately walked out of the camp. I didn't want him to think I was afraid of him.

When I got back to the plane, I was shaking. The guys were already onboard—Uncle Chris and Ammo in the back, Grandpa in the right-hand seat again. The pilot seat was waiting for me. After climbing in, I put on my headset and asked if a preflight inspection had been done.

"Yep," Grandpa said.

Looking out my window, I saw the wreck in the lake and then asked, "Did anyone check the flap actuator rods?" Silence. I hopped out and inspected them both.

Strapping myself back in, I asked everyone if they'd gone pee. Uncle Chris said, "Yeah, all three of us."

I told Grandpa I thought I could get us back home, but I needed my V-speeds.

"What for?" he said. "It's going to take every bit of this beach to get off the ground. When we get there, you'll either have the airspeed or not."

I took a moment to process that, but I just wasn't in the mood. I snapped, "It was a simple question," and snatched the checklist off his lap.

He simply said, "Page four." When I asked if twenty degrees of flaps was right, they both said yes. I ran my before-start checklist, opened my window, and hollered "Clear prop!" I hit the starter, and the engine came to life.

I started to run the before-takeoff check, but Grandpa took it from me. Irritated, I looked at him, and he said, "It's the same checklist you're used to using. Think you can do it without this?"

I thought about it for a moment. "Yes, I can."

I fell back on a little ritual my flight instructor in Utah had taught me, whispering to myself as I go through the steps. Pointing to the fuel selector switch, I whispered, "Set to Both." Pointing to my mixture lever, I whispered, "Full Rich." Grandpa silently touched my prop control. I looked at him and said, "Thanks." Then, pointing to my heading indicator, I whispered, "Set to . . . ?"

Grandpa told me that since I didn't have a runway, I should just set it to my whiskey compass.

I touched my trim wheel and said, "Set for takeoff."

Grandpa reached up and pointed to my head. "Set to fly?"

I angrily said, "Yes."

"Are you? Are you set to fly? You seem a little tense."

I realized I was still wound up pretty tight, so I paused and took a deep cleansing breath. Once again I looked at Grandpa and said, "I've got the airplane." Then I added, "I'd appreciate it if you would follow through on the controls."

"All right."

I got on the radio, identified myself to local traffic, and started to announce my location, when I realized I had no idea where we were. When I asked Grandpa, he just shrugged and waved his hand like a wagon master, in an old cowboy movie.

I released the brakes, and we started rolling. It seemed to take forever, but the tail finally lifted off. I could now see the trees at the end of the beach. I started to pull back on the yoke, but Grandpa calmly said, "Wait." I didn't know why—all I could think of were those trees coming at me.

Finally he said, "Now!"

I pulled back a little, but I felt Grandpa pull his yoke back much farther than I would have. The aircraft just jumped into the sky. We cleared the trees with twenty feet to spare. My airspeed started dropping off real quick.

"Push it over a little."

I lowered the nose a little, and right away my airspeed came back. I brought the flap control up one notch. I watched my airspeed increase and then brought the flaps all the way up.

Looking over at Grandpa and sporting a big grin, I said, "I like it!" Then I looked back at Uncle Chris and said it again. They both grinned back at me.

The aircraft responded very nicely. We had dropped a lot of weight when Uncle Chris had unloaded the supplies back on the beach. I continued my climb out and was about to ask for a vector when Uncle Chris said, "Aren't you going to say good-bye?"

I didn't understand, so he asked Grandpa to show me how it's done.

Grandpa pursed his lips together and did one of those little dry spits to get rid of a raspberry seed and said, "It is my airplane." Looking at me, he said, "Stay on the controls but do not fight me." Then he reemphasized, "I do not want to feel you on the controls."

I nodded and said, "It's your airplane."

Grandpa circled the lake twice as we gained altitude. He told me to make a note of our airspeed and altitude.

We were doing one hundred knots and were at three thousand feet.

Grandpa reduced power back to idle and then did the most graceful descending turn I'd ever experienced. He was headed right for the buses. I pretended to squeeze an imaginary machine gun trigger. I really wanted to see the whole place vaporize. We got lower and lower, and our airspeed got faster and faster. Next, I dropped some imaginary bombs on the place. When I looked at the airspeed indicator, I saw we were in the red arc!

Just when I thought we couldn't pull up in time, Grandpa pulled so hard on his yoke that mine came back into my lap. I could feel G-forces I had only felt before on a theme park ride. Ammo started barking unhappily.

Grandpa just kept the yoke back, and the plane climbed up at an impossible angle. I knew our airspeed was now dropping dangerously low, but Grandpa never touched the throttle. Just when I thought for sure we were going to stall, he kicked the left-rudder pedal hard and turned the yoke to the right.

We did a cartwheel! Suddenly, we were pointed back toward the ground. We just hung there for a second. I looked over my shoulder and saw Ammo floating above his seat. I squealed like the happy, excited girl I usually was. We were headed down toward the camp again. Grandpa did another graceful descending turn over the camp and out over the lake, and then he pulled back on the yoke and climbed until we were well above the lake, where he leveled off again.

"It is your airplane," he said and let go of the controls. "Check your airspeed and altitude."

I grabbed the controls and saw that once again we going one hundred knots per hour and at twenty-five hundred feet. I looked over at Grandpa with my mouth open. He said, "You might want to add some power."

That's when it finally sunk in that we'd just dived and climbed, did an aerobatic maneuver, dived again and climbed again—all without relying on the engine. We were back at our original airspeed but only about five hundred feet lower than when we started! My mind went reeling through my ground-school lessons. "We just traded airspeed for altitude and then altitude for airspeed, didn't we?"

"Yes . . . now would you add some power, please?"

I quickly added power. We'd dropped down almost three hundred feet while I was figuring out what we'd just done. I was speechless. I'm sure my mouth was wide open as I stared at him.

He said, "What!? Did you think I spent the last seven thousand hours shooting touch-and-goes and practicing emergency procedures? Sweetie, you've got sixty hours, but you still have no idea what flying is really about."

I just looked at him for a moment and said, "Uh, yeah!"

He told me to climb to three thousand and to head for the large lake I could see off the nose. This time I managed my own power. I did forget the cowl flaps, but Grandpa took care of that for me.

Uncle Chris asked, "I didn't see Louie, did either of you?"

Grandpa said he hadn't. I just remained silent.

"Grandpa, what was that maneuver you did back there over the camp?"

"That was the most basic aerobatic maneuver you'll learn someday. It's called a Hammerhead Turn. Not exactly an authorized maneuver in the Skywagon, but it could save your life if you ever fly up a blind canyon."

We all got a little quiet as we flew over the big lake. I broke the silence by announcing we had traffic just above us about a mile off our nose. I then called local traffic and asked if anyone had a good local barometric pressure.

A pilot called back and reported that Homer was reporting three-zero-zero-five a half hour ago.

Thanking him, I adjusted my altimeter to the new setting. It was then that I realized my tongue had found another raspberry seed and was working in harmony with my lip to get it free. I also realized that wonderful taste was still in my mouth. Pretty soon I could see a large valley off the nose at the end of the lake. I pointed toward it.

Grandpa shook his head and said, "Not today. That's Lake Clark Pass. If you look off to the right, you can see Mt. St. Augustine way off on the horizon. If we take Lake Clark Pass, we'd miss it."

Uncle Chris said, "There was a midair collision recently in Lake Clark Pass."

"Really? What happened?"

"A Piper Navajo and a Cessna 206 actually clipped each other as they met in the pass," he said. "Both aircraft made it back safely, but the 206 had a messed up float and the Navajo had a pranged rudder and stabilizer. They just didn't see each other until it was too late."

Grandpa said, "You've got to keep your head on a swivel and your eyes outside the cockpit." Then he asked me, "Do you see the volcano?"

"Yes, sir, I do. How tall do you think it is?"

Uncle Chris chimed in. "The last time they measured, it was 4,134 feet tall." We both turned around and looked at him. "More or less. What? It's a hobby of mine."

I climbed to five thousand feet and adjusted my power for cruising. Grandpa complimented me and then reminded me to bring my cowl flaps to full closed.

"Let's both keep our eyes open," he said. "This is a popular place for sightseeing." Grandpa shouted, *"Holy smokes!* Look at your oil pressure!"

I didn't even need to look at the gauge but instead looked straight into Grandpa's eyes. Calmly, I said, "There's nothing wrong with my oil pressure or oil temperature—and my manifold pressure is spot on."

Uncle Chris blasted out a single "Ha!" and clapped his hands one time. I turned around and gave him a grin. Grandpa bowed his head and in his best Yoda voice said, "Learn fast, you do, young Padawan."

It got quiet again. I looked in the back and saw that Ammo had climbed into the luggage compartment, and Uncle Chris was sprawled out on the seats.

"Grandpa, what's a 'featherweight'?

"It's a lightweight .38 or .357 caliber, five-shot revolver. Most guys carry them on their belt, in the small of their back. They're the last line of defense for bears—to use *after* the bear has already got you in a hug."

That was not a pleasant thought. *There are too many bears in this country!*

It got quiet again, and I started thinking about what had happened with Louie. I got a sick feeling in my stomach and tensed up.

Grandpa reached over and pried the fingers of my right hand off the yoke. He looked at me with sincere concern. "You're frowning again. Why are you so tense? Is something wrong?"

I bit my lip and said, "No, Grandpa, I'm fine." I wanted to forget what had happened and I sure didn't feel like talking about it. I just wanted to fly and see the beauty all around me. I guessed it was going to take another half hour to get to the volcano, so I forced myself to think about other things.

"What about you, Grandpa? Are you okay?"

"Yeah, I'm just getting old, that's all."

It didn't take as long to get close to the volcano as I'd thought. After checking for traffic and announcing my intentions over the radio, I flew just to the right of the peak and looked straight down into the crater. What I saw was pretty much what you might expect—a well-defined gravel covered . . . crater. Some thin clouds inside the crater kept me from seeing the very bottom. I was disappointed—I didn't see any lava or even a red glow. I'm not sure what I was expecting see—I mean, I'd never looked into a volcano before.

I looked over at Grandpa. He was looking at me and smiling. "Grandpa, would you take the airplane and do one more pass so I can get a picture?"

"Yah, fur sure, you betcha." I got my picture, took back control of the aircraft, and headed up the inlet. Grandpa pointed out two more volcanoes as we flew by—Iliamna and Redoubt.

Then Grandpa surprised me. He got out a cursed rubber suction cup thingy and covered up my right fuel gauge. Then he asked, "How much fuel do you have in your right tank?"

I realized I had no idea.

"I've been watching you. You haven't looked at your fuel gauges once since we took off."

Suddenly, I ripped off my headset and screamed, "*Yeah, well, why weren't you watching when I went back to get my sunglasses?* I asked you to go back with me! If you or Uncle Chris had been there . . ." I'd said enough. I'd said too much.

Uncle Chris nearly climbed into the front seat. "What happened? Did Louie do something to you?"

"*Yes! He did something to me!*" I shouted. Then I took a few deep breaths and said, "I'm not hurt. But you *should* have been there—both of you. Just forget it, all right. Just forget it. I'm okay."

I could tell I'd shocked Grandpa—and Uncle Chris too. I didn't mean to. I guess I was kind of shocked too—that burst of emotion came from somewhere deep down. I'd hurt Grandpa, and he didn't even know what he'd done—or *not* done. I looked back at Uncle Chris. He had a worried, reflective expression on his face.

I put my headset back on, changed radio frequencies, and got us safely through the control airspace in Anchorage and past Birchwood Airport. Grandpa just sat there silently. When I turned up the Matsu Valley, I gently touched his left hand and asked him to stay with me on the landing. He looked over at me and nodded. Then he started talking again. "If there is any wind, it will be coming down the river, so let's just set up a long final on the sandbar. We already know there are no logs or other debris. Do you see the Suburban?"

"Yeah, I see it." I called local traffic and let them know my intentions and then ran my prelanding checklist from memory.

"Talk to me, Granddaughter."

I said, "This is just like landing at the camp."

"Actually," Grandpa said, "this sandbar is a little longer, but I want wheels on the ground as quickly as you can get them there after we clear the trees."

We talked to each other like student and instructor all the way in. I brought it in like I'd been flying a Skywagon forever. I pivoted the aircraft around on the upriver end of the bar—Grandpa told me to not stop, or we might get stuck—and taxied back to the other end. Once we were at the downriver end, I spun the aircraft around again and lined it up for Uncle Chris.

Uncle Chris said, "It's getting late. I can't stay. I'm just going to fly back to the cabin."

As I started to get out, Grandpa said, "Hobbs meter." I looked back in and checked our time en route, so I could add it to my flight logbook. Grandpa didn't get out right away, so I slid my seat forward, letting Ammo and Uncle Chris get out on my side. Then I went around and stood by the right wheel to watch Grandpa. He managed to get out by himself but stumbled a little with his first couple of steps. He reassured me, saying his leg had just gone to sleep.

Grandpa limped all the way over to the Suburban and asked me to drive home. Before I got into the driver's seat, I gave Uncle Chris a proper ladylike hug and thanked him for a most remarkable day.

We stuck around until Uncle Chris had taken off, and then I drove back home. When we got to the cabin, Grandpa got out of the car just fine and seemed to be okay. He went straight to the kitchen and took out a carton of ice cream and two bowls.

Later, when we said our good-nights, we both knew there were things left unsaid. I cleaned up our ice cream dishes, along with the morning's breakfast mess. Grandpa took his turn in the bathroom first and quietly went to his room.

I headed for the shower. I took off my shirt and stood in front of the mirror as I brushed my teeth. Something caught my eye. There were smears of jam on both cups of my bra—fingerprints—and I hadn't put them there.

As I showered, I thought about the incident with Louie. I hadn't actually been harmed. I didn't feel like I needed counseling or anything. But what Louie had done was wrong. It may not have even been illegal, but he had crossed a boundary. I felt like there needed to be consequences.

CHAPTER 13

A STRANGE CALL IN THE
MIDDLE OF THE NIGHT

A week had passed. I went to church with Grandpa the previous Sunday. I enjoyed meeting some of the kids I knew. Service was okay, but I did not partake of the sacrament. I was still feeling pretty guilty about being so angry at Heavenly Father.

It is amazing how the length of the days changed so rapidly this time of year. Grandpa showed me a graph that showed an eight-minute-a-day change. That is almost an hour every week. Anyway, it was starting to actually get dark at night.

I was woken in the middle of the night by the phone ringing. A few minutes later, I heard Grandpa moving around in the kitchen. It was one o'clock and totally dark outside. Ammo got up and ambled out into the light—he usually liked to stick by Grandpa if something was going on. Covering up my head, I tried to go back to sleep, but before I had a chance I heard the side door open and Grandpa talking to someone. I was kind of groggy, so at first I couldn't figure out whose voice I was hearing. Then I realized it was Sister Baker.

I lay there a few minutes longer until I heard the door close again. Getting out of bed, I shuffled into the kitchen. On the kitchen table, I saw a box and a bunch of knives and other things—rags and rubber gloves and a couple of wash basins. Sister Baker was reaching into the box, pulling out more gloves and a bottle of bleach.

"What's going on, Sister Baker?" I asked sleepily. "Where's Grandpa?"

She smiled at me and said, "Why don't you just call me Cam when we're alone? That's short for Camilla."

I rubbed my eyes. "Okay." Yawning, I asked, "Cam, doesn't anybody sleep in Alaska?"

She chuckled and flashed those deep-green eyes at me. "Sure, we sleep in the winter."

I managed a little laugh. "Really, what's going on?"

"Your grandfather's out in the shed, and your uncle will be here in a few minutes."

"Uncle Chris? Why is Uncle Chris coming over in the middle of the night?"

"He's bringing over a moose."

"A moose?" I asked in a squeaky voice. "What . . . ? Why . . . ?"

Just then Grandpa stepped into the kitchen carrying a chain saw. "Roadkill," he said, laying the chain saw on the kitchen counter. "It looks like you're about to lose another bag of doughnuts." Then he went back outside.

When Cam saw the look on my face, she said, "I'll explain everything, but first, why don't you go freshen up, and I'll make us some cocoa."

I went into the bathroom and looked at myself in the mirror. I was a mess. I brushed my hair and pulled it back with a scrunchie and then swirled some mouthwash and spit it into the sink.

When I walked back into the kitchen, Cam was setting two cups of cocoa on the table. She pointed me to a chair and sat in one across from me. "So, you don't know about the roadkill list?"

I raised my eyebrows and sat there blowing on my hot chocolate.

"Well, where do I start? Let's start with the moose. The problem with moose is they're dumber than a sack of hammers. I've driven up behind a moose on a narrow road, and the silly thing just would just run down the road right in front of my truck. If I honked, it would just run faster. If I stopped, it would run a little farther and then stop and look back at me. When I started moving again, it would start running down the road again!"

I wasn't sure what I was supposed to understand about the moose's behavior. I guess I looked a little stumped.

She said, "A deer would never do that. It would simply run off into the woods."

"Ohhh," I said, finally understanding.

"Moose are so dumb they'll try to outrun a train. They run right down the tracks until the train knocks them ass over tea kettle."

I almost spewed out a snootful of hot chocolate. I was still giggling when Grandpa walked in and said, "I've had this idea for a long time, but no one will listen." He put his fists on his hips. "I think we should tie a telephone pole to the front of train engines. That way we could have moose-kabobs."

I wasn't sure if he was kidding, but then he winked at me, and I started to giggle even harder.

Cam gave Grandpa a look and then said, "August Porter Rockwell, why don't you go out and move your vehicles or something."

I suddenly realized I was again being treated like an adult. Cam and I were sitting in the kitchen drinking hot chocolate and having an adult conversation. I was really beginning to like her.

After Grandpa went back outside, Cam swallowed the last of her hot chocolate and then got up and started working again. She reached into the box and pulled out the funniest-looking tool I'd ever seen. It looked like a cross between a screwdriver, a socket wrench, and a corncob pipe. Walking over to the chain saw, she looked back over her shoulder and said, "You can help out, Summer Rose—would you mix up some bleach water in one of those plastic basins?"

I got up and took a basin to the sink, filled it with water, and poured in about a cup of bleach. Cam started taking the chain saw apart—using just that one funny looking tool—and told me about the roadkill list.

"Because they're so stupid, moose are killed around here pretty frequently. The state of Alaska has a program to prevent the wanton waste of perfectly salvageable meat. Groups like churches and other agencies that help feed people can volunteer to be put on the roadkill list."

Cam started putting pieces of the bar and chain into the bleach water. "When a moose goes down, the Alaska State Troopers or Alaska Railroad dispatchers call the first agency on the list. You have to be fast. You've got to be able to get to the animal within thirty minutes. If the first agency on the list can't get the moose fast enough, they call the next agency. Once an agency gets a moose, they move back to the bottom of the list, in rotation."

Cam dropped the last piece of the chain saw bar into the basin. Wiping her hands on a rag, she lifted her chin toward the pantry and said, "Hey, Summer Rose, get that big jug of cooking oil out of there for me, will you?"

Cam had removed a small lid on the body of the chain saw and was draining the old oil.

"Your Uncle Chris is on the church's rapid response team. He and two other men are out picking up the moose right now. They use Chris's snowmobile trailer with the winch." She shook the saw a couple of times and wiped everything down. "It's taking them a while because the accident happened out on the Park's Highway almost to Honolulu Creek."

"Honolulu Creek? That's funny."

"Yeah, but not as funny as Chicken, Alaska."

I decided not to ask! I handed Cam the jug of cooking oil, and she refilled the tank. Then she asked me to take the parts out of the bleach water, rinse them off, and hand them to her when she asked.

In just a few minutes, Cam had put all the pieces of the saw back together. I watched her closely—it didn't look that hard.

"This is called the tensioner," she said, pointing to a screw on the chain saw. She used the tool to adjust the tension on the chain and showed me how much slack there should be. Then she handed me the tool. "Here, why don't you put the cover back on?"

I finished the job while she dried off her hands and put the jug of cooking oil back into the pantry.

When she came back into the kitchen, I finally had to ask, "What are we doing this for?"

"Oh, we use this saw for fieldstripping the moose when it gets here," Cam said matter-of-factly. "It's never used for anything else. That's why we use cooking oil to lubricate the bar, instead of regular bar oil."

Fieldstripping? I was afraid to ask what that meant, so I didn't.

Just then, three people walked into the house from the front porch, without even knocking or announcing themselves, which kind of surprised me. When they came into the kitchen, I recognized Danny Larkins, a boy I'd met at one of the church dances when we came up Christmas before last.

Danny turned excitedly to the taller man and said, "Hey, Mom and Dad! This is Summer Rose. She's Brother Rockwell's granddaughter."

They smiled and shook my hand, saying, "Hi, Summer Rose!" They said hello to Sister Baker and excused themselves to go out and help Grandpa.

"So, you two know each other," Cam said, raising her eyebrows.

We both said, "Yes, ma'am," at the same time and sort of laughed.

I got butterflies from seeing Danny again. He had such sincere eyes and wavy dark hair. He looked even cuter than I remembered, and taller.

"Hey, Danny, I didn't see you at church last Sunday."

"Yeah, we moved and I attend a different ward, but we still meet in the same building." Then he sort of looked me over and said, "Wow, you've gotten . . . taller!"

That's when I realized I was standing there in my kitten pajamas and fluffy moose slippers! I felt my face getting red. I think Cam realized what was happening because she suggested Danny go outside and help the men.

I muttered, "Excuse me," and hurried into my bedroom.

I was looking through my closet trying to figure out what to wear when Cam came to my door and apologized. "Summer, I'm so sorry! I never thought twice about what you were wearing. I should have told you some of the brothers would be coming in."

"That's okay." I shrugged. "I didn't think of it either until Danny looked at me. I just need to make up for it now!"

"Well, I wouldn't get too fancy if I were you. It's one thirty in the morning. Besides, as soon as the moose gets here, everyone's going to get a little messy. I suggest a sweatshirt and a pair of jeans." Then she closed the door and went back into the kitchen.

I quickly put on a brand new pair of jeans I had bought at the mall in Anchorage last week when Grandpa had an appointment at the VA hospital. I also slipped on my favorite sweat shirt, one with beautiful sparkly designs. After putting on my Adidas, I went to the bathroom and worked on my hair a little more. I took out the scrunchie and brushed my hair down smooth. *Not too bad considering it's the middle of the night.*

When I went back into the kitchen, Cam smiled and shook her head once. "You look beautiful, Summer, but I don't think you understand what's about to happen. Those clothes are *waayyy* too nice for what we'll be doing. Think of it this way . . . what would you wear to work in the garden?"

I definitely didn't like the way this conversation was going. Cam must have sensed this because she said, "Summer Rose, there are two kinds of nice. There's just plain nice and there's 'Alaska nice.' So if you really want to impress that young man out there, you want to look 'Alaska nice' tonight."

"Really?" I asked.

"Really. I raised three daughters. Would you like some help?"

We went into my room and started looking through my closet. Cam pulled out a pair of faded jeans and asked, "What about these?"

"They're kind of tight," I replied.

"Good," she said with a grin and tossed them on the bed. She found an old pink tank top and tossed it on the bed too, and then held up a gray hoody. "Wear this halfway zipped up." She looked around for something else and then said, "I'll be right back."

About thirty seconds later she came back with one of Grandpa's faded blue-denim shirts. "Wear this over the hoody, but don't button it up. Put on your work shoes, and meet me in the bathroom." She closed the door and was gone.

After changing, I checked myself out in the mirror. *Ohhhh, layers—I get it. Why didn't she just say that?* I reached inside the front pockets of the jeans and turned them inside out.

In the bathroom, Cam brushed my hair up into a high ponytail, twisted it into a bun, and pinned it to the top of my head with about a thousand bobby pins. We were at the bathroom mirror with her standing behind me, and I watched her face as she worked. She was really concentrating, and it gave me a chance to see how pretty she was, especially for someone so old.

"Comb," she commanded, smiling at me in the mirror. I handed her the rattail and she started picking at the hair until she got three or four strands to hang in wisps around my face.

"Hairspray," she said, like a doctor asking for an instrument. I slapped it into her hand and repeated, "Hairspray." We both laughed.

"Lip gloss," she snapped.

I held one up and said, "Very, Very Cherry?"

"Nope," she said.

I held up another. "Burnt Sienna."

"Uh-*uh*," and she curled up one side of her lip in mock disgust.

I held up my last one. "Pink Poppy?"

She smiled and said, "*Perfect!* You put it on, and I'll take some of it off." I put it on and pretended to kiss myself in the mirror.

"Turn around." I gave her my best pooch, and she started dabbing at my lips with a tissue. She stepped back and looked me over from top to toe. "Boy! Those jeans *are* tight. Just don't take off your overshirt." We both laughed. "Girl, you look really 'Alaskan nice' now, but what's with the pockets?"

I grinned. "Trust me on that one."

She shrugged and said, "I'll bet the men would really like some hot chocolate about now."

As I watched her walk out of the bathroom, I thought she would make a pretty cool grandma.

Back in the kitchen, Cam got down a giant tea kettle made out of heavy metal like an old-fashioned skillet—but it was shiny, not black. She filled it, and using both hands, put it on the stove.

Just about then Uncle Chris drove up with the moose. Two other cars and a police cruiser showed up too.

"Is something wrong?" I asked Cam.

"No, I don't think so."

We stepped out onto the side porch as Uncle Chris backed the trailer up past us, almost to the shed. The moose took up almost the whole trailer. I noticed that its left front leg was missing and the right front leg was badly broken. I had never been this close to a moose before. I had no idea they were so huge.

Uncle Chris got out and walked up to the porch. "Hi, Sister Baker . . . hey, Summer. You going to help out?"

"Hey, Uncle Chris," I said casually. "Maybe—I'm not sure what I can do."

Sister Baker smiled and said, "Hello, Christian."

Ammo came running from the shed and went around sniffing everybody, begging for pats on the head. Then suddenly he scented the moose. Crouching down, the hair on his back standing up, he growled and started circling the trailer. When he came around and saw the moose's head, he started barking angrily and did little false charges, never getting too close.

Uncle Chris picked up a handful of gravel and tossed it at him. "Go on, git or I will turn you into Ammo Mark two, mod *two*." Ammo slunk away, and I didn't see him outside for the rest of the night.

A state trooper walked up into the light. He was wearing a really nice uniform with a dark-blue Smokey Bear hat. His shirt was light blue and his trousers were like those old-fashioned riding pants—fat on his thighs but skinny below the knees. They were the same color as his hat, with double yellow stripes down the outside seams. His black, high-top boots were the shiniest I'd ever seen. Broad shoulders, a square jaw with just a little cleft in it, and eyes were the same color as his shirt—he was *cute*! No, handsome—brutally handsome.

Uncle Chris said, "Sister Baker, Summer Rose—this is Dudley Do-Right."

The trooper just grinned and said, "It's Tom. Tom Atwater." He took off his hat and nodded to Cam and me. "Ladies."

Then Uncle Chris asked, "Sister Baker, do you know where Dad keeps the authorization letter?"

"Sure," she said. "It's right in here with the other things." She went in and got a letter out of the box on the kitchen table. When she brought it back out and handed it to the trooper, he pulled a long black flashlight out of its holster on his wide belt and casually looked it over. "Thank you, ma'am."

Tom's holster belt creaked as he moved around.

"You're welcome, *Tom*." She emphasized his name and gave Uncle Chris a sideways look. "I don't believe I've seen you before, Tom."

"No, ma'am. I recently moved down from the post in Cantwell."

"Well, it's nice to know you're out there," Cam said. "I'm the third house down over on Yellow Rock Road. I'm a hospice caregiver for an elderly lady who lives with me. Her red sheet is on the side of the refrigerator. Stop in any time to get a drink or whatever."

"Thank you, I'll remember that," he said. "By the way, what is with that yellow rock?"

"It's simple, Tom. The state can't seem to keep the birch trees trimmed, and most of the year, it's really hard to see the road, even if you know where it is. It's kind of hard to tell people how to find the road, so we painted the boulder bright yellow to help people find us."

"Well, that makes sense—thank you." He handed the letter back to Cam, put his hat back on, and said, "If you'll excuse me, ladies, I have to go take a quick look at the operation."

As he walked out back, I smelled his cologne. It was really, really nice. I whispered to Cam, "He called us ladies!"

"Well, we are, aren't we?"

"I guess we are." Then I whispered, "Is he cute or what?"

Cam said, "Yeah, Bing Crosby eyes."

"Who's Bing Crosby?"

She laughed a little and said, "My, you make me feel old." Then she added, "I'll bet Danny is ready for that hot chocolate."

We walked back into the kitchen. The water was almost boiling. Cam went to the pantry and got out a big silver can, the same size as the ones in the school cafeteria. She popped the plastic lid off and started pouring hot chocolate powder into the pot, without using a measuring cup or anything. She poured and stirred and blew and tasted three times before she was satisfied.

Reaching on top of the refrigerator, she got down a big restaurant-style serving tray and then reached in the box and pulled out a bunch of *huge* hot drink cups. She asked me to set about a dozen of them on the serving tray, and then she used both hands to pour chocolate into the cups. She said, "You know, Danny is the captain of the JV football team over at Colony."

"He is?"

"Yes, and the season is just starting."

"Already?"

"Yes, they've got their first game next week. If they don't start in the summer, the weather gets too cold to finish out a full season. And hockey practice starts as soon as the rinks freeze over." Then she asked if I'd like to go to the game.

"With you?"

"Sure. That lunkhead grandfather of yours would never think to take you."

I looked at Cam for a moment then said, "You really like him, don't you?" She looked at me, got a big smile on her face, and said, "It's a little more than 'like.'"

I said, "Really?"

She put her finger to her lips and said, "Shhhhhh . . . girl's secret. He hasn't figured it out yet."

"Boy, he *is* a lunkhead," I said, and promised not to tell.

"Okay, you grab the chain saw," she said, "and I'll carry the chocolate. Lips?" I pooched them out for inspection and she said, "Perfect."

While Uncle Chris's rapid response team was out getting the moose, another team had shown up. Danny and his parents were just the first three to arrive. I said hi to everybody and handed the chain saw to Brother Larkins. Then I grabbed one of the cups and took it over to Tom.

He looked at me with his dreamy eyes and said, "Thank you, Summer Rose," speaking real slow with his deep voice.

As I was talking to Danny, two men spread a giant-sized blue tarp on the ground right behind the trailer. I was in the way, so I stepped closer to the porch, reaching down to straighten out one of its corners. They put a smaller blue tarp on top of the giant one. Uncle Chris got in his truck and backed up until the end of trailer was over the top of the tarps. Several of the men tied a strap around part of the moose and hooked a gasoline-powered winch to the strap. The winch was sort of like a chain saw. The noisy little motor revved up, and the moose started moving. When the moose was almost off the trailer, one of the men hollered, "Hike!"

Uncle Chris jerked the truck forward, and the moose fell onto the tarps. It was lying on its right side with its legs pointed toward the trailer. Uncle Chris got out of the truck with an older blue tarp, handed it to me, and asked me to cover the bed of his trailer with it. He pointed to four bags of kitty litter and asked me to dump one of them out on the tarp.

As I was finishing up, I watched as Danny knelt by the moose's belly. He and his dad were wearing disposable plastic raincoats. He started cutting the moose close to its rib cage. Another man grabbed the moose's head and kind of wrestled it around until it was where he wanted it. He had a knife too. Cam came back with the empty tray and stood next to me.

"What are they doing?" I asked.

"Getting the two choicest pieces of meat—the heart and the tongue."

"Totally gross!" I squealed.

Danny looked up at me, and suddenly I felt silly.

Cam said, "The heart and the tongue really are the best parts of the animal. They always go to whoever does the gutting. This time it's the Larkins family."

I couldn't watch the man working on the head, but I worked up the courage to watch as Danny reached deep into the animal's chest. He was in almost to his shoulder. Brother Larkins was talking to Danny as he worked. Just about a minute later, Danny brought out the heart and handed it to his dad. Brother Larkins handed it to a sister who was also wearing a cheap little raincoat. She quickly carried it over to Uncle Chris's trailer. Leaning over the tarp I'd spread out, she massaged the heart until all the blood had dripped onto the kitty litter.

Another sister had taken the tongue from the man who was butchering the head. She placed it in a large clear plastic sack and then carried it over to the sister with the heart, who put the heart in with the tongue. That sack then went into another sack and was closed with a twist tie. When they finished, there wasn't a drop of blood on the outside bag. They'd done it all without saying a single word to each other.

"Who is that with Sister Larkins?" I asked.

Cam said, "That's sister Gregory." She and her husband just got married a month ago in the Hawaii Temple. Brother Gregory is the one who cut the tongue out."

Brother Gregory had moved to the animal's back and was starting to skin it. Trading places with Danny, Brother Larkins opened up the animal's belly. I noticed the men were working as smoothly as Sister Larkins and Sister Gregory had. No one seemed to be in charge, and no one had to tell anyone else what to do. Several of the other men were standing around, watching.

Cam sent me to get Grandpa's shotgun and the box of shells by the front door. When I brought them to her, I asked, "What are these for?"

"Bear." Then she asked if I knew how to handle a shotgun.

I told her Grandpa had taught me.

"Think you'd like to help fieldstrip the moose?"

"*Ugh*, no . . . I don't think I'm ready for that."

"Well, then, you can earn your keep as the bear guard."

She told me to load six slugs into the receiver and one round of buckshot in the chamber. She watched me closely as I worked all the shells in. "You need to stay alert and always be right here, near the men. You're doing a real job here. If you see a bear, throw the safety and fire the buckshot into the air. Don't wait for someone to tell you to shoot. Chamber a new round and get the gun to one of the adults immediately."

We were both still standing on the porch when Tom walked by. He stopped and told Cam that this was the most organized group of roadkill people he'd ever seen. Touching the brim of his hat, he wished us both a good night. As he walked away, he turned to me and said, "Keep your powder dry." Then he walked off into the night, got into his cruiser, and left. His cologne lingered for a moment or two after he left.

Cam went inside, and I assumed my post.

I watched as Brother Larkins started pulling the steaming pile of guts out onto the smaller tarp. Uncle Chris walked up to the truck with two more bags of kitty litter and poured them out on the wet pile.

Cam came back out and inspected the scene. "Good, they didn't nick the intestines."

"How do you know that?"

She took in a deep, exaggerated breath through her nose. "Smell anything?"

I shook my head.

"That's how I know," she said and walked down the steps to the shed. She said something to Danny, who passed it on to his dad. Brother Larkins turned and looked up at me. He nodded and then went back to work inside the moose.

Pretty soon two men hooked up the straps to the moose's legs and fired up the motorized winch again. Others pushed against the moose's back as they winched the animal over onto its other side. Several men and Sister Gregory then began to skin the moose's left side. I noticed Sister Gregory was dressed "Alaskan nice."

Cam came back up the stairs. I felt a little silly standing there with the shotgun. "Is a bear guard really necessary?"

"Oh, Summer! You have no idea how many hunters have been mauled or killed because a bear smelled a kill. A bear out there has plenty of berries to eat, but he'd never turn down fresh meat. Look at Danny and Brother Larkins, covered in blood. A big brown would just as soon eat Danny instead of that moose—that way he could *play* with his food first. *We* may not be able to smell anything, but if that bear is out there, *he* can smell the kill." She patted my shoulder and went back into the kitchen.

The shotgun was getting heavy, so I rested the butt on the porch rail, leaving the muzzle pointed up. I looked to the east and was able to see the outline of the jagged peaks against the sky, which was just starting to show a hint of light.

After the moose had been rolled over, there was just the pile of guts lying on the smaller tarp. Danny and Brother and Sister Larkins started gathering the corners of the tarp and tying them together. Then they—along with a couple of the men who had been standing around—wrestled the bundle onto Uncle Chris's trailer. I was only a few feet from the trailer, and I caught a strange smell coming from the bundle. It wasn't really stinky, but it was strange, and I didn't like it. That's when I realized *I* would now smell like a fresh kill too. I hoped Grandpa was right about me being too skinny to eat.

I was startled by the sound of the winch firing up. At least, I thought it was the winch, but this time it was the chain saw. Grandpa was about to cut off the animal's head. The neck had been skinned right where the saw cut was to be. The little engine revved, and I looked away.

As soon as the saw was shut off, Brother and Sister Gregory brought the head over to the trailer. They plopped it down next to the bundle of guts. Another bag of litter was poured around the animal's neck. The next thing they brought over was the animal's hide. It had been cut into a number of pieces, but they still struggled with the weight of it. Then the saw started back up again. Pretty soon there were three forelegs lying on top of the hide.

Cam came out with another tray of hot chocolate, and everyone took a break. I sat down on the steps. I crooked the shotgun in my left arm and drank the chocolate with my right hand. Danny came to sit by me.

He told me there are a lot of moose-car collisions in the Anchorage and Mat-Su areas. "When a car hits a moose, it usually totals the car. People in the car can be seriously hurt or killed. The tall moose get knocked off their feet, and their bodies fall onto the car. Trooper Atwater told me two people died in the collision with this moose."

"Oh, no—that's so sad!"

"Yeah, it is. He told me this moose had been injured but wasn't dead, so Tom had to dispatch it with his pistol. The state tries to keep moose off the highway. They've even installed a very high moose fence on the Glenn, between Eagle River and Anchorage."

"Is that what that is? What are those funny-looking breaks in the fence?"

"Moose gates. Those curved bars you see act like tree branches, but they only swing outward, letting moose *off* the highway right-of-way but not letting them *in*. Funny thing is, we go to so much trouble to put up a moose fence, and then we spread salt all over the roads, and the moose come down to lick the salt. They're a lot like giraffes—they have a real hard time touching the ground with their mouths, so they have to kneel down on their front knees. When a car comes around the corner, the moose can't get up off its knees and out of the way before the car hits it.

"There are a lot of moose-train collisions also. The moose use the tracks to get around, because there is no deep snow on the tracks. They'll try to outrun the train when it comes along instead of just stepping off the tracks. You know, I have an idea! They should put a telephone pole on the front of the train; that way they could—"

I interrupted and said, "Make moose kabobs."

Danny looked up at me and said, "I see you've heard that one before."

Uncle Chris walked up and announced he was ready to leave. Cleaning his hands with some wipes Cam had set on the porch rail, he said good night to everyone and got into his truck like he had just been to the grocery store. He hadn't done any butchering, so he wasn't bloody. This was a totally new experience for me, but obviously they'd become quite used to this kind of thing.

Uncle Chris stuck a hand out of his window and waved at no one in particular. I watched as he drove out of the driveway, pulling the trailer load of guts and stuff.

I guess I'd never actually watched the sun come up before. I was surprised at how quickly the sky changed colors. I could now clearly see the Chugach Mountains, including Pioneer Peak, to the south of us. The Talkeetnas, to our north, were still just silhouettes against the now-pinkening sky. There was a wispy layer of fog on the lake.

Looking down at the shotgun, I realized it was wet and so were the porch railings. A dew had settled onto everything. *Wow!* I'd gotten up on a lot of mornings and seen the dew already on the grass and porch rails and the windshield of a car. I guess I'd never thought about the process that put it there. I decided I would have to look that up when I had time.

Two more people left, saying good night to me as they walked down the drive. I was amazed at how "not bloody" everyone was, except for the two butchers.

The Larkins removed and bagged their raincoats, along with any outer clothing that might have blood on it. Sister Larkins tied up the bag and took it along with the sack with the heart and tongue over to their car. Then she, Danny, and Mr. Larkins walked inside the cabin.

Before long, Grandpa fired up the chain saw again. This time he cut the carcass into quarters. It took several people, but each quarter was hung from the rafters in the shed. They put tarps under the meat and spread the last bag of litter to catch any remaining blood. When the doors were closed, absolutely no trace was left of what had just happened.

Grandpa Gus was limping a lot as he walked toward me.

Just then Tom pulled back into the driveway. He looked surprised. He greeted Grandpa and asked, "Are you done already?"

"Had a good crew. I'll let Summer Rose show you the shed." Grandpa took the shotgun from me and ejected the shells.

When Tom and I walked back to the shed, I opened the doors and he stuck his head in to look around. He again looked surprised and said, "Thanks, Summer Rose. That's all I need."

As I closed the doors again, I asked, "Tom, do you guys have to come out to every one of these?"

"No. But we have a new policy that before the annual letter can be renewed, we need to make sure everything is being done to properly save the meat. Your letter is about to expire."

As we walked in the cabin, everyone was sitting around the table eating bacon and egg sandwiches. Cam had also set up little cups of applesauce sprinkled with cinnamon. She asked, "Tom, what time does your shift end?"

He looked at his watch. "A half hour ago."

Without even asking, she pointed to an empty seat and started frying up a couple more eggs.

A few minutes later, Tom stopped eating long enough to say, "I've been doing this for a while and hunting since I was boy, but I've never seen a more organized and efficient operation."

Grandpa spoke for the group. "Thanks, Tom. That's nice to hear. I'll pass that along at church."

Tom fingered one of the slices of bread from the sandwich and asked, "Is this homemade?"

Cam asked, "Like it?"

"Yes, I do."

Cam said, "I made this batch two days ago."

When he'd finished his applesauce, Tom asked to see the authorization letter again. Cam handed it him, and he applied a little yellow sticky label and signed it. She then took the letter back, slipped it into its sleeve, and dropped it into the box that was now on the floor beside her chair.

Brother Larkins came out of the bathroom, his hair still wet. Danny got up and took his turn in the shower. Again, Cam got up and made another sandwich.

As we all sat there relaxing, Tom asked Grandpa, "Could your church use another moose, right away?"

"Why do you ask?"

"Well, our game troopers have had to take letters away from three different agencies because they had terrible organization. One of them lost an entire carcass because they couldn't get their butchering team together in time. These are good agencies that help feed a lot of folks. They were really disappointed to lose their authorization letters. I'll bet we could put you back at the top of the list if you'd be willing to train them."

"Well, I can speak to the rapid response effort," Grandpa said. "I have at least three complete recovery teams I can count on. I even have a small annual budget for the supplies we use. But you'll also need to talk to Sister Larkins—our Stake Relief Society president. She oversees eight ward Relief Society presidents who are responsible for both the needs assessment in each of our wards and also assembling our butchering crews. Each of those ward presidents also has a budget for the supplies they use."

"Very impressive!" Tom said. "How can I reach her?"

Grandpa pointed across the table.

Sister Larkins waved at Tom and said, "We can always use more meat. I'd say we could handle another moose in three or four days. We still have to butcher and wrap the meat that's out in the shed now."

Tom nodded. "All right then. I'll run it up the flagpole and get back with you, Mrs. Larkins."

I looked out the window and saw the sky had changed from pink to light blue. I could now see details on the Talkeetnas. In two more hours, the sun would be peeking over their tops. The mist was sitting heavy on the lake.

CHAPTER 14

GOOD FOR HELGA

Looking out the window, I noticed a woman walking around the edge of the lake from the direction of Yellow Rock Road. She walked up to the house, came up the porch steps, and just walked in.

Cam turned from the stove and said, "Hi, Judy. What's up? Everybody, this is Judy Marx. She is a hospice aide who is helping me with—" Cam stopped midsentence.

"Cam . . ." Judy said, "Helga died last night. When I went in to wake her for breakfast, she was just lying in bed with the covers tucked around her. She fell asleep and never woke up."

Everyone fell silent for a moment.

Then Cam sucked in a breath and said, "Well, good . . . good for Helga."

Everyone around the table repeated, "Good for Helga."

They were all smiling at each other like they knew a secret. Nobody cried.

Cam turned to me and said, "You'll have to clean things up here, sweetie. I have to go make some calls." She got up and gave Grandpa a kiss on the cheek.

Tom stood and asked if he could be of any help.

Cam said, "No, Tom, there's nothing for you to do. All that was taken care of weeks ago."

Cam and Mrs. Marx walked out and headed back to Cam's house. About halfway to the lake, I saw them take each other by the hand as they walked. Then they stopped by the lake and bowed their heads in prayer. Before long, they started walking again and disappeared from sight.

Danny came out of the bathroom, and the Larkins all excused themselves. Brother Larkins thanked Grandpa for the use of his shed. I caught Danny's eyes and gave him the universal "call me" sign.

Tom thanked everyone for the hospitality.

Grandpa said, "You're welcome." I noticed he didn't get up as he shook hands with Tom.

After everyone left, Grandpa was really having a hard time getting up out of his chair. He told me he was going to go soak his bones as soon as there was enough hot water. I said I'd finish up in the kitchen and take care of the saw and things. He put his hand on my shoulder and without saying anything shuffled down the hall. Later, I heard him close his bedroom door.

I'd washed all the remaining tools and the dishes from breakfast but decided to wait to reassemble the saw until later. I walked over to Cam's house. As I arrived, a funny-looking station wagon was pulling out of the driveway. All the rear and side windows were painted the same silver-gray color as the rest of the car. It didn't have emergency lights and apparently no siren. I realized it was a special car for picking up dead people. I'd never thought about how a dead body gets to the funeral home.

Walking up to Cam's porch, I called out, "Hello?" and walked into the living room. I saw the glider Sister Knudtson had been sitting in during my last visit. Cam and Judy had already stripped and remade the bed in Sister Knudtson's room. They were straightening out the duvet. A small box with some toiletry items sat on top of the dresser. The dresser drawers were neatly left open just a little, in a stair-step fashion. A medium-sized, old-fashioned suitcase and a decorated garment bag were next to the closet door. I realized this was all that was left of Sister Knudtson's possessions.

I asked, "What happens next?"

"Nothing now," Cam said. "All the arrangements have been made. I've done my job. The Relief Society president is going to make the last calls to the family and arrange for chaperones for the body. Judy's taking Helga's things to the thrift store."

Just then, Judy came back in and picked up the garment bag and suitcase, saying, "You need anything else?"

Cam thanked her and said no, and Judy left. It was all so businesslike.

We walked into the kitchen, where I saw the red sheet stuck to the side of the refrigerator. I removed it and handed it to Cam. I watched her drop it into the recycle can.

When the paper disappeared into the can, my eyes began to tear up. "This is really scary, Cam."

She stopped and looked at me and said, "What part is scary, sweetie?"

"I'm not sure. I guess the fact there's nothing left to show another person was here. You could have a houseguest tomorrow, and they wouldn't even know Sister Knudtson had sat in that chair or lived in that room."

"And died in that bed," Cam said, so matter-of-factly.

"Cam, is that what's going to happen when I die?"

"No," she said, putting her arm around my shoulders. "You're just too close to what's happened here. Helga's life was like climbing a very long set of stairs. You only saw her take the last few steps. Hundreds or maybe even thousands of people watched her climbing all those other steps—all but the last couple. She has almost three hundred living descendants and many, many friends who love her so much. She won't be forgotten, and neither will you."

She suggested we go sit on Helga's bed—the bed she'd died in. She stopped in the bathroom and picked up a comb, a brush, and an old-fashioned tin that breath mints had come in. She joined me on the edge of the bed.

"I'm not surprised you have these concerns. Death is a topic that's just not talked about much in our culture. Most young people in America are given a few platitudes about death, but for the most part they're wholly unprepared when a loved one or a family friend or classmate dies. The proof for this is so obvious.

"You've probably seen on the news when something terrible happened to a school child. The first thing the school does is bring in counselors. Counselors are good, but why are they necessary? Why haven't students already learned at home about some of the unhappy aspects of the human condition? I believe the answer is because parents are as poorly prepared for these kinds of tragedies as their kids are. And the grandparents are as poorly prepared as the parents. We all know death is a certainty, yet we Americans, for the most part, are in denial.

"It's a curious thing. Many other cultures treat death so differently, and in my opinion, in much healthier ways. Many cultures celebrate death. Hispanic people even have a holiday for it known as *dia de los muertos*."

I said, "That means day of the dead. We studied about it in Spanish class. It's a big celebration with cake and ice cream."

"That's right. Did you know in Muslim cultures the body is supposed to be buried within twenty-four hours? The Irish throw celebrations called wakes. In the Jewish tradition, close family members grieve by 'sitting shiva' for a week, never leaving the house. When shiva is over, so is the grieving."

She reached out and started pulling the bobby pins from my hair as we talked, stopping just long enough to open the breath mint tin.

I loved the contact—it reminded me of how my mother used to fix my hair when I was much younger.

She continued. "I believe this lack of preparation is because of modern medicine and technologies. We tend to live longer and healthier lives than our great-grandparents did. Our infant mortality rate is low, although higher than in many other developed countries. It's now less than seven in a thousand. In the middle of the last century, that rate was closer to thirty in a thousand. Put another way, these days most of us will not see a young brother or sister die."

I held up the tin, and she put the last of the bobby pins in it. She then took down my ponytail and used her fingers to comb through my hair. I handed her the brush, and she started brushing my hair in long motions followed by a similar stroke with her other hand.

She went on. "Our parents and grandparents and even our great-grandparents live to ripe old ages—the average being older than seventy years. This means the majority of us will not lose a parent until we ourselves are grown adults. And then there's the peaceful nature of our society. We rarely hear about neighbors or friends or family being killed in an enemy or terrorist attack. The same cannot be said about many countries, even some with advanced societies."

I was beginning to understand her line of reasoning and spoke up. "But none of these things change the fact that we're going to die. Right?"

"Right," she said.

Cam really surprised me with what she did next. She reached under the bedspread and pulled out a pillow. She held it out to me and said, "This is the pillow Helga used last night."

I unconsciously leaned away from it.

I think she was expecting that reaction from me. She encouraged me to touch it, saying, "It's just a pillow, Summer Rose. There's nothing scary about it."

With some reluctance, I took the pillow from her and held it in my lap. At first I could only imagine Helga's head lying on it. I think Cam expected that too. She took the pillow and fluffed it up and then laid it back in my lap. Then she turned it into a little lap table by setting the comb and tin on it.

Cam pushed my head forward and began reverse brushing my hair, over the top of my head. She took a moment to caress the back of my neck. Then she said, "Happily, our culture is slowly changing. More and more people are actually preparing themselves to face the death of a dear one. Some, like me, turn to religion. Others approach the matter-of-factness of death using logic, metaphysics, or education. What's important is that, as a society, we're starting to remember that death is part of life."

Then she leaned out of the way, lightly patted my back, and said, "Okay."

I flipped my hair back. She then brushed my hair some more, letting the brush dig deeply into my now tangle-free hair. The bristles felt good on my scalp. She laid the brush on the pillow, and I handed her the comb, which she used to pull down a hank of hair on both of my temples. She tossed the comb down on the pillow and I held up the tin. She pulled out two rubber bands and started braiding the hair above my temples.

I said, "We learn about the Plan of Salvation in Sunday School. It's laid out like a roadmap, so we can see where we came from, why we're here, and where we're going. All of the drawings are of happy babies and happy parents and happy old people. I'm glad I understand all of that, but no one's ever taught us about how painful it might be or how we might feel when someone dies."

She said, "I know."

"Cam, Sister Knudtson's death is the first death I've ever been associated with. I didn't really know her, yet I felt like I was supposed to cry and lock myself in my room and, in general, be in a state of shock."

Cam said, "You mean wailing and gnashing teeth."

"Yeah, and I think I would have, if it weren't for how all of you took the news this morning. You set an example."

Cam pulled the two braids back and brought them together. I held up the tin again, and she pulled out another rubber band. "Each of us knew her death was close, although none of us was expecting her to die this morning. When the news came, we were all happy for her. Because of those Sunday-school lessons, we all knew what happened to her—she'd just traveled a little farther down the road we're all on. I went to a funeral once where one of the adult children of the dead man looked at the coffin and said, 'See you later, Dad.'

"Summer, you need to remember that not all people quietly fall asleep and never wake up. Some people die sudden and horrifically violent deaths. Some people die agonizingly slow and painful deaths. But all deaths leave us with a sense of loss and a desire to understand why they died or when and how they did. And we do feel sorrow. But who are we sorry for? In my own case, I allow myself to feel sorry for those friends and loved ones who were closest to the departed one. But I never feel sorry for the ones who have died.

"I must confess I feel a little twinge of anger when I see someone on the news moaning how they never had a chance to say good-bye or was unable to tell someone they loved them before they died. To me, that's a sign of a life not well lived. I've always made sure that everyone I love knows it. I always give my loved ones sincere farewells when we are forced to be apart."

She gave my shoulders a squeeze and asked me to hand her the pillow.

I stood up and held it out to her.

She looked at me and asked, "What is this?"

I smiled at her and said, "It's just a pillow. Nothing scary."

She put the pillow back in its place and tucked the bedspread neatly around it. "You may be able to survive on three hours of sleep, but I can't. I need to take a nap, but I'd like to read something to you before you leave."

Cam went to her bookcase and pulled out a big volume of William Shakespeare's plays. After laying it on top of the case, she took only a minute to find what she was looking for. She said, "Old Bill here has given me an example on how to prepare for death. In Act V, Scene I of *Julius Caesar*, two soldiers—Cassius and Brutus—are about to ride into battle, not knowing if either of them would survive. They turn to each other, and Brutus says to Cassius—"

"O, that a man might know
The end of this day's business ere it come!
But it sufficeth that the day will end,
And then the end is known. Come, ho! Away!
And whether we shall meet again I know not.
Therefore my everlasting farewell take.
For ever, and for ever, farewell, Cassius!
If we do meet again, why, we shall smile;
If not, why then this parting was well made."

"Did they survive the battle?" I asked her.

"I won't tell you that—you'll just have to read for yourself!"

Leading me to the door, she said, "Summer Rose, I'm sad Helga is gone. I've known her for a lot of years. I saw her walking up some of those stairs I told you about.

"It gets pretty lonesome over here sometimes. I'm really glad you dropped in—you helped me a lot this morning."

She gave me a long hug and then opened the screen door.

I wished her a good night—I mean *good day*—and walked back to the cabin. Ammo met me about halfway, and we walked back together. I thought it was silly to go to bed just when the day was starting. Besides, this was the first time I'd ever stayed up all night, and I wanted to see how long I could stay awake. Ammo and I quietly went into my room and I got out my journal. I had a lot to write about today.

After I finished journaling, we went out to the porch. I opened *Moby Dick* and turned to where Cam had left off at our picnic. I was in Chapter XCVIII. It was called "Stowing Down and Cleaning Up." I was totally blown away by the similarities between the slaughter of the whale and the butchering of the moose. More particularly, the clean up afterward.

> *In the sperm fishery, this is perhaps one of the most remarkable incidents in all of the business of whaling. One day the planks stream with freshets of blood and oil; on the sacred quarterdeck, enormous masses of the whale's head are profanely piled; great rusty casks lie about . . . the smoke from the triworks has besooted all of the bulwarks . . .*

Hands go diligently along the bulwarks, and with buckets
of water and rags restore them to their full tidiness. The
soot is brushed from the lower rigging. All of the numerous
implements which have been in use are likewise faithfully
cleansed and put away. The great hatch is scrubbed and
placed upon the triworks, completely hiding the pots; every
cask is out of sight; all tackles are coiled in unseen nooks, and
when by the combined and simultaneous industry of almost
the entire ship's company, the whole of this conscientious duty
is at last concluded, then the crew themselves proceed to their
own ablutions; shift themselves from top to toe; and finally
issue to the immaculate deck, fresh and all aglow . . .

It was amazing how something that was written more than a century and a half ago could come so close to describing last night and this morning's clean up.

I think I must have fallen asleep shortly after I finished the chapter. About ten o'clock I was awakened when three people I didn't know walked up onto the porch. It was obvious Ammo knew them because he didn't bark and his tail was thumping on the floor. I was starting to figure out how things worked, so I just asked if they'd come about the moose. When they said yes, I told them everything was already cleaned up and put away—and Grandpa was probably still asleep.

It turned out that they were there to cut away the bruised meat to cook up for their sled dogs. They had their own tools and knew where everything was. "No need to wake August," they said.

After they walked out back, I fell back to sleep on the swing. About an hour later, when I heard the three loading up and getting ready to leave, I waved good-bye and then went back to my room and, like, totally crashed.

I slept on and off for the rest of the day. I thought Grandpa was in his room asleep, but around three o'clock I went out to the road to get the mail and saw a note from Grandpa on the bulletin board. It said he had an appointment at the VA and wanted to be alone for a while. That's when I noticed Bubble Truck was gone. I was a little bummed that he hadn't taken me, but then I thought I'd give Danny a call.

CHAPTER 15

AND THEN HE KISSED ME

I didn't have Danny's number—but I *did* know he was named after his dad, and they lived on Knik-Goose Bay Road. I got the phone book and sat down in the big chair next to the living room phone. There it was—D. J. Larkins on Knik-Goose Bay Road. When I called the number, Danny answered.

We talked for about an hour. I let him know Sister Baker and I were coming to the game on Friday. Then he asked if he could come over and visit this evening. I told him I'd enjoy that. After hanging up, I went back and lay across my bed.

About an hour later, I heard Bubble Truck pull up in the drive. I had to smile when I heard the brake pedal go *thunk*. Grandpa came in and knocked at my door, looking really tired. I was awake and dressed, so I patted the bed, and he came in and sat on the edge.

"Sorry, sweetie," he said, "but I don't feel like cooking."

I smiled at him and said, "Pizza?"

He smiled back and said, "All righty then."

When I told Grandpa about Danny wanting to come over, he slapped the bed and said that would work out great, since he'd already planned on asking Cam to come over. "We will get enough pizza for the five of us. You call Danny and tell him seven o'clock. I'll call Cam."

After I called to invite Danny to dinner, I went out on the porch with my e-reader and sat on the swing to read. A few minutes later, Grandpa came out with a bowl of veggie chips.

I knew Grandpa was worn out, but I put my book aside and brought up his promised trip to Lake Eklutna. It had been a while since we'd talked about it, but it was already mid-August. In a few weeks, I'd have to go back to Utah until Dad redeployed and we could move up here. Before he said anything, I could tell by the look on his face that I was really going to have to put some pressure on him.

Then he said, "I do not know, sweetie. I have really not felt well this week. I just do not know if I am up to it."

"Oh, Grandpa, if we don't go soon I might not get to go this year. I'm running out of summer. I can row really well now. I've been practicing all summer on your lake."

"True. I have watched you."

"Grandpa, I'll even load the car," I whined.

He finally said, "Let me sleep on it tonight. We will see how I feel in the morning."

It wasn't the yes I was hoping for, but, unlike many adults, when Grandpa said he'd think on it, he really meant it. It wasn't just a code word for no.

I got up and kissed him on the forehead, picked up the remains of our snack, and went into the house. After rinsing the dishes, I went to my room. Thinking about Danny coming over changed my mood for the better. I put on a long, crushed skirt and a really awesome peasant blouse. I liked what Cam had done to my hair—I just had to fix it up a little, and I put on some more of that Pink Poppy lip gloss. I pretended to kiss the mirror again, only this time I was thinking about Danny.

Grandpa interrupted my fantasy by hollering, *"Tout de suite!"*

It wasn't hard to figure out that was French for "let's go" or "hurry up." I took one last look in the mirror and did the kissy lips one more time. I pointed at the mirror and said with a sultry voice, "And I'll see you later, captain of the football team."

When I stepped out, Grandpa said, "Ohhh, Granddaughter, you look like a hippy chick."

He took me out to the garden and picked some tiny little white flowers and then asked my permission to put them in my hair.

"They're beautiful, Grandpa. What are they?"

"Chamomile. Now you look like a flower child from the sixties."

He looked at his watch and said, "The pizzas are supposed to be ready at six thirty, and I would like to stop at Carr's. We are out of ice cream."

When we got back, Danny was already parked in the drive!

Grandpa said, "Would you take the food in? I need to talk to Danny for a moment, and then I will walk over and get Cam."

I watched through the kitchen window. Danny got out of his car as Grandpa walked over to him.

While they talked, I looked down at Ammo, puffed up as big as I could, and shook my finger at him. In an exaggerated deep voice, I said, "You'd better be a perfect gentleman while I'm gone." Ammo looked up at me and tilted his head to the left. I looked out just in time to see Grandpa heading across the field toward Cam's house.

Danny came in and said, "Grandpa Gus is so cool. He said he and Sister Baker will be back in about fifteen minutes."

Fifteen minutes! Fifteen real minutes totally alone with a boy. Like, totally alone with the captain of the JV football squad! My girlfriends at church back home will just die when they hear this!

Danny walked over to me and took my hands. He really seemed taller from this perspective. We kind of fumbled around until we got our fingers right. Then he spread his long arms out, and my arms went out with his. Taking a little step backward, he looked down into my face. He said, "Hello, Summer Rose. You really look nice this evening."

I don't think either of us knew what to do next, so we just let go of each other's hands.

"And I can't believe how nice you looked last night when you were standing bear guard."

Hmm, "Alaskan nice" worked.

He stuttered a little and said, "What I meant to say was I was glad to see you standing there while I was working on the moose. One of the kids over at Colony got killed last year when he and his dad were field-stripping a caribou. I never thought a girl from Salt Lake would know anything about guns and stuff."

"Grandpa's taught me a lot of things. I've fired several of his guns, including the 12-gauge. I know all about range safety and stuff. Shooting is okay I guess, but I really don't like the shotgun very much." I told him it had left a big bruise on my shoulder. He looked down at the soft part of my right shoulder, just below the collarbone. Then he quickly looked back up at my face, like he'd committed some kind of sin.

We moved to the kitchen table and sat down. He took my hand—just one this time—as we sat there looking at each other.

"I'm sorry," he finally said.

"For what?"

He cleared his throat and said, "You know, for looking at your . . ." He cleared his throat again and said, "That sure is a nice blouse."

I suddenly realized this big jock was putty in my hands. "Why, thank you, Brother Larkins."

He paused for a second and asked, "Can you really fly an airplane? You know, actually drive one?"

"Yes, I can pilot an airplane."

"What's it like, Summer Rose? What's it really like?"

"It's so exciting, and I feel so powerful!" I said. "And there's something else," I said looking down at the table.

"What?" he asked, trying to coax the answer out of me.

"There's something else I just can't explain. Leonardo Da Vinci said, 'For once you have tasted flight, you will walk the earth with your eyes turned skyward, for there you have been and there you will long to return.' That's how I feel."

But this wasn't how I wanted my fifteen minutes alone with the captain of the JV team to be going. We were still holding hands, so I pulled him up off his chair and took him to the front porch. I got kind of really close beside him, so he either had to keep his arm straight down—like a board between us—or put his arm around my shoulder.

"Do you see Pioneer Peak over there?" I asked.

"Sure," he said, and he put his arm around me.

"Well, I've flown around that peak like a bird. I could see Denali and the Knik Arm and Lake Eklutna and the Matanuska Glacier. All from right up there."

"Wow!" He looked down at me and pulled me in a little closer—and I let him. My heart was beating about ninety miles an hour. We both got very quiet. I looked into his eyes and he started to lean in to kiss me when we heard the side screen door slam closed, and Cam shouted, "Grandpa alert!"

Man! I don't know what he and Grandpa talked about earlier, but Danny almost knocked me down as he turned toward the front door. I couldn't believe how close he came to kissing me! He was like an inch away.

Turning back to me, he whispered, "I'll go in first. You wait a minute." He looked like the kid who got caught with his hand in the cookie jar. Opening the door, he went inside and cheerfully said, "Hello, Sister Baker."

It was going to take me more than a minute to come back to Earth. My heart still racing, I sat down on the swing. I wanted to let the whole "almost kiss" event burn itself into my memory. I didn't ever want to forget that feeling.

Cam opened the screen door and peeked out. She had this great big smile spread across her face. She knew! I don't know how, but she knew! She looked at me and paused for a moment and said, almost to herself, "August was right."

She raised her eyebrows, pooched her lips, and pointed at her mouth. We were, like, somehow totally communicating. I shook my head and held up my thumb and finger, giving her the "so close" sign. She did a silent snap of her fingers and waved me in. I held up one finger letting her know I needed a little more time.

A few moments later, I walked into the cabin and had the most unusual feeling—almost like I was having an out-of-body experience. I became acutely aware of the sounds and smells and even the quality of light in the room. I was very aware of myself—how I was dressed and how I looked as I stood in the kitchen door.

There was pleasant laughter. The food smelled extra delicious. The light seemed to be especially rich and golden. Everything seemed to be in almost slow motion. Cam was serving the pizzas. Danny was rubbing Ammo's ears. Grandpa was sitting at the head of the table, looking content. The room was filled with a remarkable peace and quiet joy. There was sense that all was right. It was if my brain was saying, *Remember . . . remember this night.*

Cam opened another pie and said "EBA . . . I believe that's yours, Summer Rose."

I stepped into the room, and as I did the magic dissolved. Everything returned to normal.

Danny asked, "What's an EBA?"

Grandpa looked at him with a fake expression of disbelief and said, "Everything but anchovies!" We all laughed.

The evening was a blast. When we'd finished eating, Cam and I cleaned up the mess and Grandpa got out a game of Balderdash. To our surprise, Cam was clearly the best liar in the room. She got us all with the word "zeteties," convincing us all that it was the scientific name for bees' knees.

After about an hour of playing, Grandpa asked Danny to join him in the kitchen. Pretty soon they came out with four bowls of ice cream. Danny served me and started to sit. Grandpa stopped him and suggested he take me out to the porch. My heart started pounding again.

Danny stepped up to me and asked, "Would you like to go outside?"

I didn't answer but just got up.

We walked out to the porch, and I sat down in the center of the swing so Danny would have to sit close to me no matter which side he chose. He handed me a bowl and sat down on my left. Then he looked in the window and switched to my right side. Leaning forward, I looked in the window. I could just barely see Grandpa at the table. I realized neither he nor Cam could see us if we sat back in the swing.

We sat there eating our ice cream. We talked and talked, but Danny didn't try to kiss me again. I was going crazy! I wanted him to kiss me so bad! I snuggled up closer, but then I couldn't see his face. He finally readjusted his position so he could put his arm around me. When his hand touched my arm, he could feel my goose bumps. Like a gentleman, he asked if I wanted a sweater.

I kind of did, but I didn't want to break our mood. I leaned forward to look through the window—to check on Grandpa and Cam—and I couldn't believe what I saw! Cam was kneeling in front of Grandpa. She was crying, and Grandpa was holding her head and caressing the back of her neck. I couldn't hear anything they were saying, but I could hear Cam sobbing. I saw Grandpa nodding.

I quickly leaned back and said, "Danny, something's wrong with Sister Baker!"

He leaned forward and peeked in. "Oh, man, I wonder it is."

"I don't know, but I think we should leave them alone."

"I've got an idea," he said. "Dad has an emergency kit in the trunk of our car, with some extra blankets in it. Let's sneak off the porch, get a couple of those blankets, and walk down to the dock."

Suddenly I wasn't thinking about what was going on in the cabin. I slowly leaned forward, got off the swing, and crouched down, waving for Danny to follow me. We tippy-toe-ran out to his car, where he got a blanket out of the trunk and quietly closed it. Then we ran, I mean really *ran*, for the dock. About halfway there, we were laughing.

When we got to the dock, we hopped down into the boat. It rocked back and forth while we tried to get seated. I untied the boat from the dock, and Danny quietly rowed us out to the middle of the lake.

We moved to the back bench and snuggled under the blanket. It wasn't as nice as the swing, but it would have to do. Danny put his arms around me and drew me in close.

He looked at me and just kept looking. It was like he didn't know what to do—or maybe he was afraid to do it. Our church looks down on dating before age eighteen. We understand why—we're not stupid!—but all I wanted was a kiss. Maybe he wanted to ask my permission. Maybe he thought I would be offended or tell his dad or something. So I *carpe'd* some *diem* and whispered, "Kiss me." And he did.

It was a long kiss. I suppose in the history of kisses it wasn't a record breaker, but it was my first kiss, and I'll never forget it. And my bishop would have been happy to know it was *just* a kiss. When we came up for air, I told Danny that was my first kiss.

He said, "Mine too."

He kissed me several more times—and I kissed him a couple more after that.

There was, however, a problem. Sitting in the back of a row boat, there was simply no way to get comfortable. Danny finally had to stand up and straighten his back. When he did, he said, "Summer Rose! Check it out!"

I looked back toward the cabin and was totally blown away. Northern lights! And not just *any* northern nights.

I'd seen them before, and they'd been beautiful—sort of shapeless, wispy clouds that glowed a blue-green color. Sometimes they were easier to see with your peripheral vision than looking straight at them.

But *these* lights must have been what Grandpa called "traffic stoppers." They were *amazing*—mostly red and very bright. They looked like red drapes hanging in the sky. They truly looked like curtains . . . curtains with folds . . . curtains that were blowing in a gentle breeze. Then it was like Tinkerbell flew across the sky splashing color everywhere. A few moments later, the lights calmed down and formed a rope of green light whipping across the sky from horizon to horizon, wriggling like a snake.

Danny and I sat back down on the center bench and watched some more. Even with a blanket around us, I shivered a little from the coolness of the evening. Danny wrapped it tighter around me. We got off balance for a moment, and he shifted around until he got comfortable. Then he put his face close to my ear. I leaned my head toward his face and nuzzled him back. We sat that way for a long time.

Eventually, I saw the side porch light come on. I watched as Cam left and walked by the end of the lake. I couldn't really see her, but she was carrying a flashlight. I don't think she could see us either but we heard her call out, "Danny, your folks called. It's time to go home."

Danny leaned away from me and hollered back, "Yes, ma'am. Have a nice night." Then he asked me how she knew where we were. I said, "I dunno. Kind of spooky, huh?"

"Yeah," he said. "Spooky."

Danny and I kissed a long good-night kiss and then made our way back to the cabin. He walked me to the side door. He hesitated, and we heard Grandpa say, "Good night, Danny."

"Good night, sir." Danny looked at me and squeezed my hand. I told him I'd see him at the game. I stood there until he drove down the driveway. When I went in, Grandpa was already in his room.

The next day was rainy again and kind of chilly. We started the day with our morning breakfast rituals. Later, the two of us saw a movie down in Eagle River, and on the way back we stopped at the Village of Eklutna and saw the spirit houses in the village cemetery.

Grandpa checked his watch and said, "The butchering team should be at the cabin now."

I asked, "Does that mean we have to leave?"

"No. We did our jobs the first night. It's someone else's turn to work."

Then we went to the Palmer Library. Grandpa pulled a copy of *Moby Dick* off the shelf, and we settled down on a big stack of pillows and beanbags in the reading pit. He started to read aloud from where I last left off. I showed him the passage I'd discovered yesterday, and he read it carefully and deliberately.

He said, "That's funny—every time I read this, I find something new."

Grandpa was lying flat on his back like a little kid. Before long a small crowd was gathered around, listening to him read. It was great. We stayed there until about dinnertime.

As we started for home, I asked if he would stop at Carr's for a minute. I went in and bought a box of doughnuts. I showed them to Grandpa when I got back in.

"I was wondering when you were going to pay up." When we got home, Grandpa said he felt like having a meatless dinner.

Wow, I guess Cam is having some sort of influence on him.

He set out some yellow meat potatoes and a turnip. I'd never eaten a turnip until I came to visit Grandpa. We also cut up some grocery store broccoli and cauliflower. Anyway, we boiled the potatoes and the turnip and mashed them together. We steamed the broccoli and cauliflower and sprinkled them across the top of the potato-turnip mash. Of course, it was all covered with cheese—and it was delicious!

After dinner, Grandpa asked if I had ever looked up "epiphany."

"No, I guess I forgot."

"If you go look it up now, I'll finish the dishes."

I hopped up from the table and went into the study. I couldn't find the word in the dictionary. Grandpa must have figured that out, because he hollered, "It's Greek."

Oh yeah, "ph." I found it and saw the definition I was looking for. After studying it for a minute, I realized I'd had several epiphanies.

I went back into the kitchen and told Grandpa.

"Really? I'd like to hear about them. Just give me a few minutes first." Grandpa went into the bathroom but didn't close the door all the way. I heard him open the medicine cabinet and shake out some pills. I knew Grandpa took pills every morning, but I'd never known him to take pills this time of day.

Going into the living room, I arranged wood in the fireplace and lit it. Ammo came over and bumped me. "You want to go out, boy?" But he just lay down and rolled over on his back. "Oh, you want a belly rub."

When Grandpa finally came into the living room, Ammo and I were lying on the floor. We'd been wrestling, and I had him in a bear hug. I slapped the floor three times, saying, "Ding, ding, ding," and then let him up. After Ammo went over by Grandpa, I got up and sat cross-legged on the couch.

Grandpa slowly sank into his chair. Before he was totally settled down, he said, "So, tell me about your epiphanies."

"Well, they both happened in sixth grade. My teacher's name was Mrs. Michaels. She was from New Zealand. It happened at sixth-grade science camp, and she wasn't even talking to me. A parent volunteer had just given us a class on orienteering. After the class, one of my friends ran up to Mrs. Michaels and told her we'd just learned that moss grows on the north side of trees. Mrs. Michaels looked at him and said, with a big smile on her face, 'Only in the Northern Hemisphere.'"

"I'm not sure my friend really heard what she said, but I did. I thought about it for a moment and said, 'Oh, I get it, Mrs. Michaels.' Suddenly I understood the relative motion of the earth and the sun. No one taught it to me. I just came to understand it."

Grandpa smiled. "You said there were others?"

"Well, I can only think of one other right now, and Mrs. Michaels was also responsible for that one. She had a large poster of a picture of Earth, taken from space, tacked up in the corner of our classroom. It stayed up all year. It was printed in a strange way—Earth was upside down, but all of the writing was right-side up. I mean, like the North Pole was at the bottom of the poster, but you didn't have to turn your head upside down to read the words North Pole. Mrs. Michaels had never once commented on it.

"One day our class was working quietly on some assignment. I went up to sharpen my pencil, and I started looking at the poster. I must have stood there long enough that some of my friends noticed and were giggling at me. Mrs. Michaels came over to me and asked if I was all right. I looked up at her with a big smile and said, 'I get it, Mrs. Michaels.'

"That's when I figured out why people don't fall off the bottom of the earth. Gravity doesn't pull you *down*—it pulls you toward the *center*. She just hung up a funny poster, and somewhere inside me was a knowledge that was waiting for me to discover it.

"Grandpa, as near as I can figure, everything else I learned came from an outside source of knowledge. For instance, learning my ABCs was not an epiphany. Someone had to pound that little jingle in my head."

Then Grandpa said, "I'm sure if you tried a little harder you could think of other epiphanies."

His voice was a little stressed, in that Grandpa kind of way. You know what I mean—sort of like when someone says something while they're picking up something heavy. Then he made an "old man" kind of sound, somewhere between a grunt and a puff and a throat-clearing sound.

"Grandpa, are you okay?"

He looked at me for a second without answering, and asked, "Do you have any plans for tomorrow evening?"

"No, nothing planned, but it'd be nice to see Danny or something."

"Well, Cam and I are going to the temple tomorrow. How about we drop you off at the Dimond Mall? You want to call Danny and see if he'd like to go with you? I need to be sure it's okay with his parents."

"Thanks, Grandpa! I'll call right now." I hopped over to the chair by the phone. I turned to Grandpa and started to ask . . .

"Tell him we're leaving this house at exactly seventeen hundred, local. Cam and I need to make the seven o'clock session at the temple." Then he added, "The temple doesn't run on PST—*that's Procrastinator Standard Time.*"

I called Danny and set it up, and then handed the phone to Grandpa so he could clear our plans with the Larkins.

When he got off the phone, Grandpa said, "Cam baked an apple crisp for us. Let's heat some up and eat it *a la mode.*"

We put on our anoraks and ate our desserts on the front porch. It was almost dark. As we sat quietly on the swing, Ammo's radar came on—first, his left ear and then his right moved toward the side of the porch. Grandpa noticed it too. Then Ammo growled a very low growl and gave a quiet "woof" . . . not quite a bark.

Grandpa said, "I think there's moose in the garden!" He leaped to his feet and hollered, "*No! Not Big Bertha!*"

Ammo jumped up from his spot and tried to run on the smooth porch deck. He was like a cartoon dog whose feet were going ninety miles an hour but not getting anywhere. He finally made it to the porch rail and let out an honest bark.

Before I could get off the swing, Grandpa hollered again, "*Not Big Bertha!*" When I got to the rail, I saw a cow moose and twin calves. They were in the garden and headed for one of Grandpa's giant cabbages!

Mother moose with calves can be very dangerous. Grandpa knew this—and so did Ammo. It was against the law to shoot the moose, and you can't just run out to the garden and shoo them away. Ammo kept barking, but he never left the porch. He'd learned his lesson as a puppy. Even though Ammo's bark sounded mean, the moose never even turned around to look at him. The three moose slowly ambled closer to the cabbages.

Grandpa grumbled, "Doggone garden varmints!"

He jumped over to an old wooden box on the porch with a bunch of gardening magazines on top of it. I'd never looked to see what was inside. When he flopped open the lid, magazines went flying everywhere. He reached in and pulled out an old hot chocolate can, which he set on the porch rail. Reaching back into the box, he brought out several bunches of bottle rockets. He opened one package and set them in the can so they sort of leaned toward the garden. Then he grabbed a lighter and hollered at the top of his lungs, "*Not Big Bertha!*"

Then he started lighting the bottle rockets. The first one hissed out of the can and headed for the garden. While it was still high in the air, it whistled and popped—then another and another, and then several at a time.

Grandpa said, "Quick, girl, open another bunch!" I did what Grandpa asked, and he fired another volley of the little rockets into the air.

I hadn't heard so much noise since I arrived in Alaska. The rockets whistled and popped, Ammo barked at the top of his lungs, and of course Grandpa was shouting. The young moose got a little nervous, but mama just kept munching on whatever caught her attention.

Grandpa then reached into the box and pulled out a long string of little firecrackers—hundreds of them all tied together in a string. Lighting the fuse, he dropped them over the rail, where they started going off like little machine guns. While the little firecrackers were still popping, Grandpa reached into the box and grabbed a big firecracker.

"Stay on the porch," Grandpa said as he stepped out into the yard. He laid the big firecracker in the grass and lit the fuse, and then hurried back onto the porch, holding his ears.

KA-BOOM!

"That did it, Grandpa!"

The moose started to trot out of the garden, but they didn't go down one of the neat little paths—they tramped across the garden, three abreast, trampling vegetables and flowers all the way. It was only after the moose were gone that Ammo left the porch, still barking quite courageously.

I saw Grandpa's shoulders slump, and he flatly said, "Let's go take a look. I guess we'll be eating moose stomp soup for a couple of days."

We walked out and examined the garden in the near darkness. There was damage everywhere. I bent over and straightened one of the shepherd's crooks that had been knocked sideways.

Grandpa went to inspect the cabbages. "At least they didn't get Bertha," he said. "It's too late this evening, but I'm going to have to come out here and work early in the morning."

The next morning I was surprised to see Cam making breakfast. She was in what I figured were her gardening clothes. The four of us ate breakfast together. It was a nice change to have another person with us.

After breakfast, I lost track of Cam and Grandpa as I cleaned up the kitchen. When I went back to my room to change into gardening clothes, I spotted them kneeling in prayer beside his bed. I'd seen my parents doing this a thousand times. I was beginning to suspect something was going on, but I wasn't yet sure what it was.

Soon we were all out at the scene of the crime. The garden was a terrible mess. Grandpa gave Cam and me our marching orders. My job was to pick out anything that was obviously destroyed and put it into the mulch boxes. He was going to straighten up anything that had just been bumped around, and Cam was to harvest anything that could not be put back into the ground but was ready to go into Grandpa's famous Moose Stomp Soup.

I noticed they stayed pretty much shoulder to shoulder as they worked. I moved all around the garden to pick out the destroyed plants. In about an hour, the garden was as good as it was going to get. They had collected two washtubs full of broken but edible vegetables. One washtub was full of nothing but the broken pieces of one of Big Bertha's little sisters.

They carried the tubs into the shed and prepared the vegetables to be taken into the kitchen, chopping away everything inedible and using a garden hose to wash away the dirt. When they'd finished, there was another bucket of scraps and bottle rocket sticks to take to the mulch boxes.

Then the real processing started in the kitchen. Cam rewashed the salvaged vegetables, and then sliced, diced, and chopped, putting them into a giant oval-shaped pan she got from the floor of the pantry. It was so big it sat on two burners of the stove.

Cam put water in the pot and started adding the vegetables. For a while I thought it was just going to be a fancy cabbage soup—most of what we had was broken cabbage leaves—until Grandpa got a still unfrozen package of the new moose meat out of the refrigerator. It was wrapped in fresh white paper, marked as stew meat. He cubed it up and seared it in a pan.

I offered to help any way I could, but they were content just working with each other and said they didn't need me. I happily sat at the table reading *Moby Dick*.

When everything was in one pot and under cover, they went out to the front porch. Ammo and I left them alone. About noon, Cam went home, and Grandpa said he was going to get cleaned up for the temple. That meant his Sunday best.

When he came out, he told me he was going to drive over to Cam's house. Ammo and I passed the afternoon quietly until it was time to get ready to go to the mall. I wanted to look "regular" nice for Danny. I picked out another peasant blouse because I knew he liked them. Then I put on a new pair of jeans.

I noticed Grandpa had stripped his bed, and the dirty sheets were piled on the floor.

Grandpa was gone an extra long time, and when he drove back, Cam was with him. She had never looked prettier, and I told her so—and

Grandpa agreed with me. Cam asked me if I'd take a picture of the two of them together.

Hmm . . . I wonder . . .

After picture time, we all went inside. The cabin smelled wonderful. Cam went straight to the kitchen and dished us each a big bowl of soup with a slice of fresh-baked bread. Man! The Moose Stomp Soup was good.

A little later Danny showed up, and the first thing he said was "Wow, something smells delicious!" Sister Baker ladled him a bowl of soup.

An hour later, Cam and Grandpa dropped us off at the theater entrance to the mall, saying they would meet us right here in four hours. Then off they went to the temple.

Danny and I caught a movie and did some shopping, and then we ducked into a photo booth and took pictures of us posing cheek to cheek. Then we met Grandpa and Cam and headed back to the cabin.

After Danny left for home, Grandpa said he was going over to Cam's, telling me and Ammo not to wait up. Handing me a box of one-gallon freezer bags, he asked me to bag up all but one big bowlful of soup and then leave the bags on the counter to cool off.

After they left for Cam's house, I got into some knock-around clothes. I stripped my bed and washed all the linen. I remade both beds and turned down Grandpa's linen. I found a mint and placed it on his pillow, like they do in motels.

It took an hour to get everything done and cleaned up in the kitchen. As I put the big pan back into its place, I looked up and saw the box with all of the stuff for fieldstripping the moose. I thought about Tom's card—which I knew was in the box—and made a decision.

I called him and asked him to come over.

CHAPTER 16

JUST FIFTEEN MINUTES FROM THE REST OF ALASKA

T he next day, Ammo woke me in his usual way. I talked to Ammo for a few minutes and then got up to let him out. Grandpa's door was still open and I saw the mint still lying on his pillow. *What is going on here?*

I was hungry, so I decided to go ahead and make breakfast without Grandpa. I grabbed an orange, a biscuit, and several slices of crisp bacon, and then Ammo and I went out onto the porch. I'd prepared Ammo's breakfast snack. When we reached the porch, he stared at that greasy biscuit like a laser beam—that really cracked me up. When his tail started bumping the floor, I reached down and flicked the biscuit with my finger. It was a pretty sad little flick—the biscuit sort of fell off the swing instead of flying through the air. Ammo had to reach a little to get it, but he gulped it down and gave the usual burp before heading off to the lake.

I was getting impatient for Grandpa to show up. I had big plans. I thought this would be the day we would go to Lake Eklutna. I knew I was going to have to work on him to get him to give in. So I decided to make my own opportunity. I would get everything ready myself! Then he couldn't possibly say no.

I started gathering everything I thought we'd need for the trip. In about twenty minutes I had everything loaded in the boat. Grandpa actually has two boats. There is the flat-bottom boat on the lake and a slightly larger V bottom, which he keeps on a small trailer. It had a small outboard motor hooked to the transom.

I decided to try to hook the trailer up to the Suburban. I'd never done it before, but I'd seen it done several times, so I decided to try it myself. It wasn't as easy as I'd hoped—I tried five times to get the ball and hitch to line up. Once I thought I had it, I cranked the trailer down onto the ball, but it got hung up. The hitch ended up sitting on top of the ball instead of falling into place. I'd seen Uncle Chris get this far and then just kick the trailer to get it to fall onto the ball, but that didn't work for me, so I just stood there.

Suddenly I heard, "Get in the Suburban and put it in reverse. Don't use any gas and let the clutch out slowly." Grandpa had walked up behind me from the direction of Cam's house.

Hey, wait a minute?

I hopped in the front seat and did as Grandpa said. I heard and felt the hitch fall onto the ball and I let out a little, "Woo hoo!"

Grandpa went in the side door without saying anything more. When I went in, I found him sitting at the table. He'd helped himself to some bacon and a biscuit. Without looking up, he asked, "Did Ammo get his biscuit?"

"Yes, sir."

He seemed to be studying his biscuit between bites. "I don't suppose there is any way I can talk you out of this trip?"

My heart sank a little and I fell back on an old technique that most little girls are familiar with. I began to beg. "Grandpa, I've explored every *inch* of your lake. I really, *really* want to explore Lake Eklutna before I have to go back to Utah. I'll do *all* the work. *Pleeeeease?*"

He took a fast cleansing breath through his nose. "Did you hook up the chains and lights?"

I realized he wouldn't have asked if we weren't going. Trying not to sound too excited, I told him I had.

He said, "Give me a few minutes," and then he walked into his room.

I cleaned up after Grandpa and then headed to my room. That is when I saw him kneeling at his bedside.

A few minutes later he came out of his room and seemed to be his old self. "Thank you for changing my bed. When did you do that?"

"Last night."

He paused for a second and then asked, "Are you sure you packed everything?"

"Yes, sir, and I have even written a trip plan for the bulletin board."

"Very nice. I still have a few things I would like to throw together and had better call Cam. Would you get the wool army blanket off the line and the aviator's kit bag that is on the floor in the laundry room?"

I grabbed the things Grandpa asked me to get and dragged them out to the Suburban. "Come on, Ammo!" I yelled. "We're going for a boat ride!" The kit bag was too heavy for me to load so I waited for Grandpa's help. Ammo jumped into the backseat and started sniffing around.

Pretty soon Grandpa came out and we walked around the entire rig, kicking tires and rattling chains. We checked the taillights, and he put the kit bag up into the boat.

"You'll need to crank the jack wheel up higher. It's too low and will drag the first time we go over a dip in the road. We also need to pull the outboard off. There are no motorboats allowed on Lake Eklutna."

"Why?"

"Oh, I don't know, I guess they just want to keep it pristine and it is part of Anchorage's water supply.

Grandpa then got into the driver's seat while I cranked up the wheel. By airplane, Lake Eklutna is just a few minutes away. It is just behind Pioneer Peak. But by car it took almost an hour to get there. When we arrived, Grandpa and I worked as a team to get the boat into the water.

Grandpa seemed to be in more of a hurry than usual. He tossed me my life vest. He already had his on and was about to get in the boat. I looked at him and said, with an exaggerated tone, "Graaaandpa!" He looked at me and I said, "Please come here."

He walked over and asked, "What is it?"

"Look how beautiful," I said.

He looked at me and said, "Yes, it is. You can get used to all this beauty and forget to look."

I spread my arms in a grand gesture and said, "Look at this place!"

He turned to see the entire panorama. He stood beside me and hugged me with his right arm.

We stood there for a moment, and then he said, "You have a long row ahead of you, and there will be plenty of time to see the whole valley from the boat. If we are going to make the back side of the lake, we need to get those oars of yours in the water."

Grandpa and Ammo got in the boat. I grabbed the gunwale of the boat and shoved us off. We all got settled. I grabbed the oars and we were off. It seemed we moved away from the launch site really fast. I mentioned this to Grandpa, and he asked if I had noticed which way the wind was blowing. As a pilot I should have been more aware of things like the wind, but I confessed I hadn't noticed.

Grandpa then told me that, as usual, the wind was blowing in from the northwest, or up the valley. Grandpa explained how the lake and valley breathed throughout the day. He explained that as air warmed during the day, it rose up, or in this case moved up, the valley. Later in the evening, as the air cooled off and became denser, the wind would flow down valley. Grandpa said if things worked as usual we would have following winds going both ways.

As I rowed, Grandpa told me there was a popular trail along the north side of the lake and recommended I steer closer to the south side of the valley. After about an hour I was getting a little tired of rowing and asked if he would take over for a while. He said he would, and we traded places.

The kit bag was in an awkward place, so I moved it around a little. "What's in this thing, anyway?"

He said, "Everything but the kitchen sink. We have a saying up here: 'Anchorage is just fifteen minutes from the rest of Alaska.'"

"What does that mean?"

"Just that we need to be prepared even though Anchorage is right over that mountain."

Grandpa asked if I had brought any sunscreen.

"I never leave home without it." I smiled broadly at him. "And I have my own bug spray."

He reached down somewhere in his little backpack and found his old camouflage jungle hat. It had an elastic band around it. That band held two little bottles. One was his bug repellent and the other was his sunscreen.

Grandpa asked me which way I wanted to go.

I said, "That way," pointing to an interesting feature I could see on the mountain ahead of us.

Grandpa said, "Aye-aye, sou-sou-east."

As we got closer, I realized what it was. "Grandpa, this valley was carved by a glacier; look at those marks on the side of the mountain!"

It was good to see he seemed to be back to his old self again. Using his pirate's voice, he asked, "Do ye know, missy, what a pirate's favorite vegetable is?"

I giggled and said, "No—what is a pirate's favorite vegetable?"

"It be an arrrrrtichoke."

What a corny joke. But I started laughing. I started having a giggle fit. Grandpa started laughing too. I don't think he was laughing at his own joke; he was laughing at me. Before long he was laughing as hard as me. He could barely get out the next joke.

"Matey, do ye know what is a pirate's favorite pet?"

I started belly laughing because I knew the answer was going to be just as corny. We were both laughing so hard.

He finally got out the answer. "An aarrrrdvark."

It was so stupid but I laughed even harder. I thought I was going to pee in my pants. Grandpa reached in his little backpack and handed me a liter of water. I started to drink and then had another giggle fit. Water squirted out of my nose. Poor Ammo didn't know what was going on. Grandpa started rowing again, and I started to calm down. I watched the scenery go by. It was so beautiful. When I had finally calmed down completely, he did it again.

"Do ye know what a pirate's favorite fast-food restaurant is?"

I started laughing and stomping my feet on the bottom of the boat. I covered my ears and begged him not to tell me.

Instead he shouted out the answer. "Arrrrbys!"

"No more!" I begged. "No more, I have to go pee!"

"Okay," he said, "I promise." I think we laughed for another minute. Even Ammo had figured out we were having fun. He first started licking Grandpa and then would lick me. His tail was wagging and you could see he had on his happy face.

There was a very high peak to our east. Grandpa said that was Bold Peak.

A little farther, the lake bent to the right. Before long I saw the back side of the lake. Grandpa rowed to a place where the lake got really narrow and stowed the oars for a little while.

We were just drifting along when I heard a bird call—at least I thought it was a bird. It sounded like a cross between a coyote and a ghost. "Grandpa, what's making that sound? I've heard the same thing around the cabin."

"It is those loons over there by the edge of the lake."

"Loons?"

"They're a water fowl. Daffy Duck was supposed to be a loon."

I thought about that for a minute and then said, "Ohh, I get it—Looney Tunes."

Grandpa explained that, unlike Daffy, real loons have four distinct calls. He suggested we sit and listen for a minute. We heard two different calls while we drifted slowly toward them.

From a distance, they just looked like any other duck. They were mostly black with a white ring around their necks, paddling around the reeds near the edge of the lake. Then I saw the most amazing thing! Both loons suddenly rose up, started splashing, and then started dancing right across the top of the water! They weren't flying. Their wings were not open—not even a little. They were *dancing*! They moved in a straight line, with their necks bent into a tight S curve.

"Grandpa, how wonderful! Why do they do that?"

"That is a territorial threat. We are probably looking at one male and one female. My guess is their chicks are in that stand of reeds over there, and we have drifted a little too close to them."

"Grandpa, that's the most *amazing* thing I've ever seen."

Grandpa just smiled and said, "You say that a lot up here in Alaska, don't you?"

"Grandpa, look! What is that?" Before he could answer, I shouted, "It's an island!"

Grandpa used his fake pirate's voice and asked, "Where-away, me hearty?"

"Over there, over there!" I hollered.

Grandpa didn't turn around to see. Squinting one eye he asked slowly, "*Where*-away-me-hearty?"

I whispered to myself, "Let's see, let's see . . . right is starboard and left is port." Then I jumped up and shouted, in my best pirate's voice, "Off the starboard bow, Captain!"

He reached into his little backpack and pulled out a newspaper. He rolled it up and looked through it like it was a spy glass. Then he hollered, "Land ho! Missy, ye have discovered an uncharrrrrrted island!" Then he looked down at Ammo and said, "Avast, me Bucko, prepare ye to go ashore."

"Grandpa, it's the most beautiful island I have ever seen," I said gleefully. Then I said that it was the first island I could actually get on. The island was small. It had five little trees and some bushes. It was just big enough for two people and a dog—I mean three pirates. It had a little dirt cliff on one end and a little beach on the other.

"It is tradition, ye know, that the discoverer gets to name the island . . . arrrr." He found a rag in the stern of the boat and tied it to a piece of broken fishing pole, like a little flag.

Grandpa . . . I mean me Capt'n Gus . . . commanded, "Prepare ye to claim this island for king and country—arrrrr." He handed me the flag and then rowed us right up onto the beach.

Using my best pirate voice, I said, "I am Summer Rose the navigator, and I name this island 'Isla de la Rosa'—arrrrrrr." Then I coughed a little. I stepped onto the island and planted the flag.

Capt'n Gus stood up and shouted, "Hip-hip-hooray!" and took me picture. Then he commanded Ammo, "Go to me cabin aft, lad, and break open me chest and bring out the booty. This calls for celebration! Arrrrr." He then reached into his backpack and held up a bag of Oreos and said, "Thank ye, lad."

The three of us explored the whole island. That took about five minutes. We named the little cliff North Head and the little beach South Point. Ammo was running all over the island sniffing and marking every tree and rock. It was kind of funny because Ammo had to pee like a puppy because he only had one front leg. He could not lift a hind leg like an adult dog. (Think about it.)

Finally, we sat down with our feet dangling over North Head. Grandpa and I had some cookies and Ammo got some dried fish treats. All three of us shared milk from a thermos.

Grandpa grabbed a stick, waved it in front of Ammo's face, and then threw it into the lake. Ammo almost knocked me over as he ran past me and jumped off North Head. He splashed into the lake and went swimming for the stick. He got it and then brought it back to me, shaking water all over us.

I did this two more times. On the last time, old Ammo decided not to jump off the cliff. Instead he rolled over on his back and wriggled around. He was making a kind of growling sound, but I could tell it was a happy sound. When he stopped, all three of his feet were up in the air. He just lay there looking at me through his upside-down eyes. Then he sneezed, and his big old dog lips flapped open. It looked like he was smiling. When he got tired of that, he rolled over and started giving himself a bath.

We all got quiet for a few minutes, and then I asked Grandpa if he had any more stories.

"I got a million of 'em. Let's see. I know. Do you remember the Great Goose Chase story?"

"Sure, Grandpa; that was a good one."

"Well, a lot more happened before I got back to the mainland.

"After the *Tiĝlax* picked us up off Amchitka, there were still many projects the scientists had to complete before they could return to Adak. They went to one small island named Buldir. This is one of the islands that never had a fox population. Two volunteers had been camped on this little island for six weeks and would remain for another month. They were surveying the bird population. They needed to be resupplied with food, fuel, and batteries for their radio. The supplies and a few volunteers were brought to the beach.

"Once that was done we headed east. We stopped at the Island of Kiska. This is an island the Japanese occupied during their invasion of America, during World War Two. All of the stuff the Japanese left was still there; even a submarine in a submarine pen.

"Another thing was a dock. This dock is on the National Register of Historic Places. It had been reported that crabbing vessels were illegally using the dock to store their pots. When we pulled into the harbor, a crabber was actually unloading his pots. The director had enforcement powers and he cited the captain of the vessel.

"We had just a short time to tour a little of the island. One of the things that left a great impression on me was a Shinto shrine. We couldn't stay long because the scientists had one more stop to make. That was on the island called Little Tanaga. When we got there, we could not even see the island because the fog was so thick. The *Tiĝlax* could not get too close to the island or it might run aground and get stuck or even sink, but the captain had used his radar to put the ship directly out from the landing beach."

Grandpa explained that the men and women of the shore party had to put on Mustang Suits that would keep them dry if they fell overboard. "The suits are bright red and have lights that will flash automatically if it senses saltwater. There is also a whistle to blow to help searchers find you.

"I got permission to go ashore with the other seven team members. The driver of the Zodiac squared up with the hull of the ship, which would point him in the direction of the beach.

"We climbed over the edge of the *Tiĝlax* and down into the Zodiac. When everything and everyone was secured, the helmsman started the large outboard motor, and we headed off into the fog.

"We traveled into the fog for about two minutes, and then he shut off the engine and told us all to be quiet. He was trying to hear the surf breaking on the beach. He did this twice more. On the third stop everyone heard the surf. The beach was made of large smooth cobbles, and the surf made a thunderous noise when it hit the cobbles.

"We knew we were close to the island even though we still could not see it. The driver told us the plan would be to jump out of the boat as soon as the Zodiac hit the beach. We then had to haul the heavy rubber boat up the beach before the next wave broke and swamped it. If the motor on the Zodiac got swamped, we would have been stuck on the island.

"He started the powerful motor and let it idle. He was watching the swells pass by the boat. He was like a surfer who was 'sitting outside,' waiting to catch the right wave. Suddenly he hollered, 'Here we go!' He revved up the engine and the Zodiac went racing toward the beach, which was still hidden by the fog. The Zodiac was running right behind the swell in front of us.

"Slowly, the shadowy outline of some high cliffs became visible. Then we could see the beach. When the wave broke, it set the Zodiac on the beach. We all jumped out and struggled to pull it up the very steep beach. Everything worked out just like it was supposed to. We had pulled the Zodiac above the surf line before the next big wave came crashing in.

"The scientists did their jobs. When they were finished, we just sat and watched the wonders around us. The melon sized cobbles on the beach were all black and smooth and shiny.

"On those few days when the sun shines in the Aleutians, the water is a beautiful turquoise color, but because of the usual fog, the water seemed to be gray. Since the water and the fog were the same color, we could not see the horizon.

"All of us were in awe of this tiny little part of the world that consisted of a thin sliver of cobble beach in the Bering Sea. Behind and on either side of us the cliffs reached all the way into the fog. In front of us was the thunderous surf that seemed to come out of a mysterious gray void that was neither air nor water. After the waves broke, the water made a sucking sound as it retreated between the cobbles and back out to sea.

"Occasionally, a brightly colored tufted puffin dived down from the cliffs, somewhere up in the fog. Their small little wings seemed to beat as fast as a hummingbird's. The only thing to be heard was the surf and the call of gulls that were circling somewhere above us, in the fog." He said it was a magical place. Then Grandpa stopped talking for a few minutes.

I looked into Grandpa's scratchy face. I could tell he was looking at something far, far away and a long time ago. You could say he was just remembering something, but I think Grandpa could really see that place again. Then he looked at me and said, "Not very many people have ever seen a sight like that, nor likely will. I hope you get to go there someday."

Grandpa took a deep breath and then continued his story. "Getting off the island was even scarier than getting on. The Zodiac pilot gave us the plan. He would sit in the boat and start the motor even before it was in the water. The rest of us were to take up positions on either side of the boat. On his command, everyone had to pull the boat down the beach and into the surf and then jump onboard.

"Everyone was ready and waiting for the command. He watched several waves come crashing onto the beach and then hollered, 'Go, go, go, go, go!' We all did what we were supposed to. The Zodiac was in the water and racing right into the big waves. Just after we pulled the last person onboard, the next wave came rushing right at us, and the Zodiac climbed up the wave just before it broke over the boat.

"It felt like we were climbing straight up the wave, but the boat did not flip over, and no one fell overboard. We had to ride over two more waves before we were safely out of the surf zone."

He continued. "None of us looked back because we were all looking forward into the fog to find the *Tiĝlax*. The driver slowed the boat and took out a pocket-sized air horn. He let go a blast and waited for the reply. The crew aboard the *Tiĝlax* was waiting to hear the horn, and when they did, the captain of the *Tiĝlax* blew a long low blast on his big foghorn. The pilot steered toward the sound, and it did not take long before the ghostly image of the big ship came into view.

"On our last full day out, the sea was very rough. Almost everyone got sick as the ship heaved into giant waves. Everyone had gone below decks to try to sleep through the heavy seas. Even the cook had gone to her cabin after she had made a stack of sandwiches, which were left in the empty galley.

"I didn't get sick and spent most of the day up on the bridge talking to the captain and looking at each beautiful island as they slid by. We saw giant cliffs and waterfalls and several sleeping volcanoes and sea lion rookeries and more orcas and a pod of humpbacks. It was almost like I was getting a private tour of the chain. When things got boring, we would just let the porpoises entertain us.

"By evening, the seas had calmed quite a bit. The smell of steak was coming up from the galley. Nearly everyone came up for another excellent meal. Everyone else had been asleep all day so they stayed up to play cards and watch videos and write in their journals. But I had had a full day, so I went below and climbed into my berth and fell asleep.

"The next morning at breakfast everyone was talking about the exploding volcano. At first I thought they were talking about a movie or something. Then I learned the entire ship's complement had watched the volcano on the Island of Kanaga actively erupting! Kevin, the first mate, was in command of the ship at night, but the show was so amazing he even woke up the captain.

"They talked about the lava and rocks tumbling into the sea. They said the volcano whistled and roared and the lava was pouring down two sides of the island at the same time. There were clouds around the top of the volcanoes, and the lava made it look like the volcano was wearing a glowing red crown. All the red hot lava was reflected in the black sea. They all said it was the most spectacular thing any of them had ever seen.

"But no one had realized I was asleep, below decks. It was a big ship, and everyone must have thought I was someplace else watching the eruption. But I had slept through the whole thing!"

Grandpa then said the next day the *Tiĝlax* was home at its dock on Adak. But he was still a long way from Anchorage. He caught a ride on a Coast Guard C-130. The big cargo plane took him to Kodiak Island. From there he rode a ferry to Seward, on the mainland. The last leg of his journey was made by hitchhiking back to Anchorage. He told me that was a whole other story.

He said, "When I got home I smelled of the sea and had many stories to tell my family." He looked at me and said, "This was is just one of them," and winked at me.

CHAPTER 17

SHIPWRECKED!

I noticed Grandpa had been watching the sky to our east. He seemed a little worried and finally said, "I think we've stayed a little too long. We'd better get back to the cabin." We gathered up everything we'd brought to the island. Grandpa had taught me to take nothing but pictures and leave nothing but footprints whenever in the wild.

I manned the oars as we started back, and I did pretty well for a while—but rowing back was hard work, and I was getting tired again. I realized I had been fighting a slight headwind.

So I stopped rowing in the middle of the lake and asked Grandpa if he'd take over again. I moved to the seat at the stern, and Grandpa moved from the bow to the center bench. Sitting this way, we could see each other's faces.

As I rested I let my mind wander until it finally fell on the pillow mint on Grandpa's bed.

Then I started playing events backward in my head. Grandpa's un-slept-in bed . . . Grandpa coming back from Cam's house early this morning . . . "Don't wait up for me" . . . their trip to the temple last night . . . their bedside companion prayer . . . Cam kneeling in front of him a couple of nights ago.

It had to be. I jumped up and shouted, "Grandpa! Did you get married last night?"

He just smiled and said, "I can't get anything by you, can I?"

"She's my grandmother! Really, Grandpa, no joking, right? Does anyone know?"

Grandpa said, "Yes. No. Just the bishop."

My mom answers me this way when I ask more than one question at a time.

"Grandpa, why haven't you told anybody?"

"We did not want any fuss. We are too old for bridal showers and bachelor parties. We did not want bridesmaids and best men and the whole lot of it."

"But, Grandpa, did she have a wedding dress?"

He smiled and said, "She wore a nice veil."

Then it hit me. This is the first day of their honeymoon, and here he was out on a boating trip with me!

I apologized to him for taking him away from his new bride.

"It's all right, sweetie. Besides, we didn't want anyone to know until we announced it at church on Sunday."

"But, Grandpa, we could have at least invited her to come along with us today."

"That wouldn't have been possible. Someone had to be home to accept our new bed. And she is pretty busy packing."

"*Packing!*"

"Well, you didn't think we were going to live in two houses anymore, did you?"

I squealed with delight. "She's moving in with us?"

He chuckled and asked, "We? Are you staying with us?"

I guess that is really when it hit me. I had to go back to school in Salt Lake City in a little more than a week, and they would really start their new lives together.

"It's funny, Grandpa, when I first got here I felt like I was going to jail. Now Salt Lake City is going to feel like a six-month jail term. Do you realize Cam and I became friends first and then she became my grandmother? How many kids are that lucky? Oh no! What am I going to call her now?"

Grandpa just smiled at my ramblings.

I noticed the lake's surface had become flat and smooth. It was, as they say, smooth as glass—a mirror, reflecting all the mountains and trees around us. It looked just like a jigsaw puzzle picture.

Without my even asking, Grandpa explained, "The wind has gone slack. Before long we should start picking up the down-valley wind." As he rowed, he squinted through one eye, and in his pirate's voice, recited part of a poem—

> "Day after day, day after day
> We stuck, nor breath nor motion
> As idle as a painted ship on a painted ocean
> Water, water everywhere, and all the boards did shrink
> Water, water, everywhere; Nor any drop to drink."

He continued on, but his voice got very quiet. Both eyes were closed, but he seemed to know where he was going. Then his lips stopped moving, and he began pulling harder on the oars.

The lowering sun painted his face, and for the first time I was struck by its ruggedness. You don't normally study a man's face, but his eyes were closed. For the very first time, I noticed—I mean *really noticed*—the age around his eyes. As I examined his face, I noticed the gray in his beard was creeping up to his temples. I'd never paid attention to the hint of gray that was starting to soften the light brown of his thick hair. I watched, as with each pull of the oars the loose skin on his neck tightened and traces of unnamed tendons briefly appeared. Even his beard changed shape slightly, as he tightened his jaw with every stroke.

That's when I noticed the boat was no longer gliding smoothly along but instead moved in spurts as the oars bit more deeply into the water. There seemed to be some urgency in his labor, but his face was calm. I got the impression he was silently praying.

After a few more minutes, I saw some dark clouds coming around either side of Bold Peak. Then I saw something I didn't understand—the surface of the lake was somehow *changing*. Grandpa still had his eyes closed and didn't see it. A little frightened, I said, "Grandpa, look!"

Grandpa opened his eyes and said, "Oh, no!"

I watched as the change came closer and closer. It was a little scary because I didn't know what I was seeing.

"What is it, Grandpa?"

Before he could answer me, a big wind hit us. *That's* what I'd been seeing—the wind coming across the lake. It was like someone turned on a giant fan. One minute it was calm and the water was smooth, and then—*bam!*—the wind hit us and the water got choppy.

Grandpa said, "Damn! I thought it would hold off a bit longer."

"Grandpa, what is it?"

Shouting over the wind, he said, "We call them Chinooks around here. On the coast they call them williwaws."

That word I knew, and it struck me with fear. It was a williwaw that almost killed Ivan and September in Tom Bodett's book called *Williwaw*. It had flipped their boat over.

We'd almost reached the big bend in the lake. If we could just get a little farther the wind would blow us all of the way back to our launch point. But Grandpa suddenly turned the boat around and headed back into the wind and for the north shore.

He was rowing really hard. "Damn! We are going to have to walk the shore trail back to the car. There is a park service cabin about halfway to the parking lot. We will be wet but all right."

Grandpa was rowing as hard as he could, but the wind seemed to be pushing us back toward the south shore and away from the trail. The waves started building up. The ride was getting rough, and water started splashing into the front of the boat.

"I am scared, Grandpa!"

"Just get down low."

Grandpa rowed as hard as he could for about another minute. I heard him grunting with each stroke. Then he hollered at me, "I can't do it. I'm going to have to turn back around again."

The boat almost flipped as he made the turn, but now the wind was at our stern. It wasn't raining, but I was getting wet from the splashing waves. And what was worse was the wind was pushing us away from the big bend in the lake. We were going to get trapped on the back side of the lake. Several times Grandpa tried to tack toward the big bend, but each time he did, the waves splashed over the side. Water sloshed around in the bottom of the boat. I looked at Ammo and saw he was shaking. That didn't make me feel any better.

"Granddaughter, I need you in move to the front of the boat and cover up with the army blanket." He stopped rowing long enough for me to get around him. Then he hollered at me to make sure the bitter end of the rope was tied tightly to the boat. I made sure it was.

Just then the wind ripped the blanket right off me and out of the boat. Grandpa rowed hard for a few more minutes. When we got within ten feet of the shore, he stopped rowing and started to stow the oars. As soon as he stopped rowing, the waves starting coming in over the transom. We were being swamped! The boat bumped against a snag. The bow of the boat was still about five feet from the edge of the lake, but the snag wouldn't allow the boat to run up on the beach.

Grandpa hollered, "Take the backpacks and get out now!"

The boat was sinking fast. I threw the backpacks toward the beach, but they both fell into the water. As I attempted to jump out of the boat, it lurched. I landed feet first but fell to my knees in the shallow water. I still had the bow line in my left hand. I turned around just in time to see the back of the boat go completely under as the bow rode up onto the snag. Rising up, the bow was caught by the wind, causing the boat to twist around and roll over. The rope was ripped right out of my hand. Ammo had already bailed out, but Grandpa was trapped under the boat! I started screaming. Ammo was splashing around and barking his head off.

Grandpa didn't come up right away. In fact, at one point I saw his feet come out of the water like he was trying to dive to the bottom of the lake. He came up and I saw him tear off his life jacket and dive down again. Finally, he popped up, coughing and spitting up water.

He crawled out of the lake, dragging that heavy old aviator's kit bag. The boat didn't completely sink—it was upside down and sort of halfway sunk. The wind was blowing it away from us, but it stayed close to shore as it bumped along. I saw one of the oars floating away faster than the boat.

Grandpa's shirt was torn on the right arm, and he had a bad cut just above his elbow. His arm was, like, totally bloody. He also had a cut on his forehead right above his left eye. He sat at the edge of the water, looking down between his feet as he continued to catch his breath. Ammo was whining and moving around him.

Then Grandpa looked up at me and yelled above the wind, "Are you okay?"

"Yes, sir," I hollered. The wind was gusting so hard, it kept knocking me off balance.

Then he sounded really mad and barked, "Are you sure?"

"Yes, sir! I'm just really cold, and I hurt my ankle getting out of the boat."

"All right, we will take care of you in a minute."

He kept holding his head like he had a headache. His arm was bleeding a lot. He grabbed his arm and squeezed it with his good hand.

"Listen to me! You're going to have to take care of me first."

"All right, but I don't know what to do." I was crying. "Grandpa, I'm really scared!"

Grandpa still sounded mad. "Just listen to me! We are going to be all right."

"Okay," I whimpered.

Then, just as fast as the wind had come upon us, it stopped blowing, but I was absolutely certain it had gotten a lot colder.

Grandpa stopped shouting, but he still sounded upset. "We need to get up a little bit farther from the water."

We were on a cobble beach. About ten feet up, the slope leveled out and was covered with pebbles and sand with some small scrubby trees. The real tree line started just a little farther up. I grabbed both backpacks, and we hobbled over the rocks and climbed up to the flatter sandy shelf. We settled down among some young birch trees that were about my height. Except for the beach directly in front of us, I couldn't see anything. It made a really cool hideout. Stephen Nephi would love it.

Grandpa's eyes looked weird. He said, "We have got to stop this bleeding. And I think I have a concussion. We both also have to get warm, or we will be in real trouble. I want you to come over here with my backpack. Let's see what we have left."

"Yes, sir." I added, "I'm sorry, Grandpa, I didn't mean to . . ."

Suddenly Grandpa threw up! It looked black—I was terrified, until I realized it was the Oreo cookies. He wiped his mouth with his good arm and said angrily, "Stop whining, girl! It was not your fault. It is *my* fault. I knew better than to be out today. I knew the weather was about . . . was about to . . ." Then Grandpa slumped over and fell silent.

"Grandpa, Grandpa!" I went to him and realized he was unconscious. He was soaking wet from head to toe. I started crying and put my arms around him. "What do I do, Ammo?" I sobbed. "I don't know what to do." I hugged Grandpa and prayed.

Then I realized he had already told me almost everything I needed to do. He said we had to stop his bleeding and that he thought he had a concussion and that we needed to get warm. He also told me there was some stuff in the backpack that would help us. I was so scared, but Grandpa was the answer to my prayer. Now I knew what had to be done—but I wasn't sure I could remember how to do it.

Something I'd learned in sixth-grade health class suddenly came to mind—the ABCs of first aid. A stood for airway. I was remembering now! I knew Grandpa was breathing because he was mumbling. B stood for bleeding. Grandpa's arm was bleeding badly. I remembered that a compress is a good way to stop bleeding, if it wasn't arterial. I looked at his arm again and saw the blood wasn't spurting—just coming out in a fast, dark flow.

I had to find some serious bandages. I tore open Grandpa's backpack, but all I saw was a half-eaten bag of cookies and the empty thermos bottle the milk had been in. There were some napkins and toilet paper, but everything was soaking wet.

What? I thought. *There's nothing in here to help me!*

Then I opened *my* backpack. I had my iPod, but it was ruined. I had a lipstick, a candy bar, and a couple of tampons, as well as my address book and a pen with purple ink and a little plastic flower on top. Everything was wet. I got so angry at myself.

Then I remembered the kit bag Grandpa had saved from the sinking boat. It was still down by the water. I went down to get it, and my ankle really hurt as I walked over the cobbles. I started dragging it back up to where Grandpa was—but it was *so heavy*. It took a while, and I hurt my ankle even worse, but I dragged it over close to Grandpa and unzipped it. There was some water on the inside but not a lot.

The first thing I saw was a package of white cotton socks—five pair, still sealed up in the store package. They were still dry! I opened up the package, took one pair, and put them right on the cut. Then I took three more socks and tied them together into a sock rope. I tried to tie it really tight, but one of the knots came undone. When I tried again, it worked. The bleeding stopped.

I went back to the kit bag and found an old army poncho and some green packages called MREs—which I later learned were military rations, and MRE stood for Meals, Ready to Eat. I put the army poncho on right away. Then I saw a small orange backpack on an aluminum frame down at the bottom of the larger kit bag—maybe that was the backpack Grandpa was talking about. I had to wrestle with it, but it finally came out with a bunch of other loose stuff.

When I opened the main flap on the backpack, I saw it was, like, totally full of stuff. Almost everything was sealed in plastic bags. There were two compact flashlights and two-liter bottles of water. I saw a complete change of Grandpa's clothes and a couple of other things, but I didn't know what they were.

I was beginning to shiver, and my toes and fingers were really getting cold. Now I was sure the temperature had dropped way below what it had been before the wind came. Even though I had the poncho on, the wetness from my pant legs was slowly spreading up almost to my waist. But I didn't have time to worry about that now.

I remembered that C of the ABCs stood for control shock. The treatment for shock was to elevate the feet and keep the victim warm. I went down to Grandpa's feet and tried to raise them, but his legs were too heavy, and I didn't have anything to put his feet on anyway. In the classroom, we used a stack of school books—now I thought how stupid that was. That's when I remembered something else about shock—one of the symptoms we were supposed to look for was irritability. *That's why Grandpa had sounded so angry*. It was just another symptom of shock.

I was wasting time. I decided to take off Grandpa's wet clothes and put him in the dry clothes that were smashed flat in one of those vacuum bags. I started with his boots. My fingers were so cold I could barely get them off—he had tied them so tightly. The fact that my hands were shaking didn't help either.

When I finally got his wet socks off, I could see his feet were blue! I started crying again and said, "Oh, Grandpa, what do I do?" I continued to cry as I put a pair of dry socks on his feet. My fingers and toes were starting to sting.

Then I went over to the pile of stuff that I'd dumped out of the kit bag. There was a silver blanket-looking thingy called a space blanket. My hands were now shaking so bad I could barely hold the package steady. On the back was a series of pictures showing a man sitting against a tree with the blanket wrapped around him.

I looked at the rest of the stuff and saw a gun! It was the biggest gun I'd ever seen, much bigger than the guns Grandpa and I had used at the firing range. Like everything else, it was in a sealed bag. *It's for bears!*

It was starting to get dark. The sun was well behind the mountains and thick clouds covered the whole sky. *It must be about eight.*

I remembered that shock could kill a person, and I still had to get Grandpa warm. I tried to take off his shirt, but I found out that changing a man's clothes was not like changing clothes on a Ken doll. I couldn't do it. The shirt was stuck to him like glue and he was too heavy to move. I was sure I could never get his pants off.

Everything I was doing was difficult because my fingers were now almost totally numb, and my ankle was really starting to throb with pain, even when I wasn't standing on it.

When Grandpa had slumped over, he had fallen on his left side—like he was sitting on a chair, only lying on his side. I took the space blanket out of its wrapper and laid it on the ground behind him. Then I went around his other side, and using all my strength, I rolled him over onto the blanket. Now he was lying on his back and just on the edge of the blanket. I had to push him some more to finally get him rolled over onto his right side. He was closer to the middle of the blanket but not quite. I decided to wrap him up like a burrito. The blanket was just big enough to do that, except his feet and head were sticking out.

I was so cold! I realized *I* had to get warm too, so I decided to put on Grandpa's dry clothes. First I took off my wet shoes and socks. My ankle was turning black and blue, and it hurt so bad, even just to touch it. I pulled off my wet pants—funny, I felt warmer as soon as I did—and pulled on Grandpa's pants. My shirt sleeves had gotten wet when I fell out of the boat and my arms were now freezing cold. I still had the life vest on, which I think was helping me stay warm. Taking the poncho off for a minute, I put the spare shirt on right over the vest, like it was a coat—it was big enough. After I slipped the poncho back on, I put on a pair of the socks, but there was no way I could get my shoes back on.

I was a lot warmer—but not warm enough.

Scooting over to the backpack again, I slid right out of the big pants. To hold them on, I had to keep one hand on my pants. This time I found some candy bars and gobbled down two of them. I also found a string of bear bells and some little flat packages of something. My hands were shaking so bad, I could only read the word "Heat." I also found some toilet paper zipped up in a plastic bag. *Thanks, Grandpa.*

I put the one leftover sock on my right hand like a mitten and then stuck both hands inside my pants and curled up next to Grandpa to rest for a few minutes. I called Ammo to come over and got him to lie down by me. I was like a girl sandwich. I started talking to Ammo again, like he was a person. I told him how scared I was, how cold I was, and how my ankle hurt. When I asked him if he would protect us from bears, he rolled his head up and kissed my face.

After about a half hour, I wasn't quite as cold, and I wasn't shaking as bad—but it had started to drizzle. *That's just great.* I got up to checked on Grandpa. I tried to wake him but he just lay there. His face was covered in dried blood that was now running down his face as red-tinted rain. He wasn't moaning anymore, but he'd thrown up again. He was lying on his cut arm, and I noticed there wasn't a pool of blood inside the space blanket, so I knew my sock bandage had worked. Grandpa looked so pale; I knew I still needed to raise his feet.

It was now totally dark, so I had to use one of the flashlights to see what I was doing. Using one hand to hold the light and the other to hold up my pants, I didn't have any way to carry the heavy gun—so I laid it in plain sight near Grandpa, in case I needed to get to it quickly. I didn't feel safe searching in the woods, so I went out on the beach, even though I could barely put any weight on my injured ankle. I shined the light around until I saw the scariest looking tree stump I'd ever seen.

It had washed way up on the beach about twenty yards from our little camp. Four or five hard, gnarly roots stuck out in all directions at the bottom. Four feet of the old trunk remained, about as big around as my arm, and near the end it split into three branches. The whole thing was sort of like a little sawhorse. I figured I could use it to put Grandpa's feet on.

It took all the strength I had—and I lost my pants three times—but I managed to drag the stump up to where Grandpa was. I decided it was probably safe now to put him on his back. Anyway, that was the only way I could elevate his feet. I had to unwrap the burrito and work with just one leg at a time, but I managed to get both of his legs raised a little. After I rewrapped the burrito, I kissed Grandpa's forehead and whispered in his ear that everything was going to be all right.

I was getting tired of my Grandpa pants falling off, so I made a pair of suspenders out of Grandpa's boot laces. I was pretty proud of myself. But my clothes, including my new pants were now, like, totally damp.

Rummaging around in the backpack to see what I might have missed, I found some zippered pockets on the outside that I hadn't opened before. I found more of those packages that said "Heat" and also a silver tube that was a little bigger than a lipstick tube. When I shook it, it rattled, but it didn't have a label, and I couldn't figure out how to open it. (I later found out it was a watertight container with matches inside.) The last pocket held a rolled-up knit hat, a whistle, and a compass. I also knew Grandpa carried a sportsman's knife on his belt.

Since Grandpa's head and feet were still sticking out of the space blanket, I put the knit hat on his head. His hair was still wet, but I figured it might help. I used the flashlight to start reading one of the packages that said "Heat." I couldn't believe it! They were called Red-E-Heat—all I had to do was tear open the plastic wrapper, and they'd get warm all on their own! The instructions said they could be put inside your gloves or shoes or in your pockets, and they'd stay warm for hours!

Grandpa had eight of the packs. I used his knife to open up two and put one in each of his socks. About then it started to rain harder, so I took the two small, empty backpacks and put them over Grandpa's feet, like giant galoshes. I opened another pack of Red-E-Heat and put it inside his knit cap. Then I used the plastic bag the space blanket had come in to make a little tent over Grandpa's head. Next, I opened up the burrito blanket and stuck a heat pack inside his wet shirt and another one in his lap. Finally, I put one in each of his armpits and then closed the space blanket back up.

I was so cold. I only had one pack left and decided to put it inside my sock mitten. The bottoms of my new socks were totally wet and muddy, and I couldn't feel my toes—but at least they didn't hurt anymore. Suddenly, I felt the heat pack getting warm inside my sock mitten. I held it against my ears and my neck, and then I put it inside my shirt—it felt so good. After a while, I put the sock mitten on my other hand.

There didn't appear to be anything else I could do for Grandpa, so I decided it was time to finishing taking care of myself. I took off the army poncho and spread it out right next to Grandpa. I gathered everything up and laid it all in a neat pile on the poncho—MREs, cheese sticks, jerky, two flashlights, a whistle, a compass, and Grandpa's knife. I also had the gun and a pouch of extra bullets. I put the flashlights in my shirt pockets and hung the whistle around my neck. I looked at Ammo and said, "Sorry, boy." Then I shook the kit bag and turned it upside down over me like a sad little tent.

I couldn't get totally inside, so it was more like an umbrella for a troll. But at least Grandpa and I and all our stuff were under cover. I turned on one of the flashlights and leaned back against Grandpa. I heard the rain hitting my makeshift tent. Up until then I'd only worried about first aid and shelter and—oh, yeah, bears. I finally had time to think about our situation.

I knew Grandpa was in bad shape. I *had* to get help for him. I thought about walking along the shore, but then I remembered what the south side of the lake looked like—in a lot of places the mountains came right down to the water. I reached down to rub my ankle, but it hurt too bad to even touch. I used the light to look at it. It was way swollen now, so walking was out of the question.

I thought about the boat but decided it wasn't an option either. Even if I could find it, it was upside down, and I had no idea where the oars were.

Despite the overwhelming cold, I would just have to stay here with Grandpa. Somebody would certainly come looking for us in the morning. I decided to just wait.

Just when I thought we were at least safe for the night, I felt water sneaking under my legs and butt. The poncho was catching the water and bringing it right into my little tent. Within a minute I was actually sitting in a puddle of cold rainwater. I tried to bunch the poncho up. That helped some, but the damage was already done. My Grandpa pants were now soaking wet.

This made me unhappy, but more than that, it made me afraid. There were no more dry clothes, and I was starting to shiver again. And just sitting around being miserable gave me time to start thinking about bears. I reached for the gun. I knew how to handle a gun, but I had no idea how to kill a bear. That's when I thought about featherweight pistols and when they were to be used.

But this was no featherweight. I had a hard time holding it out in front of me. I checked—it was loaded with five rounds. I took out one of the bullets—it read .41 Mag—and then put it back in and rotated the cylinder so the empty chamber was under the hammer, like Grandpa had taught me.

I remembered something else Grandpa taught me about bears. They could smell a candy wrapper a mile away. I quickly found my candy wrappers and put them in my pocket. *That's really dumb!* I pulled the wrappers out of my pocket and buried them, right beside my little tent thingy. After thinking about that for a minute, I dug them up and stuffed them inside a spare plastic bag. I scraped up some dirt and rocks to fill the bag and then tried to zip it closed, but I was shaking too badly again.

Gritting my teeth, I flipped the kit bag off and crawled thirty feet down to the cobble beach. I threw the little bag as hard as I could, but I wasn't sure it even hit the water. What's worse, when I threw the bag I also accidentally threw my only mitten and the heat pack that was in it.

It was raining harder, and I was freezing! My little trip to the beach had gotten me even wetter than I'd been before. Realizing just how warm my little troll tent was, I crawled back and pulled it over me again. I snuggled back up against Grandpa. My hands were stinging so bad, I put them down my pants to help keep them from freezing.

One more thing Grandpa told me about bear attacks is that bears don't like people and usually only attack if they come upon you unexpectedly. I called Ammo over and had him lie down where I could see his radar ears. If a bear was coming, Ammo would hear him—and then I would make a lot of noise.

The problem was Ammo's radar ears worked too well and would swing around in all directions, constantly. Sometimes he'd lift his head and look out into the trees. I had no idea the woods were so full of noises—little noises like two trees rubbing against each other, or a squirrel running through dead leaves, or a couple of birds squawking at each other.

Since I couldn't use Ammo's radar, I had to come up with another plan. Grandpa had taught me to be noisy if I thought I might be in bear country, so I started singing as loud as I could. But my lips were so stiff the songs came out more like, "This old nan he hlayd hon nnnnuh-nuh-nuh-nnnnuh." I couldn't say *p*s or *m*s or *f*s or any other letter where you had to close your lips. I had to keep wiping the drool off my chin, and my nose was running. I knew because I could taste the salt. I sang until it got too hard.

My flashlight started to flicker, so I felt for the other one in my shirt pocket. I would only use it if I needed to. When the first flashlight finally failed, I was surprised to see it wasn't quite as dark outside as I'd thought. The clouds seemed to be slightly glowing, but I was sure it was way too late to be the sun. I then realized the clouds were being lit by city lights. Now I understood what they meant when they said Anchorage is just fifteen minutes from the rest of Alaska. Anchorage was so close I could see the glow from the city lights, but I was beginning to fear we were going to freeze to death or be eaten by a bear in the wilderness.

The rain slowed to a drizzle. I needed to check on Grandpa, but I felt a little like a kid who's afraid there's a monster under the bed. Silly, I know—but somehow I felt safer under my tent. I shook the bear bells and yelled as loud as I could and then peeked out from under the troll tent. I shined the flashlight around, but I didn't see any bear—or monsters. Finally, I built up enough courage to take my tent off. I tried to wake Grandpa, but it was no use. At least his heat packs were still working.

That's when I started to shake violently. It started with my jaw and spread to the rest of my body. *If I grab the bear bells, they'll shake without me even trying.* I tried to laugh at my own joke, but I did shake the belt, and the bells made a real racket. *Better than singing.* It was obvious that Ammo didn't care for the noise. He got up and went over and lay down on the other side of Grandpa. *Good. If Ammo doesn't like the noise, neither will a bear.*

I was sore and cold, but all I wanted to do was sleep. I got back into my troll tent, and when I did, I realized I wasn't shaking anymore. In fact, I felt pretty good and drifted off to sleep.

I don't know how long I was asleep, but I woke up when I heard Ammo let out a little growl. He bumped into my little tent—he was backed right up against me. When I peeked out, I saw he was looking down the beach and to our right. His ears were standing up and pointing forward. All I could see were trees silhouetted by clouds in the near total darkness.

Then Ammo started really barking. He started doing little false charges, and then he'd back up again until he bumped into me. He was making that really scary sound between barks—like a backward growl when he breathed in—and the hair on his back was standing up. I shook Grandpa and begged him to wake up, but he was still unconscious. I turned on the remaining flashlight and put it back in my shirt pocket. Ammo started for the beach.

I was sure a bear was coming. I grabbed the gun and then got out from under my tent and managed to stand up. I guess I was so cold I couldn't feel the pain in my ankle. Terrified, I started screaming as loud as I could, "*Go away, go away!*"

I decided to shoot the gun straight up into the air. Maybe that would scare him away. I did everything Grandpa had taught me, but it took both my hands to cock the hammer. I pointed it up in the air, held my breath, and squeezed the trigger—*kablooey!* I'd never heard such a loud explosion. There was a bright flash of light and then the gun kicked and hit me in the face. I was knocked back onto my butt and dropped the gun. *Holy cow!* My wrists hurt, my face hurt, and my ears were ringing. Something was running into my eye, so I rubbed it. When I put my hand in the beam of my flashlight, I saw it was covered with blood and snot.

Ammo was out of sight, in the darkness. My ears were still ringing, but I did hear Ammo start barking again. He was sure something was still out there.

I found the gun lying in the mud. I had to cock it while it was still on the ground because my hands didn't seem to want to work. I managed to stand up and—holding on to the gun even tighter this time—I squeezed the trigger again. There was another explosion and flash of light. This time the gun flew right of my hands and hit me squarely on top of my head. I think I blacked out for a second.

When I came to, I saw something—coming right at me! It was . . . it was a . . . it was a light! Out on the water was a light!

"Anno! Anno! We're sayied!" I tried to yell, "Ammo! Ammo! We're saved," but my lips could hardly move. I tried to get the flashlight out of my pocket but couldn't get my fingers to work at all. I did manage to get the whistle in my mouth and blew it once, but then I blew it right out of my mouth.

I managed to stand up again and started waving my arms. I was crying and laughing, and I tried to hop, but the only thing that happened was . . . my pants fell off! I tried to pull them up, but they were soaking wet, and it was like I was wearing boxing gloves. Then I fell into the mud.

I saw three lights out in the lake, all pointed right at me. I couldn't see their faces, but from their voices I could tell it was Cam and Grandpa's two home teachers in a small flat-bottomed motor boat. Cam came running right to me with a great big Hudson's Bay blanket. She kept asking over and over, "Are you all right, Summer? Are you all right?"

"Hi Gwadna, I luh loo. I'n 'kkkk." She hung the blanket in the branch of a tree and started taking off all my clothes. "Gggwanta Guzis hurdt. I gggayied him hirst aid ut he won wake uhd."

When I fell down again, Cam called one of the men over. Between the two of them, they got the rest of my wet clothes off and pulled me to my feet. Then she wrapped me in that wonderful blanket, and they carried me down to the beach, away from the mud, and laid me down on the sand. They opened the blanket and looked for other injuries. I was embarrassed and tried to cover myself up, but by that point even my arms wouldn't work right. They rewrapped me and started to inspect my head and face injuries.

"I'n kkkay. Thuh gggun jus kickkt laaack and hit ne, that all." I added, "It gnus a wwordy-wone Nagnun."

The man started laughing and said, "A .41 magnum! So *that's* what that was. We heard the shots and saw two bright flashes over here."

I tried to smile and said, "Yeah." I recognized his voice. He was Brother Carpenter.

They seemed to be most concerned about my head and face wounds so I told them, "I hurdttt ny ankkkle lut itz kkkkay nnnow." They both looked at my ankle. Then Cam left us, went over, and knelt down beside Grandpa.

Brother Swenson stood up and took out a walkie-talkie. I heard him say, "Rescue One, Rescue One—this is team three. We have them. Still assessing injuries. We definitely have severe, repeat, severe hypothermia. We're on the south shore. I'm firing a flare now."

He hollered, "Flare!" and then fired into the air. It was just like a Fourth of July sky rocket, curving high up into the air and then exploding into a bright shower of sparks over the lake.

I heard a voice on the radio, "We have you, Rescue Three. We're on the way. Say again, injuries."

Brother Swenson said, "Female is semiconscious, definitely in stage-three hypothermia. She also has unknown head injuries. Male is unconscious with multiple injuries." Then he added, "Don't waste any time."

The man said, "Give us another flare."

Brother Swenson fired the flare gun again.

I could now hear a motorboat approaching. I started trying to take my covers off. Brother Swenson called to Cam, asking her come back and help him. She knelt and rewrapped me, but I kept trying to take it back off. I started fighting her. I just wanted to get out from under the blanket. I wanted to tell Brother Swenson he wasn't supposed to have a motorboat on this lake.

Cam grabbed me by my face and yelled, "Summer Rose Watson. You've got to stay covered up!"

Hearing my name seemed to clear my head a little. "Howz Gwanddnna, howzs Gwranddnna?"

She said, "We don't know yet," then asked me, "Did you give him first aid?"

"Yeah," I said. "Oh no, dddid I do zonethink wongh?"

"Something wrong?" she asked with surprise. "No, honey, you did everything just right. Where did you learn first aid?"

"In heald cccclass," I said, and then I flipped my blanket off again and said, "Cahn! Cahn! They're not suddost to have a notorgoat on this lake!"

A big red rubber boat with a little tent-like covering and a small windshield drove right up onto the beach. It was the rescue squad. A man jumped out of the boat and came over to me. He was wearing one of those headlights, so every time he looked at me I was blinded.

That's all I remember, until we were in the rubber boat racing back to the parking lot. I saw lots of red emergency lights way down at the end of lake. Their reflection on the water was beautiful.

A man said, "Base, any word on the helicopter?"

"Rescue One, ETA two minutes. We're setting up a clear LZ now." I could see Cam holding Grandpa's head in her lap. I was wrapped in someone's arms, and together we were wrapped up in blankets and tarps. He was holding me tight, trying to keep me warm and out of the wind. I felt the warmth from his body heat. Actually, he felt hot—like *really* hot. That's when I realized he didn't have on a shirt or coat. We were skin-to-skin. His body heat felt so good. Then I smelled his cologne. It was Tom!

"Ttton, zzat yyyou?"

"It sure is, Summer. You know us Mounties—we always get our man."

"Ttton, tanannk yyyyou so nnuch wor saiying us."

Cam leaned over and started kissing me. I heard her say, "Hold her tighter, Tom. Hold her as close as you can."

I struggled to look around the boat. "Tton, is zis a Zodiak?"

"It sure is."

"C-c-cool. Wherez Anno? Wherez Anno?"

Cam tried to calm me down. She adjusted the tarp so that it covered my face again. My arms were around Tom, and my face was buried in his chest. I pulled him in as close as I could get, feeling his strong muscles. He smelled so nice.

That must have been when I passed out for good.

CHAPTER 18

I WANT A REAL DOCTOR!

E verything was really confusing. I thought I was in a cage—then I realized I was in a hospital bed with really weird bed rails. I couldn't talk—some kind of tube was stuck down my throat—and I couldn't move. At first I thought I was paralyzed, but slowly I came to realize I was tied down. When I began to struggle, I could see my arms were restrained at the wrists. I also realized I could only see out of my right eye.

When I tried to kick free, my right leg moved fine, but a giant pain shot up my left leg. Looking down, I saw it was braced between pillows with a blue cold pack arranged across my ankle. As soon as I'd started thrashing around, a little alarm went off on some equipment above my head. A doctor came in right away. I tried to sit up as he lowered the bed rail.

"Whoa! Nurse, help me out," he said.

He stepped up again and pulled down the top of my hospital gown without so much as a howdy-do or thank-you, ma'am. I tried to scream and pull away, but all I could do was glare at him as he used a stethoscope on my exposed chest. Then he took out one of those pen lights and shined it into my right eye. I felt him mess around with my left eye, and then he shined the light into it too. I was grateful I could see out of that eye as long as he had his hand on my face.

The doctor said, "Equal and reactive."

I was terrified and mortified. What was this thing in my throat? Why was I tied down? Where was I? What was wrong with me? Ohhh, my head hurt so bad. What gave him the right to pull down my gown?

The doctor was speaking to the nurse and completely ignoring me. Then he got right in my face and asked, "Do you know where you are?"

I didn't like him—he frightened me—and I tried to pull away.

"I was told she was feisty. You try."

Then the nurse stepped up to my bed, refastened my gown, and *also* got right in my face. She was wearing way too much makeup. She scared me almost as much as the doctor.

"You, missy, have had a couple of bad days. Do you know where you are?"

I shook my head no. Man, it really hurt!

"Do you know who you are?"

I nodded yes.

"Do you know why you're here?"

Then, in a flash, it all came back to me. "*Grandpa!*" I tried to scream, but the tube wouldn't let me. *Where's Grandpa? Is he okay?* I tried to sit up again, which made my head start pounding and pain shoot up my leg.

She told the doctor, "We've just called for her mother. She'll be here in a minute. I think that'll calm her down."

What's this lady talking about? Mom's in Utah.

I looked at them in confusion.

The doctor put two of his fingers in my right hand and asked me to squeeze. If my wrists hadn't been restrained, I would have tried to break them. He extracted his fingers and tested the grip in my left hand—and I tried again to break his fingers, without any luck.

He turned to the nurse and said, "Equal and strong."

Then he took some sort of instrument and rubbed it hard against the bottom of my right foot, which made my leg jerk in a most unladylike fashion. Then the dope did the same thing to my left foot! My left leg jerked, and the pain almost made me pass out. All I could do was move around in my restraints, although I did try to kick him with my free foot.

I was crying with pain, but I couldn't say anything.

The doctor said, "Looks like that hurt."

Do you think?!

"Nurse, put fresh cold packs on her ankle. I suspect the orthopedist will want to wait to operate until after some of the swelling goes down."

Operate? Oh, no! I was still very groggy, and these two people were really freaking me out.

Then the doctor told the nurse, "Go ahead and extubate her."

What did he just say?

A few seconds later they were standing on either side of me. The nurse got right in my face again and said, "I am going to pull that mean old thing out of your mouth now. When I tell you, I want you to cough for me. Can you do that?"

I nodded.

"You might feel like gagging, but I really want you to try not to throw up, okay?"

The nurse removed tape from my face—the tape holding the tube in my throat. Then she said, "Okay, cough."

The tube came right out. I did have an involuntary gag, but I didn't throw up. I coughed a couple of times and then hoarsely whispered, "Will I still be able to fly?"

Looking over at the nurse, the doctored sarcastically said, "She's going to be an astronaut."

I didn't like his tone at all.

I barely got out, "I can be if I want to!" Then I asked for some water. The nurse poured some ice chips into a cup and held it to my mouth. Well, at least my throat still worked—but it was sore, and I added that to my list of aches and pains.

Before I even knew what she was doing, the nurse put one of those little plastic tubes around my face that blows oxygen up your nose. After she got it adjusted, she reached over my head and turned a valve. I could hear a little bubbling noise, and the oxygen started flowing into my nostrils.

Then I looked at the doctor and said, "Yes, by the way, that *did* hurt. I'd appreciate it if you wouldn't do that again. *And* leave my gown *alone!*" No reaction. I might as well have been talking to a brick wall!

Oh, my head!

Looking around the room, I saw princesses and floating castles painted on the walls. A teddy bear sat on one of my bedside tables. When I looked at my gown, I saw it was covered with little puppies and kittens. With a sinking feeling, I began to realize where I was. I croaked out, "What kind of doctor are you?"

The nurse answered for him and said, "Darling, he's the head of pediatrics."

"Pediatrics!" I howled. *Owww.* "Pediatrics!" I said a little softer. Feeling furious, I demanded, "I want a real doctor!"

Just then, Mom stepped in and came right over to my bed. I cried out a barely audible, "Mom! Where's Grandpa? Is he all right?"

Mom saw me struggling in my restraints and asked the doctor if he could remove them.

"Sorry, not yet. She has a central line in her femoral vein. If she tears at it, we could end up with a real emergency here. Once her blood gasses come back from the lab, we'll know if we can remove the central line. Then can we remove her restraints."

Mom bent over and hugged me, careful not to disturb all the wires and tubes hooked to me. The doctor and nurse must have stepped out, because we were suddenly alone. We whispered "I love you" to each other, and then she just hung on to me. We stayed that way until Cam came in and walked over to my bed, standing on the side opposite Mom.

I started to cry. "Thank you, Cam. Thank you for saving me and Grandpa." I saw that she was crying too. She reached in and hugged whatever part of me could be reached. She and Mom started rocking. They rocked back and forth like I was a baby, but I didn't mind.

I refocused my thoughts. "How's Grandpa?" Cam stood up, but Mom stayed bent over my bed.

"He's in stable but guarded condition," Cam said. "He hasn't regained consciousness, but the doctor told us not to worry about that yet." Through her tears, she added, "We were afraid we were going to lose you both that first night."

At that moment, the doctor stepped back in. He seemed to be annoyed by Mom's and Cam's presence. Coming up to the side of my bed, he practically pushed Cam out of the way, trying to explain away his rudeness by saying, to no one in particular, "This is the PICU, and I need to assess my patient's neurologic signs."

Holding up one finger, he asked me, "How many fingers do you see?"

This guy was the rudest doctor I'd ever seen. I looked at him hard and said, "Four," which wasn't the answer he expected! He started to write something on my chart, so I added, "I saw one pointed up and three pointed down. Oh, yeah, there was a thumb too."

I guess I surprised everyone—including myself—with my flippancy, because it got real quiet in the room. He clicked his pen twice for no apparent reason and with a stern expression, asked, "What's your name?"

"Summer Rose," I said, and then broke into a coughing fit. Mom had already reached for my cup of ice. I took a few and then finished, "Watson."

"Where are you?"

Other than the obvious—in the pediatric ward—I didn't know. Cam was here, so I assumed I was in Palmer, but Mom was here too. *Maybe I'm in Utah.* I just hesitated and then asked, "I don't know—where am I?"

"What year is it?"

I just wanted him to go away so I snapped, "Two thousand—and-twelve," and added, "C.E."

He stuck his pen back in his breast pocket, announcing he'd be back in fifteen minutes. Partially blocked by Cam, he grudgingly made a sidestep to get around her.

Just then, an automatic blood pressure cuff started to inflate around my left arm. Things were still very foggy in my head. I asked, "What did you mean, 'That first night'? Mom, what day is it? Where are we?"

Mom said, "Sweetheart, you've been unconscious for almost four days. The accident happened three nights ago."

"Are we in Utah?"

Cam walked over to the window and opened the blinds. I could see Pioneer Peak. There was snow on it! She said, "Termination dust."

"What's termination dust?"

"That snow up there means summer is over," Mom said.

Cam added, "Terminated! And it's a couple of weeks early."

"The snow level got down to about three thousand feet the night of your accident," Mom said. "The lake is at about a thousand feet. The weatherman said it got down to thirty-five degrees on the lake that night."

Mom started doing "mom stuff" to me. She started fixing tape on my bandages that probably didn't need to be fixed in the first place. Then she checked for a fever with the back of her hand. She picked at my hair and examined my eye. "I think you're going to have a scar there," she said.

Cam said, "Oh, don't worry about that. The doctor said your little scar will be quite appealing to men of action."

"Scar?" I whined.

Mom was wiping her nose and said, "Well, not exactly a scar. The gun hit you right on your brow ridge." She reached up and touched my other eyebrow. "The doctor said the wound was not a simple cut—a little piece of your eyebrow was actually torn away. There'll be a tiny little spot where your eyebrow won't grow back."

"Doctor? You mean that stupid pediatrician?" My voice still sounded like I had laryngitis.

"No, I've never seen *him* before." She leaned over close and whispered, "It was a *real* doctor down in the trauma center." I looked at her and we both laughed.

Cam added, "It'll make you look quite mysterious. That same trauma doctor is the one who put the central line in your leg instead of your neck. That would've been another scar."

"Mom, why can't I see out of my left eye?"

"Your eye is totally swollen closed, sweetie. You have a black eye that would make any schoolyard bully envious."

"A world-class shiner!" Cam added.

Suddenly, something started squeezing my legs. It scared me to death. "Mom! What's wrong with my legs?" Mom and Cam didn't know what I was talking about. I started freaking out, and Mom pulled back my covers.

Cam stepped up and said, "Summer! It's okay, it's okay! Those are called an 'intermittent compression device.' They help stop blood clots from forming in your legs. You've been lying here unconscious for four days, sweetie. You needed something to help your blood circulate."

Man, all of this was almost too much. I just didn't understand what they were telling me.

"Summer Rose, I'm going back up to sit with your grandfather," Cam said. She came over, kissed me on the forehead, and left.

We both watched as she left. "Mom, isn't she wonderful?"

"She sure is," she said, and then added, "She'll make a wonderful grandmother."

I looked at her. "You know?"

"Yes, your new grandmother and I have had almost two days and nights to get to know each other, ever since I flew in from Salt Lake."

She reached out and cradled my face with her hands and told me how much she loved me. She started crying again and said, "I was so afraid for you."

"I'll be okay. I'm just worried about Grandpa."

"Me too," Mom said, starting to cry all over again.

The "king of pediatrics" came in and stepped between me and Mom, who quietly walked over to the windows and cried some more. The doctor seemed to be deliberately trying to create stress.

He held out his hand and asked, "How many fingers am I *holding up*?"

"Three."

"What is your name?"

"Summer Rose Watson, future astronaut."

"Do you know why you're here?"

"Yes. Well, actually, I'm still trying to figure out why I'm in the PICU instead of the adult ICU."

"Do you know where you are?"

"Latitude sixty-one degrees, thirty-six minutes north and longitude one hundred forty-nine degrees, seven minutes west."

He looked at me, confused.

"Palmer, Alaska."

He clicked his pen twice, put it in his pocket, and said, "I'm just trying to do my job."

My head was pounding in pain. Mom came over and took my hand in hers. "Mom, what happened to my head?"

"It looks like the gun hit you. You've got a skull fracture."

"Yeah, that was the second shot."

"It's just a hairline fracture, but you have a concussion. They've been a little worried about brain swelling. At least they didn't install an intercranial pressure monitor, like they did for your grandfather."

"Oh, no! Mom, what's that?"

"They had to drill a hole in Dad's skull and insert a pressure monitor in his brain. His pressure was a little bit too high, so they actually drained some fluid from around his brain."

"What about me?"

"They've been monitoring you in other ways—like loud noises and bright lights—and they've been poking you and tickling you. That's why they're asking you all those silly questions now that you're awake."

I was becoming aware of just how bad I felt. I had a headache from out of this world. I was hungry. My mouth was dry, and my lips were cracked. And my ankle! Man, did that really hurt. When I told Mom how I felt, she called the nurse.

While we waited for the nurse, I noticed I had a pulse/ox meter clipped to my right index finger and a blood pressure cuff on my left arm. I also had some electrodes attached both on my chest and apparently on my scalp under the bandage. I saw an extremely scary-looking IV line going up under my gown, way up high on the inside of my left thigh. I also saw another tube taped to my leg, coming from the side of my bed and running all the way up my leg. I mean *alllll* the way up my leg.

"Mother! What is *that*?" *Oww, I have got to stop yelling.*

"They've catheterized your bladder."

I thought about that for a moment and asked, "Why?"

Mom said, "Well, your body was still producing urine while you were unconscious. If they hadn't inserted the catheter, you would've wet the bed like a sleeping baby."

"Mom? Inserted it where?"

"Well, sweetie, there's only one place to insert it."

"Oh, Mom! That's so totally gross."

"Is it bothering you?"

"Well, yeah! It's embarrassing."

"No, I mean, is it physically hurting you?"

"No. I didn't even know it was there until I just now saw it."

The nurse came in just then and said, "The doctor said we can remove her fancy pants and some of her monitoring equipment. He will be in in a few minutes to remove her central line." I noticed she was talking to Mom instead of me.

Mom drew the curtain around my bed, and then she and the nurse worked together to remove the compression devices that had been massaging my legs. It was a most undignified procedure and all the effort had worn me out and made me aware of all my soreness. All I really wanted to do was go back to sleep, but the nurse told Mom, "The doctor wants her to stay awake."

The nurse began to unwrap the gauze turban off my head. I could see yellow stains all over the bandage as she removed it, but I was afraid to ask what the stains were. Then the nurse started removing the electrodes off my scalp. I was surprised at just how roughly she treated me as she got each one to come off. She also removed about a half-dozen electrodes from my torso. Again, she handled me very roughly, but I figured better her than the pediatrician.

Then the nurse went into the bathroom and came out with a plastic basin full of water, a spongy cloth, and a small bottle of soap called Neo-wash. "I need to give her a sponge bath and change her gown," she said to my mother.

I finally had enough and said, "Hey, I'm right here. You can talk to *me*, you know." I looked at Mom and said, "Please get me out of the pediatric ward. They keep treating me like I'm a baby."

"I'll do what I can," Mom said.

"Ma'am, your daughter can't be in an adult ward until she is eighteen years of age. We'll move her out of the PICU into a regular peds room as soon as the doctor is sure there isn't going to be any brain swelling."

Once again, she acted like I wasn't even in the room. I did a slow burn, but I was so miserable I didn't have the strength to fight.

Mom and the nurse started undressing me. I finally said, to no one in particular, "I'm getting tired of being naked in front of strangers." Mom looked at the nurse and said, "I'll call you when we're done."

The nurse left, closing the curtain as she did. I was now crying out loud but not from the embarrassment. I was really hurting, and I was starting to feel nauseous. I was still very confused and really didn't understand what had happened to me or what to expect next. The wrist restraints were really bugging me.

Mom said, "I'm going to give you a 'possible' bath." When I looked at her questioningly, she said, "I'll wash you *down* as far as possible, then I'll wash you *up* as far as possible. Later you can wash *'possible'* yourself."

"Thank you, Mom." I was still crying. Mom squeezed my arm and started out the door, saying she was going to ask the nurse for something to ease my pain.

When she came back into the room, Mom started getting me ready for my "possible" bath. "I'm so worried about Grandpa," I cried.

She said, "We all are, baby."

She pulled down the top of my gown so just the lower part of my body was covered. She was washing me down as far as possible. I was surprised to see how much mud there still was on my body. Just then the doctor slid the curtain back and barged in. Mom quickly pulled the gown up and snapped at the doctor, "Did you ever hear of knocking?"

Whoa! You go, Mom!

But the doctor never even acknowledged his rudeness. He just told Mom he needed to inspect my sutures. He did so without comment. Then he tugged at my swollen eyelid. As he did I could see light out of that eye.

"We have your daughter scheduled for another MRI in the morning," he told Mom. "The orthopedist will be in shortly. I've instructed the nurse to bring in some new cold packs for the edema on her ankle and facial injuries."

A few moments later, the nurse came in with the cold packs and a tray of surgical instruments and supplies. When no one offered any explanation, Mom was forced to ask, "Is that for removing the central line?"

The doctor continued to examine me and just said, "Uh-hum." He then directed the nurse to put a pad under my bottom and prep the site.

He then asked me, "Who is Mickey Mouse's girlfriend?"

"Minnie."

"What is twenty-one minus fourteen?"

"Seven." Then I added, "Seven is the fifth prime number."

He turned to my mom and said, "All right, I'm going to remove her central line. Some girls are embarrassed by my presence down there. I'd appreciate it if you'd stand by the bed, over on the other side and up close to her head. My nurse will be assisting me. There will be some bleeding until we get her sutured back up so you may not want to watch."

I asked, "Can the nurse do it?"

No one answered. The doctor just pulled up my gown. Mom squeezed my hand as a sign. It took quite a bit longer than I imagined, but I got through it okay. I was, however, seriously embarrassed and more than a little angry at the doctor.

When he finished, he directed the nurse to clean me up and dress the wound. Then he said to my mom, "The orthopedist should be here in just a few minutes."

As he left, I growled at him, "Tell the orthopedist to knock first. Also, I could really use some pain medication here!"

Mom looked at me with love in her face and said, "Wait till you have a baby, baby."

Gross!

When the nurse finished, she asked Mom if we had finished my bath. Mom told her, "No, I still have to wash her up as far as possible. Could you bring a fresh basin of warm water?"

The nurse never answered but went into the bathroom again with the wash basin. A minute later she returned and set the basin on my bedside table. Then she finally undid my wrist restraints and warned me to leave my bandages alone. Finally, she pulled off the automatic blood pressure cuff and left us.

Mother finished washing me. No matter how gentle she was, I involuntarily jerked as she worked on my left leg. Mom then dressed me in a fresh gown—one with teddy bears on it. It was entirely too short.

"Mom," I whined, "would you bring my real pajamas when you come back to visit?"

"Sure, baby. I'm staying in your room at the cabin. I'll bring everything you need."

"Please bring my journal too."

"Okay, I sure will. You know, I had the last of a really great soup at the cabin. Cam told me there is a story behind it."

"There is, Mom, but I'd like to tell you about it later."

She stroked my face and said, "Sure, honey, that'll be fine." Then she touched my hair, tilted her head a little sideways, and said, "We really need to do something with your hair."

"Can I look at myself in a mirror?"

Mom got out her little makeup mirror and handed it to me. It was really nice to have the use of my hands back. I was shocked. My right eye was totally swollen shut. Most of that side of my face was black and purple and green. The suture line ran right through my eyebrow like she'd told me. My hair looked like Medusa's. It was all knotted up and matted to my head. They had shaved a great big patch of my hair along the suture line on my skull. The skin was purple and green there too. I found four other smaller spots that had been shaved. That must've been where the electrodes were.

My whole head was covered in this orangey-yellow stuff. I asked Mom what it was.

"That's Betadine. It's just an antiseptic soap. It has some iodine in it."

It looked like they had put in on with a turkey baster. It had run down my left cheek and into my ear. Half of my forehead was also yellow, and my hair looked like an old string mop that had been used to clean up a big spaghetti sauce spill.

The nurse came back in and introduced a man in scrubs. He looked like he was about Uncle Chris's age—he had a friendly face. The nurse told Mom that she was going off shift and that Nurse Larry would be my new nurse.

No way!

She took my vitals and gave me a cup of Jell-O, which I immediately wolfed down. When I asked for more, she told *my mother* we'd have to wait to see if I could hold down the first cup.

Man, that woman is really starting to make me mad.

The nurse inserted a needle and installed an IV port on the back of my left hand, telling my *mom* (*naturally!*) it was to replace the central line they had just removed. She hung a bag on my IV pole and then asked me those same dumb questions again. I was trying to be polite and was doing okay until she asked me what day it was.

"*I don't know!* You do realize I've been unconscious for the last couple of days, right?" I said sarcastically.

When she was finished, she stepped out of the way, and Nurse Larry stepped in and injected some medicine into the IV port.

He looked at me as he was doing so and said, "This is for your pain. Now, I don't want you going to sleep right now, okay? I'll be back as soon as shift change is over."

Well, at least he's talking directly to me.

As they stepped out of the room, Nurse Larry picked up my Jell-O cup. He pointed to it and silently mouthed the words, "Want some more?" I nodded; he held up five fingers and pointed at his watch. Then we smiled at each other.

CHAPTER 19

WE GOT OUR MAN

A few minutes later, Uncle Chris walked in. He did this dramatic double take, walked back out the door, and shouted, "Oh, Momma!" A moment later, he peeked back in and said, "Girl, you look like you been in a fight with a buzz saw!"

He's a riot.

I cracked up, even though it hurt. "Uncle Chris, please don't make me laugh. Please don't . . . *oooww!*"

Walking into the room, he hugged Mom, gave her a kiss on the cheek, and said, "Hi, Sis." Then he leaned over to give me a kiss but jerked back. Covering his face, he said, "I can't, I just can't—there's no way I can kiss that face."

I started laughing again. "Stop it, Uncle Chris!"

Then Mom leaned over and said, "This is a face only a mother could love." She kissed me on my yellow forehead, looked up at Uncle Chris, and said, "But I could be lying too." That got Uncle Chris laughing.

Then he said, "I've just came down from the ICU. There's been no change in Dad's condition."

Smiling at me, Mom said, "I want to go sit with Dad. I'm hoping Cam will go home and get some rest. She's been in this hospital for four straight days and nights. I'll be back later." I blew her a kiss. She pointed at her ring finger and then at Uncle Chris. She mouthed the words, "He knows."

Uncle Chris said, "Love you, Sis."

Digging around in my bedside table, Uncle Chris pulled out a little package with tooth paste and a brush in it, along with a tiny little bottle of mouthwash and some lip balm. "You really need these," he said with his nose scrunched up, and then he winked and tore open the package for me. Smiling, he brought over a little U-shaped bowl and a wet washrag and poured water out of my little water bottle.

While I brushed my teeth, he pulled up a chair close to the bed and dramatically unfolded a newspaper, casually asking, "Seen today's paper?"

"*Duh!*" I said, in my best Valley Girl accent, drooling some toothpaste down my chin. I spit the rest out, rinsed my mouth, and wiped my face with the washrag. "I've been, like, totally unconscious for four days."

"What*ever*," he said in a mocking valley girl accent. "The news people think you're the cat's meow."

"What?"

"Yeah, girl, you're *fay-moose*. I go around bragging to everybody that I'm your uncle."

"No way!" I said.

He remained silent and dramatically turned to the sports page. I leaned over and tried to see the paper, but that made my head spin. I fell back onto my pillow. *Uggh.* I wouldn't do that again. "Uncle Chris, you're joking, right?"

He folded up the paper and said, feigning disinterest, "All I know is that there've been reporters in the lobby for the last three days. They all want to interview you."

"Are you serious?"

"You're crazy famous!" he said, turning around. "All three TV stations are begging to get a look at you and hear your story. They've all been feeding updates to the national news networks. When they found out how old you are and the fact that you're a pilot, the media went nuts! By the way, I'm officially your press agent. And get this, there's a production company that wants to do a one-hour reality show and recreate the whole thing, showing how you and Dad were prepared and filed a trip plan, how you saved Dad and fought off the bear! By the way, did I mention I'm your press agent? Tom is also being called a hero."

"Don't joke, Uncle Chris—was there really a bear?"

"*Yes*, there was a bear! Didn't you see it?"

"Ammo and I thought it was out there, but I never saw it. How do you know it was there?"

"Well, I went out to find Ammo and I saw bear sign everywhere."

I was feeling pretty confused. I still didn't know if Uncle Chris was pulling my leg or what.

"Well, how do you know the bear didn't come later?"

He got silent for a minute, looking down at his feet, and then said, "I'm sorry to tell you this, Summer Rose, but the bear got Ammo."

"What? Oh, *no!* What happened?"

"It looks like Ammo worried the bear away from you, because his paw prints were on top of the bear's tracks. But the bear must have turned on him."

"Oh, no . . . *oh, Ammo!* Is he dead?" I cried.

"He's alive—but his face and head look a lot like yours, and he has some broken ribs. The worst thing is his front leg is busted up real bad."

I thought about that for a moment and then realized the worst. He was already missing one of his front legs.

"We'll just have to see what happens, but if that leg doesn't heal right, we'll have to put him down."

"Oh, Uncle Chris," I said, starting to cry. "Poor Ammo. That makes me so sad."

"We're doing everything we can for him. Like I said, we'll just have to wait and see." He touched my shoulder. "The media has already done several updates on Ammo from my clinic. He's just as famous as you and Dad and Tom Atwood."

Then I freaked. "Did you say the reporters are talking to Tom too?"

"Dudley has already been interviewed on all the channels."

"Oh, no!"

Uncle Chris got really serious and moved closer to me. He started talking in a really low voice and said, "Summer Rose, everything went right that night. You and Dad left a trip plan. You did everything you'd learned about first aid. Cam didn't hesitate. Dad's home teachers didn't hesitate. The rescue squad was there. Ammo fought off the bear."

Then he wet the washrag and started working on my face. He talked to me as he soaped up the tape marks around my mouth. "You've got to understand this. It was *you* who saved Dad and it was *Tom* who saved *you.* They said your body core temperature was down to eighty-seven degrees when you got here. They said, for sure, if Tom hadn't done what he did, you wouldn't have made it. And just so you know, what he did for you is a standard way to treat hypothermia victims. And don't worry, he's been very discrete. I promise you, he would never say a word."

Then he slid his chair back and looked down at the floor. I could tell he was starting to choke up. He turned to me and asked, "Do you know what Dad's temperature was when they brought him in?" He didn't wait for me to guess. "It was 98.2 degrees. You saved him and almost gave *your* life doing it." Then he broke into tears and turned away.

I was crying too. "Uncle Chris, I never thought I was giving up my life for him. I just love him and wanted to take care of him."

The pediatrician came in again and saw us crying. When he asked Uncle Chris if anything was wrong, Uncle Chris just waved him off. The doctor announced that he was going home and would be back in the morning. As usual, he never once spoke to me.

Just then Nurse Larry came in pushing a cart. The doctor had to pause for a moment because Larry didn't yield. I caught the doctor's eye with the evilest stare I could muster and said in the gravelly-est voice I could, "*Kahb HukSII' Qojad!*" The doctor just turned and left.

I shyly looked over at Uncle Chris, and he was staring at me with his mouth wide open.

Nurse Larry asked, "What did you just say?" His eyes were big and round.

"That was a Klingon insult!"

Nurse Larry repeated, "A Klingon insult!"

Uncle Chris got a little smile on his face and then asked, "What does it mean?"

I folded my arms across my chest, stared out into space, and said, "Your sister has a smooth forehead."

Uncle Chris folded over with laughter.

Nurse Larry repeated, "Your sister has a smooth forehead!" and busted out laughing.

It took a minute for them to calm down. They'd both get quiet, and then they'd look at each other and start another round of laughter. Finally, I started laughing a little too—at *them*—but, *ohhh*, it made my head hurt! It took like two minutes for us to finally calm down. Nurse Larry was leaning over the cart. Uncle Chris had slipped out of his chair, and I was sitting there in bed holding my throbbing head. I guess a little laughter was exactly what we all needed.

Nurse Larry finally caught his breath and said, "*Girrrrrl!* They warned me you had an attitude. Hey, can you teach me how to say that?"

"Sure, but can we wait till later? It takes practice to pronounce some of the syllables. And right now I can't think with this headache I've got."

Then Nurse Larry said, "I just got a report from the ICU—your grandfather has been moving! That's a very good sign. He might wake pretty soon, and girl, we have *got* to do something with your hair before he sees you! And what's with all these news people? We've been fighting them back with a stick, but I said, '*Unh-huh,* you ain't goin' anywhere near my patient until I get her cleaned up.' And what is with that hospital gown?"

He reached into the cart and pulled out a set of lavender scrubs. He held them up for me and swished them around, saying, "I think these will fit you." He leaned out the door and hollered, "Nancy, get your size two butt down here and change this girl's clothes."

A moment later, a very pleasant-looking young woman stepped in like she was walking down a runway. Nurse Larry said, in a grand voice, "*Lady* and *gentleman*, I give you Nancy, nurses' aide *extraordinaire*."

Then he said, "Now, I have some good news and some bad news. The good news is, Nancy will get you into these in just a moment. The bad news is, I have to remove your catheter first. Doctor's orders. You can't leave the PICU until we know you can pee like a big dog."

"Can Nancy do it?"

"No, I'm sorry. It has to be done by a nurse."

"Can't you bring in a female nurse?"

"I'm sorry, it's a slow night in the PICU, but they're pretty busy in the NICU. The only female nurse on duty on this side of the hall was detailed over to help them out. I'm the only nurse over here tonight—and *you're* my only patient."

I said, "I just want you to know, I'm not too excited about this."

"I know you're not, but we have to get it done. It'll only take a second. Nancy will be standing right beside you. I realize this isn't going to sound exactly right, but you're not a little girl anymore. I understand that you have done some very adult things lately. I guess this is just another adult thing you have to do. Can you handle it?"

"Yes, sir."

Uncle Chris got up and said, "I'll be down in the cafeteria."

Nancy drew the curtains and came and stood beside the bed. Larry put on some latex gloves. "I'm going to have to lift your gown. I'll cut a little rubber tube that inflates a balloon in your urethra. Then I'll lay my left hand firmly on your pubis. I will have you count to three, and I'll pull it out with my right hand. Then I'll pull your gown back down and we will be finished."

"Nurse Larry, I don't want to do this."

"I know. All right, I'm lifting your gown. Okay, now I just deflated the balloon. I'm going to lay my hand on you now. Now, count to three."

I took a deep breath. Before I even said "one," Larry announced he was finished, and I felt him pull my gown back down. He handed the catheter to Nancy, who then took it and the collection bag and headed to the bathroom.

"That was probably easier than your first crosswind landing, eh?" Nurse Larry said.

Nancy asked if I was ready to change into the scrubs.

"Not quite. Only two-thirds of me has been bathed. I'd like to finish my bath before I get dressed."

"Do you need any help?"

"No, thank you, but I guess I need the wash basin and washcloth again."

"Coming right up."

Larry somehow disconnected the IV line from my hand and removed the plastic tube from under my nose. I think those were the last two things tying me to the bed and all of the equipment above my head. He excused himself about the time Nancy stepped back in with my bath supplies.

She handed me the little squeeze bottle Neo-Clean. "I think you'll like this soap. It's very mild and has moisturizer in it. I'll be right here if you need me." She closed the curtain, and then I heard her sit down in the chair beside my bed.

When I finished, Nancy stepped back in, closing the curtains behind her again. She started by pulling the old gown off of me. Then she got me straightened out, and I was able to pull on the scrubs top. The only thing she did was guide my IV port through the sleeve.

Nurse Larry and Uncle Chris tried to come back into the room, but Nancy told them to stay on the other side of the curtain—we weren't finished yet. Getting my bottoms on was a lot more difficult because of my broken ankle, but Nancy was very gentle. I was glad when we were finished, because I was finally decent again—*and* I could stop moving my leg.

She asked, "Are you ready for your big reveal?"

"Ready."

She flung open the curtain and sang out, "Ta-dah!"

Where have I heard that before?

Nurse Larry and Uncle Chris gave me a standing ovation. It's funny, when the earlier shift treated me like a kid, I hated it. When Nurse Larry and Nancy treated me like a kid, I loved it.

Nurse Larry rolled up a new piece of equipment and hooked it up to my IV. He explained that if I pushed the button it would inject a small amount of pain reliever into my line. "It's a 'pain pump.' Don't worry—it won't let you overdose."

Then he picked at my hair with his fingers and said, "I will prepare your *coiffeur, mademoiselle*."

I said, "*Très bon, monsieur.*"

Nancy brought in the funniest looking chair I'd ever seen. I soon realized it was how they were going to shampoo my hair. It was like a highchair, but it tilted back and had built-in basins to catch the runoff. They could also elevate my feet so my ankle didn't throb as bad.

Uncle Chris, Nurse Larry, and Nancy got me out of bed and into the chair, where I was seat-belted in. Nancy started on my hair, rinsing it three times before she soaped it up, doing her best to avoid my sutures. Between rinses, she worked on my yellow forehead and ear. As she worked, she told me how tough it was to get the Betadine out.

While she worked on my hair, Uncle Chris started reading aloud newspaper articles from the last two days. He even read one from the *New York Times*, but it was the exact same story, word for word, that was in the Anchorage paper. I learned a lot of stuff about that night that I didn't know—like the rescue squad also had a team on ATVs searching the trail along the north side of the lake. Uncle Chris had actually headed up the trail search.

Nancy was so gentle, I was starting to get sleepy. About that time, Nurse Larry walked in and shook his finger at me. "Sorry, you can't go to sleep yet. We've got to keep you awake for another couple of hours."

He walked up and asked me to tell him what his name was.

"Nurse Larry."

He asked what year I was born.

"In 1995."

What is the registration for the Starship *Enterprise*?"

"Which one?"

"The second one."

"NCC-1701A."

He then held up two cups of Jell-O and asked me how many cups I saw.

I smiled and said, "Two."

"If you can hold these down for at least half an hour, I'll get you some real food."

"Pizza?"

He rolled his eyes and then huffed out of the room with a smile on his face.

Nancy said, "That boy."

He came back in about the time Nancy was wringing my hair out for the third time. He said all of the NICU patients had their diapers changed and were being fed and stuff by the other nurses. He suggested Uncle Chris go up to see how Grandpa was doing and then added that he and Nancy would take good care of me.

After Uncle Chris left, they soaped up my hair with some baby shampoo. I'd never had two people shampooing my hair at the same time. It felt nice. They wrung out my hair after the final rinse and wrapped my head in a towel and got me back into bed. My leg hurt so bad that I moaned a little and tears welled up in my eyes. They cranked the bed up so that I was almost in a sitting position.

Nurse Larry said, "Push the button," pointing to the pain pump.

Nancy and Nurse Larry stood on opposite sides of the bed and started gently combing and drying my hair.

"So, Nurse Larry," I asked, "did you learn hairstyling in nursing school?"

"No, I have two daughters at home."

They worked as a team—when one was using a rattail to get out the last of the knots, the other was brushing or blowing. Finally, Nancy asked me how I wore my hair.

I looked at her and said, "Like yours."

They looked at each other and paused, and they simultaneously went back to work and corrected their errors. When they finished they gave me a mirror—I was absolutely amazed. My hair looked almost like it usually does. None of the shaved areas were visible. All the Betadine was gone from my hair and skin. There was, however, the matter of my eye.

Gross.

Seeing my reaction, Nurse Larry said, "Nancy, what do you think about an eye patch for the cameras?"

"Genius!"

When they finished, they again gave me the mirror. The eye patch covered up a little of my hair, but it completely hid my gross swollen eye.

Nurse Larry stood back and looked at me through his hands like a movie director and said, "I think you're ready for your close-up."

After he left again, Nancy cleaned up the mess and rolled the highchair out of the room.

About a half hour later, Uncle Chris came back and made an announcement—or more correctly, a pronouncement. He told us the three news stations were leading their six o'clock news programs with the fact that I was awake and alert. Then he told me that each station was going to do a short interview with me that would lead their ten o'clock news shows.

At first I was really excited, but the more I thought about it, the more unhappy I became. I told Uncle Chris that everyone was making me out to be the hero, but a lot of people helped save Grandpa.

Uncle Chris added, "They saved *you* too!"

"Yes, and me."

Before he could respond, the orthopedist *finally* arrived—eating a slice of pizza! Nurse Larry followed him in with two uneaten pizzas. Within a minute, about a dozen people were in my room—all of them eating pizza. One of them turned on the TV.

I asked "Hey, what about me?"

Nurse Larry said, "Oh, sorry about that," and handed me my own little personal-sized pizza.

I was starting to get excited and chirped, "Channel two, channel two."

At six o'clock on the dot, the news started with the dramatic announcement of breaking news out in the valley. A reporter with a microphone and an earpiece looked into the camera and said, "That's right, Hunter. We have just learned that young Summer Rose Watson is awake and eating pizza right now." Everyone in the room cheered.

I couldn't hear or see half of what was said, but I did see Tom in his uniform saying something to the reporter. Then the anchorman back in the studio said, "We expect to have a live interview with our local hero at ten p.m." Once again, everyone cheered.

Nurse Larry then spoke up and said, "All these people are just *some* of the hospital staff who've taken care of you and Grandpa Gus for the last four days." One at a time, they came to my bed to congratulate me or to say some other nice thing. Finally, Nurse Larry raised his hands and said, "All right, everyone, we've got work to do here." Everyone but Larry, Uncle Chris, and the orthopedist filed out of the room.

The doctor came over and said, "All right, let's see what this ankle of yours looks like this evening. Your X-rays are unremarkable." He carefully examined my foot and said, "You're young. This ankle will be just fine."

"But the pediatrician said I was going to need surgery," I said.

"I don't know why he told you that. It's an uncomplicated break, and your growth plates have not sealed up. A year from now, a flight surgeon won't even be able to see where the break was." He looked up at me and smiled. "Just keep off it until I tell you different. For now, we'll keep icing it down. Once the swelling is controlled, I think we'll use an air cast. If you behave, I doubt we'll need to put a hard cast on it at all. Just remember, you're the one who wants to be an astronaut."

He wasn't mocking me. He was reminding me that I could be jeopardizing my future career by not following doctor's orders. The doctor then held out his hand to shake mine. He told me what a great thing I had done and excused himself. But right after stepping out of the room, he stuck his head back in and said, "You have some visitors out here."

A very handsome man in uniform walked into the room, followed by a beautiful woman. They both came over to the bed.

I reached my arms out and hugged Tom around the neck. I held on to him for a long time, thanking him over and over. When I finally let go, he introduced the lady. "Summer Rose, this is my wife, Susan Fireweed."

That's when I realized she was Native American. I said, "I love fireweed . . . all those pink flowers. What a beautiful name."

Stepping close to the bed, she took my hand. She had the most remarkable smile and the whitest teeth. Her big brown eyes caught mine, and she said, "Summer Rose is also a beautiful name."

Looking down at my left leg, she said, "I see your ankle is hurt. May I try something?"

I looked over at Tom and he nodded. "Okay," I said and then looked at Nurse Larry. "Is it okay?"

"Only a Reiki treatment," she told Nurse Larry, and he said that was fine.

Susan carefully pulled my pant leg up above my knee. After rubbing her hands together very gently, she put them on my thigh just above the knee. Then she rocked my leg in a tender motion, like she was trying to wake a sleeping baby. Holding her hands just above my leg, she glided her hands down from my knee to my toe, never quite touching my skin but getting close enough to brush the hairs on my leg.

Then she moved back up to my knee and started doing a light stroking movement down my leg, just barely touching my skin with her fingertips. I laid my head down on my pillow. I could barely feel her touch—it almost tickled. She always stroked in a downward motion as she worked her way slowly down my leg.

As she started stroking my ankle, I felt the strangest sensation. I can't even explain what I was feeling. Like some sort of energy flowing down my leg. It was weird. I became aware that this energy was building up in my toes. I felt like my leg was being cleaned of something, something inside, something that was trying to get out through my toes.

As she continued stroking all the way down to my toes, I watched her swoosh her hands away like she was shaking water off them. As she did, my leg did an involuntary jerk. Then she leaned over and gently blew on my ankle.

I swear it was like she had just *sucked* the pain out of my leg. Quietly, she said, "Do what the doctor says, and someday you will be an astronaut."

When I thanked her, she put her finger to my lips and said, "No, thank you. You have made my husband a better man."

Susan stepped away from the bed, and then Tom came close, leaned over and whispered in my ear, "We got our man."

At first I didn't understand, but then the light came on. Straightening up, he smiled and then walked over to join his wife. They both gave me a little wave and left the room.

Suddenly I realized how bad my head was hurting. I told Nurse Larry it felt like my head was going to explode. He reminded me to use the pain pump, and then he took my blood pressure and told me it was a little high. He looked at Uncle Chris and said, "I think we need to let her rest for a while."

I asked about the ten o'clock news.

Nurse Larry said, "If your blood pressure doesn't come down in an hour, I'm sure the doctor will ground you."

Uncle Chris stood up, saying, "I'll see you later, kid."

Nurse Larry hooked me up to my pulse/ox monitor again. "Let's give it an hour and then we'll see how you're feeling."

CHAPTER 20

THREE O'CLOCK WILL BE FINE

When I woke up, I saw my bed rails had been raised again. My bed was actually just a big crib. Mom was asleep in an easy chair next to my bed. I just watched her for a minute. Then a nurse—one I hadn't seen before—came into the room and walked straight over to her. The nurse quietly woke her up and asked her to step outside. I didn't move, and they both thought I was still asleep. Mom stood up and stretched and then headed for the door. I watched them leave the room.

I really had to go pee. I knew there was supposed to be a nurse call button, but I couldn't find it. So I took the pulse/ox meter off my finger, which caused a small alarm to sound. Almost immediately, the nurse came in.

I asked her where Nurse Larry was and she told me he'd already gone off shift. I looked over at the window and realized sunlight was trying to sneak in through the blinds.

"What time is it?" I asked.

"Eight thirty."

Well, duh, that's no help. I had to ask, "In the morning?"

"Yes. Would you like some breakfast?"

"Yes, please . . . but first I really need to go to the bathroom."

"I'll be right back with some help," she said.

When she left, I started checking my injuries. I still had a headache but not as severe as last night. My eye patch had been removed. I gently played around with the swelling and could see light out of that eye if I moved things around just right. My leg was still propped up, but there was no cold pack on it. I slowly moved my leg around and discovered, to my surprise, there wasn't a lot of pain. My sore throat was better too.

My bed had been moved to the other side of the room. There was a baby next to the window to the nurse's station now. It was asleep or unconscious and had tons of wires and tubes going in or coming out of it. There was also some sort of plastic tent that was keeping in some sort of vapors. It was a pitiful sight.

My other roomy was about eight years old. I couldn't tell why he was in the PICU. He was sitting up in bed coloring something.

"Good morning. What are you working on?"

"I'm making a get-well card for Ammo." Then he asked, "Does he really just have three legs?"

I said yes.

Without taking his eyes off his work, he said, "I only have one leg. Ammo and I would probably make good friends."

I asked, "What's your name, so I can tell Ammo he has a new friend."

"LaDarian Washington. I already know your name is Summer Rose Watson."

I didn't know how to make conversation with a little boy. "It's nice to meet you LaDarian. What are you going to be when you grow up?"

"I'm going to be an astronaut just like you, or maybe I'll be a veterinarian like Doc Rock."

"Cool—was my uncle here this morning?"

"No, he was here last night, but you were sleeping. Your mom's here now. She's up with Grandpa Gus."

LaDarian was acting like such an adult—or should I say he was not acting like a kid? "That's wonderful. Thank you for telling me all of that." I was amazed at how much he seemed to know about me and my family.

The new nurse and a nurse's assistant came in with a wheelchair. Within a minute, they had me sitting up in bed and transferred to the chair. I held on to my IV machine and they rolled me into the bathroom. Gah, there were three people, a wheelchair, and an IV machine in there. Now I know why hospital bathrooms are so big. They told me not to flush and left the room.

When I'd taken care of business, I pulled the little string and they came and got me. The nurse's assistant cranked up my bed into a full sit-up position, and the two of them helped me back into bed. I brushed my teeth and used a warm washrag to wipe the sleep out of my right eye. After washing my hands, I felt a little more human.

Another aide brought in my breakfast tray. I pulled the cover off. *Hmmm, no bacon and eggs this morning.* That made me think about Grandpa.

I asked the man, "How's my grandfather?"

He said he didn't know and left.

LaDarian said, "Grandpa Gus is conscious, his vitals are normal, his eyes are equal and reactive, and he held down his Jell-O."

I realized this little man has spent a lot of time in this hospital.

When I asked the nurse about my family, I was surprised to find out that only my mother could visit me in the PICU—and that she was up in the ICU with Grandpa Gus. *The nurse called him Grandpa Gus too!*

"But I had visitors last night."

The nurse explained, "That was a special case, since you were the only patient here. But you're going to be transferred to a regular ward as soon as the doctor signs the orders."

She was about to leave the room when she said, "Oh . . . you have a visitor waiting for you downstairs."

"Really? Who is it?"

"All I know is she's an air force colonel. We told her she'd have to wait until we got you into a room on the ward. She said she'd wait."

An air force colonel?

Before long, several people in scrubs came in and told me it was time to move. I looked over at LaDarian and said, "Thanks for the update, Mr. Washington." He smiled broadly and growled a really great little laugh.

I was rolled unceremoniously out of the room and down the hall, bed and all. My new room just had two beds but was still definitely a pediatric room. All the curtains had a Disney theme. Even the bed linens had cartoon characters printed on them.

Uncle Chris was waiting in my new room when I was rolled in. He held up a hand puppet that looked like a chili pepper. He worked the mouth and said in a deep Chicano accent, "Nice ride, *chica*."

"Yeah, thanks. How is everybody?"

He continued to work the puppet. "*Muy bien. Su abuelo es mejor.*"

"Really? He's better?"

The puppet said, "*Si, mejor.*"

I looked at the puppet and said, "*Oye, Pepi, se va!*"

Uncle Chris threw the puppet into a toy box in the corner and said, "Dad was awake earlier and ate a light breakfast, but he's asleep right now. He kept asking about you and Ammo. Your mom and Cam have gone back to the house to get a bath and some rest. I'm on duty right now."

"What about the clinic?"

"Lenore is minding the store. Another vet and I help each other out at times like this, so all my patients are covered."

I took a deep breath. I was almost afraid to ask. "How's Ammo?"

"Not good, I'm afraid. We're trying everything we can, but he has sepsis. We just can't bring his fever down.

"But it's not for lack of prayers and well wishes. We've received a hundred cards for Ammo—twice that many for you. I got a call from the post office this morning. Apparently they have sacks of mail for you and Ammo and Dad that were just addressed to Palmer, Alaska." He smiled and added, "Speaking of fans, you have a visitor. I'll go get her if you like."

"Thanks."

About a minute later, I heard her walking down the hall. Her heel clicks were firm and perfectly measured. I imagined a big-boned, horse-faced woman with a large dark mole near her lip. I still had no idea why an air force colonel wanted to see me. For one silly moment, I thought I might be in trouble.

She paused outside my room for a second and then walked in. She was a mature, pleasant-looking, tall, slim woman in a dress uniform with a bunch of ribbons on her chest. She stood there with an air of confidence that I found appealing. Then she let a big smile spread across her face, and all the formality melted away.

She stepped around to the side of my bed and stuck out her hand. I saw her name tag—CARTER. "Hello, I'm Donna," she said, "and I'm really proud to finally meet you."

I was still pretty much in awe.

"You don't recognize me, do you? I'm Beaver seven-seven."

"*Oh!* Cool! I'm Local Traffic."

We both laughed. Then she said, "I heard about the accident on Lake Eklutna on the news, but I didn't realize *you* were the heroine. When they said you were a sixteen-year-old pilot, I suspected it might be you. When I heard the dog's name was Ammo, I *knew* it was you. I kind of pulled some strings to get in to see you. I told them I was your aunt."

When I looked up at her, she said, "Well, we *are* sister pilots."

That made me feel like a million bucks.

Looking around, she said, "I cannot believe they have you in the pediatric ward."

I told her about my run-in with the head of pediatrics over in the PICU *and* the fact that I'm too young to see my grandfather in the ICU. Startled, she blurted out, "What?" and then said it again, "What!" Reaching over the head of my bed, she pulled a couple of printed sheets of paper out of a little holder attached to the wall, handing me one and keeping two in her hand. Suggesting I read mine, she said she'd be back in a minute then turned on her heel and left the room.

I looked at the sheet—Patient Rights & Responsibilities. The page was formatted in two columns, but I didn't feel like reading the text. It was obvious one side was a list of rights and the other was a list of responsibilities. At the bottom was a picture of a man with the title of patient advocate and a phone number.

My headache had returned so I pushed the button and laid the paper on my covers. I sank back into my pillows and closed my eyes.

A few minutes later, Colonel Carter and Uncle Chris both came back into the room. They stood near the foot of my bed and talked quietly. Several minutes later, the king of pediatrics came into the room. He didn't look too happy to be there.

He started with his attitude on Colonel Carter. "I'm Dr. Richards, the head of pediatrics." It wasn't a greeting.

I watched as Colonel Carter began to chew him out. I later learned that in the military, this one-way communication is called a "dressing down." It was quite effective. The longer Colonel Carter went on, the humbler the doctor became. He tried to defend the "eighteen-years-old" policy, but the colonel cut him off every time he tried. She got right into his personal space and occasionally waived the Patient Bill of Rights in his direction. Even Uncle Chris had backed up a little.

Pointing at me, she said, "She saved the life of 'that man' in the ICU. If she's old enough to save his life, she's old enough to visit him." Then she raised her voice and added, "Furthermore, there is no way I'm going to stand by and see this woman interviewed by the media in a room with ducks painted on the walls."

She next gave the doctor a list of demands. She demanded a private room in the adult ward. She also said, "We need a wheelchair and an escort." She added, "And I don't want to see a wheelchair with 'Peds' printed on the back."

The doctor started to argue one more time.

Donna cut him off and barked, "If you can't handle those simple tasks, I'm sure the patient advocate can."

The doctor finally accepted defeat and weakly said, "Yes, ma'am." He turned to leave, and I was surprised to see Uncle Chris step into his path. Nothing was said between them. The doctor turned back to me, cleared his throat, and said, "Miss Watson, I apologize for my behavior yesterday." Uncle Chris stepped back, and the doctor left the room.

The colonel came over to my bed. "I'm sorry you had to see that. In my twenty-two years in the air force, I've never treated any of my subordinates that way."

"For a minute I was starting to feel sorry for him," I said with a little smile.

"Well, we won the battle, but it's doubtful he'll change his ways. All I did was make a small man even smaller than he was when he woke up this morning. What he really needs is some sensitivity training from a professional."

"I'm absolutely sure I've overstayed my welcome, but I have something here for you." She reached into her purse and pulled out several drugstore photo department envelopes. She handed me the whole bundle, and then she and Uncle Chris and I all looked at the pictures, which were like images you'd see in an Alaskan tourist magazine. There were dozens of beautiful shots of Uncle Chris's Skywagon with all kinds of mountain peaks and glaciers in the background. One especially nice shot showed the Skywagon directly in front of the sun. You could see the silhouettes of me and Uncle Chris and Grandpa.

Uncle Chris and I thanked her several times for the beautiful pictures. I tried to get her to stay longer, but she said she had to get to work. She gave me her business card and then asked, "Do you know Camilla Baker?"

I proudly said, "She's my grandmother."

"I know her from the Officers' Wives Club," she said, smiling. "I see it runs in the family."

After she left, Uncle Chris asked how I was feeling.

"This headache just won't go away, and I'm feeling dizzy again. Mostly I'm staying confused. When I woke up this morning, I thought it was still last night. What day is it?"

"Monday."

"Man, I missed Danny's game and everything."

"You didn't miss much. Chugiak won the JV *and* varsity games. I saw the highlights on the news. And by the way, Danny and Esperanza have been calling about five times a day wanting to know how you are." Pulling up his chair, Uncle Chris said, "We need to talk. Can you stay focused for a while?"

I nodded. Suddenly I felt like my heart was in my throat.

"It's not good news."

"I figured that," I whispered, "but can't we just get it over with?"

"Okay," he said, taking my hand. "I called the clinic when I went out to get the colonel. I'm sorry, Summer—Ammo died about an hour ago."

"I guess I sort of expected that." I looked at Uncle Chris and saw his eyes were moist. That's all it took. I managed to get out, "I'll miss him, Uncle Chris," before I started crying.

Uncle Chris stood up, bent over, and gave me a hug. "He didn't suffer at all. Actually, he never regained consciousness. He lost a lot of blood that first night. And like you, he was hypothermic. I'm really surprised he hung on as long as he did."

"He was strong, wasn't he, Uncle Chris? And so brave . . . *so brave.* He was taking care of us. Oh, Ammo—*I'm going to miss you so much!*"

Uncle Chris hugged me for a long time while I sobbed. I realized he seemed to need the hug as much as I did.

I finally stopped crying and pulled away. "Uncle Chris? Is there something else going on?"

Before he could answer, a smiling man knocked at my door, asking if he could come in. He was wearing a suit—and he didn't have a stethoscope around his neck.

I didn't say anything until I realized he wasn't asking Uncle Chris—he was asking *me.*

"Yes, sir. Please come in."

I guess he was confused by our tears. "Are you all right?"

"Yes, thank you. I just found out that my dog died—well, my grandpa's dog."

He surprised me with his exclamation, "Not Ammo?"

I was still recovering from the impact of the news and just nodded.

"I'm sorry. I could come back later."

I regained my composure and said, "No, it's okay." I was really curious to find out who he was.

"Miss Watson, I'm Dr. Neill, the hospital administrator. I wanted to come in and meet our most famous patient."

I grabbed a Kleenex and dabbed at my eyes.

Walking over to my bed, he stuck out his hand. He seemed sincere, so I took his hand and shook it.

He then turned to Uncle Chris and asked, "Doc Rock?"

Uncle Chris just smiled.

"Dr. Rockwell, I really admire your work." They exchanged a strong handshake; a handshake like brothers would share.

Dr. Neill then turned backed to me and said, "I believe this hospital owes you some apologies."

I had no idea what to say, but I felt both relieved and proud. *Finally*, someone was taking me seriously.

"First, may I please try to defend my staff, just a little?" Dr. Neill started. "They were, in fact, following hospital policy 'to the letter.' We have a policy that says a person must be eighteen to be in ICU or the adult ward. Even then, we have to make special arrangements and observe certain restrictions. We *can* and *have* made exceptions to this policy, but it requires an administrator's permission. Unfortunately, the on-call administrator was never contacted in your case. And for that, I'm deeply sorry.

"We now have a private room set up for you in the adult ward. Also, our public information officer will be contacting you and the press right after lunch about a news conference." He paused for a moment and then said, "I'm very sorry to tell you that we still can't allow you into the ICU—but *not* because of your age!" he added in a rush. "It's because the ICU is pretty busy right now. I have also directed that Mr. Rockwell be transferred to this room. He will be spending the night with you before he's transferred to the VA hospital tomorrow morning."

I looked at Uncle Chris. "The VA hospital?"

"I was just about to tell you," Uncle Chris said. "Give me a minute, sweetie." Then, looking at the doctor, he said, "Dr. Neill, there's still one other matter."

"Yes, there is." Facing me, he squared his shoulders and said, "I will make no excuses for Dr. Richards's behavior. I wouldn't insult you that way. I'm sure you understand that I can't discuss personnel matters, but I can tell you this—that type of misbehavior will not be tolerated in my hospital. That's really all I can say." He wished me a full and speedy recovery and excused himself.

No sooner had he stepped out than a new nurse came in, saying she had to check my vitals before I was transferred downstairs. It didn't take that long, and I took the opportunity to let her know my head was hurting a lot, plus I felt really dizzy. The nurse said she'd let the new floor nurse know.

About ten minutes later, I was helped out of my crib bed and into a real adult wheelchair. I was asked to hold on to my pain pump. After being seat-belted in, I was wheeled to the elevator and down one floor. My new room was right next to the nurses' station.

As we passed the door to a waiting room, Uncle Chris said, "I'll stay here until you get settled in."

It took about fifteen minutes to get my vitals taken again. The new staff also had to change the dressing on the incision on my leg where the central line had been. They had me fill out a form with my meal selections and finally gave me some extra pain medication. I was told several doctors would be in to examine my injuries in the afternoon and that I was scheduled for an MRI. I got the feeling no one was planning to send me home anytime soon. I asked the nurse to please let Uncle Chris know he could come in.

He came in a few minutes later and pulled up a chair close to the bed. He tossed a section of newspaper up on my bed—the special state fair section. I wasn't really interested or in the mood, but I looked at it. It only took a second for me to see the page with the produce and livestock pictures. There were cows and horses and pigs and poultry—and *right in the middle* was a picture of Big Bertha with a blue ribbon!

Uncle Chris said, "A couple of other farmers and I harvested her and entered her in Dad's name." As soon as he mentioned Grandpa, I started thinking about him and wondered again why he was being transferred to the VA hospital. But I was so tired. I laid my head back, closed my eyes, and waited for the pain medication to work. I think I was about ready to drift off when Uncle Chris startled me.

"*Holy crap!*"

I jerked awake. "What?"

He was leaning forward in his chair, rapidly scanning an article. "Louie's been arrested!"

"Oh . . . for what?" I asked very casually.

He scanned a little further. "An anonymous tip led Alaska Fish and Wildlife officers to raid his illegal fish weir."

"What?" That's not what I expected. "An illegal fish weir?"

He leaned back in his chair and said, "There were also a number of subsequent charges, to include drug possession, child pornography, and child abuse charges in at least two other states." Shaking his head, Uncle Chris muttered, "Louie, Louie, Louie."

I guess I shouldn't have been surprised that the troopers didn't arrest him for what he'd done to me. Grandpa was over at Cam's house the night I called and asked Trooper Tom to come to the cabin. I told him everything that had happened and what I'd seen. I even told him about the scanners. I was really disappointed when Tom told me there was little chance anything could be done about Louie's behavior with me. But Tom said he had an idea. I guess I was just surprised they got him on a fish and game violation.

I didn't say anything, just laid my head back down. For a minute I felt guilty about causing him to get arrested, but when Uncle Chris read he'd had all those other charges against him, my anxiety left me.

After Uncle Chris's excitement passed, the room was quiet again. I fell asleep, until I was woken by Mom and Cam coming into the room.

He greeted them. "Hi, Sis. Hi, *Grandma.*"

Cam said, "I won't call you Christian if you won't call me that." Then there was the usual kissing and hugging and a little chitchat.

I finally couldn't take it any longer. "*What's wrong with Grandpa?*"

Everybody found a chair and got seated around my bed. When they did, I started crying. "What's wrong?" I asked through my tears.

Cam was the one who started talking. She asked, "Do you remember the night Danny came over, and we all had pizza, and you two went out to the boat dock?"

I nodded.

Three o'clock will be fine

"Well, that night your grandfather told me the doctors at the VA had discovered he had bone cancer in his right leg."

I gasped and whimpered, "Oh, no."

Mom reached up, grabbed my hand, and "shushed" me. "It's all right, Summer Rose. It's going to be all right."

Cam came over to the other side of my bed and put her hand on my shoulder.

Uncle Chris spoke up and said, "His cancer is called chondrosarcoma. It's a slow-growing cancer. They caught it in time—the survival rate is about ninety percent after five years."

For a minute I got mad at the world. Looking up at Cam, I asked angrily, "Did you marry Grandpa so you could be his hospice caregiver?"

I regretted asking that question as soon as it came out of my mouth. I could see she was genuinely hurt.

She straightened up and said, "Absolutely not!" There wasn't a hint of anger in her voice. "I'd already proposed to your grandfather that night *before* he told me about the cancer. I love him very, *very* much. Honestly, I didn't find out about his diagnosis until after I'd asked him to marry me. He said he'd planned to tell me soon, but he wanted me to know before he gave me his answer—to see if I wanted to reconsider." She smiled and said. "That lunkhead."

She continued. "Girl, I plan on being with August for a long, *long* time. He was scheduled to have surgery and chemo treatments in about two weeks, but a lot depends upon how well he recovers from his injuries. Anyway, that's why he's being transferred to the VA."

Cam took hold of my hand and said, "We were going to tell everyone about the marriage and his cancer at church . . ." She paused again and then said, "Umm, yesterday."

I brought Cam's hand to my lips and kissed it. I asked about Grandpa's injuries from the accident.

Mom said, "He has a very serious concussion. They had to stitch up his arm. He's got some stitches in his forehead, but he's going to be just fine. They took his intercranial pressure monitor out this morning."

Just then they rolled Grandpa into my room. He was in a bed just like mine, and he still had an IV. We looked a little like twins, only his head was still bandaged, and he didn't have a black eye. He was smiling weakly, but it was obvious he was in pain.

Uncle Chris moved all the chairs and bedside table to make room for the technicians to roll his bed next to mine. Once it was in place, they tilted the upper part of his bed so he was almost sitting up. He held his hand out for mine, but we couldn't reach each other. Mom stepped between us and took hold of both our hands—so we were like a chain.

"I'm sorry, Grandpa. I'm *so* sorry." Then I started bawling like a little girl. I tried looking at him but couldn't, so I just closed my eyes and tried to say I was sorry again—but I couldn't talk through the tears.

"What are you sorry for?" His voice had the same hoarse whisper I had after they took out my breathing tube.

Torn with grief and remorse, I was actually ashamed to look at him. I tried to talk but couldn't. I cried for another minute and then managed to force out, "You told me . . . I'm sorry, Grandpa . . . you told me . . ." Then I just started crying all over again. I guess I finally got the crying over with and just sobbed for a while.

"Granddaughter, *what* did I tell you?"

I still couldn't look at him. "You told me you didn't feel good. I could tell you didn't want to go, but I was selfish. I was just thinking about myself. And it was your honeymoon. I *hate* myself for making you go."

In his whispery hoarse voice, he said, "Summer Rose, I would do almost anything for you, but you didn't *make* me go anywhere. I went because you asked, *and* because I wanted to go. I didn't *feel* like it, but I did *want* to go. This cancer diagnosis made me realize it may be a while before I could make another trip like that. I really did want to go." Then he said, "I have something I need to tell *you*. Please look at me so I can see your face."

I turned my face and finally raised my eyes to look at him.

"Thank you," he said. "You are a most remarkable person. Thank you for saving my life."

Then Cam said, "Thank you, Summer Rose, for saving his life."

Then Mom and Uncle Chris thanked me for saving his life. I think we all started crying again.

I finally spoke up and said, "I didn't save you, Grandpa. You saved yourself." He looked at me, nodded, and then smiled. Uncle Chris was doing exactly the same.

Mom asked, "What do you mean, sweetheart?"

I looked at her and said, "Mom, Grandpa's the one who packed the survival kit. He's the one who dived down and got it from the bottom of the lake. And he's the one who told me what to do before he passed out."

Uncle Chris said, "Everything you just said may be true, but I'm here to testify, sister. I've had the sad experience of finding the bodies of a number of grown men and women who died *despite* the fact they had everything they needed to survive. They didn't have the courage or strength or savvy to do what needed to be done to save their own lives, let alone someone else's."

We were interrupted by a man who knocked and walked in. "Hello, folks! I'm Aaron Kamp, the public information officer for the hospital. I need to know—is three o'clock okay for a joint news conference?"

"What's that?" I asked.

"All the news media want to hear your story," he replied. "They'll all be down in the media room at the same time. You know, like when there are a dozen microphones on the podium."

I looked around the room to check what everyone else thought. They were all just smiling and looking at me. Grandpa had the biggest smile of all.

I turned back to the man and said, "Three o'clock will be fine."

Epilogue

My bag of experience is overflowing now, and I hope I still have a little luck left in the other bag. I have now logged twenty-three thousand hours.

I'm looking out a viewing port of my ship the *Pequod II*. A brand-new, young flight officer named LaDarian Washington has the con.

I am watching the Earth below as I float weightlessly in my sleeping bag. I can see Alaska silently sliding by. There is the Knik Arm. I can even make out Lake Eklutna and the flats where I got some of my early flight experience. I can see the Chugach Mountains and the Talkeetnas. I can't quite make out Pioneer Peak, but its shadow is falling across the cabin where, not that long ago, I passed the time with a wonderful old pilot and a three-legged dog.

About the Author

R ocky Morrisette was born in East St. Louis, Illinois, in 1951. He was raised in a semirural county—up on the bluffs of the Mississippi River. He attended Bunkum School, a four-room schoolhouse, from first through sixth grades. In 1962, his father moved the family to Phoenix, Arizona. But he was not prepared for big-city schools. He was a terrible student but somehow managed to graduate—on the five-year plan—in 1970 from Rincon High School in Tucson, Arizona.

The Vietnam War was still ongoing, and in 1971 he joined the air force to avoid being drafted into the army. He had a supervisor named Master Sergeant Mullins who stayed on his tail until he had picked himself up by his bootstraps and earned an associate's degree from the Community College of the Air Force. Rocky separated from the air force in 1981. In 1983 he graduated from Middle Tennessee State University, having earned a BS in aerospace maintenance management as well as a commission in the air force.

In 1994, Rocky retired from the air force as a captain after twenty years of service. For nine of those years he was stationed in Fairbanks, Anchorage, and Shemya, Alaska. After retirement, he remained in Alaska and returned to school, at the University of Alaska. While earning a B.Ed in secondary education, he substitute and student taught at Chugiak and Bartlett High School, as well as A. J. Wendler, Clark, and Gruening middle schools.

He and his wife raised seven children in Alaska, the youngest having been born there. In 1999, after a total of thirteen years in Alaska, he moved his family to Illinois, back into his boyhood home. He taught science at Beaumont High School, in St. Louis, Missouri, and finally at the junior–senior high school in Okawville, Illinois—not far from the site of his old four-room schoolhouse.

It was during these teaching years that Rocky discovered the insufferable prejudice his young female students endured at the hands of male students, male teachers, and even the institutions themselves. He struggled to give his female students the same opportunities afforded the boys. He eventually quit teaching to protest what he considers society's futile attempts to ride the "dead horse"—that is, in his opinion, the American public educational system.

After leaving the workforce for good, he realized this sexism pervades society, even today. Although the book is not autobiographical, Rocky's personal experiences inform his writing as he seeks to empower young women and encourage them to consider science-oriented career paths.

As a father of four girls, a lifelong learner, a teacher, an Alaskan adventurer, and a pilot, he is uniquely qualified to tell this exciting story of an exceptional young woman in a remarkable land.

He and his wife have purchased land in Taos, New Mexico, where they plan to build their retirement home.